SEASONS OF SORCERY

A Fantasy Anthology

with stories by

JENNIFER ESTEP
GRACE DRAVEN
AMANDA BOUCHET
JEFFE KENNEDY

An anthology of fantasy novellas for all seasons from the hottest authors of fantasy romance and urban fantasy...

Credits

Cover: Ravven http://www.ravven.com

Contents

WINTER'S WEB

An Elemental Assassin Novella

BY

JENNIFER ESTEP

An assassin at a renaissance faire. What could possibly go wrong?
Everything, if you're Gin Blanco. This Spider is trapped in someone
else's icy web—and it seems like they don't want her to leave the
faire alive . . .

Dedication

To all the fans of the Elemental Assassin series who wanted more stories—this one is for you.

To all the fans—never stop enjoying the things that make you happy.

To all the folks I have gamed with over the years—thanks for the hours of entertainment, fun, food, and laughs.

To Andre—I totally rolled a twenty (not a two!) the day I met you.

Author's Note

Winter's Web takes place after the events of **Venom in the Veins**, book 17 in the **Elemental Assassin** urban fantasy series.

CHAPTER ONE

"I LOOK *RIDICULOUS*."

I stared at my reflection in the mirror above the long counter that ran along the wall. Even though I had been peering at myself for the better part of a minute, I still couldn't believe what I was seeing.

Normally, my wardrobe could best be described as *functional*. Black boots, dark jeans, a long-sleeved T-shirt, a fleece jacket if the weather was cold. I never invested a lot of time or money in my clothes, since they had an annoying tendency to get ripped, torn, and covered with other people's blood.

But today I had left functional behind for *flamboyant*.

A royal-blue silk blouse with ruffles running down the front stretched across my chest. As if the color wasn't bright and bold enough, the entire garment was also covered with shiny thread, glittering sequins, and tiny feathers, all in black. I looked like I'd killed a couple of crows and was proudly wearing their fluttering feathers as some sort of macabre trophy. Plus, the sequins caught the light with every breath I took, and they winked at me in the mirror like dozens of little evil eyes.

But that was only the beginning of my unfortunate ensemble.

In addition to the dead-bird blouse, I was also wearing a

black leather lace-up corset covered with even more black feathers and sequins. The tight corset pushed my breasts up to new and impressive heights, and my sudden abundance of cleavage was on display for all to see, thanks to the blouse's deep scooped neckline.

The plunging neckline also showed off the silverstone pendant resting in the hollow of my throat—a small circle surrounded by eight thin rays. A spider rune, my rune, and the symbol for patience. A matching ring stamped with my spider rune gleamed on my right index finger, and the same symbol was branded into each of my palms.

Tight black leather pants and knee-high black leather boots, both trimmed with royal-blue thread and even more black sequins and feathers, completed my outrageous outfit.

Normally, royal blue was one of my favorite colors, but this outfit screamed *Look at me!* in all the wrong ways. The only good thing about the atrocious ensemble was that the abundance of thread, sequins, feathers, and flounces hid the two silverstone knives I had up my sleeves. Another knife was tucked in the small of my back underneath the horrible corset, and two more rested in the sides of my boots.

"Well, I think you look great," a bright voice chirped, interrupting my dark musings. "Really in the spirit of the season."

A man stepped up beside me and checked his own reflection in the mirror. His long-sleeved shirt and pants were both made of bright green velvet trimmed with even brighter purple silk stripes, making him look like an oddly flavored candy cane. A matching green-and-purple-striped velvet hat with three long, pointed, floppy ends topped his head, while the toes of his green velvet slippers curled up to form soft purple triangles.

Finnegan Lane, my foster brother, reached up and carefully adjusted one of the shiny silver bells on the end of his hat. All that velvet made his eyes seem greener than usual, although the ridiculous hat hid most of his walnut-brown hair.

"What are you supposed to be again?" I asked.

Finn lifted his chin with pride. "*I am a court jester, ready to entertain the masses with my charming wit, amazing skills, and dashing good looks.*"

"Really? Because I think all that green velvet makes you look like one of Santa's elves who couldn't find his way back to the North Pole."

Finn glared at me, but the other people in the room snickered at my joke.

"Forget about you." I held my arms out wide. "I don't even know what character I'm supposed to be."

Finn grinned and opened his mouth, but I stabbed my finger at him in warning.

"If you say *serving wench*, then I am going to make you eat that jester's hat, velvet, bells, and all," I growled.

He cleared his throat, changing course. "Well, I was going to say *pirate queen*, but why don't we just go with *assassin*? After all, that is your usual nighttime occupation."

I made a face, but he was right. During the day, to most normal people, I was Gin Blanco, owner of the Pork Pit barbecue restaurant in downtown Ashland. But at night, to the shady folks on the wrong side of the law, I was the Spider, a deadly assassin and the supposed queen of the city's underworld.

"Well, pirate queen, assassin, or whatever else you want to

call me, I still look ridiculous," I grumbled. "Fletcher would roll over in his grave if he saw me dressed like this."

Fletcher Lane had been Finn's dad and my assassin mentor. And just like me, Fletcher had always been far more comfortable in his old blue work clothes than anything else.

"Nah," Finn said. "He'd laugh his ass off, then make us pose for pictures."

He was right again. The two of us shared a smile at the thought of the old man, and then my brother shook his head.

"Don't blame me for this," Finn said. "This was all Owen's idea."

"Oh, trust me, I haven't forgotten that."

I turned to look at the other man in the room. He too was dressed in costume, although his was far more subdued: a black silk shirt under a dark gray leather vest, along with matching gray leather pants and black boots. Like Finn, he was also wearing a hat, but his was much simpler, a black leather cap with two long flaps that covered his ears, along with most of his black hair.

Despite the costume, the sight of his strong, muscled body and handsome features, including his slightly crooked nose and the scar that cut across his chin, made my heart skip a beat, especially when he fixed his violet gaze on my gray one.

"I don't know what you're talking about," Owen Grayson, my significant other, rumbled. "I am but a humble blacksmith today, remember?"

I huffed and crossed my arms over my chest. Instead of being intimidated by my continued grumbling, Owen stepped forward, grabbed my hand, and dropped to one knee in front of me.

He grinned. "Although this humble blacksmith is always happy to serve his lady, the Spider, a fearsome pirate queen assassin and the purveyor of the finest barbecue in all the realms."

I huffed again at his cheesy words and theatrics, but I couldn't help but grin back at him. "You are getting way more into this than I expected."

Owen flashed me another grin, then climbed to his feet. He was still holding my hand, and the warmth of his skin soaked into mine. "Oh, come on. It's not every day we get to dress up and go to a renaissance faire."

"Especially one called Winter's Web," Finn chimed in. "How perfect is that? Why, it's like they picked an icy spider theme just for you, Gin."

I gave him a sour look, but I couldn't argue. The name was right on the nose, especially given my moniker as the Spider and the elemental Ice and Stone magic flowing through my veins.

From what I'd read online, the faire was a biannual event sponsored by the Ashland Renaissance Players, a group dedicated to showcasing all things medieval, magical, and the like. Winter's Web was the first faire of the year, with the second one to follow in the summer.

I shook my head. "I still can't believe you thought that going to a ren faire would be fun. Or that you actually bid on the tickets during a silent auction back during the holidays. Didn't you say the organizers had a ski trip to Snowline Ridge? Now, that's what I would have bid on. Or that spa weekend in Cypress Mountain."

"Oh, there were all kinds of trips and getaways up for grabs. I bid on several of them," Owen said. "Trust me. I know how much we could all use a vacation, especially given our latest run-in with Hugh Tucker."

Out of the corner of my eye, I spotted Finn frantically slicing his hand over his throat, not so subtly telling Owen to shut up. Owen grimaced, knowing it was too late to correct his mistake.

Saying that Hugh Tucker was my personal nemesis was putting it mildly. Tucker was the vampire enforcer of the Circle, a secret society responsible for much of the crime and corruption in Ashland. A few months ago, Tucker had tried to get me to join the Circle, and when I'd refused, he'd tried to kill me. But my relationship with the vampire was far more complicated than mere nemesis status. To my shock, I'd learned that my mother, Eira Snow, had been a member of the evil group—and that Tucker had loved her.

Tucker's feelings hadn't kept my mother from being killed on the Circle's orders, but they had led the vampire to help me more than once. Although Tucker's help always came with plenty of strings attached and usually involved him manipulating me into killing his enemies. Clever bastard.

Over the past few months, the ugly revelations about Tucker, the Circle, and my mother had just kept on coming and coming, like a freight train that kept running over the tracks of my heart no matter how hard I tried to derail it. But I'd slowly fought, clawed, and killed my way through the Circle ranks until I had finally identified the group's leader and the man ultimately responsible for the murders of my mother and my older sister, Annabella.

My uncle Mason.

That recent discovery had been a particularly surprising and brutal gut punch. My father, Tristan, had died when I was young, so I didn't remember much about him and knew nothing at all about his relatives. I was currently searching for Mason so that I could kill my mysterious uncle for everything he'd done to me and my family, but I wasn't having any luck finding him so far.

Finn kept flapping his hand at Owen, who cleared his throat, breaking the awkward silence.

"Although I have to admit that I don't remember actually bidding on the faire tickets," Owen said, changing the subject. "But at least Jo-Jo was able to find us some costumes."

"Anytime, darling," a light, feminine voice drawled. "And I think you all look fabulous."

I looked over at the middle-aged dwarf lounging on one of the cherry-red salon chairs that filled the room. Unlike the rest of us, Jolene "Jo-Jo" Deveraux wasn't wearing a costume. Instead of swaths of leather or velvet, a long white fleece housecoat patterned with tiny pink roses covered her short, stocky body. Given the early hour, her white-blond hair was still done up in pink sponge rollers, although she'd already applied her favorite pink lipstick and other makeup.

A mug of chicory coffee steamed on the table by her elbow, and the rich, dark fumes tickled my nose and overpowered the chemical scents of the perms, hair dyes, and other products that Jo-Jo used in her beauty salon.

Despite her thick housecoat, Jo-Jo's feet were bare, and she was idly rubbing her toes back and forth over the tummy of

Rosco, her beloved basset hound, who was lying on his back, with his stubby legs sticking up in the air. Every once in a while, Rosco would let out a little grunt of pleasure, but his eyes were closed, and he was fully enjoying his belly rub.

My friends and I had shown up at Jo-Jo's house about an hour ago so she could give us our costumes before she opened her salon for the day. The dwarf had also done my makeup, rimming my gray eyes with silver shadow and liner and painting my lips the same royal blue as my awful blouse. She'd also used some of her many rollers, hot irons, and combs to curl, twirl, and tease my shoulder-length dark brown hair out and up to new heights. I might be going to a renaissance faire, but this was still the South, where hair only came in two categories: big and bigger.

"At least you guys got to wear pants," another voice groused. "How did I end up in this monstrosity?"

High heels clattered on the floor, and a woman a few years younger than me stepped into the salon. She was wearing a bright, neon-pink silk dress that could best be described as *poofy*. The neckline, the sleeves, the skirt—there was some ruffle or flounce everywhere I looked. As if that wasn't bad enough, the whole thing was also covered with pale pink sequins. They matched the ones on her pink high heels, as well as the pink crystal tiara sparkling on her head.

I wasn't the only one who had shed her usual low-key look for the ren faire. Bria Coolidge, my baby sister, might be a tough-as-nails police detective, but right now, she resembled a Southern belle princess crossed with a glittering disco ball.

Jo-Jo had also done Bria's makeup, and she'd given my sister a soft, dreamy look, with pink shadow and silver liner that brought out her blue eyes. A matching pink gloss covered Bria's lips, and her blond hair had been set into loose waves. My sister was lovely as always, although I couldn't say the same thing about her dress.

"That is really . . . pink." That was the least offensive adjective that came to mind.

Bria glowered at me. "I know. I look like an oversize flamingo. With *ruffles*. And *sequins*."

I grinned back at her, not even trying to hide my amusement. Owen's lips twitched up into a smile as well, and Finn let out a loud snicker that had Bria planting her hands on her hips and turning her hot glower to him.

Finn's laughter abruptly cut off, and he went over and put his arm around her waist, drawing her close. "Well, I think you look smashing no matter what you wear," he said, trying to be diplomatic, since he was her significant other. "Besides, I've always had this court jester and princess fantasy . . ." He let his voice trail off and suggestively waggled his eyebrows.

Bria crinkled her nose. "Ewww."

But Finn was not deterred. He never was. He bent down and whispered something in her ear that made Bria's glower melt into a speculative look.

"Later," she murmured.

Finn kissed her cheek. Bria smiled, then reached up and flicked one of the bells on his jester's hat, making it *ting-ting-ting* out a merry tune.

Jo-Jo took a sip of her chicory coffee to hide her own smile. "I'm sorry, darling, but that was the only princess dress I could find on such short notice. There weren't many costumes to choose from, which is why your outfits don't exactly match the Renaissance period."

"It could be worse." I pointed at my own hideous shirt. "You could be wearing feathers, like me."

"At least you get to hide in the Pork Pit truck most of the day." Bria sighed and picked at one of the sequins on her poofy skirt. "I have to walk around and let people take pictures of me in this thing. Pictures that will be online *forever*. Xavier is never going to let me live this down."

Xavier was Bria's partner on the force and another one of our friends, although he was missing the faire. Lucky, lucky man.

Finn held up his hands. "Hey, it wasn't my idea to pimp us out and make us actually work at the faire. That was all Grayson's genius plan."

"As I've told you many, many times now, the Ashland Renaissance Players donate part of the proceeds from their ticket and concession sales to food banks, homeless shelters, and other charities," Owen said. "Darrell, one of the guys in my office, is really into the whole ren-faire scene. When I told him about the tickets I'd won, he said that the Renaissance Players were having trouble finding volunteers. So I thought we could help out."

I put my arm around his waist. "And that's one of the reasons I love you."

He grinned back and pulled me closer. "Don't worry. We're only volunteering for a couple of hours. We'll still have plenty of time to walk around and enjoy the faire."

"*Volunteer?*" Finn shuddered, as though the word was some

awful curse. "Don't you know that I only play the part of the fool for money?"

"And here I thought you did it for free every single day," I drawled.

Finn rolled his eyes at my teasing, then turned back to the mirror and checked the bells on his jester's hat again, making sure they were perfectly draped in place.

"We need to get going," a low, eerie voice rasped. "Gotta get the truck set up."

More footsteps sounded, and another woman entered the salon. Sophia Deveraux was a dwarf like her sister, Jo-Jo, although she was much younger, with a thicker, stronger, more muscled body. Sophia was wearing a ruffled white silk shirt patterned with tiny grinning black skulls, along with black leather pants. The tops of her knee-high black leather boots were turned down, revealing the soft white interior, which was also patterned with black skulls. A large black crystal skull pendant with royal-blue heart-shaped eyes hung from her neck, while a silver cutlass dangled from her black leather belt, along with a small old-fashioned spyglass.

A white bandanna patterned with small black skulls covered her head, and the ends of her black hair had been dyed a bright blue and dusted with matching glitter. Smoky shadow rimmed Sophia's black eyes, and her lips were the same royal blue as mine.

Sophia had kicked her usual Goth style up several notches for the ren faire. The rest of us might look like we were playing dress-up, but not her. Sophia totally owned that outfit from top to bottom.

I let out a low, appreciative whistle. "Now, *that* is what a badass Goth dwarf pirate queen assassin is supposed to look like."

Sophia winked at me, then grabbed the cutlass off her belt and brandished it high in the air, as though she was calling her rowdy pirate crew to order.

"Yargh!" she cried out, shepherding us out of the salon. "To the faire!"

CHAPTER TWO

THIRTY MINUTES LATER, Finn pulled his Aston Martin into a gravel parking lot, and he, Bria, Owen, and I got out of the car.

Even though it was a cold, blustery January morning, hundreds of people had still come out for the Winter's Web Renaissance Faire in Riverfront Park, and Finn had snagged one of the few remaining parking spots. We fell in with the flow of people streaming toward a black wrought-iron fence that marked the park entrance. Brightly colored ribbons had been woven through the bars, along with strings of silver bells, as if to add a bit of jingling cheer to the winter day.

Beyond the fence was a flat, grassy space that was serving as the concessions area. Food trucks, vans, and carts lined both sides of the expanse, with several wooden picnic tables and metal trash cans clustered in the middle. I focused on a white truck that featured a logo of a pig holding a platter of food, along with the words *Pork Pit* on the side. Sophia had already found a spot among the other trucks, although she wouldn't open for business until I came to help her.

Many of the other trucks, vans, and carts were already serving food, and the sticky-sweet smells of kettle corn and cotton candy curled through the air, along with the warm, rich scents of hot chocolate and cinnamon-apple cider and the harsher, greasier aromas of French fries and funnel cakes.

Finn drew in a deep appreciative breath, then sighed it out. "Ah. I love the smell of faire food in the morning."

Bria elbowed him in the side. "We're here to volunteer, remember? Not eat ourselves into a sugar coma."

Finn pouted, but then he spotted a guy dressed like a barbarian gnawing on an enormous turkey leg, and he perked right back up again. "I am *totally* getting one of those for lunch."

Bria rolled her eyes, while Owen and I laughed. We walked through the concessions area and stopped, staring out at the scene before us.

As its name implied, Riverfront Park fronted the Aneirin River as it cut through Ashland, and the grass spread out in all directions like a dull green picnic blanket. Stone paths wound through much of the park, many of them leading to water fountains, swing sets, and more picnic tables. Several rhododendron and other bushes dotted the landscape, along with a few towering maples with bare, skeletal branches.

The east side of the park butted up against the city, with metal-and-glass skyscrapers looming just a few blocks away. Over there, a low stone wall cordoned off the grass from the river below before opening up into a wide pedestrian bridge that crossed the water and led into the downtown area.

On the west side of the park, the stone paths winnowed to dirt hiking trails that vanished into the thick brown woods. Beyond the trees, an old rust-colored barn perched on a hill in the distance, like a weary, worn-out soldier keeping watch on all the activities below.

The park itself was pretty enough, but what made it truly interesting were the people roaming around inside.

Especially since most of them were in costume.

Jesters, princesses, pirates, wizards, minstrels, witches, and more had gathered for the renaissance faire. Most of the outfits were simple—crystal tiaras, plastic swords, and black eye patches paired with store-bought velvet shirts and leather pants and boots.

But some of the ensembles were quite elaborate and hand-crafted with obvious, impressive skill, like the exquisite embroidery of winter snowflakes, spring flowers, summer suns, and autumn leaves on a sorceress's long, flowing blue cloak. Or the knight encased in a full suit of armor that featured jagged marks carved into the metal, along with streaks of red paint, as though he had barely survived being attacked by some monster with extremely sharp claws.

Even the folks who weren't dressed in bona fide costumes were still sporting superhero and other fantasy T-shirts, jackets, and hoodies, while many of the kids were waving sparkling magic wands and running around with glittery fairy wings attached to their backs.

"Well," Bria said, "at least we're not the only ones in costume."

"There is that small favor," I agreed.

Whether they were in costume or not, people were already moving from one wooden booth and tented area to the next. Vendors manned many of the booths, selling everything from old-fashioned jewelry and replica weapons to handmade soaps and perfumes, while the tents were spaces for face painting, storytelling, and other activities.

In keeping with the *Winter's Web* theme, all the booths and tents had been decorated with plastic silver snowflakes and icicles, pale blue cobwebs, and strings of white and blue fairy lights. Snowflakes, icicles, and cobwebs also decorated many of the water fountains, swing sets, and picnic tables, while lights had been wrapped around several trees and bushes. A few machines were scattered about, blowing fake flakes of white and blue snow up into the air. Despite my earlier grumblings, even I had to admit that it made for a lovely, enchanting scene.

"We just need to find Darrell, and he'll tell us where to go," Owen said.

He'd barely finished speaking when a voice rose above the chattering crowd.

"Owen! There you are!"

A forty-something man stepped around a passel of giggling teenage princesses and hurried over to us. He was tall and thin, with shaggy, sandy-brown hair, hazel eyes, and silver glasses. Like Finn, he was dressed in a green velvet shirt, along with matching pants and boots, although his outfit was much more muted and practical than my brother's striped jester costume. An old-fashioned wooden bow was strapped to the man's back, along with a black leather quiver full of arrows, as though he was some ren-faire Robin Hood.

He would have looked really cool, except for two things: the clipboard he was clutching and the white paper tag on his shirt that read *Ashland Renaissance Players, Event Staff.* The modern touches totally ruined the derring-do vibe of his costume.

Owen smiled and stepped forward to shake the other man's

hand. "Hey, Darrell. Looks like you're going to have a great turnout for the faire, despite the cold weather."

"Well, it is called Winter's Web," the other man joked. "I guess it would be false advertising if it wasn't cold. Ha-ha-ha-ha."

Darrell Kline was an accountant who worked for Owen and the reason we were here. In addition to managing money, Darrell was also one of the board members of the Ashland Renaissance Players and was heavily involved in staging the faire. He had been talking to Owen about volunteering at the event ever since Owen had won the tickets.

I had met Darrell a few weeks ago at the holiday party Owen hosted for his workers at the Pork Pit. He had seemed like a nice enough guy, but he had lit up like, well, a Christmas tree once he started talking about his passion.

Darrell was into ren faires the way people in Bigtime were into superheroes or the folks in Cloudburst Falls were into monsters. During the holiday party, he had talked my ear off about all the faires, festivals, and other events he attended in Ashland and beyond. He'd also whipped out his phone and shown me photos of the costumes, weapons, and more that he wore to the events, along with his other collectibles.

Darrell had proudly revealed that he had an entire room in his house devoted to his ren-faire treasures. One-of-a-kind this, limited-edition that, hard-to-come-by thingamabob. All his photos, items, and excited chatter had blurred together after a while, although I'd been shocked at how much some of the swords, jewelry, and costumes had cost. Darrell's taste for the finer (medieval) things in life was right up there with Finn's insatiable appetite for Fiona Fine designer suits. Then again, Darrell and Finn were far less likely to get blood on their fancy costumes and sleek suits than I was on my generic clothes. But it was their money, not mine. To each his own.

"Thanks so much for coming," Darrell said. "I know you won the tickets, but I think it's so great that you and your friends wanted to volunteer."

"Volunteer?" Finn muttered. "More like being coerced—"

Bria elbowed him in the side again, cutting off his complaint. Finn let out a strangled cough and rubbed his ribs. Darrell glanced at the two of them, but Bria gave him a bright, sunny smile, as though nothing was wrong.

Owen introduced Bria and Finn, then gestured at me. "And of course, you remember Gin from the holiday party."

Darrell faced me. He drew in a breath as though he was going to murmur a greeting, but then his hazel gaze locked onto my royal-blue blouse with its shiny black thread, winking sequins, and mounds of fluttering feathers. His eyes widened, and his lips puckered into a silent O of surprise. I sighed. I had a feeling I was going to get a lot of those looks today. Even among all the costumes here, mine was truly horrific.

Darrell quickly smiled and stretched out his hand. "Gin, it's nice to see you again."

Despite the cold air, his hand was surprisingly warm and sticky, and I had to hold back a grimace as I shook it. "You too. Have you added any new treasures to your collection lately?"

He blinked, and his head jerked back, as if the question surprised him. But after a moment, he smiled again. "Oh, just a few things. Nothing too spectacular. Although there is something here today that I have my eye on."

I smiled. "Well, I hope you get it."

"Me too," he murmured. "Me too."

Darrell stared at me a moment longer before turning back to Owen. "Actually, before we get started, I was hoping to steal you away so we could discuss the Harrison account. I want to talk about how to get the forensic accountant set up when she comes in on Monday to review the files. Your friends could check out the faire while we talk. It shouldn't take more than five or ten minutes."

Owen shook his head and clapped the other man on the shoulder. "No business today. We're here to help you, remember? We can talk about the account audit when we're back in the office on Monday."

Darrell nodded. "Okay, then. First things first. We ask that volunteers turn off their phones while they're working so that they can really focus on the crowd. It also helps to promote the magical atmosphere."

"Turn off my phone? Kill me now," Finn muttered.

Bria drew back her arm like she was going to elbow him again. Finn knew when he was beaten, and he quickly sidestepped her, pulled his phone out of his pocket, and powered it down. The rest of us turned off our phones as well.

Darrell nodded again and looked at his clipboard. "Okay, let's get you guys to your stations."

We followed him deeper into the park. In addition to the booths and tents, several small wooden stages had been set up so that minstrels, magicians, jugglers, and others could perform. Soft strains of music floated through the air, along with appreciative cheers, claps, and whistles.

But the pièce de résistance was the ship.

Well, it wasn't an actual ship but rather an enormous stage that had been built to look like the deck of a ship, complete with a wooden railing, a brass steering wheel, and several small cannons. People dressed like sailors were scurrying around, checking the ropes and pulleys that hung across the stage like thick brown spiderwebs, as though they were preparing the vessel to set sail. In the center of the deck, a woman was hoisting a traditional skull-and-crossbones flag up the main mast.

"Is that a pirate ship?" Bria asked.

Darrell beamed at her. "It is. Well, not a real ship, of course. I couldn't get one of those." His lips puckered in disappointment. "But the highlight of the faire is our noon show, where the beautiful Pirate Queen Celeste will fight the evil Captain Walls."

"It sounds like quite a production," Finn said.

Darrell beamed again. "Oh, it is. You guys don't want to miss it. But for right now, let's get you settled."

We dropped Bria off at Princess Penelope's Pink Wardrobe, a tented area where children could try on everything from princess dresses to tiaras to fairy wings. Several kids were getting their faces painted, while others were running around with plastic swords and shields, as though they were gallant knights in search of monsters to slay.

A couple of little girls squealed with delight when they caught sight of Bria. "Look! Look!" one of them shouted. "It's Princess Penelope!"

Bria smiled and stepped forward to talk to the girls.

Next, Darrell led us over to the Jesters Court, another tented area, which was full of, you guessed it, jesters. Men and women wearing costumes similar to Finn's were juggling balls, engaging in acrobatics, performing pratfalls, and generally making fools of themselves, much to the delight and laughter of the onlookers.

"Oh, Finn," I drawled. "You're going to fit right in here."

My brother gave me a dirty look. "You owe me dinner at Underwood's for this humiliation."

I waggled my fingers at him. "Go on, now. Have fun."

Finn glowered at me another moment, but he plastered a smile on his face, stepped into the court, and started hamming it up with the other jesters. Despite his horror of volunteering and turning off his phone, he really was a good sport.

Darrell checked something off on his clipboard, then gestured at Owen and me. "This way, guys."

He led us back to the front of the park and over to a large open-air pavilion that was close to the food trucks. A makeshift forge had been set up inside, and a couple of blacksmiths were already hammering away and demonstrating how horseshoes, swords, and other items had been made back in the olden days. It was the perfect spot for Owen, who was a metal elemental and had his own forge at home, where he crafted all sorts of weapons, including the five silverstone knives I was wearing.

"I thought this would be right up your alley," Darrell said.

Owen grinned. "You know me too well."

Darrell grinned back at him, then turned to me. "And Gin, you're manning the Pork Pit food truck with your friend Sophia."

"That's right."

He nodded and checked off something else on his clipboard. "Perfect. I need to go back to the main stage to help set up for the noon show, but I'll try to swing back around later to see how you guys are doing. Okay?"

Owen and I both nodded, and Darrell moved off into the crowd, still clutching his clipboard.

"Hear ye! Hear ye!" a loud voice boomed out, drawing my attention. "The Pirate Queen Celeste has arrived, along with her royal court!"

People stepped back, and a woman strode forward. She was quite beautiful, with hazel eyes and glossy black hair that had been wound up into a crownlike braid that arched across her head. She was dressed in blood-red leather from head to toe, and the tight garments showed off her muscled body and generous curves. I might have looked like a laughable pretender in my dead-bird blouse, but Celeste truly resembled a fearsome pirate queen.

A silver tiara glittered on her head, while two silver swords with large rubies set into their hilts hung from her red leather belt. Thanks to my elemental Stone magic, I could hear the gems singing about how real, pretty, and expensive they were. Seemed like Darrell wasn't the only one who spent a fortune on ren-faire treasures.

Several people dressed in red velvet shirts, pants, and gowns were following Celeste, and they smiled and waved to the crowd, as though they were real royal lords and ladies. But my gaze skipped past them and landed on the giants at the tail end of Celeste's entourage—tall, strong giants clad in black leather shirts, pants, and boots. Most of the knights, barbarians, and other costumed characters were carrying plastic weapons, but not these guys. I could tell by the way their silver swords glinted in the sunlight that the blades were the real deal.

Pirate Queen Celeste stopped in an open space on the grass, grabbed her two swords off her belt, and started twirling them around and around in her hands, putting on an impromptu show. She definitely knew what she was doing, and she spun the blades around with smooth, easy grace. A minute later, she stabbed both of her swords high up into the air, finishing her flashy routine. People clapped and cheered, and Celeste bowed low, acknowledging their applause. Then she straightened up, holstered her swords, and started posing for pictures.

Owen noticed my curious look. "Darrell said that the pirate queen roams around the faire, showing off her sword skills, judging the jesters, crowning knights, stuff like that. It's just a way to make the event more fun and to get people excited about the noon show."

"And what about the giants?" I asked, jerking my head in their direction.

"I think they're supposed to be the pirate queen's personal guard."

A couple of the giants did stay close to Celeste, but the rest moved away and started roaming through the crowd.

"What are they doing?" I asked. "Why aren't the giants staying with the queen if they're supposed to be her guards?"

"Oh, Darrell told me that he hired some giants to work security."

I frowned. "Why would you need so much security at a ren faire?"

Owen shrugged. "Darrell said that folks can drink a little too much at the ale garden. They also had problems with people challenging each other to duels and real fights breaking out at the summer faire last year, so he thought it would be a good idea to have some giants around for this one. But he didn't want to make a big deal about it, so he had them dress up like the pirate queen's guards. Nothing to worry about."

I eyed one of the giants as he walked past us. That was a very strong giant carrying a very real and very sharp sword. In my experience, that was *plenty* to worry about.

"I should go to the forge and get started. I'll come over to the Pork Pit truck later, and we'll watch the noon show. Okay?"

I dipped into a low curtsy, with my hand pressed to my heart, as though I was a courtly lady. "As my humble blacksmith wishes."

Owen laughed. I straightened up, and the two of us shared a quick kiss. Owen winked at me, then headed toward the forge. I watched him go with a smile on my face, but I couldn't quite ignore the cold finger of unease that slid down my spine.

Perhaps it was my constant paranoia, but I couldn't help thinking that something wasn't quite right here—and that we were already trapped in Winter's Web.

CHAPTER THREE

I WAITED UNTIL Owen was safely ensconced in the forge with the other blacksmiths, then headed over to the concessions area.

By this point, almost all the food trucks, vans, and carts were open, and people were already standing in line to get everything from gourmet tacos to old-fashioned cheeseburgers to home-made ice cream, despite the cold weather.

The Pork Pit truck was parked at an angle across from the blacksmith forge on the far side of the picnic tables. In keeping with the ren-faire spirit, Sophia had hung out a large piece of poster board with the words *Ye Olde Pork Pit* written in fancy cursive with thick black marker. She'd also decorated the board with black skulls and silver hearts stuck in royal-blue cobwebs. I grinned. More like *Ye Olde Goth Pork Pit*.

The food truck had been Sophia's idea, a way for us to get out and about in the community and remind people about the good food we cooked at the restaurant. I had bought the truck and given it to her as a Christmas present, and she'd been cleaning and fixing it up ever since. We hadn't had a chance to try it out yet, and the faire was going to be our test run.

I knocked on the back door, and Sophia unlocked it. The inside of the Pork Pit food truck was like any other. A sink, a refrigerator, a freezer, a couple of stoves, several cabinets and drawers, lots of cooking gizmos, utensils, and containers. Everything you would need to make good, hot, hearty meals out of the back of a truck.

Sophia handed me a black apron patterned with tiny white skulls. "You ready?" she rasped.

I eagerly tied on the apron, since it helped to cover up my dead-bird blouse. "Let's get cooking."

Sophia rolled up the metal cover on the service window, and we were officially open for business. We'd done a lot of prep work last night at the restaurant, and Sophia started heating things up, while I sliced potatoes, onions, cabbage, and carrots.

We were going with a limited menu—pulled beef, pork, and chicken drenched in Fletcher's secret sweet-and-spicy barbecue sauce and piled high on Sophia's warm, yummy sourdough rolls. Our sides were creamy coleslaw, baked beans, and homemade potato chips sprinkled with dill weed and blue cheese crumbles. We had also made sweet tea and cherry limeade to quench everyone's thirst and oatmeal-cherry crumbles to satisfy everyone's sweet tooth.

Finn could keep his giant turkey legs. I would much rather have Pork Pit barbecue any day of the week and twice on Sundays. And plenty of other folks agreed with me, judging by the crowd that quickly formed outside the truck.

An hour later, after that initial rush, Sophia and I finally had some time to relax. Sophia made another batch of coleslaw, while I hung my arms out the service window and stared out at the booths and tents. The faire really was something to see, and I found myself smiling as I watched the people ambling around in their colorful costumes.

At least, I was smiling until I spotted the giants.

They were still roaming around the park, looking tall, strong, and intimidating in their black leather. But what truly caught my attention was the fact that the giants had their hands on the silver swords hooked to their belts, as though they were old-fashioned executioners about to whip out their blades and strike down anyone who displeased them.

Oh, I knew that the giants were probably just doing their jobs as members of the security staff. Or maybe they were playing their parts to the fullest and were determined not to break their gruff, dangerous characters during the faire.

Or maybe, just maybe, they were up to something.

Stop it, Gin! I mentally chided myself. *Stop it! Stop looking for trouble around every corner!*

Finn often said that I was totally paranoid, and he was absolutely right in his assessment. Even here, at a fun, innocent faire, I couldn't fully relax. Because this was Ashland, and someone was *always* up to something shady here. Most of the time, it was me. Maybe that was why I was always so worried—because I knew all the bad, deadly things that I'd gotten away with as the Spider when no one was looking.

"Something wrong?" Sophia rasped, now squeezing some limes and pouring their juice in a pitcher.

"Nope," I said in a breezy tone. "Just people-watching."

She eyed me a moment, clearly not believing me, but she went back to her limes.

I might not have shared my worries about the giants with Sophia, but I couldn't stop myself from tracking the men as they moved from one tent, booth, and area to the next. They didn't do anything overtly suspicious, but they didn't make an effort to participate in the faire activities either, and they didn't play to the crowd or pose for pictures like the other costumed characters were doing. It was almost like they were waiting for something to happen before they revealed their true intentions.

But what trouble could they possibly cause at a ren faire? Steal the more expensive swords and jewelry? Crack some skulls and make off with people's wallets and phones? Swipe the cash from the food trucks? Each new possibility that popped into my mind only increased my worry.

A few of the giants wandered by the Pork Pit truck, and one of them stopped and peered up at me. He was taller than the other giants and quite handsome, with golden hair, tan skin, and pale blue eyes.

I smiled at him, trying to be friendly and not paranoid, but he gave me a flat stare and moved on.

That giant and two others rounded the side of the blacksmith forge and disappeared. They might have been out of sight, but they were definitely not out of my mind—

A light trill of laughter caught my ear, interrupting my thoughts.

Pirate Queen Celeste's royal rounds had finally taken her over to the blacksmith forge, and she was standing next to Owen, who was showing her a dagger he'd made. Owen also showed the blade to the other people gathered around and answered a few questions. Once he was finished, everyone in the crowd clapped in appreciation, then moved on to check out the rest of the faire.

Everyone except Celeste.

The lords and ladies in her court drifted away to browse through the soaps, perfumes, and more in some nearby booths. But not Celeste. She sidled closer to Owen and smiled, clearly interested in all the wares he had to offer. Seemed I wasn't the only one who was into humble blacksmiths.

She said something, but Owen immediately shook his head and stepped away, turning down her proposal. Celeste smiled again and shrugged, as if to say there were no hard feelings.

Owen nodded, then moved away. Celeste stared at him a moment longer, her red lips puckered in thought, then headed back into the crowd. The lords and ladies left their browsing behind and followed her, playing their parts again. A couple of the giants trailed after them as well, their hands still on their swords.

Owen saw me watching them and jogged across the grass to me.

"What was that about?" I asked.

"Oh, Her Majesty Celeste was wondering if I could make a custom set of swords for her, but I told her that I just craft weapons for myself these days. And for my favorite Spider, of course." He winked at me.

I smiled back at him. Owen always knew just what to say to make me feel better. Still, something about Celeste and the giants made me uneasy.

"It's almost time for the noon show, if my pirate queen assassin will let this humble blacksmith escort her to the stage." Owen grinned and bowed low.

My smile widened. "This pirate queen assassin would like

that very much."

SOPHIA AND I closed up the Pork Pit truck and hung out a sign saying that we would be back after the show. Then Owen offered us each an arm, and we strolled over to the main stage.

Almost everyone in the park had gathered here for the show, including Finn and Bria. Finn was chomping down on a giant turkey leg, with grease already smeared all over his face, while Bria had a funnel cake topped with fresh blackberries and raspberries and generously dusted with powdered sugar. She was using a fork to daintily cut into and then eat her fried treat, just like a proper princess would.

I waved at them, and they toasted me with their food.

"Here we go," Owen murmured, drawing my attention back to the stage.

Darrell Kline strolled out to the middle of the pirate ship deck. As if on cue, the wind picked up just enough to flutter the black flag with its white skull-and-crossbones that topped the main mast.

Darrell was still clutching his clipboard and wearing his green velvet Robin Hood costume. He smiled and waved, and everyone quieted down.

"Thank you so much for stepping back in time with us today." He beamed at the crowd. "On behalf of the Ashland Renaissance Players and all our volunteers, sponsors, and vendors, we're so happy that you decided to get tangled up in Winter's Web. Ha-ha-ha-ha."

No one really laughed at his joke, so Darrell cleared his throat and moved on. "And now, ladies and gentlemen, for your entertainment . . . the Pirate Queen Celeste and her Marvelous Marauders!"

Darrell swept his hand out to the side, then hurried off the stage. The second he disappeared, Celeste strolled into view. She plucked her two silver swords out of their scabbards and went through a much longer, more detailed routine than what she'd done in the park earlier. The crowd started *oohing* and *aahing*, and Celeste grinned and spun her swords even faster.

Maybe it was my imagination or some trick of the noon sun, but it almost seemed like the weapons were sparking and glowing in her hands, and I could have sworn that I felt a faint gust of *real* magic in the air. My eyes narrowed, but Celeste was spinning, whirling, and twirling her body and blades around so fast that I couldn't quite tell what, if any, elemental power she might have.

A cheery sea shanty started playing, and a plethora of pirates raced into view. In an instant, they had swarmed all over the stage, standing on the railing, hanging off the netting, and even scaling the main mast up to the crow's nest at the very top. They rose and fell on ropes and pulleys and did somersaults and other tricks that had the kids squealing with delight.

After that initial blast of action, the music died down, and Celeste and the pirates put on a brief play. The story revolved around the villainous Captain Walls trying to take Celeste's ship, but it was really just an excuse for Celeste to show off her sword skills again by defeating the other pirate in one-on-one combat.

Several characters also gave long-winded, flowery speeches

JENNIFER ESTEP

about doing one's duty, living by the pirate's code, and dying with honor—usually right before they were forced to walk the plank to meet a grisly death at the teeth of the sharks supposedly swimming below. The two rival crews also clashed in a massive final battle, and they even set off the cannons, which belched out loud, thunderous *booms* and thick plumes of black smoke.

All put together, it was a fun, lively, impressive show, and I smiled and clapped along to the jaunty music with everyone else.

Thirty minutes later, the show ended, and Celeste and the pirates joined hands, walked to the front of the stage, and took a well-deserved bow. The performers smiled and took another bow, soaking up the enthusiastic applause.

Several kids ran up to the bottom of the stage and held out faire flyers, and the performers, including Celeste, left the stage and came down to autograph the papers and pose for pictures.

Darrell hurried back out to the middle of the stage, still clutching his clipboard. "Be sure to come back for our three o'clock show!" he yelled, although no one paid any attention to him as they drifted away from the stage and back over to the booths and tents.

I turned to Sophia and Owen. "That was actually really cool."

"You sound surprised," Owen said.

I shrugged. "I didn't know what to expect."

Sophia jerked her thumb over her shoulder. "Back to work?"

"Yeah, I'm right behind you."

She nodded and headed toward the concessions area.

Owen held out his arm to me again. "Shall I escort my pirate queen assassin back to her own ship?"

I laughed and threaded my arm through his. "I don't think the food truck would float very well, but escort me, you may."

He grinned, laid his hand over mine, and gently squeezed my fingers. I curled my fingers into his and squeezed back—

I spotted a flash of silver out of the corner of my eye, so I looked in that direction. Pirate Queen Celeste was twirling one of her swords around in her hand again.

And she was watching me.

Celeste kept spinning her sword around in a smooth, lazy motion as though it was a baton instead of a deadly weapon. She realized that I was watching her watch me and did an elaborate flourish with the blade before bowing low. The gesture was more mocking than not. Then she straightened up, slid her sword back into its scabbard, and turned to sign a little girl's flyer.

Celeste didn't look at me again, but I couldn't help but feel like she was still aware of me, the same way that I was aware of her.

"Gin? Is something wrong?" Owen asked.

I focused on him. "Nope, nothing at all. Escort away."

He led me away from the stage. I didn't look back, but I would have bet that Celeste was watching us again—and that her interest in me was far from casual.

CHAPTER FOUR

O WEN ESCORTED ME back to the Pork Pit truck. He had to give another demonstration, but we made plans to meet up later to check out the rest of the faire.

I kissed him on the cheek and watched to make sure that he got back to the blacksmith forge okay. Then I knocked on the door, and Sophia let me into the truck.

Sophia and I hit another busy patch, and I spent the next hour dishing up barbecue, sweet tea, and oatmeal-cherry crumbles before the crowd finally died down again.

"Are you okay here by yourself for a little while?" I asked. "Owen should be done with his demonstration by now, and he wanted to explore the faire."

Sophia grunted, which was her way of saying *yes*, and put another pot of baked beans on one of the burners to simmer. I pulled off my apron and hung it on a hook on the wall before opening the back door of the truck and stepping outside.

I had started to head over to the blacksmith forge when a sharp jerk of movement caught my eye. I looked to my right.

The blond giant I'd seen earlier was sitting at a nearby picnic table, along with two other men. Ostensibly, the three giants were taking a break from their security duties and eating lunch, given the drinks, containers, and crumpled napkins clustered around them. But all three men were trying very hard not to stare at me, and they all had their hands on their swords, even though the blades were lying out flat on the table.

I stayed where I was and pulled my phone out of the back pocket of my leather pants, pretending to check my messages, even though I'd turned the device off earlier. All the while, though, I discreetly watched the three giants.

They got up from the table and slid their swords back into their scabbards. Then they took their drinks, containers, and napkins over to a trash can and dumped their food into the garbage, even though they'd barely touched their cheeseburgers and fries.

That vague, uneasy dread I'd been feeling all day solidified into cold certainty. The giants hadn't been interested in their food. Not at all. It had just been an excuse so they could sit by the Pork Pit truck and keep an eye on me.

Why? What did they want? Had Hugh Tucker sent them? Maybe Uncle Mason had finally realized that I was on to him and had dispatched some goons to eliminate me. Or maybe they were working for another one of my many enemies, like Jonah McAllister. It could be any one of those things or another possibility that I hadn't even considered yet.

I glanced around, wondering if my friends had clocked the giants. Sophia was busy helping some customers, while Owen was still over at the forge, showing a little girl the four-leaf clover he'd made. I didn't see Bria or Finn anywhere, but they were probably still at their princess and jester stations deeper in the park.

I didn't want to bother my friends, so I decided to go it

alone. There were only three giants. That was hardly a workout after Alanna Eaton, Bruce Porter, and some of the other vicious folks I'd battled recently.

Besides, I was the only one who should have to get blood on her costume today.

So I slid my phone back into my pocket, then strolled away from the Pork Pit truck. Instead of going into the crowded park, I veered in the opposite direction, heading toward one of the dirt hiking trails that led into the woods. I smiled and nodded at the people I passed, but I quickly left the noise, crowd, and commotion of the faire behind and stepped into the trees.

Time to see if the giants would follow the Spider into her own Winter's Web.

I AMBLED ALONG the trail as though I didn't have a care in the world. No clouds marred the clear blue canvas of the sky, although the weak winter sun did little to drive away the perpetual chill in the air. Trees rose all around me, their bare brown branches making them look like skeleton sentinels silently studying me. A few hardy evergreen bushes also dotted the landscape, along with small patches of ice and snow that were tucked back in the dappled shadows. The rich, dark scents of the earth and dried leaves filled the air, and I drew in a breath, letting the aromas wash away the fried-food stench of the faire.

It would have been a lovely, quiet walk—if I wasn't being followed.

I didn't hear footsteps behind me, but that didn't really mean anything, so I waited until I reached a bend in the trail, then discreetly glanced back over my shoulder.

Through the trees, I spotted the three giants on the trail a couple hundred feet behind me. They were definitely following me.

Worst mistake they'd ever made.

I kept going at my slow, steady pace, looking for a good spot to confront my enemies. Once I found it, I could slip off the trail, come up behind the men, and make them tell me who had sent them. And if it was Hugh Tucker or dear Uncle Mason, then I would use the giants—and their bodies—to send a bloody message right back to the Circle.

So I headed deeper into the woods, as though I didn't even notice the three giants creeping along behind me. A couple of minutes later, the trail turned again and led to a stone bridge that arched over a small, gurgling creek that trickled off from the nearby Aneirin River. I quickly scanned the area, then grinned. Perfect.

I held up my hand and waved. "Owen!" I called out in a loud voice. "Hey, Owen! Wait for me!"

And then I picked up my pace, jogging away from the giants. I discreetly glanced back over my shoulder again.

The giants hadn't been expecting my outburst or my sudden surge of speed, and they stopped, not sure if they should keep pretending they weren't following me or give up the ghost and chase after me. I increased my speed, rounding another bend in the trail and leaving them completely behind. The moment the giants were out of sight, I sprinted toward the bridge. I only had a few seconds to get into place.

I ran all the way across the bridge and darted around one side of the railing. I quickly jogged down the cold, frozen creek bank, then plastered myself up against one of the gray stone supports so that I was standing underneath the far right corner of the bridge.

I glanced up through the railing. I didn't have the best angle, but the view was good enough to let me see the giants racing toward the bridge. Their shouts drifted down to me.

"Where did she go?"

"I don't see her!"

"We can't lose her!"

All three giants ran onto the bridge, each one now clutching a sword in his hand. Whoever the giants were, they didn't want me to leave the woods alive.

They just didn't realize that I felt the exact same way about them.

I palmed one of my silverstone knives, curling my fingers around the hilt so that the spider rune stamped into the metal pressed into the larger matching scar embedded in my palm. The sensation comforted and steadied me the way it always did.

I studied the giants, plotting the best way to take them down. Normally, I would have just dived into the pack and hacked and slashed my way through them until they were all dead. But we were still fairly close to the ren faire, and I didn't want anyone to hear the men's screams and come to investigate—or worse, call the police. No, this needed to be done as quietly as possible.

Good thing quietly was one of my specialties.

"Let's split up," the golden-haired giant suggested. "She can't have gotten far. Arthur, you come with me. We'll check the trail and the woods up ahead. Galahad, you stay here in case she comes back this way."

Galahad nodded. "Got it, Lancelot."

Lancelot? Arthur? Galahad? And here I thought the Knights of the Round Table were supposed to be the good guys. Seemed like the giants were determined to stay in character right up until they killed me.

The three giants split up. Lancelot and Arthur jogged off the bridge and back out onto the trail, disappearing deeper into the woods. Galahad stayed behind, his head snapping back and forth in time to his quick, worried pacing.

"Where are you?" Galahad muttered. "Where are you?"

He kept pacing back and forth, his boots *snap-snap-snap-snapping* against the flagstones. But he quickly grew tired of that and headed toward the opposite side of the bridge, as though he was going to check the trail we'd all used to get here.

I waited until his back was to me, then eased around the support, climbed up the creek bank, and crouched down beside the bridge.

I paused a moment, but Galahad was still turned away from me, so I tightened my grip on my knife, got to my feet, and sidled forward, determined to bury my blade in his back before he realized what was happening.

But I wasn't quite quick enough.

Galahad must have heard the soft *thud-thud-thud-thud* of my footsteps, or perhaps he spotted my shadow slinking up on the bridge beside him. Either way, he turned around before I could strike.

Galahad sucked in a breath, probably to scream for his friends. Not very brave or knightly of him. I surged forward, closed the distance between us, and sliced my knife across his neck. The giant let out a choked, bloody gurgle, then pitched forward and landed in the middle of the bridge with a loud, heavy *thump*.

"Hey! There she is!"

"Get her!"

I whirled around.

Lancelot and Arthur must have realized that I hadn't gone deeper into the woods, because they'd doubled back. They raised their swords and rushed onto the bridge. I growled, palmed another knife, and stepped up to meet them.

Clash!

Clash-clash!

Clash!

Lancelot and Arthur swung their swords at me over and over again. I spun, whirled, and twirled between the two men, using my knives to keep their blades from cutting into me. But the giants were much bigger and stronger, and their arms and swords gave them a much longer reach than I had with my knives. Despite all my years as an assassin, I barely managed to keep the giants from skewering me.

I blocked an attack from Arthur, but Lancelot came up beside me and lashed out with his sword. I twisted my body to the side, avoiding most of the blow, but the edge of his blade still sliced across my left forearm, opening up a deep gash.

I hissed and staggered back, moving away from the giants and their swords.

"Not so tough now, are you, Spider?" Lancelot sneered, twirling his sword around in his hand.

Arthur grinned and did the same thing. Then the two of them advanced on me again. I was really starting to hate these so-called knights.

My gaze snapped back and forth, flicking from one giant to the other and back again. Despite their heavy swords, the two men were barely winded thanks to their great strength, but I was sucking down air, trying to get my breath back after using so much energy to block their hard, furious attacks. My knives weren't going to get the job done, not in this situation, so I tucked them back up my sleeves.

"Aw, are you giving up already, little Spider?" Lancelot sneered at me again. "If you raise your hands and surrender, we might just do you a favor and kill you quickly. Give you an honorable death, at least."

An honorable death? There was no such fucking thing. These guys had been hanging around the ren faire too long. All those pretty proclamations and flowery words about honor, codes, and duty had addled their minds—and were going to get them killed in another minute, two tops.

I smiled at him. "You want me to raise my hands? You got it, Sir Knight."

I reached for my magic, snapped up my hands, and flung a spray of Ice daggers out at them. Given their big, strong bodies and thick, heavy leather outfits, the daggers didn't have much chance of hurting the giants, but Lancelot and Arthur didn't realize that, and they both yelped in surprise, lifted their arms, and turned away from my frosty blast of magic.

The sharp shards of elemental Ice splintered against their massive biceps and shoulders and dropped harmlessly to the ground, but the giants' distraction let me close the distance between us. I went left, targeting Lancelot first, since he was the better fighter and far more dangerous than Arthur. I leaped up, grabbed hold of the bridge railing, and kicked out, slamming my boot into his sword hand.

Lancelot yelped, staggered back, and dropped his weapon.

Arthur snarled, stepped up, and swung his blade at me, but I avoided his vicious blow, darted forward, and scooped Lancelot's sword up off the bridge.

The weapon was far, far heavier than I'd expected it to be. I had to wrap both hands around the hilt, but I managed to hoist it up. Arthur raised his sword high overhead, giving me an easy opening, and I stepped up, whirled around, and sliced the stolen blade across his stomach.

The giant screamed and staggered back against the railing. Arthur's feet flew out from under him, and he collapsed to the ground. His sword dropped from his hand and skittered across the flagstones, shooting off a few hot silver sparks.

Arthur's panicked gaze dropped to his stomach, and he clamped his hands over the deep, gruesome wound, trying to keep his blood and guts from leaking out. I could have told him that it was a losing battle and not to bother, but I went for the more direct approach of lashing out with my sword again. This time, I buried the blade in the side of the giant's neck, cutting off his screams.

I tried to yank the sword free so that I could turn my attention back to Lancelot, but I couldn't quite manage it. I grunted and tried again, but the blade was firmly stuck in Arthur, like, well, a sword in a stone.

"You bitch!" Lancelot screamed. "You killed him!"

The giant charged at me, his arms outstretched like he wanted to wrap me up in a bear hug and crush me to death. I couldn't let that happen, so I let go of the sword and lurched away from Arthur. But once again, I wasn't quite quick enough, and Lancelot plowed into me. I barely had time to grab hold of my Stone magic to harden my skin into an impenetrable shell before the giant body-slammed me down onto the bridge.

Despite my Stone magic, the bruising blow still hurt, and I let out a low groan of pain.

"You bitch!" he screamed again, wrapping his hands around my throat. "You killed them!"

Lancelot started squeezing my neck, trying to choke me to death. At the same time, he lifted my shoulders and chest up off the bridge, getting ready to slam my head back against the stone, probably over and over again until he cracked my skull open like an egg.

I couldn't let that happen either, so I reached for even more of my Stone magic. There was no time to be subtle, so I focused on the closest part of the bridge railing. Then I lashed out with my magic, hammering my Stone power into the supports the way Owen and the other blacksmiths had been hammering their weapons and other metal creations in the forge earlier.

CRACK!

Several pieces of stone exploded out of the railing. I put a lot of magic into the blast, and one of the chunks zipped across the open space and hit Lancelot in the side of his neck. The giant let out a choked cry. He toppled off me and flopped over onto his back, wheezing and clutching his throat.

I sucked down some much-needed air, then forced myself to roll over and get back up onto my knees. I palmed a knife and loomed over Lancelot, ready to drive the blade into his ribs if he came at me again, but I didn't have to.

I'd already killed him with my Stone magic.

That chunk of railing hadn't just made Lancelot choke and gasp for air. Part of the stone had shattered and driven itself deep into his neck, wounding him just as badly as my knife would have. A steady stream of blood was pouring down his throat, and it had already started pooling around his head like he was lying on a scarlet cloak.

I leaned over the giant and fisted my hand in the front of his leather shirt, shaking him and trying to get him to focus on me before he bled out.

"Who sent you?" I hissed. "Was it Tucker? Mason? Are they here? Are they watching us right now?"

But I'd done too good a job with my Stone magic, and it was too late to get any answers from Lancelot. The giant gurgled and stretched up an arm like he was going to shove me away, but his strength gave out, and his hand flopped back down onto the bridge. A moment later, his body sagged, and his blue eyes became fixed and frozen.

A knight no more, Lancelot was dead.

CHAPTER FIVE

I SLUMPED DOWN on the bridge beside the dead giant, still trying to get my breath back, even as I scanned the surrounding woods.

The fight hadn't been nearly as quiet as I'd wanted it to be, but I didn't see anyone running through the trees, and I didn't hear any shouts that would indicate that someone had heard the giants' yells and screams and was coming to investigate.

Since I was relatively safe, at least for the moment, I glanced at the three giants, but they all lay where they had fallen, as dead as dead could be. They couldn't give me any answers about who had sent them and why.

But maybe their phones could.

I got up on my knees again, tucked my knife back up my sleeve, and started patting down Lancelot. Despite the fact that he was gussied up in black leather for the faire, he still had his phone in his pants pocket, and it was still on. The honorable knight had done the not-so-honorable thing of ignoring Darrell's request to turn it off. Luckily, the device hadn't been damaged during our fight, and I hit the button on the side. The phone was locked, but maybe I could fix that.

I grabbed Lancelot's right hand, which was covered in blood and bruises, much like the rest of him was. The left sleeve of my dead-bird blouse was already torn from where I'd been cut during the fight, so I ripped off some of the loose fabric and used it to wipe the blood off Lancelot's index finger. Then I pressed his slightly cleaner finger onto the screen. A moment later, the device unlocked, and I let the giant's hand flop back down to the bridge.

The first thing I did was change the settings so that the phone would stay unlocked. Then I scrolled through Lancelot's contacts, but I didn't recognize any of the names. No Tucker, no Mason, no mysterious initials, although there were several odd monikers like the Mesmerizing Magician, the Red Queen, the Bloody Barbarian, and so on.

Lancelot had really been into the whole ren-faire scene. No wonder he'd been so good with that sword. He'd actually learned how to use the long, heavy blade. I made a mental note to add medieval weapons to my assassin training regimen.

Since I didn't recognize any of the contact names, I moved on to the call log. But none of the phone numbers jumped out at me, so I pulled up his texts. And I finally found something interesting.

Someone called the Black Rook had sent Lancelot several messages over the past few months. In fact, it looked like the giant had been texting with this person more than anyone else. Most of the texts were about the renaissance faire and focused on costumes, weapons, and the like. I was just about to give up and search the other two giants for their phones when I spotted a final text that was part of a new chain. So I opened it.

Target will be at Winter's Web as planned, along with friends. We need to separate and isolate the target. You know what to do.

Well, that was some pretty ominous bad-guy talk. This text also had a photo attachment, so I clicked on the file and waited for it to download and then pop up on the screen. I fully expected to see some shot of myself walking down the sidewalk or maybe even cooking inside the Pork Pit. But my smiling face wasn't the one that appeared on the screen.

It was Owen's.

I blinked and blinked, but the image didn't change. The picture looked like it had been taken at some recent charity event, given the red and green holiday lights glowing in the background. Owen was wearing a black tuxedo and grinning at someone I couldn't see, but he was most definitely the focus of the photo.

Owen? Why would the giant have a picture of Owen instead of me—

Horrible understanding slammed into my brain, while sick certainty curdled in my stomach. The giants might have been watching me, but only to make sure that I didn't interfere with their plans. This wasn't about me. For once, I didn't seem to be the main target.

Owen was.

Fear, worry, and dread punched me in the heart, one right after another, leaving me dizzy, shaking, and breathless. For a moment, everything inside me lurched to a cold, hard, painful stop. Then my mind kicked into gear again, and my body zoomed into overdrive.

I got to my feet, stuffed the giant's phone into my pants pocket, and started running.

I LEFT THE dead giants where they had fallen on the bridge. I didn't care if anyone found them and realized what had happened, that I had killed them.

Right now, the only thing that mattered was getting to Owen.

So I ran, ran, ran, as fast as I could, my boots pounding along the trail in perfect time to the frantic fear pulsing through my heart.

Must save Owen . . . must save Owen . . . must save Owen . . .

It became like a mantra running through my mind, and I used it to block out everything else. The cold air searing my lungs, the growing stitch in my side, the throbbing sting in my forearm, the blood still sliding down my skin from where Lancelot had cut me with his sword. I ignored it all, sucked down another breath, and forced myself to move even faster.

I hadn't gone as far into the woods as I'd thought, and I quickly made it back to the end of the trail. I sprinted out into the grassy park and had to stop short to let a group of boys dressed like Vikings pass by. The second they were out of the way, I started running again.

Well, I tried to run. The park was even more crowded than before, and I had to slow down to a fast walk so that I wouldn't bowl people over. Even then, I still had to pull up, sidestep, and dart around person after person after person, and I had to bite my tongue to keep from screaming at each and every delay.

I finally made it back to the concessions area. Sophia was still inside the Pork Pit truck, and she leaned out the window as I raced by, obviously wondering what going on, but I didn't have time to stop and explain.

Must save Owen . . . must save Owen . . . must save Owen . . .

The mantra kept pounding in my head, getting a little louder, quicker, and more frantic with each passing second, and I hurried across the grass and over to the blacksmith forge.

A large crowd was gathered around the front of the forge for the latest demonstration. I stood on my tiptoes, but I couldn't see if Owen was leading the event, and I couldn't hear his voice over the loud, constant hammering. So I skirted around the edge of the crowd, then zipped through a gap between two people. Eventually, I wound up on the left side of the forge.

It wasn't as crowded back here, and I spotted a guy in the rear wearing a black leather cap and using a hammer to shape a red-hot sword. Relief filled me, but I forced myself to wait until he'd plunged the blade into a trough of water before I hurried over to him.

I grabbed his arm and turned him around. "Owen! I'm so glad I found you—"

The words died on my lips, and my relief was snuffed out just like the heat from the sword had been in the water.

It wasn't Owen.

The blacksmith stared at me, obviously wondering who I was and why I was babbling about some guy named Owen.

I dropped his arm, stepped back, and gave him a sheepish grimace. "Sorry. I thought you were someone else."

The guy shrugged, accepting my apology, and went back to work.

I turned around, scanning the area. Another blacksmith was

at the front of the forge, although he'd finally stopped the loud hammering and was now explaining his process to the crowd. A couple of other blacksmiths were also working on their own projects. Kids were running around, while their parents were admiring the weapons, horseshoes, and other items on display. Everything was perfectly normal except for one thing: I didn't see Owen anywhere.

"Owen!" I called out. "Owen!"

No answer.

I was getting more and more worried and more and more desperate, so I went around to the back of the forge, hoping that he was taking a break. But of course, he wasn't out here either.

I looked out into the park beyond, but it was more of the same. Kids playing, adults shopping, costumed characters posing for pictures.

No Owen.

I turned around in a slow circle, just in case I'd missed anything, but I hadn't. I stepped forward and opened my mouth to call out to him again, and my boot scuffed across something on the grass.

A black leather cap with long ear flaps was lying on the ground—the same sort of hat that Owen had been wearing.

Icy dread flooded my heart, but I crouched down and picked up the cap. The leather was crumpled, as though it had been snatched off someone's head, thrown down, and then stomped on for good measure. Part of the leather looked a bit darker and shinier than the rest, so I rubbed my fingers over that spot. Sticky moisture clung to my skin in a sickening, familiar sensation. I froze a moment, then slowly pulled my hand up where I could see it.

Faint smears of blood were streaked across my fingertips.

I sucked in a ragged breath, even as more and more worry shot through my body.

Owen was gone.

Chapter Six

A s much as I wanted to surge to my feet, run around, and scream Owen's name, I forced myself to calmly, slowly, carefully examine the ground where I'd found his hat.

The grass had been flattened in patches and churned up in others, along with the dirt underneath, indicating a struggle. Owen had come here for some reason, or had been lured here, and then he'd been attacked. In addition to being a metal elemental, Owen was also a good, strong fighter. Even if he'd been taken by surprise, he still would have put up a fierce struggle, and all the flattened grass and disturbed earth told me that he'd been attacked by at least a couple of guys. Probably more of the black-leather-clad giants.

With a heavy heart, I also forced myself to search the ground for more blood, but thankfully, the smears on Owen's cap were all I found.

I stood up, thinking about what I knew. Owen had definitely been attacked here and then taken somewhere else. Despite the crowds, a snatch-and-grab would have been easy enough to pull off. A couple of the costumed giants could have bashed Owen over the head and carted him off in plain sight simply by making the whole thing seem like an act and part of the ren-faire fun instead of the kidnapping it truly was.

And it *was* a kidnapping. If someone had just wanted to kill Owen, they could have shoved a knife in his back and left his body here. But there was no body, which told me that Owen was still alive.

For now.

But why kidnap him? Was this some ploy by Hugh Tucker to get leverage over me? To force me to kill another one of the vampire's Circle enemies? And why grab Owen at the faire with so many potential witnesses around? Why not snatch him when he was coming out of his office late one night? Or from his house, where there was far less chance of someone realizing what was going on?

My hand fisted tight around the bloody leather cap. I didn't know the answers to my questions, but I was damn sure going to find them out.

And when I found the people who had taken Owen, they were the ones who were going to fucking *bleed*.

STILL CLUTCHING OWEN'S hat, I skirted around the blacksmith forge, threaded my way through the crowd, and hurried back over to the Pork Pit truck. Sophia had fed the latest wave of customers, and she leaned out the window again, a concerned look on her face.

"What's wrong?" she rasped.

I quickly told her about the giants following me into the woods and then handed her Owen's bloody hat.

Sophia studied the hat a moment, then set it aside. Her face darkened, and her black eyes glittered with anger. "What do you want me to do?"

"Call Finn and Bria—" I stopped and let out a vicious curse.

Calling them wouldn't do any good, since they'd turned their phones off earlier, just like Owen and I had.

"Close up the truck, then go find Finn and Bria and tell them what's going on," I said. "Spread out and start looking for Owen. Ask around, and see if anyone remembers some giants in black leather carrying another guy. Whoever took him couldn't have gotten too far away yet."

"What are you going to do?" she rasped.

"I'm going to find another giant dressed like the ones who attacked me and squeeze him for answers. I don't know that all those giants are working together, but it's a place to start."

Sophia nodded and started closing up the truck. I left her there and hurried over to the wrought-iron fence that cordoned off the park from the gravel lot beyond. I looked out over the rows of cars, trucks, and vans, but I didn't see anything suspicious, and there were no empty spaces to indicate that a vehicle had recently left.

The kidnappers could have taken Owen out of the park, put him in a car, and driven away, but it would have been much more conspicuous, and they would have had to walk right by the Pork Pit truck to do it. Whoever had planned this had been very careful and smart so far, and I doubted they would have wanted to risk Sophia seeing and stopping them. No, my gut was telling me that Owen was still nearby.

That was my hope, anyway. I wasn't going to think about all the awful things that might have already happened, all the ways that he could have been horribly hurt and brutally tortured. My stomach roiled with fear, but I pushed it away and instead focused on the cold determination surging through me. I didn't know what this was about yet, but I *was* going to find Owen, and the people who took him *were* going to pay for what they'd done.

With that dark and deadly promise beating in my heart, I moved away from the fence, walked back through the concessions area, and started doing a sweep of the front part of the park, searching for the black-leather-clad giants.

But I couldn't find them—not a single one.

Earlier today, the giants had been *everywhere*, but now there was nary a one in sight. That only confirmed my suspicion that they were working together. After all, why stick around the scene of your crime when you'd already abducted your victim?

Still, I kept scanning the throngs of people, desperately hoping I'd spot the giants. All I needed was one of them to talk and tell me where they'd taken Owen. Just one.

No giants magically appeared to answer my silent plea, but as I looked around, I realized that someone else was also missing from the faire.

Pirate Queen Celeste.

My head snapped back and forth, and I scanned the crowd, but I didn't see Celeste anywhere either. She had vanished, along with the giants.

Oh, I supposed that Celeste could have been taking a break, hanging out somewhere deeper in the park, or maybe even over at the stage, preparing for the next show. But mine was a suspicious mind, and I remembered how the giants had entered the faire as part of her entourage this morning, almost as if they worked for her in real life.

Maybe they did.

Even more telling was the fact that Celeste had tried to cozy up to Owen earlier at the forge. Sure, Owen had said that Celeste had wanted some custom swords, but what if that had just been an excuse to get him alone? I didn't know that I was right, but I wasn't going to take a chance that I was wrong either. Not when Owen's life was hanging in the balance.

So I quit looking for the giants and started searching for Celeste instead.

I went over to a group of people standing in front of a jewelry booth. "Excuse me, have you seen Pirate Queen Celeste?"

I didn't think a more ridiculous sentence had ever come out of my mouth. Then again, this had started out as a ridiculous day, although it had quickly turned into a bloody one—and would probably get bloodier still, before all was said and done.

Those folks shook their heads, so I moved on. I asked the same thing over and over again of all the kids, teens, and adults who crossed my path, but they all kept shaking their heads *no-no-no*. Despite the throngs of people, no one remembered seeing Celeste recently or knew where she might have gone—

I spotted a flash of red out of the corner of my eye. I whirled around in that direction, and I saw Celeste disappearing behind one of the vendor booths about twenty feet away.

I glanced around, but I didn't see Sophia, Finn, or Bria anywhere. I couldn't wait for my friends. I had to act now or risk losing Celeste, so I headed after the pirate queen.

"Hey!"

"Watch it!"

"Rude much?"

A few people let out angry mutters as I shoved past them, but I didn't dare slow down to apologize. The only thing that mattered was tracking Celeste back to Owen before it was too late.

I reached the booth where Celeste had disappeared, and I finally did slow down, creeping up to the corner and peering around the side. I didn't see Celeste or any of the giants, but the booth was close to one of the hiking trails that led into the woods on the west side of the park.

I hadn't seen any buildings or other structures during my earlier hike through the woods, but this trail was about a quarter mile away from the one that I'd used. Either way, it was the most likely place for Celeste to have gone, so I stepped around the booth, jogged over to the trail, and plunged back into the trees.

I palmed a knife and moved quickly and quietly along the path. Every once in a while, I stopped to look and listen, but I didn't see anyone on the trail ahead of me or hunkered down in the surrounding woods, and the thick tangle of trees blocked out the clatter and commotion from the faire.

A couple of hundred feet into the woods, I came across another stone bridge that arched over the same creek that I'd seen before. I approached the bridge with caution, but Celeste wasn't lying in wait underneath it to attack me like a troll, so I crossed it.

I was just about to step off the far side of the bridge when the phone in my pocket started buzzing.

I frowned, wondering why the device was buzzing instead of playing one of the ring tones that Silvio Sanchez, my personal assistant, had programmed into my phone. Silvio and I both loved movie music, and he'd downloaded a bunch of classic cinematic themes into my device.

Then I realized it wasn't my phone—it was the phone I'd taken off Lancelot.

The phone buzzed a moment longer, then fell silent. I pulled the device out of my pocket and stared at the screen. It was another message from the mysterious Black Rook.

Did you take care of the assassin?

More ominous bad-guy speak, asking if the giants had killed me yet.

I hesitated. I didn't know if Lancelot and the Black Rook were using keywords or some other code, but it would be more suspicious if there was no response, so I sent back a generic bad-guy answer.

It's done.

I waited, holding my breath and hoping I'd made the right choice. The phone buzzed again a few seconds later with another message.

Good. Meet us at the barn to get your cut.

The barn? What barn?

Then I remembered the old barn I'd seen perched on the hill beyond the woods when we first arrived at the park this morning. That must be where this trail led and where the kidnappers had taken Owen.

I switched the phone to silent, shoved it back into my pocket, and hurried along. A few hundred feet later, the path started climbing, and that old barn came into view through the trees.

As soon as I spotted the structure, I stepped off the trail and started moving from one tree to the next, steadily and silently making my way up the incline. I didn't spot Celeste or any of the giants lurking in the woods, and no trip-wires littered the ground. Sloppy, sloppy, sloppy of the kidnappers not to leave a rear guard behind or at least a few rune booby traps buried in the leaves in case someone like me came creeping up behind them.

A few minutes later, I crested the top of the hill and hunkered down behind a large boulder at the edge of the woods. The trail I'd been on before ran out of the trees and snaked through an overgrown field choked with tall grasses, winter wildflowers, and other vegetation before ending at a small mowed yard that surrounded the barn.

I studied the structure, but it looked like any other barn in the Ashland countryside—a two-story building that had probably been painted a bright, glossy red at one time but whose color had slowly faded to a dull, rusty brown. The double doors on the front were closed, and shades had been pulled down over the windows, but a faint, steady hum sounded in the distance. Probably a generator to power the lights and pump some heat into the barn.

The double doors were the only way in on the ground level that I could see, so I looked up at the second story, which featured a couple of windows, along with a large single door that probably led to a hayloft. No shades covered the glass on the second-story windows, and I didn't see anyone moving around up there.

Fletcher had always said it was better to come at your enemies from an unexpected angle, and the old man's words of
wisdom were especially true in this case, when Owen was
trapped inside the barn with who knew how many giants. So I
started looking for a way to get up to the second level, and my
gaze locked onto a drainpipe at one corner of the building.
Perfect.

I didn't want to waste time turning my phone on, so I pulled
the dead giant's phone out of my pocket and texted Sophia,
telling her where I was and what was going on. I also sent the
same message to Finn and Bria, even though I doubted they had
switched their phones back on yet. Once that was done, I slid
the device back into my pocket.

I looked around again, but the barn remained silent and shut
up, so I surged to my feet, plowed my way through the
overgrown field, crossed the mowed yard, and plastered myself
up against the side of the building. I drew in quick, steady
breaths through my nose, trying to listen above the roar of my
heart, but no shouts sounded, and no one seemed to have
spotted me.

I took hold of the drainpipe and gave it a hard, sharp tug to
determine if it would hold my weight. The dull gray pipe looked
as old and run-down as the rest of the barn, but it didn't budge,
squeak, or protest, so I wrapped both hands around it and
started climbing.

I dug my boots into the wood on either side of the drainpipe,
using my feet to help support me as I reached higher and higher
and shimmied up the pipe. The metal was so cold that it burned
my hands, but I didn't dare use my Stone magic to harden my

skin.

If an elemental was inside the barn, they might sense me using my magic and come outside to investigate. I didn't want that. Not until Owen was safe. Then I would take on anybody here who had an ounce of magic, along with everyone who didn't.

As an assassin, I'd done my fair share of spidery climbing, and it didn't take me long to reach the second level. One of the windows was right beside the drainpipe, so I grabbed hold of the wooden frame. I was only mildly surprised when it easily slid up. People thought that locking the doors and windows on the first floor was enough to keep out bad folks. And it usually was, but most folks weren't the Spider, and I was just about the baddest of them all.

I slid the window up as high as it would go, then grabbed the bottom of the frame with both hands, pulled myself forward, and slithered through the opening. I went headfirst, and I ended up sliding down into a loose mound of old, moldy hay. Ugh. The hay scratched my face and tickled my nose, and I had to swallow down a sneeze. I waited a moment, lying there, but no shouts or alarms sounded, so I slowly sat up.

I was in a hayloft, surrounded by, you guessed it, hay. Several bales were stacked up along the walls, while more loose hay covered the floor, including the spot where I was sitting. The inside of the barn looked just as decrepit as the outside, and several of the wooden floorboards were cracked or missing, while others sagged underneath the weight of the bales.

The only good thing about the loft was that it didn't look like anyone had been up there in ages, given the thick layer of dust that coated everything. Even more dust motes swirled through the air like mosquitoes, and I had to swallow down another sneeze.

I reached out and closed the open window behind me. Then I palmed a knife and slowly, carefully, quietly crawled out of the hay.

The loft was shaped like a giant U, with a set of stairs in the middle leading down to the ground. I crept over to the wooden railing that cordoned off the right side of the loft and peered down at the first floor.

I wasn't sure what I'd been expecting. Some old, forgotten farm equipment slowly rusting away. Maybe an old junker car with flat tires that had been stripped for parts and left to rot. Maybe even some barn cats sleeping in the dusty piles of hay.

What I didn't expect were the thick brown leather couches arranged around low tables full of laptops, monitors, keyboards, gaming consoles, and other high-tech computer equipment. A couple of refrigerators lined one of the walls, with cases of beer piled on top of them, along with bags of potato chips, pretzels, candy bars, and other snacks. Several bales of hay were also scattered around, with swords, daggers, spears, and other sharp, pointy, medieval weapons sticking out of them, as though the bales were oversize pincushions.

But the centerpiece of the first floor was a long, wide table covered with bright green felt that held an enormous diorama of a medieval landscape. Miniature gray stone castles, green paper mountains with painted white peaks, blue-tinted water in little rivers that snaked across the landscape, even dwarves, giants, sorcerers, and other metal figurines clutching small silver swords, shields, and magic wands. The diorama featured all that and more, and it was an impressive, museum-quality display.

Several cushioned chairs were spaced around the diorama, along with smaller tables covered with pens, notepads, and plastic containers filled with neon-colored, multi-sided dice. Still more tables bristled with bottles of paint, brushes, colored paper, and other art supplies.

This wasn't a barn—it was a ren-faire, role-playing, model-making gamer's paradise.

Definitely *not* what I had expected, and the jumble of items only made me more confused. Who owned all this stuff? And why keep it in a decrepit old barn? And what did any of this have to do with kidnapping Owen?

The low murmur of voices sounded down below, and a door creaked open somewhere in the back of the first floor, out of my line of sight. Then the distinctive *slap-slap-slap-slap* of boots against concrete rang out.

A few seconds later, Pirate Queen Celeste strolled into view. She was still wearing her red leather costume, along with her two ruby-studded swords, and that silver tiara still glinted on her head.

And she wasn't alone.

Four black-leather-clad giants followed her into the front part of the barn. Two of the men sat down next to each other and started typing on two separate laptops that were perched at one end of the diorama table. For a moment, I thought they were booting up some game, but rows of text and numbers filled their screens, not bright, flashy graphics. The other two giants lounged on one of the couches.

"Did anyone follow you?" Celeste asked. "Or try to stop you?"

One of the giants on the couch shook his head. "Nope. I waited until Grayson took a break from the forge, then bashed him upside the head just like you told me to. The boys helped me carry him through the park. We told everyone that he was drunk and played it for laughs, and they all thought it was part of the show. We walked right through the crowd, and no one batted an eye."

Celeste nodded her approval.

"What about Blanco?" another giant piped up.

Celeste shrugged. "Lancelot took care of her. We're free and clear."

I let out a quiet sigh of relief. Apparently, Celeste had believed my fake text claiming that Lancelot and his friends had eliminated me. Good. That at least gave me the small advantage of surprise.

"But it's a shame that Lancelot got to kill her instead of me. After all this work and training, I wanted to go a few rounds with the infamous Spider." Celeste stuck out her red lips in an exaggerated pout.

My hand tightened around my knife. She didn't realize it yet, but she was going to get her wish to tangle with me—and she was going to bleed out all over that concrete floor.

"All right, then," Celeste said. "Let's get on with it."

She turned to the giants on the couch and made a sharp, sweeping motion with her hand, as though she really was a queen telling her minions to scuttle away. The giants nodded, got to their feet, and disappeared into the back of the barn. A few seconds later, they reappeared, carrying a third man between them.

Owen.

CHAPTER SEVEN

T HE TWO GIANTS half dragged, half carried Owen over to a
wooden chair close to the diorama and threw him down
into the seat.

An ugly bruise had bloomed like a purple pansy on the left
side of Owen's face, and blood had oozed out of a deep, nasty
cut in the center of the swelling, trickled down his cheek, and
dried on his skin like rusty paint. Owen blinked and blinked, but
he didn't resist as the giants tied his arms down to the chair with
thick, heavy ropes. He was still clearly dazed from the hard hit
he'd taken when the men attacked him behind the blacksmith
forge.

Some of the tension in my chest eased, and my breath escaped in a relieved rush that sent the dust motes spinning
through the air. Yes, Owen was injured, but Jo-Jo could use her
Air magic to heal his head, along with all the other damage the
giants had done. I just needed to get him out of the barn first—
and figure out exactly who these people were and why they had
kidnapped him.

I could understand Hugh Tucker, Mason, or some other
Circle member snatching Owen to lure me into a trap, but it
sounded like Lancelot had been ordered to kill me outright,
while Owen was still alive. Why eliminate me and keep him

alive? Unless . . .

Unless this was all about *Owen*.

This whole time, I'd thought someone had been using Owen to get to me. But these people didn't care about me at all, other than making sure that I stayed out of their way. No, they had been after Owen this whole time. But why?

I studied Celeste and the four giants, but I had never seen any of them before today. I was certain of it. I also didn't remember seeing their faces in the files Fletcher had kept on Ashland's many criminals. These were either low-level players or new folks in town. But that still didn't answer the question of why they had kidnapped Owen.

Celeste glanced over at the two giants in front of the laptops. "Aren't you ready yet?" she snapped, an impatient note in her voice. "How long does it take to type in a few passwords?"

"A few *dozen* passwords," one of the giants corrected her, still tapping keys the whole time. "And we're almost ready. We're just logging into all the accounts so that we can see the transactions and make sure that everything processes correctly."

My eyes narrowed. Accounts? Transactions?

The giant was making it sound like this was all about . . . *money*.

Kidnapping someone and cleaning out their personal and business holdings was a common enough scheme, especially in a place as corrupt and violent as Ashland, but I still wondered exactly *why* Celeste and the giants had chosen Owen out of all the businesspeople in the city.

It wasn't like they'd seen Owen walking down a dark street at midnight and decided to grab him on the spur of the moment.

This whole setup reeked of weeks, if not months, of careful planning. But how had Celeste and her men even known that Owen was going to be at the renaissance faire? It wasn't like he'd posted photos of his blacksmith costume on social media like his younger sister, Eva, would have. The only people who had known that Owen was going to be here were me and my friends and of course—

A faint, ominous *creak* sounded. I froze, as did Celeste and the giants on the first floor.

She yanked her two swords out of their scabbards and snapped them up. "What was that?"

The two giants who'd dragged Owen in here drew their own swords and started looking around, while the other two men in front of the computers stopped their staccato typing, their heads swiveling left and right, searching for the source of the noise.

A bad, bad feeling filled my stomach. I shifted my weight the tiniest bit to the right. Sure enough, another faint, ominous *creak* sounded.

I was the one making the telltale noise.

I grimaced and glanced down. For the first time, I noticed that the boards under my feet contained several deep, jagged cracks, far more cracks than the surrounding wood. My grimace deepened. I'd picked exactly the wrong spot to crouch down and spy on my enemies.

I slid my knife back up my sleeve, then slowly stood up and scooted one of my feet to the side. I was trying to get off the weakest-looking board, but the next one I stepped onto wasn't any better, and a third ominous *creak* rang out. I scooted my foot to a different board, and that *creak* cranked up into a low, steady whine.

I grimaced again and glanced around, trying to find a sturdier board to stand on, but there was nowhere for me to go. All the wood up here was cracked and rotten. So I changed tactics, leaning forward and stretching my hand out toward the window. Maybe I could at least grab hold of the windowsill and take some of my weight off the weak wood—

Too late.

Crack! Crack! Crack!

One after another, the boards splintered, and the entire floor gave way beneath my feet.

APPARENTLY, I WAS the straw that broke the hayloft.

For a moment, I had the weightless sensation of falling, but then gravity set in, sucking me down, down, down. It all happened so fast that I didn't have time to grab hold of my Stone magic and harden my skin, but I landed on one of the bales that wasn't filled with weapons, and the hay softened my landing.

But smacking onto a solid surface was never pleasant, and pain spiked through my back. The blow also punched the breath out of my body, and I lay there sprawled across the hay bale and broken boards for several seconds, just trying to get air back down into my lungs.

While I sucked down breath after breath, two of the giants rushed forward and flanked me, their swords still clutched in their hands.

When I felt steady enough, I slowly sat up and dusted the splinters of wood and bits of hay off my clothes. Then I looked at the giants.

"Hey, fellas," I wheezed. "What's up?"

Celeste stepped forward, both of her swords still in her hands. She eyed me a moment, then jerked her head at the giants. "Get her up."

The two men holstered their weapons, stepped forward, and hauled me to my feet. One of them held me still while the other man patted me down. He found all five of my knives, which he tossed onto the top of the hay bale. Once that man had gotten rid of my knives, the other giant let go of my arm, and they both stepped back. Fools. They should have realized that I didn't need my blades to kill them.

I looked over at Owen. "You okay?"

He blinked away the rest of his daze and focused on me. "Just a little headache. You?" He nodded, and I realized that he was staring at my left arm.

"Oh, just a little slice with a sword. Nothing to worry about. You know I've had worse." I winked at him, and Owen grinned back at me.

"Well, if I were the two of you, I would be very worried right now," Celeste purred.

She started twirling her swords around in her hands, just as she had done earlier during the pirate show, and her hazel eyes started glowing with a bright, golden light. And just like at the pirate show, I sensed a faint gust of magic, one that slowly grew stronger and stronger the longer and faster Celeste spun her weapons around.

A sharp static charge filled the air, raising the hair on my arms and neck. In an instant, I felt like dozens of tiny invisible needles were stabbing into my skin over and over again, and I had to grind my teeth to keep from snarling. The uncomfortable pricking sensation reminded me of Jo-Jo's Air magic, but it wasn't quite the same.

It was *worse*.

Celeste was still twirling her swords around, but the blades seemed much brighter than before, almost as if they were . . . *glowing*. That bad, bad feeling filled my stomach again, and I peered at her weapons more closely.

Hot golden sparks of electricity popped, crackled, and sizzled up and down the two blades, streaking from the hilts to the points and back again in explosive waves. Most elementals were gifted in Air, Fire, Ice, or Stone, but Celeste's power was electricity, an offshoot of Air, just like Owen's metal magic was an offshoot of Stone. I grimaced again. Of course, she had electrical magic. Because she wasn't nearly dangerous enough with those swords already.

Celeste must have gotten tired of showing off, because she stopped spinning her swords around and slowly lowered the weapons to her sides, although those golden sparks kept dancing up and down the lengths of the blades.

"I can't believe you're an assassin, much less the Spider, the queen of the Ashland underworld." She sneered. "And to think that I used to be your biggest fan. I got into sword fighting because of you, and I even dressed up like you at the summer faire last year. What a fucking disappointment."

My fan? Training with swords? Dressing up like me? I'd expected threats of violence and promises of pain, torture, and death. Not . . . whatever this was.

"You're my fan? How do you even know who I am?"

Celeste arched an eyebrow. "Are you kidding? You're a real-life assassin who supposedly has a heart of gold and helps people who can't help themselves. Of course I know who you are. *Everyone* on the ren-faire circuit knows who you are. You're practically a fucking folk hero."

All four of the giants nodded, confirming her words, and a couple of them gave me sly, goofy grins. I glanced over at Owen, who looked as bewildered as I felt.

Celeste shook her head. "But I guess this just goes to show that the old saying is true and that you should never meet your idols, because they'll only end up disappointing you."

"And how have I disappointed you?"

She let out a loud, derisive snort. "Forgive me for not admiring someone stupid enough to fall through a rickety old hayloft."

She had a point, although I would never admit it. Plunging through the hayloft hadn't been one of my finest moments, but sometimes Lady Luck just screwed me over like that. What mattered was picking myself up again and getting back into the fight, and I was an expert at both of those things.

Unlike these people, who seemed to be . . . *amateurs.*

All the talk of being my fan and dressing up made me think that Celeste and her friends were only playing at being hardened criminals instead of being bona fide villains. I eyed the golden sparks of magic still shooting off her swords. Well, she wasn't playing. She definitely wanted to murder me in the most painful manner possible.

Had Owen and I really been captured by some weekend ren-faire players? I bit back a groan. Finn would *never* let me live this down—provided Owen and I made it out of here alive.

"Complete and utter disappointment," Celeste said for the third time.

Fan or not, I'd had enough of her snide criticism. She thought she was better than me? Well, we'd see about that.

"I bet Lancelot and his two friends were disappointed in me too—right up until I killed them."

My harsh words wiped the goofy grins off the giants' faces, although they didn't seem to faze Celeste.

"You guys don't know what you've gotten yourself into. This is real life, not some game you're playing on that diorama," I snarled. "You're right. I am the Spider, I am a real assassin, and I am really, truly going to *kill you all dead* unless you leave right now."

I turned my cold, wintry gray gaze to first one giant, then another. The two standing near me shifted nervously on their feet, but they didn't back away, while the other two in front of the laptops stayed in their seats. I'd given them a chance to save themselves, and they hadn't taken it. What happened next was on them.

Celeste snorted again. "Lancelot was an idiot who barely knew the sharp end of his sword from his ass. I won't make the same mistake. Trust me on that."

She spun her swords around again, putting even more flashy flourish into her smooth moves, along with another wave of bright, crackling electricity. Arrogant show-off.

Still, as much as I would have liked to charge across the barn, wrest one of those swords away from her, and bury the blade in her heart, I held my position. Celeste was close to Owen, and she could easily slice one of her swords across his throat before I could get to him.

I looked at Owen, who nodded back. He realized that I was going to have to wait for the right moment to strike, just like he was waiting.

I focused on Celeste again. When in doubt, start talking to stall for some more time. I hoped she wouldn't be too disappointed in me for using the oldest trick in the book.

"What do you want?" I asked. "Why did you kidnap Owen, and why did you order your goons to try to kill me? And why are you calling yourself the Black Rook?"

Celeste frowned a moment, as if she didn't know what I was talking about, but then her pretty face creased into a smug smile, and she let out a light, pealing laugh. The giants joined in with hearty chuckles. The mocking sounds grated on my nerves even more than the awful feel of her electrical magic did.

"What's so funny?" I growled.

"Oh, you dumb little Spider," Celeste purred, smiling even wider than before. "Whoever said that *I* was the Black Rook?"

Confusion filled me, but then I looked at her costume again. No black feathers adorned her red leather, and she wasn't wearing any sort of bird symbols. More confusion filled me. But if Celeste wasn't the Black Rook, then who was? And what did they want from Owen?

"Oh, Gin," a low voice called out. "I was actually hoping not to involve you in this, but you just wouldn't stay out of the way. Then again, I had heard that was one of your more annoying traits."

I didn't recognize the voice, but Owen jerked back in his chair as though he'd just been slapped across the face. His head whipped to the left, and I followed his gaze.

Footsteps sounded in the back of the barn, and a figure wearing a long, hooded black cloak stepped out from behind another stack of hay bales. This must be the mysterious Black Rook.

Owen's jaw clenched, and his eyes glittered with anger, but I still didn't understand what was going on. Who was this person?

The Black Rook stopped in an open space near the middle of the barn and pushed back the hood of his cloak, revealing a very familiar face.

Darrell Kline.

CHAPTER EIGHT

D ARRELL HAD DRASTICALLY changed since the last time I'd seen him during the pirate show.

His green velvet derring-do Robin Hood costume had vanished, along with his silver glasses and clipboard, and he was now wearing a far more badass ensemble of a black leather shirt, pants, and boots. Soft, glossy black feathers trimmed his black cloak, adding to his dark, ominous look. A large silver pin shaped like a cawing bird with ruby eyes hooked the front of the cloak together just below his throat. Not just any bird, I realized.

A rook.

"*You're* the Black Rook?" I asked.

He lifted his chin and gave me a cold, razor-thin smile. His clothes weren't the only thing that had changed—so had Darrell himself.

Gone was the nice, polite accountant who volunteered at the faire, and in his place was a much harder, more confident man. His body seemed bigger and stronger, his hazel eyes were brighter, and even his previously shaggy sandy-brown hair had been slicked back into a smoother, more menacing style. I felt like I'd just seen a snake shed its skin, and I got the impression that I was finally seeing the true Darrell Kline, or Black Rook, or whatever he was calling himself.

Darrell held his hands out wide, preening and showing off
his costume. "Well, I imagine my outfit gave it away, but yes,
Gin. *I* am the Black Rook. Just like you're the assassin the Spider.
Only today, you got caught in my web. Ha-ha-ha-ha."

I rolled my eyes at his bad pun, but Darrell ignored me and
turned to Celeste, who came over, leaned forward, and pressed
a loud, smacking kiss to his lips. Darrell grinned and slipped an
arm around her waist, careful of her two swords as he hugged
her close. Celeste let out a little giggle and kissed him again
before stepping away.

So not only did Celeste work for Darrell, but the two of
them were involved as well, like an evil, ren-faire Maid Marian
and Robin Hood come to life. Terrific. Just terrific. As if this
wasn't weird enough already.

Darrell reached into his pants pocket. I tensed, thinking that
he was grabbing a dagger or some other weapon, but he only
pulled out his phone and started swiping through screens.

"I thought volunteers were supposed to turn off their
phones," I sniped. "In order to add to the magical *atmosphere*."

Darrell shrugged. "Normally, I would do that, but you can't
steal millions of dollars just by brandishing a sword at someone.
These days, you need computers for that sort of thing."

Owen glanced over at the two giants still typing on their
laptops, then focused on Darrell again. Owen's violet eyes
narrowed in understanding.

"This is about the Harrison account, isn't it?" he accused. "I
knew there was something wrong with the numbers. I *knew* it."

Darrell shrugged again. "Of course there's something wrong
with the numbers. I've been cooking the books and siphoning

money from that account and a few others for months now. Five thousand here, ten thousand there. Not too much at one time, but it started to add up. I was hoping to get a few more weeks and paydays out of the accounts before slipping quietly off into the night, but then you announced that you were bringing in that outside forensic accountant to go over everything on Monday."

He shook his head as though he was deeply disappointed in Owen's thoroughness. "I knew the game was up, but instead of taking a few more thousand dollars and disappearing, I decided to double down and go for one last big score. Besides, why just steal from a few measly accounts when I can clean out everything you have? *All* the accounts, *all* at once."

"You bastard," Owen growled. "You're nothing but a damn thief."

Despite his harsh tone and fierce words, worry still filled his face. Owen was a successful businessman with stakes in mining, lumber, and other operations in Ashland and beyond, and he had access to accounts and assets that were worth millions of dollars. If Darrell stole all that money . . . Well, bankruptcy wouldn't be the worst part of it. Owen's reputation would be ruined, and a lot of people who worked with him or for him could also lose everything.

"Why?" Owen asked the inevitable question. "Why are you doing this? Why are you stealing from me?"

"It's been obvious for quite some time that I'd gone as high in your company as I could and that I was never going to get out of middle management." Darrell stabbed his finger at me, as if that was my fault. "Something that became crystal clear after you and Gin hooked up. You started taking more and more of your business to Finnegan fucking Lane and asking *his* advice about various accounts and investments instead of *mine*."

So this was all about money. It usually was in Ashland.

Something that Owen had said in Jo-Jo's salon this morning popped into my mind. "Wait a second. You were at that charity auction a few weeks ago, weren't you? Owen said he didn't even remember bidding on the faire tickets. That's because he *never* bid on them. *You* did. You just needed Owen to supposedly win the tickets in order to get him here."

Darrell grinned, as though he was pleased that I'd figured out his scheme. "Exactly! I needed to get Owen out of his comfort zone and into mine. Of course, I expected him to bring Eva today—not you, Finnegan Lane, and your sister the detective. But I knew that my plan would still work. I just had to get you out of the way first."

So that was why he'd posted the giants outside the Pork Pit food truck: to keep me busy and stop me from interfering while the rest of his men kidnapped Owen.

"I wasn't paying and promoting you enough, so you decided to steal from me?" Owen growled again.

Instead of answering Owen's accusation, Darrell shifted on his feet and adjusted the silver rook pin at his throat. I focused on the bird's ruby eyes and reached out with my Stone magic. The rubies were whispering about how pretty and expensive they were, just like the jewels embedded in the hilts of Celeste's swords still were. Their outfits had both cost a pretty penny too, as had all the fancy gaming equipment and the diorama.

"You're broke," I said. "That's why you're really doing this."

Owen frowned. "What do you mean?"

I held my hands out wide. "Look at this place. All the monitors and gaming equipment, all the paint and art supplies for the diorama. None of that stuff is cheap. Neither are their costumes and weapons."

I snapped my fingers, remembering something else. "And Darrell has even more of this stuff at home. He showed me pictures of his collectibles during the holiday party at the Pork Pit."

Darrell didn't respond, but a pink flush crept up his neck, his lips pinched together into a tight, thin line, and he crossed his arms over his chest in a defensive motion. Guilty as charged.

"Gin's right. You're doing this because you're a greedy bastard, not because I hurt your feelings." Owen shook his head. "And here I thought you actually believed in all this medieval, ren-faire stuff about duty and honor and loyalty."

"Oh, I do believe in it, but my favorite characters to play have always been the rogues, the thieves, the pirates." Darrell tipped his head to me. "And especially the assassins who take what they want and kill whomever they like."

"Gin has more honor and loyalty in her pinkie than you will ever have," Owen snarled.

Darrell gave him an amused look. "Aw, how noble of you to defend your lady's honor. I hope Gin appreciates the gesture, especially since it's the last thing you'll ever do for her."

He slid his phone back into his pocket, then walked over to the two giants still sitting at the computers. "Are we ready to transfer the money?"

One of the giants flashed him a thumbs-up and handed him a

tablet. Darrell clutched the device in the crook of his elbow, then strolled back over to Owen.

"And now, boss, it's time to give me access to your accounts—all of them." Darrell loomed over him. "I need your master login and password, as well as your personal authentication keywords."

"Fuck off," Owen snarled. "I'm not giving you a thing—not one damn thing."

"I thought you might say that."

Darrell stepped back and jerked his head at Celeste, who twirled her swords around in her hands again. I knew what she was going to do, and I took a step forward to try to stop her, but the two giants raised their fists and cracked their knuckles in warning. They were standing between me and Owen, as were Darrell and Celeste, and any one of them could easily kill Owen before I could get to him. So as much as I hated it, I stopped, gritted my teeth, and held up my hands, surrendering to the bastards.

For now.

Celeste made sure that I wasn't going to interfere, then whipped around and slammed the hilt of her first sword straight into Owen's face.

Crunch.

The sound of his nose breaking seemed as loud as a clap of thunder in the barn. Owen let out a low groan of pain, and blood gushed down his face.

Celeste hummed with happiness. And then she hit him again. And then again and then again.

She slammed the hilts of her swords into Owen's face, chest, and arms over and over, like he was a dummy she was practicing her moves on. Each pain-filled grunt that escaped his lips was like a punch to my own heart. Celeste also put a bit of her electrical magic into the blows, making Owen's entire body twitch and jerk and his skin blister and burn.

The acrid stench of his singed flesh was one of the worst things I had ever smelled in my entire life.

Through it all, Owen stared at me, his violet gaze steady on mine. The absolute love and trust shining in his eyes made my own heart squeeze tight in response. Despite our dire situation, he still believed that I would get us out of this. That I would save us. His unwavering trust filled me with a warm rush of love, along with an iron determination not to let him down.

But Celeste could still slit Owen's throat before I could reach him, so I had to stand there and watch while the bitch tortured him.

After a few minutes, Celeste finally lowered her weapons and stepped back. Owen coughed and coughed, trying to get his breath back after all the brutal blows, and his arms and legs kept twitching from the lingering stings of her electricity. After the better part of a minute, he finally stopped coughing, although the faint hitch and wheeze in his breath indicated that he probably had at least one cracked or broken rib, if not more.

Celeste smirked at me. My hands clenched into tight fists. She was going to die for hurting him—she just didn't realize it yet.

Darrell gestured at his partner in crime. "I like to play the part of a thief, but Celeste here, well, she's more of a barbarian at heart. I love that about her."

He gave an elaborate hand flourish and bowed low to her, as though he really was a gallant knight and she was some fair maiden, instead of them both being rotten and treacherous to the core. Darrell straightened back up, and Celeste blew him an air kiss, which he caught and dramatically pressed to his heart. Ugh. *Kill me now*, just like Finn had said.

Owen looked up at the two of them. Then he leaned forward and spat out a mouthful of blood right onto Darrell's shiny black boots. I grinned. And that was one of the reasons I loved him.

"How's that for barbaric?" Owen rasped.

Darrell's nose crinkled with disgust. Celeste stepped forward and hit Owen again, making him cough up more blood. Worry twisted my chest, but I didn't move. I couldn't risk attacking while Celeste and her swords were still that close to Owen.

Darrell eyed his former boss a moment longer, then smiled, as if some new, horrible thought had occurred to him.

"Well, if you won't give up the information to save yourself, then maybe you'll give it up to save your own precious assassin queen." Darrell jerked his head at Celeste, who grinned and stalked over to me.

She gestured at the two giants, who stepped forward and latched onto my arms. I didn't resist, even though I knew how much this was going to hurt.

Celeste moved so that she was standing right in front of me, still clutching her two swords. Her lips puckered as she studied me, clearly thinking about where and how badly to hurt me. She tilted her head to the side, then snapped her hand forward and slammed her sword hilt into my face, just like she'd done to

Owen.

Pain erupted in my left cheek and quickly radiated out through my skull like a string of grenades exploding one after another. I staggered back, and I would have fallen on my ass if the giants hadn't been holding on to me. Even then, I listed around like a ship on a stormy sea, and more than a few white stars winked on and off in my field of vision.

"Wait!" Owen yelled. "Stop!"

But Celeste didn't stop. Instead, she lashed out with one of her blades, opening up a gash along my left bicep. The deep cut was bad enough, but she also put some of her electricity into the blow, and the stinging jolts blasted over me like I'd just touched a live wire.

Sweat popped out on my forehead, my teeth rattled together, and I accidentally bit my own tongue, adding to my misery. My body involuntarily jerked and flailed, but the giants held me fast until the electricity faded away. Somehow I swallowed down a scream of pain, even though I felt like my left arm was on fire.

Celeste smirked and drew her sword back for another strike, but Darrell held out his hand, stopping her.

"I think that's enough for now. Let's see if hurting Gin has made Owen more cooperative." He turned to the other man. "Well, Owen? What do you say? Do you feel like giving up those passwords now?"

Owen glared at his former accountant, his violet eyes practically glowing with fury. "I'm going to kill you for hurting Gin," he growled.

Darrell laughed. "Oh, I doubt that. As soon as I have your

money, Celeste and I are leaving Ashland for good. In a few hours, we'll be on a Caribbean island, shopping for yachts and whatever else strikes our fancy, and drinking and spending all our cares away. Isn't that right, my queen?"

Celeste beamed at him. "Absolutely."

Shopping for yachts? Well, someone was taking their pirate fantasy a little too far, but I hoped they enjoyed it—because it was going to be the last thing they ever enjoyed.

Darrell went back over to Owen and bent down, waggling his tablet in Owen's face. "The passwords. Or Celeste goes back to practicing her sword and magic skills on Gin."

Owen looked at me, then at my two giant guards, then at Celeste, who was still standing in front of me with her swords clutched in her hands. Finally, he focused on me again.

Worry, fear, and concern tightened his face, but they weren't nearly as strong as the other two emotions burning in his violet gaze: his love for me and his determination that we were both getting out of this alive.

I nodded, telling him that I was ready to move. "It's all right, Owen. Just give him the passwords."

"Yes, Owen," Darrell sneered. "Give me the passwords. *Now.* Or your precious Gin dies."

Celeste stepped closer to me and lifted one of her swords, resting the sharp blade up against my throat. She smirked, then pressed the edge into my neck, nicking my skin and drawing a bit of blood. She was going to slit my throat the second Darrell had what he needed from Owen. Well, let her try. She was the one who wouldn't be getting out of here alive.

Darrell glanced over at the two giants in front of the computers. This time, they both flashed him a thumbs-up, telling him they were ready to rock 'n' roll and steal everything from Owen. He nodded, then turned back to Owen.

"Give me your master password," Darrell demanded.

Owen wet his lips, but he didn't say anything.

Darrell sighed, then lifted his arm and backhanded Owen. The sharp *crack* of the blow echoed through the barn, further hardening my resolve.

Owen bent over double, coughing and coughing. That went on for several seconds before he finally got his breath back and straightened up.

"The password," Darrell demanded again. "This is your last chance. Otherwise, Celeste starts cutting off pieces of Gin."

Owen mumbled something unintelligible.

Darrell frowned and leaned down. "What? What did you say?"

Owen mumbled again. This time, everyone looked at him, including Celeste, who shifted on her feet and lowered her sword one precious inch away from my throat. Amateurs. They should have known better than to take their eyes off me.

"What did you say?" Darrell asked again.

Owen lifted his head and smiled. "I said I'm going to enjoy watching you die, you backstabbing son of a bitch."

Before Darrell could move or react, Owen snapped his head forward.

Crunch.

This time, Darrell's nose was the one that broke. He screamed and stumbled away, blood gushing down his face and his tablet slipping from his hand. He sucked down a breath, probably to order Celeste to cut my throat, but Owen let out a loud roar and surged to his feet, even though his arms were still tied down to the chair. He ran forward and smashed his body—chair and all—straight into Darrell.

And that's when the real ren-faire battle began.

CHAPTER NINE

OWEN AND DARRELL crashed to the floor with a loud, thunderous roar.

The wooden chair must have been as rickety as the hayloft boards, because it splintered to pieces under Owen's weight. He rolled over and up onto his knees, then ripped the ropes off his arms. The second he was free, Owen threw himself on top of Darrell and started punching him.

Celeste cursed and started in that direction to help Darrell, but I kicked out and drove my foot into the back of her left thigh. She let out a loud, surprised shriek and tumbled to ground, although she managed to hang on to her swords.

Those two giants were still holding on to me, so I turned to the one on my right and drove my foot into the side of his ankle, which let out a loud, sickening *pop!* The giant screamed and loosened his grip. I shoved my hand down between us and grabbed the silver sword out of the scabbard on his belt. It was heavy, just like all the giants' weapons were, but I managed to slice it across his stomach, and he dropped to the ground, screaming and clutching at the wound.

I turned toward the second giant, who was still hanging on to me, his mouth gaping open in shock. I yanked my arm free of his grip, wrapped both hands around the hilt of my stolen sword, and sliced it across his chest. He too screamed and fell to the ground.

The two giants might be out of the fight, but Celeste was definitely not.

She surged back to her feet and whirled around to me. She was still clutching her swords, and golden sparks of electricity started sizzling up and down the blades again. I reached for my own Stone magic, using it to harden my skin, although Celeste didn't seem to notice.

"I'm going to cut you to pieces for that!" she hissed.

"Do your worst!" I hissed right back at her.

Celeste let out a shriek of rage and charged forward. I also screamed with rage and stepped up to meet her.

Celeste whirled and twirled her swords every which way, slicing out with them over and over again. I might be skilled with my knives, but it was all I could do to lift the giant's heavy sword and block her vicious blows. Yep, I definitely needed to add medieval weapons to my training regimen. Some heavier weights too.

After a particularly fast, vigorous exchange, Celeste managed to knock my stolen sword out of my hand. The weapon sailed away and landed point-down in one of the hay bales. Ah, the irony. I couldn't have done that if I'd tried a hundred times.

Celeste tightened her grip on her swords and reached for even more of her magic, so that the blades seemed to be made of golden electricity instead of metal. "Now there's nothing to keep me from slicing you to ribbons and then frying your weak, clumsy ass."

She let out a loud yell and charged forward, slashing her

swords through the air as fast as she could. I spun out of the way of her first attack, then her second one, but I couldn't avoid her third strike, and she sliced one of her swords across the back of my thigh.

The hard, bruising blow made me stumble, but thanks to my Stone magic, the blade didn't actually bite into my flesh, and her electricity only scorched my costume, not my skin. Still, I let out a loud, agonized scream, flailed around, and dropped to one knee, as though I was severely injured.

Celeste thought she'd won, and she started circling me, still clutching her swords. Electrical sparks fell off the blades like acid raindrops and crackled against the floor. I felt like I was trapped in a fireworks show, although I maintained my grip on my Stone magic to protect my skin from her hot, burning power.

She was savoring the moment. Well, I hoped she enjoyed it. Because I was a long way from done, something she was going to realize in another minute, two tops.

"I don't see why Darrell was so worried about you," she said. "Sure, you're a good fighter, but I'm better, especially with my swords. And my electricity gives me a clear advantage."

I could have told her that the better fighter didn't always win and that I'd killed a whole lot of people who'd been stronger than me in their magic, but I didn't waste my breath. She was already dead. She just didn't know it yet.

Instead, I looked past Celeste at Owen, who was still pummeling Darrell. The two giants who'd been sitting in front of the computers finally realized that their boss was going to lose the fight, and they surged to their feet and headed in that direction. Owen saw them coming, picked up one of the broken pieces of his chair, and threw it at them. Even though it was just a harmless piece of wood, the two giants still lurched back out of the way.

Celeste finally noticed that Owen was beating the shit out of her boyfriend, but instead of going over to help him, she turned back to me instead.

"Time to die, little Spider," she snarled.

She lifted one of her swords and then snapped it down. I didn't even try to avoid the blow. Instead, I reached for even more of my Stone magic, closed my hand into a fist, and smashed it up against her weapon.

CLANG!

Celeste wasn't expecting the concrete resistance of my Stone-hardened fist, and she lost her grip on her sword, which sailed through the air before landing point-down in that same hay bale right next to my weapon. Bull's-eye for a second time. Even Robin Hood would have been impressed with my aim today.

Surprise flickered in Celeste's hazel eyes, and she lashed out with her other sword, trying to drive it into my heart. This time, I reached out, wrapped my fingers around the blade, and used it like a lever to pull myself back up and onto my feet. Celeste snarled, gripped the hilt with both hands, and tried to wrest her sword free, but my Stone magic gave me a cement grip that she just couldn't break.

I dropped my free hand down by my side, this time reaching for my Ice magic. In an instant, I had formed a long, jagged Ice knife.

Celeste tried one last time to wrest her sword away, but I

tightened my grip on the blade and yanked, pulling her toward me. Celeste growled and raised one of her hands to blast me in the face with her electricity, but I was quicker. I snapped up the Ice knife in my other hand and buried the cold shard in the side of her neck.

Her eyes bulged, and the golden glow of her electrical magic snuffed out of her gaze like a fire doused by a wet blanket. I twisted the cold shard in even deeper, staring at her the whole time.

"If you were a true fan, then you would know that no one does my job better than me," I hissed.

Celeste let out a strangled scream, almost as if she was agreeing with me. Then her eyes rolled up in the back of her head, and she crumpled to the ground with my Ice knife still stuck in her neck. Blood started pooling under her body. The scarlet sheen matched her fancy costume.

The pirate queen was dead.

"Celeste!" Darrell shouted. "No!"

He had finally managed to scramble away from Owen, who was now battling the two giants. Owen had gotten his hands on someone's sword, and one of the giants already lay dead at his feet. Owen snarled and engaged the second giant, swinging his stolen sword like it was his more familiar blacksmith hammer.

"Celeste!" Darrell shouted again. "Celeste!"

He raced in my direction. I reached for my Ice magic again, but before I could make another knife, he plowed into me. My legs hit something, and Darrell bent me backward. An instant later, my head snapped back against a hard surface, making me lose my grip on my Stone magic. White stars flashed in front of my eyes, and my skin reverted to its normal vulnerable texture.

It took me a moment to realize that I was now sprawled across the table with the fancy medieval diorama. Judging from the hard lumps poking into my back, I'd just flattened a couple of mountains and several legions of dwarves and giants.

I tried to rise, but Darrell shoved me right back down again, then grabbed one of the gray stone castles off the table.

"You bitch!" he screamed, his voice teetering on a plaintive wail. "You killed Celeste! You killed my pirate queen!"

He snapped the castle down, aiming for my nose, but I managed to catch his wrist in my hand and stop him from hitting me. But that was only part of the problem. The castle also featured a flag pole with a very long, very sharp point. Darrell snarled and pressed down, trying to drive the needlelike tip into my right eye.

My head was still spinning, and I was having trouble grabbing hold of my magic so I could blast him with my Ice power. He might be an amateur, but he could still kill me if he hit me in just the right spot—

Something silver glinted behind Darrell, who suddenly screamed and arched back. The miniature castle slipped from his hand, hit the side of the table, and bounced off, dropping to the floor. A hand grabbed Darrell's shoulder, yanking him away from me.

Owen was here.

I rolled off the table, landing hard on my knees on the floor. The fall rattled my brain again, making a few more white stars wink on and off in front of my eyes. I forced myself to scoot away from Darrell, but I didn't have to worry about him any longer.

Owen spun Darrell around, then stepped up and rammed his sword into the other man's stomach.

Darrell screamed again and clutched at Owen's costume, his face white with shock and pain.

"That's for hurting Gin," Owen growled. "And this is for hurting me."

He shoved the sword in even deeper, then yanked it out and pushed the other man away.

Darrell screamed again and stumbled back against the table hard enough to jostle the remaining castles, mountains, and figurines on the diorama. Het let out another strangled cry, then his legs went out from under him, and he sank to the floor. He tried to clamp his hands down over the wound, but he didn't have the strength for it, and he slowly pitched over onto his side.

Darrell landed right next to that gray stone castle he'd tried to stab into my face, and he lifted his arm, as though he was going to reach for it. But he was even weaker than before, and his hand flopped to the floor well short of the castle. He didn't move after that.

The Black Rook was dead.

OWEN STOOD OVER Darrell, wheezing for breath and still clutching his stolen sword. He kicked Darrell in the ribs to make sure he was dead, then staggered over and dropped to his knees beside me.

"Gin! Are you okay?"

I blinked the last few stars out of my eyes and focused on him. Owen's face was a mess of cuts, blood, and bruises from fighting Darrell, and his broken nose had swelled up to almost twice its normal size, but he was as handsome as ever to me.

Owen leaned forward and cupped my cheek with his bloody hand, gently stroking his thumb across my skin. "Gin? Are you okay?" he repeated.

I reached up and grabbed his hand, squeezing it in my equally bloody one. "I'm okay. Thanks to you."

Owen grinned, his eyes glowing like beautiful violet moons. His grin widened, and he leaned down to kiss me—

The main barn doors burst open, and Finn, Bria, and Sophia charged inside. Finn and Bria were both clutching swords, while Sophia was holding her silver cutlass.

My friends skidded to a stop, their heads snapping from side to side as they took in the four dead giants, along with Celeste and Darrell and the fantasy diorama I'd flattened during the fight.

"Aw, man," Finn said, lowering his sword to his side. "We missed it! I totally wanted to engage in an old-fashioned sword duel!"

Sophia sighed with regret. "Me too."

I glanced at Celeste, who was lying on the floor a few feet away. She was still clutching one of her swords, and the blade gleamed with a bright, eerie light, as though it was going to start crackling with electricity again, even though she was dead.

I shuddered at the memory of her hot magic jolting through me. "Trust me. It's not as much fun as you'd think it would be."

"Are you guys okay?" Bria asked. "And who are these people, and why did they kidnap Owen?"

She came over and helped me to my feet, while Finn did the same for Owen.

"I'll tell you all about it," I answered my sister. "After we get out of here. I've had enough swords, pirate queens, and ren-faire goons to last me a lifetime."

"Me too," Owen murmured. "Me too."

I held out my hand, and Owen stepped forward and put his arm around me. Still holding on to each other, the two of us limped out of the barn.

CHAPTER TEN

S INCE WE DIDN'T want to ruin the rest of the ren faire for everyone else, Sophia agreed to dispose of the bodies in the barn, as well as the three giants I'd killed in the woods earlier. Finn stayed behind to help her, while Bria drove Owen and me over to Jo-Jo's salon.

We had to wait until Jo-Jo finished with her latest round of clients, but the dwarf healed Owen and me with her Air magic and sent us on our way. We ended up back at my house late that afternoon.

Owen was in the den, talking on the phone to Stuart Mosley at First Trust bank and trying to figure out just how much money Darrell had stolen and if he could get any of it back. While he hashed things out with Stuart, I went into the kitchen to make dinner.

Last night, I'd brought home some of the faire food that Sophia and I had prepared, and I quickly reheated the pulled chicken in some of Fletcher's barbecue sauce.

While the chicken was warming up, I microwaved a couple of potatoes until they were almost done, then sliced them in half and scooped out most of the insides. I combined the potato innards with sharp cheddar cheese, sour cream, green onions, and crumbled pieces of crispy applewood-smoked bacon. Then I refilled the potato boats with the mixture, sprinkled them with even more cheese, and slid them into the oven to finish baking.

After everything that had happened today, I wanted some warm comfort food, and barbecue chicken and twice-baked potatoes seemed like a good place to start.

I also sliced, buttered, and toasted some of Sophia's sourdough rolls in the oven and threw together a green salad filled with cherry tomatoes, carrots, and red onions and topped with a creamy blue-cheese dressing.

I had just finished putting everything on the kitchen table, along with a pitcher of raspberry lemonade, when Owen came in, sat down, and set his phone aside. I sat down with him, and we both tucked into our food.

The sweet and spicy barbecue chicken. Potatoes loaded with cheese and bacon. The warm toasted rolls. The crunchy, crispy salad with its blue-cheese tang. The fruity tartness of the lemonade. It was a delicious combination of flavors, aromas, and textures, and I enjoyed every single bite. Owen did too, judging by the fact that he went back for seconds, just like I did.

We didn't talk much during the meal, just enjoying the food, each other's company, and the fact that we had both survived another dangerous situation that we probably shouldn't have.

"What did Stuart say?" I asked after we'd taken the edge off our hunger.

"He agreed to let me access Darrell's accounts on Monday so I can recover some of the money he stole." Owen sighed and set his fork down. "There's not much left of it, though. Only a few thousand in his checking account. You were right about him spending it all. I'll have to cover most of the difference out of my own pocket."

"No, you won't."

He frowned. "What? Why not?"

I jerked my head over at one of the kitchen counters. "Because Sophia stopped by while you were talking to Stuart, and she brought you some presents."

Owen followed my gaze. Celeste's swords were sitting on the counter, along with the rook pin that Darrell had been wearing on his cloak.

"How is that going to help?" Owen asked.

"The rubies in the swords and the pin are worth quite a bit. We can go to Darrell's house tomorrow, break in, and loot the rest of his stuff. It shouldn't be too hard to find some buyers for his collectibles. I've already got Finn working on it. He's pitching it as an estate sale, and he'll run everything through First Trust. I don't know that we'll get all your money back, but we should be able to recover a good chunk of it."

Some of the tension eased out of Owen's shoulders, and a smile spread across his face. "Have I told you lately how much I love you?"

"Not nearly enough," I teased. "You know, a girl does like to hear those things from time to time."

His smile widened. "Well, I'll be sure to mention it more often, then. At the very least, every time you save me from renfaire assassins."

My heart squeezed tight at how close I'd come to losing him to the Black Rook and Pirate Queen Celeste, but I winked, not wanting to ruin the lighthearted mood. "I'll hold you to that. And there is something else you could do for me."

"Name it."

I stabbed my finger at Celeste's swords. "Make me a pair of those. Just in case we ever do run into more ren-faire assassins. You never know in Ashland."

Owen nodded, and his eyes narrowed, as if he was already mentally designing the weapons. "Two silverstone swords. With long, sharp, plain blades. And some sapphires fitted together in the hilts to form your spider runes."

I could already see the weapons in my mind, and I knew they would be just as exquisite as the knives Owen had made for me. I grinned. "You certainly know the way to this assassin's heart."

FOR DESSERT, WE had warm oatmeal-cherry crumble topped with vanilla-bean ice cream and drizzled with my homemade chocolate sauce. After we finished, Owen cleared the table while I lit a fire in the den. Then we curled up on the couch together, our arms wrapped around each other, staring into the bright, cheery flames and lost in our own thoughts.

"Do you want to talk about it?" I finally asked. "About Darrell? I know the two of you weren't all that close, but what he did still had to hurt."

A betrayal by someone you knew and considered a friend always left a far deeper mark than a random attack by a stranger.

"I liked Darrell. He was always nice, polite, and friendly, and I thought he was good at his job. I just didn't realize that he was a little *too* good at it." Owen grimaced. "I still can't believe he was plotting behind my back this whole time. And not just to steal money but to kidnap and kill me."

He fell silent, still staring into the flames. Several seconds passed before he spoke again.

"I guess it just goes to show that you don't really know some people the way you think you do. Maybe the ren faire should have a new theme next year. Maybe instead of *Winter's Web*, the organizers should call it *The Ides of Winter*." He let out a low, bitter laugh. "Hey, maybe I'll even dress up like Julius Caesar next year. After all, I've been betrayed, just like he was."

I kept quiet, sensing there was more he needed to say.

"And I can't help but feel stupid that I fell into Darrell's trap. I should have known something weird was going on when I supposedly won the faire tickets." He shook his head. "And I can't help but think that I could have done things differently. That if I'd just known how unhappy Darrell was, I could have done something to help him." His voice dropped. "Instead of killing him."

I sat up and looked at him. "It is *not* your fault that Darrell did what he did. People make their own choices, and they are responsible for their own actions and the consequences that come along with them. Darrell could have come to you and told you he'd made a mistake embezzling the money, and you would have helped him. I *know* you would have, because that's the kind of good, decent, honorable man you are. But Darrell was arrogant and stupid and greedy, and he decided to take what he wanted no matter how many people he had to hurt. That was his biggest mistake, and it ended up costing him everything."

Owen nodded, and some of the tension eased out of his

body. "How did I ever get so lucky as to have you in my life?"

I grinned. "I could say the same thing about me having you."

He leaned over and kissed me. The brief brush of his lips against mine sent warmth shooting through my body and ignited a spark of desire deep in my stomach.

I drew back, then grinned again and clasped my hands to my heart. "Oh, my dear, sweet, humble blacksmith!" I cooed in a high, falsetto voice. "Oh, how you make me *swoon!*"

I put my hand up to my forehead, let out a long, loud, dramatic sigh, and then flopped back against the couch cushions, as though I was a genteel lady overcome with a case of the vapors.

Owen laughed and then bent forward at the waist, as though he was taking a bow. "Why, thank you, fair lady. This humble blacksmith always aims to please his pirate queen assassin."

I crooked my finger at him. "Then come here and prove it," I murmured in a low, husky voice.

Owen grinned, leaned forward, and lowered himself on top of me so that we were both stretched out on the couch. I threaded my hands through his silky black hair and pulled his head down to mine. Our lips met, and I swiped my tongue against his. He deepened the kiss, plunging his tongue into my mouth. More sparks exploded in my stomach, and I sighed with happiness, wrapped my arms around his neck, and pulled him closer.

Owen kissed his way across my cheek, then sucked on the side of my neck. I drew in a breath, drawing his rich metallic scent deep into my lungs. He kept kissing my neck, even as his hands slid up my shirt. I wasn't wearing a bra, and he cupped my breasts, gently tweaking my nipples with his thumbs. Those sparks burned even brighter and coalesced into a liquid heat that flooded my entire body.

"You are wearing entirely too many clothes," Owen rumbled, still kneading my breasts.

"I was just thinking the same thing about you," I murmured back, running my hands down his strong, muscled back.

"Then let's fix that."

Owen grabbed me around the waist and sat up, pulling me up along with him. I lifted my arms over my head, and he stripped off my shirt, exposing my bare breasts.

His violet gaze darkened with desire. "Now, that's more like it."

He dipped his head to my right breast and gently caught my nipple between his teeth. Then he sucked on it hard before doing the same thing to my other breast. I gasped with pleasure and arched back to give him better access.

Owen kept sucking, licking, and kissing my breasts. That liquid heat in my body burned a little hotter with every sure stroke of his fingers and every sly slide of his tongue. I reached down to get rid of his shirt the way he'd gotten rid of mine, but Owen caught my hand in his and pressed a kiss to my knuckles.

"Not yet," he murmured. "This blacksmith wants to thoroughly pleasure his lady first."

He gave me a wicked grin, then laid me back down on the couch and undid my jeans. I lifted my hips, and Owen slid the jeans off me, along with my underwear and socks. I lay there and watched while he got rid of his own clothes, then grabbed a condom from his wallet. I took my little white pills, but we always used extra protection.

The crackling flames bathed Owen in a soft glow, outlining his broad shoulders, his strong biceps, his muscled chest, and his long, hard erection. I let out a low wolf whistle of appreciation.

"Not so humble after all," I purred.

Owen winked. "Like I said before, I aim to please."

He got down on his knees beside the couch. He smoothed his hands down my thighs and eased them apart. My breath caught in my throat. I knew what was coming next and just how good it would be.

Owen gave me another wicked grin, then bent forward and put his mouth on me, sucking, licking, and kissing just as he'd done to my breasts. I moaned with pleasure and rocked forward, and he plunged his tongue even deeper inside me.

That liquid heat in my veins flared up into something hotter and far more intense, the pressure and the pleasure built and built, and it wasn't long before I cried out and exploded.

Owen kept right on sucking, licking, and kissing as the orgasm ripped through me, trying to bring me as much pleasure as possible. Finally, when my body had stilled, he lifted his head and looked at me.

"Is my lady pleased?" he murmured.

"Exceptionally. Now, come here, you," I growled.

I grabbed his hand and pulled him toward me. Owen laughed and climbed back onto the couch with me. Our mouths locked together, our tongues dueled back and forth, and our caresses became quicker, harder, and more intense.

Eventually, I flipped him over and teased his long, hard length with my tongue and mouth the same way he had teased me, trying to bring him as much pleasure as he had given me, as though this was the first time we'd been together instead of the hundredth. But in some ways, every time with Owen felt like the first time, and I always loved exploring all the hard, muscled planes of his body, from the scar that cut across his chin to his broad shoulders and all the way down his chest.

When Owen was ready, he covered himself with the condom, then picked me up and settled me on his lap. I looked into his eyes, then rocked forward, taking him deep inside me with one smooth motion. We both groaned, and he held on to my hips, urging me on as I surged forward time and time again, taking him deeper and deeper inside me, until we both reached the very peak of our pleasure and plunged over the edge together.

The humble blacksmith and the pirate queen assassin had pleased each other very much indeed.

Afterward, we lay tangled up together on the couch, covered with a soft blanket, basking in the afterglow, as well as the flames still crackling in the fireplace.

Owen drifted off to sleep with his arms wrapped around me. I put my head on his chest and let the strong, steady beat of his heart lull me to sleep as well. My last thought before I slipped into the quiet, soothing blackness was about the ren faire.

Winter's Web, The Ides of Winter, whatever you wanted to call it. The name didn't matter, only the fact that Owen and I had survived it the way we always did, just as we would survive all the challenges with Tucker, Mason, and the Circle that were looming on the horizon.

Together.

About the Author

Jennifer Estep is a *New York Times, USA Today*, and international bestselling author, prowling the streets of her imagination in search of her next fantasy idea.

Jennifer is the author of the **Elemental Assassin**, **Crown of Shards**, **Mythos Academy**, **Bigtime**, and **Black Blade** fantasy series. She has written more than thirty books, along with numerous novellas and stories.

For more information on Jennifer and her books, visit her website at www.JenniferEstep.com. You can also follow her on Facebook, Goodreads, and Twitter and sign up for her newsletter.

Happy reading, everyone! ☺

A Wilderness of Glass

A Novella in the World of the Wraith Kings

BY

GRACE DRAVEN

The stretch of sea known as the Gray rules the lives of those in the village of Ancilar, including widow Brida Gazi. In the aftermath of an autumn storm, Brida discovers one of the sea's secrets cast onto the shore—a discovery that will change her world, mend her soul, and put her in the greatest danger she's ever faced.

Acknowledgements

A sincere and heartfelt thank you to Mel Sterling and RJ Blain for their patience with the 11th hour.

CHAPTER ONE

THE VESTIBULE JUST outside the busy kitchens hummed with conversation and the thump of wet boots. One by one, the musicians shed their footwear for the clean shoes they'd carried with them during the slow wagon ride up the castle hill.

Brida Gazi laced her shoes with shaking fingers, still cold from the winds blowing off the Gray to scour the bluff on which Castle Banat perched. She blew on her hands to warm them before tucking them under her arms for additional heat. "I can hardly tie my shoes," she complained to the woman seated next to her. "I won't be much good on the flute if I can't move my fingers."

Haniss nodded, eyeing the fire they glimpsed in the kitchen with a longing gaze, flames dancing merrily in the giant hearth. "Maybe they'll let us stand by the cooking hearth for a few moments to warm up and dry off a little." She caressed the mandolin in her lap as if it were a favorite cat. "It isn't just us who'll need warming before we play. I don't even want to hear what these strings sound like right now."

The trip had been a miserable one with the salty mists spraying off the Gray to descend upon them in a light drizzle. She had huddled in her thin cloak, clutching her flute with one hand and holding her place on the low-sided dray wagon with the other.

Autumn had brought the annual rains, and this evening had been much like the ones before it for the past fortnight—wet and chilly. It could have been worse. Thunder boomed in the distance, heard even in the depths of the keep, behind thick stone walls. At their arrival in the bailey, the wagon driver had given their troupe a brief frown and a warning as he glanced at the horizon where lightning bolts split the heavy clouds.

"Be prepared for a drenching on the way home," Odon Imre said. "And a long ride as well. I'll not be pushing Voreg here to go fast on muddy roads. I'd rather get you home late than dead."

A scullery maid appeared at the threshold between vestibule and kitchen, a spoon in one hand. She offered the musicians a quick smile. "Cook says you can gather by the fire to warm yourselves. Just don't get in the way or have a chat-up with the rest of us."

She leapt back to keep from being trampled as the five of them bolted for the kitchen and the promise of heat the hearth offered. Brida was the last to leave, and she paused before the wide-eyed maid. "I saw your mama today, Aliz. She wanted me to tell you not to forget that pot of pepper you promised when you come home in a few days." She chuckled at the maid's frustrated eyeroll.

"I wish I'd never said anything about it. You're the fourth person who's delivered that message to me. If I were my da, I'd start to feel jealous over the attention she's paying to a container of spice!"

The various scents of food stewing in pots, roasting on spits, and frying in pans made Brida's mouth water. She'd eaten at home a few hours earlier, but the meal had been nothing as tempting as the smells wafting through the great kitchen at the moment.

The castle's cook, a tall, whip-thin man with a stare sharper than the knife he currently wielded, stalked toward them. Maids and undercooks scurried out of his path. He gestured with the blade and addressed them in a startlingly dulcet voice.

"Once you get the cold out of your hands, you can have something to eat over there." He pointed the knife to a long table set against the far wall. "Lord Frantisek says a well-fed musician plays better, and he expects you to give your best tonight."

Exclamations of delight greeted his announcement, along with assurances that each musician would offer up their best performance for the pleasure of his lordship's guests.

Haniss leaned down to whisper in Brida's ear. "His lordship is much different from his wife, I think. If it were up to Ziga's sister, we'd be playing in the bailey in the downpour."

"If it were up to Lady Frantisek, we wouldn't be here at all." Brida had met the lady of the castle very briefly years earlier, before her marriage to Andras Frantisek. A brittle, high-born girl, very aware of her station in life, she had grown into a beauty who captured the attention of the powerful Frantisek family as a possible bride for the heir before their fall from grace. Sometimes Brida found it hard to believe the pragmatic Zigana Imre was her ladyship's bastard sister. The two women were nothing alike in character.

After time in front of the hearth and a quick supper, the castle steward appeared to escort them to a chamber similar to the first vestibule, except that it was much warmer and contained a staircase that led to a balcony overlooking the great hall. Another doorway opening to the hall itself gave Brida a glimpse of the guests gathering for Lord Frantisek's party to celebrate his wife's naming day.

These were not the elite aristocracy who populated King Sangur's court in Pricid. None of those nobles would deign to travel so far—or even so near—to attend a celebration hosted by the Frantisek Exile. Tonight's guests were the more lowly gentry from the towns and villages within the lord's demesne, eager to brush shoulders and have conversation with the last remaining members of a once-powerful family.

Regardless of their lower ranking, Brida was in awe of the gathering. Many who couldn't claim elevated bloodlines possessed fat purses, and their adornment tonight—silks and fine linens, sparkling jewels, and rare perfumes that scented the air— proved lower-born didn't equate to poverty-stricken.

She would have been content to stare at the pageantry all evening if she wasn't here to perform a task. She turned her attention to the steward when he cleared his throat.

"You may tune your instruments in here. Lord Frantisek has said he will speak with you all. Once he's finished, you'll climb to the balcony and begin your performance." He left them to disappear amid the growing crowd of guests filling the great hall.

"Best get to it then," Janen said as he unpacked his fiddle from its case and prepared to rosin his bow. "Once his lordship arrives, we won't have any more time to tune."

As the oldest and most skilled musician in Ancilar, Janen had accepted Lord Frantisek's invitation on the group's behalf and immediately selected the other four musicians who would join him in a quintet to perform at the castle. He'd approached Brida last.

"Are you interested?" he'd asked once she listened to the details such as payment and what was expected.

His offer had surprised her. She wasn't the only flautist in the village, nor was she the best, and she told Janen so.

He'd shrugged. "Onastis is a better flute player, but there's something about your flute, and the way you play it, Brida, that makes one either weep or laugh, depending on the music. This is what I want played at his lordship's celebration."

She'd agreed, nervous about performing for a crowd of strangers in an unfamiliar environment but grateful for the money she would earn from the event. Every little bit would help her brother and his wife. There were a lot of children to feed.

She unwrapped her flute from its protective covering of cloth that kept it dry. Made from a bone her father had found on the beach and brought back with him, he'd spent hours of drilling out the chamber and finger holes, carving the designs and sanding the bone smooth before presenting it to Brida. It had been his gift to her on her wedding day, the last one he gave her before his death, and she treasured it above all her other possessions.

Klen Gazi had no idea what creature the bone had belonged to, only that he thought it might be something which once lived in the Gray instead of drowned in it. Whatever it was, the flute produced ethereal notes that bewitched people when Brida played it. She didn't fool herself that it was her playing affecting people so much. The flute possessed a magic of its own. She felt it in her fingers and on her lips every time she played.

Despite its sorcery, it was still a flute, and a cold one never sounded good. Brida joined the other troubadours in tuning their instruments, the sounds they produced a discordant cacophony that both drew people to investigate or flinch and flee to the other side of the hall, away from the noise.

As the flute warmed beneath her tuning, the shrieking true notes lowered, and the sharp harmonics softened. It was as if the flute were a living creature, settling with her breath and touch. She played a set of scales and then a short sea shanty before settling on a quartet of notes that had haunted her since she first learned of her husband's death a few years earlier and stood on the shore, contemplating the vast and merciless expanse of the Gray at night.

A sound had rolled off the water then, rising above the surf's low thunder, a tuneless song built on the trough of loss and the crest of hope. It arrowed straight through her soul. She had wept then, for Talmai who had drowned in the Gray's depths, the doomed ship and the men who died alongside him, his eternal companions. Somewhere within the solemn waves, something wept with her.

No other flute she'd ever played could reproduce those four notes exactly. Only this one, strengthening Brida's belief in its mysterious power. She played the notes several times in a row, noting from the corner of her eye the way the other players slowed and finally halted their own tuning to listen. Magic, she thought. There was magic here. She stopped when Janen raised a hand to signal enough.

He opened his mouth to speak, but before he could say

anything, another more strident voice interrupted him. "Where did you learn to play that?"

Brida pivoted to face the newcomer. A man, clothed in the finery of monarchs, his hands bedecked in gold rings, strode into the room. Brida's eyes widened as she backed away to keep him from treading on her feet. He reached for her flute. Only her quick reflexes stopped him from snatching it out of her hands. Janen and the harpist Arpath closed ranks in front of her, creating a living wall to block the stranger.

"Where did you get that flute?" He almost snarled the words, face bloodless with shock, mouth thinned with rage. "Where did you learn those notes?"

Behind Janen's and Arpath's shoulders, Brida gaped, clutching her flute even tighter. Stunned by the unwarranted attack, she struggled to give a coherent reply.

Another, deeper voice joined the fray. "Ospodine, I didn't invite you here to assault the musicians." Andras Frantisek, new lord and tenant of Castle Banat, stood behind the man he called Ospodine, his own sun-kissed features set in grim lines. "What are you doing here?" His tone warned he wouldn't suffer any blather.

Ospodine half turned to answer, still glaring at Brida. "I want to know where she learned to play the song and where she got the flute." His words were accusatory, and in them, she heard the unspoken charge of "thief."

Her indignation overrode her initial surprise. She pushed her way past Janen and Arpath, careful to keep the flute out of reach. Ignoring her accuser, she sought out his lordship's gaze. "My lord, the flute was given to me by my father on my wedding day nearly a decade ago. He fashioned it himself from a bone he found on the beach." Uncaring that she, a village woman of no standing and little import, challenged one of his lordship's guests, she glared at the scowling Ospodine and said "The flute is mine and has always been mine." It was no business of his when and where she'd heard the four-note tune.

Lord Frantisek watched her for a moment, silent, before he raised an eyebrow at Ospodine. "I believe you have your answer, friend. No reason to linger now. Allow me to escort you back to the other guests." Again the implied warning that if Ospodine didn't leave of his own accord, things wouldn't go well for him.

The other man's features, made memorable by his strangely pale eyes, stiffened into lines of contempt before smoothing out to an expressionless mask. He nodded to Brida and bowed to Lord Frantisek. "My apologies for the disturbance, my lord. The flute and its music seemed familiar and startled me. I beg your forgiveness." At Frantisek's head tilt of acknowledgement, Ospodine melted back into the swirling crowd of guests, a dark figure that made Brida think of smoke and water entwined.

Janen bowed, and Brida and the others followed suit. "Thank you for the honor of your invitation, my lord," he said.

His lordship's mouth quirked at the corners, his gaze taking in the instruments in their hands, settling for just a moment longer on Brida's flute before moving on. "The gratitude is mine, especially with the promise of foul weather later. You're welcome to stay overnight if the road is too dangerous to travel home. You'll have to sleep in the kitchens or possibly the stables as we're packed to the rafters with guests, but it'll be dry and safe from lightning."

Brida hoped the weather would hold. This was her first time at Castle Banat, and while she was awed by the structure and its rich trappings, she didn't fancy spending a night under the same roof as the hostile Ospodine.

After a few more pleasantries exchanged between them, his lordship left them to tend to his hosting duties. The steward returned to lead them upstairs to the balcony where stools had been placed in preparation for their arrival. Brida claimed one placed where she could look over the balcony without standing up. The view from above turned the great hall into a sea of flickering lamplight, glittering jewels, and colorful skirts as guests mingled, conversed, and laughed.

Janen moved his seat to face the other four. "Let's start with something slow and soft. Background as they talk and eat. We'll play something livelier if and when they choose to dance."

He struck up the first chord to the first song, and Brida and her companions joined in. They played through the evening, until the candles melted low, the oil lamps burned dry, and the guests emptied the casks of wine manned by a pair of servants who refilled cups as fast as people drained them.

During the brief respites between sets, Brida dabbed at her perspiring brow and wet her lips from the cup of water a servant had brought her while she played. She was tired and on edge, the weight of one man's relentless scrutiny heavy on her skin as she played.

What about those notes had elicited such aggression from a complete stranger? Ospodine had glared at her as if he'd just discovered the thief who'd stolen all the silver from his house.

Brida bristled inwardly, even as her fingers danced down the length of the flute and her breath teased music from the hollow bone.

By the time the steward called a halt to their playing, their quintet was exhausted. Janen stood to follow the steward down the stairs. "Pack up," he instructed the group. "I'll be back with our pay."

Rejuvenated by the prospect of returning home and falling into her own bed, Brida put away her flute, tying it under her skirts as a precaution. Better it not be seen should she be unlucky enough to cross paths with Ospodine a second time this night.

Janen returned to distribute the payment they'd received, and Brida kissed the small purse of money she held before tucking it into her bodice. Despite her encounter with one of Lord Frantisek's unpleasant guests and the prospect of a wet ride home, she was glad she came. She'd made enough to repair the leak in her roof and help her brother's family with their ever-depleted larder, at least until the seaweed harvest started in earnest, and they could sell what they gathered to the farmers of adjacent towns.

A quick peek outside assured them that while the moonlit squall line in the distance still threatened, the troupe had a little longer before the line made landfall. At Odon Imre's impatient gesturing, the five settled into the dray for the trip back down the bluff. Imre's mare, Voreg stamped her hoof, splattering mud, as if to echo Odon's silent encouragement that they hurry it along. Soon they rolled out of the bailey and through the barbican, leaving behind the dark castle.

Brida turned for a last look at the majestic keep, searching for the source that created a prickling itch between her shoulder blades, the same sensation she'd experienced all evening under Ospodine's unwavering stare. Only stone stared back at her, along with a pair of guttering torches. Still, she shivered and turned away, certain down to her bones the nobleman watched her leavetaking from somewhere in the castle.

"It won't be worth going to bed if I have to be back up before the sun's rise," Haniss groused, breaking into Brida's thoughts.

Like the Imres, Haniss and her husband owned a pair of the big draught horses that trawled the Gray for shrimp during summer. With the arrival of autumn, rakes replaced nets, and they put the horses to work harvesting the seaweed that choked the shallows and shrouded the rocks in the aftermath of storms. Heavy clouds and distant lightning hanging over the Gray earlier in the evening prophesied a tempest guaranteed to hurl a rich bounty of seaweed onto the beaches by morning.

Brida patted her shoulder. "I'll meet you on the beach. I may even beat you there." She yawned. "Norinn told me Laylam plans to sleep in his boots, in the stables, with the dog beside him so all he has to do is hitch the horse to the cart and be on the road as soon as the storm has passed. I've volunteered to accompany him while Norinn gets the children ready."

Haniss laughed. "No one will ever accuse your brother of being a lay-about, that's for certain."

The sky was the color of cold ink by the time Odon Imre let Brida off at her front door. She was his last passenger, and she waved from her doorway until the dray turned a corner and disappeared from her sight. She yawned repeatedly now, and her eyelids felt scratchy, but she didn't dare lie down. If she did, she'd slip so far into slumber, she'd miss her brother's arrival, and he'd go on without her. She'd never hear the end of it from him or Norinn later.

She changed out of her clothes into her oldest frock, tucked her flute back into its customary cabinet, and hid her money purse beneath a floorboard under her bed. Afterwards, she made herself a pot of tea. She stood at her window as she drank the entire pot, watching as the storm swept in, first on a wind that bowed trees, then the lightning that flared across the sky, followed by thunder loud enough to rattle the windows. The sky finally opened, dumping a solid wall of rain onto Ancilar. Even from this distance, Brida heard the roar of the surf as it beat against the shore.

The buckets she'd placed on the floor under the roof leak in her bedroom and the parlor filled up fast. She exchanged them for empty ones and tossed the contents of the first out her back door. Rain blew into the kitchen before she managed to close the door against the wet, and she spent the next several minutes mopping up her floor.

The storm's fury lasted beyond dawn, finally lessening to a drizzle by mid morning. Sleepy, damp, and grumpy, Brida groaned at the sound of wagon wheels rolling up to her door. She opened it and leaned against the jamb to pull on her muddy boots.

"I thought you'd be ready by now," her brother said, a frown creasing lines in his brow. "We're hours past when I planned to pick you up."

Brida climbed into the driver's seat beside him. "Don't start. I've been up all night playing for his lordship's fancy guests and all morning battling roof leaks." She reached behind her to pet the head of his favorite dog where it sat behind them in the wagon. Laylam had raised Moot since she was pup, and while the dog practically worshipped Laylam, she often visited Brida for treats, affection and a quiet place to sleep before the fire.

Laylam twitched the reins. "Walk on," he instructed the horse, and the animal pulled the cart through Ancilar toward the beach, joining an ever-growing line of other carts and wagons as villagers emerged from their houses to harvest the Gray's bounty.

"I'll fix the roof for you after we harvest," Laylam said around the pipe stem held between his teeth.

Brida eyed him, concerned. "You don't have time for it, and I made enough last night to hire someone in Ancilar to do it."

His perpetual frown deepened. "You're my sister. We help each other. I would have patched it sooner if you'd told me it had gotten that bad."

"You do enough already. I can handle this. You have family to care for." She refused to acknowledge what they both knew. She feared the label of burdensome widowed relative more than a leaky roof.

Laylam's frown turned into a full-fledged glare. "You are family, Brida, and if you aren't careful, you'll choke on all that stupid pride. I'll come by later. You can feed me supper if it makes you feel better. Norinn won't mind."

Brida didn't pursue the argument any further. While she might suffer from too much pride, Laylam could put a mule to shame with his stubbornness. They completed the journey to the beach in silence, at least until they got their first look at the storm's aftermath. Laylam halted the wagon, rose from his seat and gave a celebratory whoop that startled his horse, set Moot to barking, and was echoed by the other villagers who rolled up on either side of him.

For as far as the eye could see, a carpet of seaweed in variegated shades of green to black covered the sand calf-deep, and spilled over the clusters of rocky outcroppings that tumbled from the meadows of salt grass to the foaming surf. More of it swayed in the shallow surf, so thick one could stand on it.

"Thank the gods," Brida breathed in a reverent voice. The first heavy storm had delivered a plenitude. If fate and deities remained generous, they'd have more then one good seaweed harvest like this one.

The shallows still churned in places, and gulls swarmed the sand, feasting on dead fish that had been thrown onto the land by an angry tide. That tide had pulled far back now, leaving scatterings of shells in its wake. Children who had accompanied their parents to the shore raced back and forth, gathering up cockles, conches, wings, and drill tips before tossing them back into the water in a game to see who threw the farthest.

Brida climbed down from the driver seat after her brother to join the other villagers gathered in a group to divvy up sections of the beach. Each family was assigned a spot to harvest, that lot marked by a stone set at the allotment's edge.

Once they were assigned their allotments, the siblings met at the back of their wagon where Brida unloaded a sickle and pair of baskets with straps sewn to them. Moot abandoned them on arrival. She leapt off the wagon and raced away, barking with excitement as she plunged into the knot of children gathered by the water's edge.

The wind still howled off the Gray, whipping Brida's skirts around her legs and nearly tearing the baskets out of her hands. She had to shout in order for Laylam to hear her.

"I'm off to the tidal pools!" She pointed to her allotment. Rock formations edged parts of the beach had been carved out by the sea's endless wash. The tidal pools nestled in their shelters were too hard for the horses to navigate with the cage-like rakes dragging behind them, so the seaweed piled there was cut and gathered by hand. Laylam nodded and waved her away as he unloaded his rake from the wagon and unhooked the horse from its traces.

Moot left the children to join Brida, bounding ahead only to double back and run circles around her, snapping at the fluttering hem of Brida's skirts. The dog's ears suddenly swiveled forward, and she stopped, nose raised in the air as she sniffed something more interesting than salt, seaweed, and dead fish. A curious whine escaped her mouth before she bolted for the tidal pools where Brida planned to harvest.

Brida followed at a leisurely pace, trekking over hillocks of kelp. She'd be salt-caked and sand-encrusted by the end of the day and reeking of seaweed, but for now she enjoyed the hike and the hints of sunlight breaking through the cloud cover.

She was the only one on this section of beach. The rest of the harvesters had dispersed into the shallows behind her or toward the bigger pools that lay in the opposite direction where the cups of the bluffs were deeper and trapped more of the seaweed.

Moot had mostly disappeared behind a tall shard of rock, only the last third of her tail peeking out to reveal her whereabouts. The hound's tail suddenly drooped before she backed away, teeth bared at whatever lay hidden behind the rock's shelter.

Brida slowed her approach, gripping the sickle a little harder as Moot growled low in her throat. Sometimes the Gray coughed up predators that swam too close to the shore during the storms and were slung onto the beaches where they gasped their last breaths. Alarm swirled through Brida's belly. What if it was an *obluda*? One of those foul abominations that usually lurked in the black deep?

An *obluda* had terrorized Ancilar during the long summer before Zigana Imre had dispatched it with the help of her mare Gitta and Lord Frantisek. Even now, with that thing crushed to bone splinters under Gitta's massive hooves, people still feared falling asleep, feared dreaming in case another such creature lured a grieving, unwary villager into the water to feast on them.

What had the dog found?

She peeked around the line of stone. Moot pressed against her leg, preventing Brida from getting any closer. Brida's heart surged into her throat at the sight before her.

Like the beach and shallows, the tidal pools were choked with seaweed. The stuff draped over the rocks and spilled across the sand, dotted with tiny sand crabs that skittered across the lacy leaves before burrowing under them to reach the water in the pools. Entangled within a net of the weed, a man and a child sprawled. Bright blood streaked the man's bare torso and the arm stretched across the child in a protective clasp. The pair looked asleep, their features slack, eyes closed. From her vantage point, Brida couldn't tell if they breathed.

Seeing two gravely injured people sprawled in the sand should have stunned her speechless for only a moment before she'd start screaming for help. But in *this* moment she remained silent, her shock making her doubt her own eyes.

Where there should have been hips, and legs, and feet, the two possessed tails, sleek and muscular that ended in flukes similar to those of dolphins. Their skin shimmered in the sun like the inside of an abalone shell bleached by the sun—striations of blue, indigo, silvery gray, and cascading green. Their hair was nearly indistinguishable from the leafy varieties of seaweed spilled around them, neither blond, brunet, or ginger, but multiple shades of pearlescent green and purple.

A dozen memories from childhood skated across Brida's mind, stories told by her mother and others to enthralled children, of the mysteries of the sea, of things that swam there, beautiful and dark, dangerous and benevolent. Some believed and others scoffed at such fanciful tales as nothing more than the delusions of bored sailors trapped too long on deep-water ships.

Brida wasn't a sailor, and her feet were planted firmly on the shore. She'd outgrown fairytales a long time ago, and while she was sleep-deprived, she wasn't hallucinating. Merfolk were real, and two lay before her, dead or dying.

CHAPTER TWO

B RIDA CREPT FORWARD, balanced on the balls of her feet and ready to sprint away. Despite the chilly air blowing off the Gray, her hand on the sickle handle was slippery with sweat. She used her knees to nudge Moot out of the way so she could get a closer look at the two stranded merfolk.

The child made a faint noise, a cross between a kittenish mew and a whistle. The small fluke flapped against the sand, dislodging swags of seaweed. The merman's hand flexed in response to the sound, fingers splaying wide to reveal webbing between the digits, the translucent skin patterned in a lacework of tiny blue veins.

Brida leapt back, nearly trampling Moot who'd stuck to her legs like a barnacle. The hound let loose with another round of barking, the hair on her back stiffening into a ridge that ran the length of her spine.

"Moot! Hush!"

The dog only did what instinct and training required of her, but Brida didn't want half the village running over here to see what all the commotion was about. Moot quieted, though her hackles remained high and her teeth bared as she guarded Brida.

The merman's eyelids lifted, and Brida gasped. His eyes were pale and strange, not human, yet so full of misery and pain that an involuntary moan of sympathy erupted from Brida's throat. The bloodshot whites of his eyes contrasted against irises almost silvery in color. Two pupils, one atop the other and no bigger than the heads of pins, dotted their centers.

He blinked, a rapid flutter of a double set of eyelids, one a delicate membrane nestled under a thicker-skinned lid. The movement mimicked the sudden thrash of his tail. A piercing whistle cut the air, the sound so sharp that Brida dropped the sickle to cover her ears with her hands. Next to her, Moot yelped and danced backward, shaking her head hard enough that her ears flapped like flags in a hard breeze.

Brida held out one hand, palm forward, and pressed the index finger of her other hand against her lips. "Shhh. Shhh," she told the merman. "I mean no harm."

Blood cascaded down his tail to drip off the edges of his fluke. A jagged wound, where the hip might be on a human man, pursed open with his movements. Crescent in shape, it matched another one farther down his tail. Something had bitten him. Something big.

Numerous smaller wounds marred his body, from human torso down to dolphin tail, a mural of slashes and shallow bite marks. Brida glanced at the child, noting the absence of any bites or blood. Had the merman battled a hungry predator to save the merchild and ended up stranded on the shore, too weak to propel himself and his charge back to the water?

Both were alive, but not for long by the look of them. Their breathing was shallow, barely discernible, and the merchild's newing sounded thin. Blood ran in continuous rivulets along the merman's body, tempting tiny crabs to investigate and taste the

A Wilderness of Glass

salt and iron in the red flow. The lovely abalone shell shimmer of the pair's flesh was dulling before her eyes, and flecks of skin furled off their tails and arms under the weak sun, peeling away as if they'd suffered sunburn.

She knew nothing of merfolk, but creatures born of the water belonged in the water. Beaching was a death sentence. She'd seen it firsthand as a child in the tragedy of a dying whale crushed by its own weight as it lay on the sand.

The urge to call to for help warred with the caution to remain silent. Brida's cries would bring the entire village running to her aid. Of that, she had no doubt. But she feared that call would elicit a massacre, driven by a mindless fear engendered into people still traumatized by the terror the *obluda* had subjected them too not so long ago.

She jumped again when a voice boomed over the beach. "Ziga! Odon!"

Moot renewed her frantic barking, capturing the hem of Brida's skirts in her teeth and tugging to pull her away from the tidal pools.

"Stop it, Moot!" She tugged her skirts up, lifting the dog with them as those teeth remained firmly clamped on the fabric.

Hobbled by the dog's weight, she shuffled from behind the concealing rock face to see the new arrivals on the shore. Odon Imre and his daughter Zigana had joined the harvesters, leading their two mares by tether lines into the shallows.

The villager who greeted them pointed at the water, nodding and gesturing to the water seers as they engaged in conversation. Brida was too far away to hear, but she could guess at what was said. Odon and Zigana possessed the gift of

133

water sight, an ability that allowed them to sense whether or not it was safe to trawl the waters for shrimp, fish from the boats or rake the seaweed from the shallows. The last had never required their unique assistance before. The horses and villagers harvested the kelp, wildweed, featherweed, sea whip, and pepper fern from the rocks or in the surf where the water was too shallow for predator fish to lurk. These days, however, the Imres' talent was in high demand. No one dipped a toe in the waves without their signal that all was well. Brida could only imagine the reactions if she showed them the two merfolk trapped in the tidal pools behind her.

Laylam waved to her not far away, his gelding standing patiently beside him, cage rake attached to the traces behind him, as the pair waited for the signal it was safe to harvest. "All right there, Brida?" he shouted.

The wind caught his question, whirling it toward her. She waved back. "Fine." She pointed to Moot who finally let go of her skirts. "Moot's battling crabs, and they're winning!" she shouted back to him.

He nodded and returned his attention to the Imres who stood together and gave a tandem nod. It was safe to enter the water. Like racers perched on a starting line, the harvesters guided their horses into the surf with a snap of the lead lines. Around them, women and children with baskets hoisted on their backs or strapped to their hips waded into the shallows, bending to pick the Gray's gifts washed in by the storm.

Brida strode back to the beached merfolk. They lay as she left them, the merman's webbed hand still resting on the child's small body. The pool under the adult's tail had turned a dark pink, evicting resident starfish from its tainted waters.

The merman watched her with that strange double-lidded gaze, his face a study in suffering. Discounting the most obvious physical differences, he looked mostly human. His nose was like any other she'd seen, neither too long or too broad, but his nostrils were smaller. They flared in rapid bursts as he struggled to breathe. In contrast to his nostrils, his eyes were large, sunk a little deeper in their sockets than a human's. He didn't have eyelashes, and his eyebrows were arches of rippled flesh instead of short hairs along his brow ridge. No hint of beard shadowed the sharp line of his jaw or his chin, and his partially open mouth hid his teeth from her view.

Beside him, the merchild breathed just as hard, though seemed in less pain than the adult. From the waist up, it looked much like a human child of two or three, with tiny webbed hands, rounded belly, and features still plump with baby fat. Brida couldn't tell the child's gender by the appearance of its face or torso, but there were differences between the pair on the exposed undersides of their tails not far from the flukes. The merman possessed two slits in the flesh, one long, the other much shorter and just below it. In the child, there was only the one long slit. If her assumption was right, the merchild was a girl.

Brida stared at the surf and then the distressed pair so far from it. The merman was much too big for her to move. She could see that in a glance, but if she was quick enough, she might be able to sneak the merchild into the water without the harvesters noticing.

Then what? Leave her in the water to drown? That inner voice, with its merciless reason, made her curse under her breath. She had no idea, no true plan for how she might possibly save these two on her own, and asking for help from the villagers wasn't an option.

Moot's ears pricked forward when Brida turned to her and shook her finger. "No barking, Moot. Understand? Hush." The dog cocked her head to the side as if considering, her tail wagging. Satisfied, Brida shrugged off her baskets.

She pushed one to the side and used the other as a pail to scoop water from the pools. Liquid streamed from the basket's holes, but enough stayed in for Brida to gently pour it over the merman. He gasped, a convulsive shiver rippling along his tail and up his torso. The muscles in his arms, chest, and midriff flexed, and blood streamed off his skin in pink ribbons. Still, he didn't let go of the merchild.

The little girl twitched and mewed as Brida trickled water across her body. Brida crooned to her in a sing-song voice, words of reassurance she'd sometimes used to comfort her younger nieces and nephews after a spill in the garden or a nightmare during a nap. "Easy, love. You're a brave girl. We'll get you home soon."

Lies always hung sour on the tongue, even when told with the best of intentions. Brida didn't know if she could fulfill that implied promise to the merchild. Even if she managed to get her in the water, without the merman there with her, she wouldn't survive. Some sea creature had already attacked the merman, gravely wounding him.

Overwhelmed with sympathy, Brida forgot caution, set the basket aside, and reached out a hesitant hand to push the lacy locks of seaweed hair away from the merchild's face. Another shrill whistle nearly burst her eardrums. She had only a moment to catch a glimpse from the corner of her eye of an arching fluke before a powerful force slammed into her, flinging her sideways. She smashed into the rock face concealing the pools. A shockwave of pain bolted down her spine and up the back of her head while black stars exploded across her vision.

She sprawled on the wet seaweed, breath knocked out of her lungs. Moot's frantic barking sounded far away, though the dog's face was so close, they nearly touched noses. "Moot," she whispered when she could finally breathe. "Stop."

The dog whined and leaned forward to nuzzle Brida's cheek with her wet nose. Brida turned away, wincing as the movement made her vision swim and her stomach roil. An odd set of clicks and pops sounded nearby, punctuated by a series of softer whistles that held the unmistakable tones of inquiry and regret. She must have hit her head harder than she thought if she was imagining such things.

An exploratory touch to her scalp told her she'd have a lump, but there was no blood. Her vision rapidly cleared, and her nausea faded as the pain dulled to a throbbing ache.

She met the merman's wide-eyed stare. He'd drawn the merchild closer to him, sheltering her even deeper into the cove of his body. His mouth moved, emitting more of the clicks and short whistles that carried the ring of apology.

Brida clambered to her feet, swaying. She raised both hands toward the merman in a supplicating gesture. "Forgive me," she said. "I didn't mean to frighten you."

She grabbed her basket and staggered to the pool for more

water to pour on the pair. She bore no resentment toward the merman. He had only tried to protect his charge from an entity who might be a threat, despite the benevolent gestures she'd shown so far. Had she been in his place, she didn't doubt she would have done the same. The fault was hers for being so careless.

Laylam would soon notice Brida wasn't helping to fill the family wagon, so she split her time. After each trip to the beach with loaded baskets, she poured more water over the merfolk, and cut kelp, discarded plan after plan for returning the pair back to the Gray, alive and unnoticed.

"I'll be right back," she assured the merman. Even knowing he probably didn't understand a word she said, she hoped the tone of her voice conveyed some of her intention not to abandon them.

This time her sister-in-law, Norinn, had joined the harvesters and met Brida at the back of the dray with a full basket of her own. "You didn't tell Laylam about that nobleman accosting you last night, did you?" Disapproval dripped from every word. "Haniss told me when the children and I got here."

Brida scooped out bits of kelp stuck to the bottom of one basket. "I wasn't accosted. He didn't even touch me, although I think he was on the verge of accusing me of stealing my flute. His lordship sent him on his way." She shrugged. "What's there to tell?"

The memory of Ospodine still made her uneasy. There had been about him an unnatural intensity. She'd been almost surprised not to find burn marks on her back this morning when she dressed, his regard of her had been that scorching. That hostile. Still, she didn't think it either useful or necessary to worry her brother. His lordship had expertly diffused the situation, and Brida doubted she'd ever cross path with Ospodine again.

"Laylam won't like that you didn't say anything, Brida."

Brida stiffened. She liked Norinn very much, though the woman sometimes had a bad habit of expecting Brida to report everything in her life to Laylam. "He'll adjust. He's my brother, not my keeper."

The other woman sighed, reaching out to pat Brida's shoulder in a gesture of truce. "You're his only sibling, Brida. He's just protective."

"I know, and I love him for it, even when he's being his most annoying." She offered Norinn a quick smile before shouldering her empty baskets. She didn't have time to chat. "I'll talk to you later. Over tea. I still have a lot to harvest at my allotment."

"Do you need help?" Norinn called to her as she left. Brida waved and shook her head, leaving Moot behind this time. She desperately needed help, just not the kind Norinn offered.

The dread building inside her from the moment she left the title pool eased a fraction when she discovered the merman and child still breathed.

Brida had emptied one small tidal pool trying to keep her charges wet and cool and started on the second one. The merman's closed eyelids fluttered but didn't lift as she poured water on him. Her mind raced as she did the same to the merchild.

Merfolk obviously communicated with a series of whistles and clicks, a language of the sea both mysterious and yet familiar to her. She'd heard something similar years earlier. Brief, sadly beautiful, and a balm to her soul when she was at her most wretched. She'd never forgotten those four tuneful whistles drifting off the night surf.

The whistles the merman and child made were different, frightened instead of mournful, yet Brida guessed they came from the same origin as the ones she played on her flute. She didn't have the instrument with her now and could only attempt to reproduce those sounds with her mouth.

She set her basket aside to ease a little closer to the merman's head and stay out of striking range of his powerful tail. Either he heard her approach or sensed her nearness, because his eyes opened, and the muscles in his torso visibly tensed.

Brida held up her hands once again to signal she wasn't a threat. She pursed her lips and tried to echo the four whistles she'd heard years earlier. The merman's eyes widened, his narrow nostrils flared hard, and his entire body twitched in reaction.

She had no idea what she just said and prayed it wasn't some vile insult or promise to visit some violence on the merman or merchild. She eased back a little more, away from the tail and the reach of those muscular arms and webbed hands.

The merman's chirp carried a wealth of question and surprise. Brida dared not show her relief that he didn't react with anger and kept her expression neutral. She patted her chest with her hand. "Brida." She repeated the gesture. "I'm Brida." She pointed to the merman. "You?"

His answering whistle differed from the previous ones he'd uttered. Deeper, drawn out, with a stutter in the middle. His brow knitted in a frown.

Now we're getting somewhere, Brida thought. She repeated it as best she could, only to have him shake his head and whistle again, this time without the stutter. The effort left him panting.

"I understand," she said. That stutter had been inadvert, a product of his pain and the weakening state of his body. She tried a second time, and was rewarded by a weak nod.

When Brida pointed to the merchild, the merman replied with a another higher whistle, one that made the child open her eyes and chirp at him. He chirped back, lifting one hand to cup the small face in comfort.

Brida's eyes teared up, and for a moment she could neither whistle nor speak. Somehow she had to find a way to save these two. With a series of hand gestures, spoken word and the whistling of their names, she tried to convey the beginnings of a plan to get them both to the water.

He passed out in the middle of her oration, and Brida gasped when his body went slack. The merchild echoed her alarm, tiny fluke slapping the seaweed mounded under her. Brida promptly forgot the last consequence to her mistake of getting too close and rushed forward to lift the merman in her arms. He was monstrously heavy, and her arms strained under the weight as his head lolled back.

"Oh no," Brida whispered. "No, no, no, no. Don't you dare die on me." She bent lower to listen, tears streaming down her face when no sound issued from his nose or mouth. She shook him as much as her strength allowed. He didn't even flinch, body limp as a sack of grain. The child's anguished mewing was nonstop now and growing louder.

"It's all right, little one," Brida lied. "He's just sleeping." The long sleep. The death sleep. Brida shook him even harder, panic giving her strength. A faint gasp followed by an even fainter exhalation gusting across her cheek sent a surge of relief—no, joy—coursing through her. She whistled his name, and his eyes opened. This time his pupils had changed shape, dilated so they converged to create a black horseshoe that almost eclipsed his pale irises.

Brida braced his torso on her knees and gently turned his head so that he faced the frightened merchild. His slippery hair spilled through her fingers where she cupped the back of his skull. "Show her you live."

Whether or not he understood her words, he comprehended their intentions and issued a series of weak chirps that calmed the merchild. Brida carefully lowered him to his side on the seaweed, noting for the first time the ridge of a small dorsal fin that ran the length of his spine. The change in position exposed more of the grievous bite wound but also eased his breathing.

The merman reached for the child, and Brida helped him, careful only to touch his arm as he nudged the mergirl onto her side as well. Like the adult, the child's breathing grew less labored. Brida sat back on her haunches and exhaled. Maybe, just maybe that small position change had bought them time.

She had an idea, one that held no guarantees of saving the pair, but it was better than nothing, and leaving them here on the beach. They'd be dead by the next day. If she could get both back in the water, they at least had a chance.

She spent the next hours keeping the two wet and cool with water from the diminishing tidal pools and hauling cut seaweed to the wagons farther down the beach. Brida declined offers to join others for lunch or a quick rest when she emptied her baskets at the wagon. By the time the harvesters called it a day, she was nearly seeing double from exhaustion. Still, her charges clung to life.

Cloud cover pillowed a sky the dull color of flint. Brida was grateful for it. Right now, the sun was an enemy, its warm rays punishing splinters on the beached merfolk. She briefly considered covering them both with a blanket of wet seaweed but discarded the idea. Their bodies gave off a feverish heat now, the shimmering sea colors streaking up their skin nearly gone, leaving their bodies and faces ashen. Piling on wet seaweed might camouflage them from passersby, but they'd overheat even more without the cooling breeze from the Gray drifting over them.

Brida crouched before the merman and whistled his name. His eyelids twitched but didn't lift. She touched his cheek, unsurprised at how hot it felt beneath her finger. "I'll be back when night falls. Hold on a little longer. Both of you."

It was hard to walk away from them, even harder to pretend with her brother that nothing unusual had happened while she harvested. She glanced up at the dreary sky, silently counting the hours until nightfall when she could return to the shore unobserved.

Laylam side-eyed her curiously as he drove his wagon back to the village, its box piled high with dripping seaweed. "You're far away in your head, Brida. Quieter than usual. You feeling peaky?"

She patted his arm, offering a tired smile and a yawn that

was far more sincere than affected. "Sorry. I'm just sleepy. I might even nod off on your shoulder before you drop me home." She resisted the temptation to look back to the beach slowly disappearing behind the feathery barricade of salt grass.

"Janen kept you and the others at the castle too long last night. He knew we had harvesting to tend to today." Laylam flicked the reins, coaxing the horse into a faster clip. "Don't worry about feeding me supper. Norinn said she'll have a plate ready for me when I get home. One for you too if you want."

"I just want to sleep. Tell Norinn thank you and that I'll see her tomorrow to help you both with laying out the seaweed to dry." She didn't lie. If she didn't have two merfolk to try and save, she'd fall into her solitary bed without undressing and sleep until one of her nieces or nephews pounded on her front door the next morning. But slumber was a luxury that would have to wait.

The obscured sun bloodied the western horizon by the time Laylam delivered her to her door. She waved to him from the doorstep until the wagon turned a corner and disappeared behind a row of houses along Ancilar's market road.

Hinges squeaked softly as she pushed open the door and paused. A scent of exotic spices mixed with perfume teased her nose. She'd smelled that scent before, though the memory only skated the edges of her mind before flickering away.

The house she once shared with her husband Talmai was small and sparsely furnished, the line of sight from the door stretching into parlor, kitchen, larder, and bedroom. Silence rested within the empty rooms as if waiting to greet her the moment she crossed the threshold. Dust motes danced in the air, illuminated by the last bits of fading light that speared the front window. The pair of buckets she'd set out to catch the rain from her leaking roof stood undisturbed, nor had the book she'd left in her chair by the fire been moved. Still, she hesitated at the doorway, sensing a difference in the feel of the house from when she'd left it hours earlier.

She crept across the parlor on quiet feet before easing the poker from its stand by the hearth. Only her heartbeat sounded in her ears, and she gripped the makeshift weapon with both hands, ready to bash or stab anything that leapt out at her. Fear sent a trickle of sweat down her spine despite the house's chill, but anger at the thought of someone robbing her pushed her deeper into the rooms. She refused to abide a thief. If she caught one, they'd regret ever crossing her doorstep.

No one. There was no one. Neither in the bedroom nor the larder. Not lurking under the kitchen table or hiding behind the two thorny bushes in her garden. Still she couldn't shake the sensation that someone had been here, creeping about, touching things. The thought made her skin crawl.

She closed her door and threw the bolt home. Ancilar was a small village where most everyone knew each other. People didn't steal from their neighbor, not if they wanted help for some calamity later. That someone might have done so here didn't bode well for her or anyone in the village.

Sick dread roiled in her belly. She returned the poker to its spot by the hearth and strode to the bedroom. The floorboard under her bed hadn't been moved, and she exhaled a hard breath when her hand dipped into the hiding space beneath the floor and felt the pouch of coins.

Her relief died a swift death as the memory of Lord Frantisek's aggressive guest blossomed in her mind. The nobleman named Ospodine had stared at her flute with the fixation of a zealot.

The scent. She knew it now. Ospodine had reeked of it.

"Oh gods," she muttered. "Not the flute! Not the flute!" She raced from the bedroom into the kitchen, stopping in front of the cupboard where she always stored the instrument. It lay as she'd left it, still within its protective cloth. Brida's hand closed around it in a death grip, hesitating when more of the perfume and spice combination buffeted her nose.

She almost tossed the flute from her then, furious at the idea that anyone would dare enter her home and rifle through her things while she was gone. It didn't matter that nothing was taken, she felt violated. The urge to torch the house warred with her reason that reassured her a hard day's worth of scrubbing, mopping and washing would take care of the smell.

Still clutching the flute, Brida double-checked the bolt on her front door and did the same for the back before inspecting the latch at every window.

She could tell the village council what happened, but who would believe her? Her intruder left no trace except for a distinctive scent. He'd stolen nothing except her peace of mind and sense of safety, intangible things as precious as her flute. What did he want if not the flute? Why had her practice notes drawn him like a shark to blood in the water?

Any drowsiness she suffered burned away under the heat of her rage. She almost regretted not finding Ospodine still lurking in her house just so she'd have the pleasure of beating an apology out of him with the fireplace poker.

The image of the beached merman and merchild rose in her mind's eye, cooling the fire of her anger and replacing it with an urgency of a different kind. She'd somehow deal with Ospodine later. She still had the flute, the key to her half-mad plan in saving her charges. Nightfall couldn't arrive soon enough.

Evening brought a clearing of clouds along with colder temperatures as Brida hurried through the village's deserted streets toward the distant beach. Even if she owned a horse, she'd still go on foot, unnoticed as she flitted between houses and skirted the pools of candle light spilling from windows as people settled in for the night.

She huddled in her heaviest shawl, teeth chattering as the damp breeze blowing off the Gray cut through layers of clothing to raise gooseflesh on her skin. She glanced over her shoulder every few steps to make sure no one had seen her, or worse, was following. Once past the village's perimeter, she broke into a sprint, cutting a swath through the salt grass toward the shore. Part of her prayed the two merfolk still lived, another part cautioned her not to put much hope in the notion.

The tide had come in, black waves capped in white foam creeping farther and farther up the beach with every purl of the surf. Wet sand sucked at her bare feet, and cold water swirled around her ankles as she ran toward the tidal pools concealed by the short ridge of rocks.

A chorus of whistles, carried on a brine-scented wind, rose above the surf's thunder, and Brida stumbled to a halt at the eerie sight of small, greenish lights flickering in the troughs and peaks of the waves like fireflies. Swatches of clouds floated past a bright half moon that paved a silver road on the water's surface.

"My gods," Brida breathed.

Moonlight unveiled the source of the lights. Not fireflies, but eyes, bright with the animal eyeshine that shone at night in many creatures, wild and tame alike. A cluster of the glowing eyes gathered in the water directly across from the tidal pools where the merfolk were beached, and Brida caught glimpses of flukes slapping the water as their calls grew in number and volume. Two of the whistles were repeated over and over. Names. They were the two names the merman had whistled to her on a weak breath. His kinsmen were calling to him and the wee girl trapped with him.

She resumed her sprint toward the tidal pools, splashing water as she ran. The whistles abruptly stopped, and the waves went dark. The merfolk had seen her. Brida prayed they didn't swim away. She would need their help.

The merman and child were black silhouettes under the shadows cast by the rocks that sheltered them. Seaweed floated over their bodies, lifted by the encroaching tide. It wasn't enough to make them buoyant, but Brida hoped the continued rise might aid her in moving them closer to the deeper surf. If they even still lived.

She tossed her shawl on one of the nearby rocks and crouched next to the merchild. "Please be alive, little one," she prayed to any gods who might be listening. The bright moonlight didn't reach here, and the darkness obscured details, but Brida noted the child's tail had peeled even more, her small face hollowed out under the cheekbones as if she had withered in the autumn air. Her closed eyes were sunken, her lips cracked and bleeding. The child didn't move when Brida laid a hand on her shoulder, nor did the merman beside her.

Brida's eyes teared as she touched cold, dry skin. She drew a shaky breath before tightening her lips to whistle the child's name. The mergirl didn't respond, even when Brida's tears dripped on her throat and chest.

Despairing, Brida scooped the child into her arms. Similar in size and maturity to a human toddler, the merchild was easily twice as heavy in Brida's hold. She remained limp as Brida hugged her, pressing her face against her cheek, whistling softly.

The faintest twitch made her freeze. She pulled back abruptly to stare at the mergirl's shadowed features. Her gaze traveled the length of the small body, and she swallowed back a triumphant cry when the little fluke jerked upward in an anemic flap.

She surged to her feet, staggering for a moment under the child's weight, to face the Gray. Lantern flickers of eyeshine shimmered once more among the waves. The silenced calls started again, this time shrill or mournful. Sharp clicks and chirps accompanied them, reminding Brida of the merman's vocalizations when she made the mistake of touching the merchild the first time.

Fairy tales, told by generations of mothers, grandmothers, and old salts land-bound but still sea-ensorceled, teased her memories. Leviathans that lived in the black deep and swallowed ships whole. Ancient *obludas* that lured their victims with grief and ate them with teeth like daggers. And merfolk who frolicked in the waters and rode the bow waves of ships, waiting for some unfortunate sailor to fall in the water and drown in a mermaid's seductive embrace.

Brida had never sailed on a deep water ship or seen a leviathan, but she knew the *obludas* were real, and held in her arms proof that merfolk were more than myth. And all were dangerous to a land dweller like her. She had to get the merchild into the water, back to the family who watched her from the surf, but she didn't want to die in a mermaid's lethal arms.

She waded calf-deep into the surf before stopping, her unconscious burden heavy against her. Her flute nestled in a satchel slung from her shoulder, so close but completely inaccessible unless Brida put the merchild down. She sank to her knees in the water, submerging the little girl from fluke to belly but careful to keep her shoulders and face clear of the rolling surf. With one hand she fished the flute out of the bag, pulling away the cloth cover with her teeth. She spat the cloth out. It floated away, rolling back with the tide toward the cluster of glittering eyes and flashes of silvery flesh.

Twisted in a position that kept the merchild afloat in her arms, and the flute balanced in both hands, Brida raised the instrument to her mouth and blew into the end stem in a series of bursts. The sounds the flute made were sharper than those she made with just her mouth, but the tone was the same—one for the merman's name, one for the child. He'd given her nothing else. Just their names, and she repeated them in a second burst of whistles played on the flute.

Silence greeted her playing, though she didn't imagine that the eyes drew closer. Fear coiled snakelike up her body. She was tempted to draw back, but the merchild's increasing movements against her kept Brida in place. She'd brought the flute in the fragile hope she might better communicate with the merman.

He was either dead or too far gone into delirium to whistle to her now, but those in the waves might do so if they were as willing to set aside their wariness of her as she was of them.

She repeated the names twice more before changing tactics. Five years earlier, she had stood on this very beach and wailed her grief over the loss of her husband to a deaf sky. The moon didn't answer, nor did the stars, but something in the Gray did— the four-note whistle she still played on her flute. A reply from the black waves, so full of sorrow and sympathy that Brida had fallen to her knees and sobbed until she retched.

A mysterious reply from an unseen source then. Possibly a mystery no longer. Brida braced the merchild against her knees as she swayed with the surf's infinite purling. She licked her lips before pressing them to the flute's mouthpiece again, fingertips perched on the playing holes, and played the four-note tune.

Had she lobbed a live, starving shark into the water, the reaction to the tune couldn't have been more vehement, much like the wounded merman's when she whistled it earlier. A frenzy of splashing heralded a cacophony of whistles and clicks that shrieked above the Gray's dull roar. Multiple wakes of frothing water raced toward the shore. Brida almost dropped flute and merchild as she struggled to her feet, nearly falling face first into the water amidst a tangle of soggy skirts.

A deeper, sharper whistle rose above the rest, and as one body, the merfolk splashed to a halt, their eyes shimmering green coins in the darkness. Flukes slapped impatiently at the waves, and Brida got her first clear view of the sea people who had come to claim their own.

Like the merman on the beach, and the merchild in her

arms, their kinsmen possessed the tails and flukes of dolphins instead of fish, and their skin glowed shades of silver in the moonlight. Seaweed hair spilled down their backs and shoulders, some woven with bits of shell. Like her merman, the males were muscular, with broad shoulders and powerful arms. The females in the group were smaller than the males, sleek and arresting, their long hair at times revealing or obscuring their bare breasts.

One female swam through the center of the group, moving slowly as if all the time in the world lay before them. She entered the shallows just shy of any danger of beaching herself and stared at Brida with a puzzling combination of wariness and recognition. She parted her lips and whistled the four-note tune in clear, perfect mimicry.

Brida's throat closed against an involuntary sob, and new tears coursed down her cheeks. She swallowed several times in an effort to speak. "You," she told the merwoman. "I heard you once. Long ago."

The merwoman didn't reply with either words or whistles, only watched Brida for a moment before her gaze slid to the mechild. She raised a webbed hand in an unmistakable command for Brida to bring the girl to her.

Brida's feet moved of their own accord, or at the will of a sea spell cast silently by one of its denizens. She clutched her flute in one hand and waded deeper, closer and closer until she stood directly in front of the mermaid, and stared down into a pair of sea glass eyes full of ancient secrets. She dropped to her knees and held out her arms, her muscles quivering with the effort to hold the heavy merchild.

"She lives," she told the merwoman. "For now."

Slender hands lifted the girl from Brida's embrace. The merwoman spoke in a series of soft clicks, and the child's eyes opened for just a moment before closing once more. The merfolk surrounding them trilled as the merwoman passed her to a mermaid who snatched her away before disappearing into the deep. Three more merfolk followed, but the rest stayed behind, their regard unwavering as they watched Brida.

She braced a hand in the sand to keep the waves from knocking her over. She considered standing, but something warned her to stay put, at least for now. The merwoman whose voice had haunted her all these years whistled again, a single note ending on a question, and Brida recognized it as the merman's name.

Her shoulders lifted in a shrug. "I don't know. I can't know, and I can't help unless I go back ashore."

The two stared at each other for long moments before the merwoman nodded as if she understood what Brida said. Careful to act as if negotiating with merfolk was an everyday event, Brida stood and waded steadily back to the beach where the water glossed the sand like a thin shield of glass. Here she was safe from a drowning. Here she could gather her sodden skirts in her hands and bolt for the safety of the salt grasses, leave behind a beached merman and the danger of being drowned by angry merfolk if she delivered their kinsman back to them, dead. The thought crossed her mind, brief as a candle flame flicker, before she cast it aside.

She was scared, terrified even, but she wasn't a coward. She returned to the tidal pools.

The merman was as she'd left him, sprawled across the filling pools, tangled in bloodstained seaweed. His wounds still trickled blood and a small cluster of sand fleas gathered around the jagged line of flesh that marked where sharp teeth had torn into his tail. Brida approached him far more cautiously than she did the merchild, whistling his name in a steady repetition in case he lived and could hear her. His neck, under her palm, burned hot instead of cold, and a pulse beat in a thready rhythm just below his skin.

"Thank you," Brida said, not dwelling on whether she thanked the merman for not dying on her or the gods for being merciful in keeping him alive this long.

His oddly handsome face tightened for a moment, his breathing growing louder. He convulsed, one hand digging into the seaweed beside him.

Brida stroked his smooth cheek. "Shh, your daughter is returned to your kinsmen. They're waiting for you now." His eyelids lifted a fraction, giving her a glimpse of his eyes, no longer pale, but glowing with the same eyeshine she'd seen from the merfolk in the water. She offered him a smile and whistled the merchild's name before pointing to the water.

Her heart jumped in her chest when his eyes rolled back and his body collapsed, as if her words offered not only succor but permission for him to die.

"No you don't," she snapped, her gentle caress on his cheek changing to a pair of quick slaps that made his eyelids flicker.

Inquiring whistles sounded behind her. The merwoman and her people were growing impatient. And concerned.

Brida stared at the merman. Now what? She couldn't wait for the tide to move farther inland. It would be at least two more hours before it had filled the pools enough for her to float him into the deeper surf, and by then it would be too late. He was far too heavy for her to lift, much less carry.

There was nothing for it. She'd have to drag him across the sand, risking more injury to his already battered body, and no doubt a terrible amount of pain. Brida prayed the gods would remain merciful and keep the merman unconscious through the ordeal.

Her soaked skirt impeded her movements. She stripped down to her shift, shivering hard in the cold breeze that blew off the equally cold water. The flute joined her shawl on the rocks. Her teeth clacked together as she maneuvered behind the merman and bent to slide her hands under his shoulders.

"Mother's mercy," she said between grunts. "You are heavy!"

He was dead weight in her grip as she she slowly turned his body. Her discarded skirt became a useful tool when she wove the material under his armpits, and gripped the excess to tow him toward the surf and the waiting merfolk. His head lolled, and more than once she stepped on his trailing hair, jerking his head back so hard, she feared she'd broken his neck.

Brida laid him down and straightened, pressing her hands to the screaming muscles of her lower back. Her exertions made her forget the cold, and she swiped a forearm across her sweating brow. The whistles from the surf grew demanding and ever more impatient. She spun to frown at the figures patrolling the surf. "You'll kindly hold down that racket and keep your flukes in the water, mind. This is even harder than it looks."

A sharp click followed and the whistles stopped. Brida lifted the merman's head and gathered his hair to drape it across his chest where she quickly wove it into a loose braid and tied it into a knot. That done, she resumed her task, leaving a trail of blood in their wake.

This time the merfolk didn't wait for her to wade deeper into the surf. A half dozen mermen suddenly surrounded her, and she fell back on her haunches in the water as they lifted their brother's limp body and floated him into the waves. The rest followed, their excited whistles and clicks resuming once more.

Short of breath and exhausted, Brida watched them go, both relieved the merman and merchild were no longer her responsibility and happy that she'd done all she could to save them. What a story she had to tell to her nieces and nephews, even if they thought it only an imaginative yarn spun by their eccentric aunt. Only she would know the truth of her tale or how the memory of the merman's face would haunt her for many days to come.

She was thoroughly drenched in salt water, as was everything she wore. If she didn't develop a cold after this, it would be a blessing. Dark memories of the now dead *obluda* motivated her to hurry out of the surf even more than the cold did. The merfolk hadn't tried to drown her, but that didn't mean she was safe from some other lurking danger that swam along the Gray's shores at night.

Sand slid beneath her feet as she trekked to the rocks where she'd left her skirts, shawl, and flute. A clear whistle made her turn.

The merwoman who'd approached her directly bobbed in the waves, moonlight plating her skin in dappled argentum. She raised a hand, in thanks, farewell, or both. Enchanted, Brida offered a nod and returned the gesture, watching as the merwoman turned and dove, disappearing beneath a rising hillock of water.

"You're welcome," Brida said softly, with only the wind and the moon to hear her.

It was time to go home.

CHAPTER THREE

B RIDA WALKED BAREFOOT among a flock of gulls patrolling
the beach. Some followed her in hopes of reaping scraps
she might drop as they hunted for crabs and darter fish at the
edge of the surf. She kept a close eye on those winging above
her, grateful for the kerchief she wore around her head to tame
her hair and protect her head from bird droppings.

Some of the villagers had begun giving her odd looks, pity-
ing ones even, and she'd overheard a whisper or two floating
amongst the crowds during the busy market day. They worried
the solitude of her widowhood had brought on a dangerous
melancholy. She walked the beach these days far more than a
body should, especially now that colder temperatures had
seeped in and settled, and the autumn sky was often bleak.

Brida smiled as she wrapped her shawl tightly about her
shoulders, her flute tucked under one arm. Who knew that she,
Talmai's flute-playing widow, would ever become as interesting
a topic of public house conversation a the noble family to whom
Ancilar was a vassal village? They were welcome to their
conjectures. Gossip was its own form of entertainment in
Ancilar, and she found it funny that for once, people weren't
gossiping as much about the inhabitants of Castle Banat perched
on the bluff behind her.

Her smile faded a little. Solitude wasn't a bad thing, nor did she possess an overabundance of it as her neighbors assumed. Helping her sister-in-law with her large brood of children during the day guaranteed she was rarely alone or uninterrupted. She'd resorted to spinning wool—her main source of income—at night, when she escaped to her own house for some much needed quiet.

Sometimes though, her curiosity got the best of her, along with a futile hope, and she put aside her spinning to walk the shoreline in the twilight hours before the gulls settled down to roost. Except for the birds, the beach was hers, as it was now, with only the waking stars to keep her company and the surf to sing to her.

A fortnight had passed since she'd watched the merfolk disappear into the Gray with the injured merman and child he'd done his best to protect. She thought of the two often, especially the merman. He haunted her dreams, and she found herself remembering his unique eyes and the apologetic whistles he'd uttered in a weak breath after he landed that strike on her with his tail. She'd woken the following day with a painful lump on the back of her head but nothing more, except maybe a passing uncertainty that the events of the previous night had actually happened. She told no one. Who would believe her anyway?

You know of one, her inner voice warned.

As if her uncharitable thoughts had summoned him, a familiar figure perched for a second time on her favorite lookout spot. A saddled horse grazed on sea oats growing amid the salt grass nearby. Brida paused, pondering whether to continue or turn around and go home.

"No reeking nobleman with his nose high in the wind is going to chase me away," she grumbled under her breath and continued toward the ledge. She had her spare flute with her instead of the one her father had made for her, and if Ospodine tried to take it from her, she'd willingly surrender it to him and wish him good luck and good riddance.

That pale, cool stare didn't waver as she drew closer, and the thin smile playing across his mouth was as insincere as the cheery tone of his greeting. "A pleasure to see you here again, Madam Gazi. It seems we both like to stroll the shore this time of evening."

Brida considered herself a mild-mannered woman with a wealth of patience. This man, however, made her hackles rise. He wore an air of contempt about him that belied his surface manners. She hadn't forgotten he'd entered her house to pry while she and the rest of the village harvested seaweed. She'd been startled and then dismayed to see him at Ancilar's market day a few days after Lord Frantisek's party, a guest who had not yet worn out his welcome at the castle or didn't have the sense to know when he actually had done so.

"Syr Ospodine," she said shortly, not bothering to smile in return. This was no one she wanted to befriend, even under different circumstances. He reminded her too much of a cat that played with its prey before killing it.

He unfolded his tall frame from the perch and gestured to the space. "Please, take my seat. I believe this is your favored spot, isn't it?"

An oily shiver eeled down her back. How often had he seen her sitting here this past fortnight, watching the Gray and playing her flute? Once? Twice? Every night?

"You're welcome to your privacy, syr," she said and pivoted to trek back the way she came.

The slap of footsteps in wet sand echoed behind her as Ospodine caught up with her. She jerked away when he touched her elbow, and he dropped his hand as if scalded. His expression held a mix of mutual dislike and revulsion.

She didn't stop walking until he strode ahead and stopped in front of her, blocking her path. He held up his hands in mock surrender. "Please. I mean you no harm. I only want to ask you something."

Wary, Brida tucked her hands into her shawl, using one to grasp the scissors on the chatelaine tied at her waist. "And what is that?"

"Would you play the tune I heard at Lord Frantisek's?"

"Now?" Brida stared at the nobleman, very glad for several reasons that she'd brought her spare flute with her this evening.

He nodded, an avid gleam entering his eyes. "Yes! Here. Now."

He knew. Knew just as she did that the four-note tune was something other than varied breaths blown through a musical instrument during warm-up exercises. The man vibrated with a suppressed eagerness verging on hysteria. The flatness of his mouth against his teeth and the narrow gaze he cast on her warned Brida that she might well compromise her safety if she refused.

She adopted a bored expression, matching it with an equally casual shrug. "All right. If it means that much to you. Though I can play a ballad or a plaint for you that's more entertaining."

"No," he almost snarled before remembering himself. The false smile grew ever more strained. "Just the tune, and play it more than once."

Brida didn't dare mention that only the flute her father had made could replicate the merwoman's whistles perfectly. This flute, no matter how hard or how often she played it, had never accomplished the same.

She fished the flute out of the folds of her shawl, warmed it up with a few experimental scales, and played the merwoman's short song, never taking her eyes off her audience who loomed over her like a vulture.

He flinched as if the sounds grated on his ears. "That isn't right," he complained. "Play it again. As you did at his lordship's celebration."

Brida did as he commanded, playing and replaying the notes until Ospodine cursed her and snatched the flute out of her hands. "Stupid woman," he snapped. "Like this." Instead of putting the flute to his mouth, he whistled the notes himself, and this time it was her turn to wince at the discordant sound.

She barely dodged out of the way in time when the nobleman flung the flute at her, enraged. It landed in the sand, and she left it where it lay, far too busy with keeping an eye on the red-faced Ospodine and her hand on the scissors. With her heart in her throat, she backed away from him.

"Where did you learn to play that tune?" he shouted at her, advancing on her with long strides.

"I didn't 'learn' it! I only heard it long ago and repeated it!" Her shout carried alongside his over the dunes.

"Oy!" a voice called out, making them both turn. "What are

you going on about down there?"

Brida almost burst into relieved tears at the sight of two of the village elders watching from the top of one of the dunes. She used the distraction to dart around Ospodine and run for the safety of their company.

He didn't follow, taking the opposite path to retrieve his horse and vault into the saddle before galloping back toward the castle. Brida watched him go, her heartbeat still banging inside her skull like a war drum. She and the elders watched as his figure soon diminished, becoming nothing more than a fast moving speck that disappeared behind a hillock of sand before reappearing at the bottom of the castle road.

"Trouble, that one," one of the two elders said as he squinted into the distance. "He's been roaming about the village, asking odd questions." His aging gaze drifted to Brida. "A few of those questions about you, Brida."

"What were you two arguing about?" the second elder asked. "We could hear you playing and then you both shouting afterwards."

Brida shuddered. "He's obsessed with a few notes I played at the castle during her ladyship's name day celebration. They mean nothing to me." That wasn't quite true. "But they're important to him for reasons he's chosen not to share."

"He didn't hurt you, did he?" The second elder's face bunched into a thunderous frown. "Laylam will want his head on a plate, nobleman or not, if he did."

She groaned inwardly. The last thing she needed was her brother's already overprotective instincts to flare into a bonfire. He'd try to nail her feet to the floor of her own house in a misguided attempt to keep her safe. "He didn't touch me. Just grew angry when I played what he requested, but it seems I played poorly."

Thank the gods she hadn't brought her bone flute. After discovering Ospodine had wandered uninvited through her house, Brida had taken the flute to Laylam's where Norinn had stashed it and Brida's earnings in a locked box stored beneath the kitchen floor.

The thought reminded her of her forgotten second-best flute, still in the sand where Ospodine had thrown it. She asked the elders to wait for her while she retrieved the instrument. She bent to pick up the flute and froze at the faintest sound purling toward her from the incoming tide.

A deeper whistle, drawn out in the middle, dropping off at the end, and clear as the twilight sky above her. Brida turned her head slowly, half afraid she'd see nothing except the disappointment of unacknowledged hope. A sliver of silvery tail ending in a fluke gently splashed water in her direction, and she caught a glint of twin blue-green fireflies that floated among the waves. Eye-shine in a handsome, unhuman face framed in garlands of floating seaweed hair.

Still half bent toward the flute, Brida breathed out a soft exclamation. "You."

As if he heard her, the merman edged a hand above the wave peaks in greeting. His glowing eyes shifted to the two men waiting at the dunes, their attention turned toward the castle road. Brida placed a finger to her lips in what she hoped was a universal signal for silence. He nodded and half submerged until only the crown of his head remained visible, nothing more than a ubiquitous knot of floating kelp to anyone else who might be watching the water.

Brida snatched up the flute and made her way to the elders. She wanted so badly to return to the merman, but to insist on staying alone on the beach after her confrontation with Ospodine would invite the elders' unwelcome scrutiny and a litany of questions.

"We planned to walk toward the bluff, Brida," the younger of the two men said. "You're welcome to join us. We'll see you home afterwards."

Astran was a jovial man, one of the more reasonable men on the village council, and Brida had always liked him. He'd been the one to call out when she'd faced off with Ospodine.

She smiled at him, hatching an idea. The two men planned to walk in the opposite direction to where the merman waited. They'd be more focused on the castle in the distance and watching for any sign of Ospodine's reappearance. "I thank you for the generous offers. I gladly accept the offer of the second, but would you mind if I stayed?" She held up her flute. "I like to come here in the evenings and play. It was my and Talmai's favorite place."

Their expressions softened, and both men nodded. Astran gestured to the bluff. "We'll come back for you when we're done, or if you find we're taking too long, meet us halfway."

She waved to them as they set off toward the bluff, following the fading hoofprints Ospodine's horse left in the sand. Once they'd gone a short distance, she sped back to the spot where she'd seen the merman. "Please still be there," she murmured to herself. The urge to move faster prickled across her lower back, but she kept her pace to a brisk walk instead of a sprint in case the elders turned to watch her.

Her visitor still floated in the waves, sleek tail and muscular arms flexing in the water to stay afloat. A delighted smile spread across his shadowed face, and Brida caught a glimpse of teeth shaped much like hers in the fading light. He whistled to her, an unfamiliar tune, and motioned toward the ledge Ospodine had claimed earlier.

She paced him on the shore as he swam to their meeting spot. He was much quicker than she and lolled in the shallow surf to wait, protected by the silhouette of the ledge where it jutted beyond the sand and into the water.

Brida climbed the natural ladder carved out by the sea to the flat expanse of stone and perched on the edge, tucking her legs under her. The merman swam closer, the shine of his eyes not so bright with the moon behind him. Brida set the flute to her lips and played the note he'd whistled earlier. His name. This flute lacked the other's accuracy in mimicking mer speech, but the merman didn't seem to mind.

He nodded, his smile widening even more. He tapped the water with the flat of his hand. "Brida who sings," he said in a voice soft and deep, the words a little hesitant as if his tongue still sought to work around their unfamiliarity.

She almost dropped the flute. "You speak!" She shook her head. Of course he spoke, although the whistle language was not one she understood. "You speak *my* language."

"Some," he said. "Your words are hard. This..." he whistled and followed it with a series of clicks in the back of his throat. "Is easier for us."

Delighted, Brida scooted closer to the edge. He, in turn,

swam a little more into the shallows, bracing his elbows in the sand so that he could stretch toward her. His body curved in a faint arc, his fluke lifting high to help him balance. Moonlight plated the dual tones of his skin, highlighting the darker gray of his back and the short dorsal fin that ran the length of his spine. His face, chest, belly and underside of his tail gleamed white in the water. The wounds and lacerations he'd suffered had healed or were healing, silvery flesh knitting itself together into jagged scars.

Brida patted her own hip and pointed to the spot on his tail where he'd been most grievously injured. "That looks good. No blood. No pain?" She chose her words carefully and spoke slowly, trying not to overwhelm him with rapid-fire speech. If he suddenly started whistling and chirping at her in an unending succession of sound, she'd be completely lost.

He nodded. "You saved me. Saved..." Again, a whistle, only different, higher, and she recognized the name he'd given the merchild.

It was her turn to grin. She had prayed both man and child would survive, even when her doubts about his chances made the praying seem futile at times. "I'm happy," she said. "Your daughter?" she asked.

He frowned, then shook his head. "Daughter?" He parsed out the word's two syllables carefully, as if saying them aloud might help him better comprehend its meaning.

Flummoxed by how to explain the meaning, Brida decided to put it aside. If she was fortunate enough to see the merman again, she'd figure out a way to translate words for him and have him do the same for her with whistles and clicks.

"What is Brida?" he asked.

She blinked. How to answer? She was a human, but that was obvious, and instinct told her that wasn't really his question. Comprehension dawned. She held up her arms and flexed her biceps, feeling foolish, but figuring it was the best way to impart her name's meaning. "Brida is strength." She patted one arm for emphasis. "Strength."

The merman's fluke twitched as if it waved at her. He tested the word. "Strength." This time the whistle he uttered was a burst of sound, short and sharp. "Brida," he said and repeated the whistle.

She had a mer name now. Thrilled at the idea, Brida took up her flute and played the note. It lacked the melodic tones of the four-note tune the merwoman had uttered, but it was her name in a language of the sea spoken by legendary creatures from its depths.

"What is…" She played his name on the flute.

Her companion spread his arms to indicate size, then curved one in a darting motion to indicate speed.

Brida raised an eyebrow. "Your name is Fast Fish?" This communication exchange was difficult.

Like the more abstract term for "daughter," his name defied simple translation through gestures. Brida waved a hand at him to signal it didn't matter. She was happy to call him in the language of his folk. It seemed only fair to return the courtesy.

Hints of conversation drifted toward her. The elders were returning from their short stroll. It was time to leave.

She sighed, wishing this extraordinary meeting wouldn't end. "I must go," she said and unfolded her legs to stand. A muscular arm stretched out before a webbed hand gripped her ankle, and she froze, heart leaping in her chest in a mixture of fright and a feeling she hadn't experienced in a long time.

The merman's gaze flickered in the direction of the two men before returning to her. He released her ankle. "Come back, Brida?" He clicked at her before pointing to the sky with his free hand. "When lights shine?"

A garland of seaweed hair spilled over his arm to trail across her foot. Brida looked up at the ever-darkening sky and the "lights." His expression held both hope and entreaty. "Stars," she said and singled out a few of the brighter lights sailors used to navigate over the vast expanse of ocean. "The lights are stars."

"Stars," he repeated and clicked twice. She tried to mimic him, and they both grinned at her failure.

"Come back, Brida?" He said a second time.

"I'll try." She wanted very much to say yes, but such would be a lie. With Ospodine still in Ancilar and his unwanted attention focused on her, she had to be careful. And he was only one of several challenges in returning to the beach in the evening hours without attracting notice or inviting questions.

She raised a hand, beguiled by the sight of him, so strange yet so beautiful in the Gray's shallow caress. "Goodbye."

"Wait." She halted, watching as he unwound a thin strip of dark cloth from around his upper arm and offered it to her. "For you from me and..." He whistled the merchild's name.

Brida's hand closed on the fabric, startled to discover it was the sheathe for her flute she'd lost in the waves when she carried the merchild out to her kinsmen. The cloth had seen better days, its weave unravelling in places and heavy with salt water. Something hard and weighted lay hidden in one end.

The elders were close enough now that another minute more, and they'd spot the merman where he rested in the shallows. Brida gave him a quick smile and a last wave before abandoning the ledge to meet the pair on the beach. She dared not look back, though the temptation nearly overwhelmed her.

She tucked the wet flute cover into one of the pockets of her skirt, feeling it soak through to her skin, and wondering what lay inside. A shell? A rock? A dead fish? She hoped it wasn't the last.

The two elders gave no indication they'd seen anything odd on their stroll, though they admonished her to be careful going anywhere alone and promised to keep an eye on Lord Frantisek's sinister guest should he choose to visit Ancilar again or the beach itself.

Alone once more in her house, she barred the door behind her, lit a few more candles, and set a kettle of water to warm on the still hot grate over the banked coals in her hearth. Her tea would be lukewarm at best, but she craved a cup, not only to warm her bones but calm her racing thoughts.

Tomorrow. The merman had pleaded with her to return tomorrow, and Brida vowed she'd find a way to do so, regardless of nosy neighbors and threatening outsiders.

She fished out the soggy bit of cloth from her pocket and set it on her kitchen table. Flickering light from a single candle cast a warm glow on the cloth and the mysterious lump in one end. Brida shook out the contents, her shocked gasp loud in the quiet room as the merman's gift rolled across the table's surface to fall into her palm.

A pearl, the size of a hazelnut, and perfectly round, gleamed a lustrous ivory in the candlelight. Beautiful. Flawless. Priceless. A gift of thanks that carried the wealth of kings. Brida, a widow of small worth had suddenly become Brida, a widow of significant means.

CHAPTER FOUR

THE CLICK OF the latch as she opened her back gate made Brida flinch, and she looked both ways into the quiet street. No one was about. She scurried along the edge of the cobblestone path, up on her tiptoes so as to make as little sound as possible. It was a sad day when she had to sneak out of her own house so as not to explain her business to every busybody who thought themselves entitled to that knowledge.

The merman's appeal of "Come back, Brida?" played inside her mind For seven evenings he'd asked the same thing each time they parted. She had yet to tell him no.

A niggling of guilt plagued her. Laylam sensed something beyond the usual preparations for winter and the upcoming harvest festival celebrated by all the villages under Castle Banat's demesne distracted her. He questioned her about it each time he saw her, and each time she lied to him without batting an eyelash.

"You've not been yourself for nearly a month now, Brida. What's wrong?"

I'm chatting with mermen at night and hiding from harassing noblemen during the day, she was tempted to reply but kept the words behind her teeth and answered with a brief shrug. "I'm fine, Laylam. I'd think you have a lot more to concern yourself with than your sister's mood." Three of his nine children had been sick with a cold the past few days, and Brida had tended to the healthy children while Norinn treated the sick ones. It had been left to Laylam to finish drying the last of their harvested seaweed, load it, and transport it to the big trading market in Galagan.

She'd left Norinn an hour ago, long enough to change clothes and bolt a cup of hot tea. The gloaming had passed. Half the village was dark, villagers finding their beds for the night. Brida didn't hold much hope that her seagoing companion still awaited her, but she intended to visit their meeting place anyway. The little time they spent together each evening had become the highlight of her life, a magic all its own beyond the fact she was visiting one of the fabled merfolk.

Her shoulders sagged when she reached the ledge and found the waters that lapped at its base empty. No silvery fluke or skin dappled by moonlight. No firefly eyes or a webbed hand raised in greeting.

"Ahtin?" she called softly. The wind caught her question, tossing it into the surf.

She'd figured out the spoken equivalent of his whistled name after more failed hand gestures and fleeting drawings dug into the sand with a stick. "Fast fish" wasn't quite right, but Brida had been close in her initial translation.

The sand drawings had done much to further their communication. She'd learned the merchild was not his daughter, but his niece, child of a sister mermaid. When the merman held out his hand for the stick, she'd passed it to him, watching as he arched his torso and tail for balance before sketching out a sleek fish with a nose that elongated into the shape of a spear or spike.

When he finished, he tapped the stick against the drawing, then tapped his chest with one finger and whistled his name.

He'd drawn an ahtin, a big, sleek, deep-water fish highly prized by fishermen, not for its meat but for the challenge of catching it. Fast and aggressive, the ahtin fought every attempt at being hooked or netted, its ferociousness legendary. More than a few fishermen had died in the attempt, impaled on the spike.

It seemed an odd name to give the merman, Brida thought. He had been anything but aggressive toward her. The name seemed more fitting for someone like Ospodine. Still, he'd managed to fight off and escape something with big teeth and a bigger appetite, saving himself and his niece, even if it had been a near death for them both.

"Ahtin," she'd told him when he gave her an inquiring look. "Your name is Ahtin."

"Ahtin," he'd repeated before nodding his approval. "Ahtin and Brida."

The pairing of their two names sent a frisson of warmth through her body, startling her. "Oh, Brida," she silently admonished herself. "Don't be a nitwit. It's simply two names and someone learning how to say them."

She hadn't echoed his words, turning her attention instead to drawing more pictographs in the sand so she and Ahtin could exchange their meanings in both spoken word and whistle. He learned her language much faster than she learned his, his fascination for this new speech reflected in the avid spark that lit his eyes and the way his gaze settled on her mouth and stayed as she spoke. It might have been disconcerting were it not for the softness of his expression, as if what she said wasn't nearly as enchanting as the way she said it.

"Vanity," that inner voice, with its relentless criticism, cautioned her. "Just your vanity."

This evening she'd promised herself not to read into Ahtin's expressions those emotions experienced by humans. He wasn't human, and his people remained a mystery to her. She'd witnessed some of their behavior when they gathered in the hope of rescuing Ahtin and the merchild Brida now called Samath, after the spirit of beaches. They displayed fear and affection, anger and worry, just like humans did, but much of that emotion had manifested audibly. The nuances of facial expression might be very different in merfolk than in humans. Though it was impossible to misinterpret the wide smile Ahtin wore every time he saw her.

No merman greeted her now with his welcoming smile, and the sea lapped solitary against the rock ledge as if to mock her. Brida climbed to the flat top anyway and peered out at the waves. Vague hints of dorsal fins rose and fell in the surf, darting one way and then the other under the dull light of stars and a fading moon. Hunting, she thought. The toothy predators that made night fishing so dangerous were out in numbers now, patrolling the waters for the unwary. Brida was suddenly glad Ahtin hadn't come, or if he had, that he chose not to stay.

The sharp whistle that was her name in the mer language proved that assumption wrong. Brida turned toward the sound coming from her left where the tidal pools in which she'd first found Ahtin were now submerged by the tide. Beyond them, a stretch of beach unfurled past the salt grass to the place where a curving ladder of rock hugged the shoreline. The black eye of a sea cave stared back at her, and in the glass-thin water kissing the entrance, a pale figure beckoned.

Brida's spirit sang with a silent joy at the sight of Ahtin waving to her, but she hesitated to join him. Ixada cave was a haunted place, a doorway to the world of the dead, or so the old stories went. Every child born and raised in Ancilar had challenged their playmates to enter the caves, including Brida. She'd only been brave enough to linger at the entrance and peer inside, at which point Laylam had leapt out of the shadows with a roar and nearly made her wet herself with terror. She'd raced home crying, unsympathetic to her brother's plight when he earned a hard swat from their father and a night without supper for scaring his sister.

Childhood was long behind her, but her wariness of the cave remained, as it did with even the most skeptical villagers. Fishermen told of hearing strange whispering from its depths during moonless nights and especially on the Day of Spirits when the year also died. Some even reported seeing vaporous shapes floating out of the blackness to fade into the waves, singing wordless songs in wailing voices.

Ahtin whistled her name a second time. Whatever spirits sheltered in Ixada Cave, they didn't seem interested in revealing themselves to him. Brida inhaled and exhaled a long breath, glanced behind her at the dark silhouette of Castle Banat atop its bluff and the empty shoreline below it before climbing down the ledge to join the merman. There were worse things than ghosts. *Obludas.*

The thought halted her for a moment before she resumed her trek, ears tuned to any melancholy dirges that might suddenly rise up from the Gray. She stepped over mounds of seaweed and skirted the corpses of jellyfish with their long tentacles stretched like venomous ribbons across the sand.

Ahtin swam parallel to the shore, powerful shoulders flexing in tandem with the rise and fall of his back and tail through the water. He paused when she did, near the cave's black maw. He gestured to the opening with a thrust of his chin. "Go inside, Brida. I want to show you."

She trusted him. Mostly. Had he wished to hurt her, the chances to do so had been many and varied since they first crossed paths. Brida didn't believe he'd lead her to an other-worldly trap where some monstrous thing waited to wrest her soul from her body and plunge it into nightmarish oblivion. But Ixada Cave...

So dark, with its untold mysteries and stories of the haunted dead.

"I have no light," she told him. "I won't be able to see any-thing in there." Things like once-dry expanses flooded with the incoming tide and the gods only knew what strange creatures that swam within it. Merfolk were almost commonplace compared to the horrors she imagined lurked in the concealing darkness.

Ahtin drew nearer, the splash of his fluke sounding close enough to touch. "Safe, Brida," he crooned to her. "You are safe with me."

In that moment, she understood what the sailors meant when they spoke of sirens' song. She set a foot down in the direction of the cave where some of her worst childhood fears waited.

"Wait." Ahtin shook his head. "Not that way. This way."

Puzzled, Brida followed him on the shore as he swam around the edge of the bluff. Her skirts dragged in the surf as she waded knee-deep through water growing colder with each passing autumnal day. She clutched the satchel she'd brought with her, its contents clinking and together. Nothing inside was of much monetary value, certainly not like the pearl he'd given her, but she didn't want to drop them and lose them to the Gray before Ahtin saw them.

She squeaked at the sight of a sharp fin slicing the water toward her. In an instant, Ahtin disappeared from her view, leaving only a temporary wake behind him that marked a path aimed directly at the fin which also dove beneath the waves. A frothing of water boiled up from the spot before dissipating. Frozen in place, Brida stared, unbreathing, until a crown of seaweed hair emerged, and Ahtin's glowing eyes stared back at her.

"Safe, Brida," he repeated and propelled himself through the surf until he floated alongside her.

"What was that?" She hated how her voice warbled, but it was hard to speak normally when her heart was still stuck in her throat.

"A hunter. It hunts something else now."

That short answer was less than comforting, and she slogged faster toward the patch of beach revealed on the other side of the bluff and a smaller entrance she assumed led into the cave. Here, the land rose more sharply, keeping the high tide at bay.

Brida looked down at her companion. "How will you go in?" She supposed he could pull himself along the sand, using the power of his arms and tail, but what a struggle that would be, even with him healed of his injuries.

He gestured toward the second entrance. "You go there. I will meet you from the other side." Before she could protest, he dove once more into the deeper waves, fluke giving a single flick before sliding under the waves.

A sliver of moonlight illuminated a patch of sand just inside the low entrance. Brida bent to enter, straightening with a gasp upon discovering a large interior space of soaring height with tidal pools closest to her and the pounding of the surf against a tumbled barrier of rock on the other side where the wider entrance faced the more level shore.

The darkness prevented her from seeing much more than the outline of curved walls and roof and the hint of reflection on the pools' surfaces. A loud splash echoed in the chamber. She tensed as verdant light spread across the cave floor, brightening the waters of a large pool surrounded on three sides by rubble, with the fourth side narrowed down to a channel where the surf spilled into the pool as a waterfall. Some of the rubble looked as if it lay in and around the water with purpose, creating an imprecise spoke pattern with the lit pool at its center.

Water lapped at the rubble shore. Brida could see all the way to the rocky bottom and track the tiny fish that darted back and forth, startled by the sudden luminescence and the addition of a much bigger occupant to their sanctuary.

Ahtin slowly revealed himself with a flex of his tail, rising above the surface until he faced her, seawater streaming down his face and torso. His hair cascaded over his broad shoulders, wrapping around his arms. In the soft light, his eyes had lost their nocturnal shine, and his double pupils shone dark within their pale irises.

Her sodden skirt slapped in rhythm with her steps as Brida picked her way across one of the spokes toward him. His mouth curved into a smile to match hers. "Your water magic?" she asked.

"One enchantment." He traced an evanescent pattern on the pool's surface with one fingertip. "There are many others."

Brida envied him the skill of water sorcery. Any sorcery for that matter. There were human mages, though they weren't common, nor had she ever met one herself. She'd heard all the Kai, the last of the Elder races not yet vanished, possessed magic that they wielded at will, but like the merfolk, they weren't human. "Do you know many enchantments?"

He shook his head. "No. The *aps* do, but they only teach all they know to the female who will become the *ap* after them."

It had taken several rounds of whistle and word exchanges as well as numerous drawings in the sand for Brida to understand the nature of an *ap*, and she still wasn't certain she had the right of it.

The merfolk were a loose confederation of several extended family units, each ruled by a matriarch they called an *ap*. At least that's what the noise Ahtin made to signify the matriarch's title sounded like to Brida. The *ap's* descendents stayed with her family, the mermen leaving only temporarily to mate with merwomen of other families. In that, Ahtin told her, the merfolk were more like the great whales than the dolphins.

Merfolk lived long lives, the *aps* even longer than the others, sustained by sea magic whose origin had long ago been lost to memory but was passed down from matriarch to oldest living daughter who carried on the heritage generation after generation.

With Ahtin's sorcerous light chasing away some of the darkness, the cave no longer seemed as sinister. Brida found the largest rock closest to the pool's edge and sat down. Ahtin glided toward her, a study in grace and power as he cleaved the water.

"I have gifts for you." She shrugged off the satchel she'd looped over her shoulder and across her chest, settling it in her lap.

Ahtin swam up next to her, so close his arm laid a wet path across the side of her skirt where he rested it on the rock shoreline. Avid curiosity glittered in his eyes as he stared at the bag, though he said nothing and waited patiently for her to reveal its contents to him.

She held up a wooden eating spoon, turning it one way, then the other before demonstrating its use. When she passed it to him, he took it as if it were a fragile piece of pottery. Brida watched, mesmerized as his fingers caressed the utensil, stroking the oval and handle in long sweeps. He then brought the oval to his mouth, pressing it down on his lower lip before sneaking a taste with the tip of his tongue. Brida forgot to breathe.

"Spoon," she said in a hoarse voice.

Both lips curved around the oval's edge in a kiss. "Spoon," he echoed, double eyelids closed as if in deep thought. He opened his eyes, heavy gaze settling on her where she sat frozen on her rock seat. "I like the spoon."

Siren's voice, siren's stare. The sea's seduction wasn't confined only to mermaids.

"I can keep it?"

Caught in that unwavering regard, Brida didn't comprehend the question at first. "Keep it?"

A knowing, closed-lip smile curved Ahtin's mouth. "The spoon."

Later, when she lay alone in her bed, contemplating the mysteries of life in the plastered divets of her ceiling, Brida thanked the gods for the cave's frigid air, otherwise she might have incinerated on the spot from embarrassment.

"Yes!" she practically shouted, flinching when her exclamation ricocheted back to her from the walls and roof. She bent her head, tempted to dive directly into the satchel and hide the heat scorching her face. Her fingers fumbled with the next item, almost dropping it in the pool. She thrust it at Ahtin who reared back to avoid being struck in the face.

Commonplace like the spoon, the comb Brida held out to him was a plain affair, carved from a splinter remnant of a shipwreck washed ashore when she was still a child. She'd done the work herself, a practice piece given to her by her father whose skilled hands would have turned it into a work of art. Brida had used it on her hair until she married, when Talmai presented her with a brush and comb set as a wedding present.

Ahtin reached for it, his expression puzzled when she suddenly pulled it out of reach. "A comb. Watch." She undid the bottom third of her plait and used the comb to tease out the small tangles created by the salt water drying there.

The same keen focus he displayed with the spoon sharpened

even more with the comb. Brida wondered if her own expression had mirrored his when the priceless pearl had rolled across her table. These things had no real value in her world, but he held them as if they were treasures like the pearl. Unique, precious, remarkable.

His inspection of the comb was less sensuous in nature than it had been with the spoon, for which Brida was glad, until he curled a hand around her loosened plait. She sat still as the stone beneath her while he twined her hair through his fingers.

"Not like us," Ahtin said, his smile telling her the observation wasn't a criticism. He used the comb as she had, running it gently through the loose strands.

"No," she agreed. "Not like you."

Did merfolk comb out their hair in some way? The ones who'd gathered to rescue their kinsmen had left theirs unbound with bits of shell woven in for ornamentation. As he'd done with her, she reached out to snare one of Ahtin's locks.

Slippery-smooth, the strands were thicker and wider than her own with a texture that made her think of a candle's surface. Water beaded on the filaments instead of soaking into them like human hair.

So intent with her inspection of his hair, Brida didn't notice Ahtin had moved until he was right in front of her, at eye level, his arms braced on either side of her, chest pressed to her bent knees. She gave a faint squeak and dropped the lock of hair, startled by his sudden closeness.

The myriad shades of pale pink, lavender, blue, and green that pulsed just under his skin deepened along his throat and across his cheekbones. Ahtin tilted his head as if considering a most unusual shell laying on the sand. He gave her the comb. "Use here," he said, fingers parting the curtain of hair that hid a portion of his face.

A steady clicking, much like a feline purr, rose in his throat as she carefully ran the comb from his scalp to the tips of his hair, and his eyes closed in quiet ecstasy. Brida glanced around him to see his fluke gently fronding the water in tandem rhythm to his clicks.

This close to him, she warmed under the heat his body radiated. She was chilled to the bone herself, holding back shivers with an effort, even as she dreaded having to leave soon and end this extraordinary interlude with her merman.

Her merman. The thought made her jerk, and the comb snagged in his hair hard enough to make his eyelids snap open. The purring click abruptly became a pained whistle.

"I'm sorry! So sorry!" She dropped the comb in her lap to pat his hair and shoulders in apology.

Ahtin whistled again, softer now, reassuring. He captured one of her fluttering hands, flattening her palm against his chest. His hand was hot, like the rest of him, and Brida was reminded that the differences between them went beyond the surface visuals to more subtle elements. She would have turned blue by now were she submerged in cold seawater for any real length of time. Her feet were already numb from wading through the surf to reach this side of the cave.

"You are cold," he said with a frown.

"And you most definitely aren't."

Maybe what she thought had been fever when he lay beached among the seaweed hadn't been from sickness or injury but simply from lack of the water to keep his body cool.

"What is Brida?" he asked, repeating the same question from their second meeting.

She shrugged. "Strength." Had he forgotten?

Ahtin shook his head and raised her hand to inspect her fingers, the slots between them where no webbing stretched, the short half moons of her nails, pale against skin still deeply brown from the vanished summer sun. The contrast between her skin and his—deep earth on shallow sea—beguiled her. They were land and water, human legs and dolphin tail with nothing in common except an abiding fascination for each other and the connection of the rescued to the rescuer.

His clear brow knitted into a frown. "No. Strength, yes, but more." He struggled to express himself. "You are this light." He gestured to the sorcerous light still shimmering around them. "This pool. The moon. The sun."

Comprehension dawned, and once more the heat of a blush crawled up her neck, into her cheeks. "Beautiful," she said. "Those things are beautiful."

Something in her tone alerted him that she understood what he tried to impart, and the frown smoothed away. "Beautiful," he echoed, reverence in every syllable. "You are beautiful, Brida."

The last time a man had called her beautiful in such a way, it had been when she lay in Talmai's arms the night before he left Ancilar to board a deep-water ship at Matalene harbor a league from Ancilar. She'd dreamed those agonizing moments more times than she cared to count after she learned he'd died at sea. Time had passed and the keen sorrow from that particular memory was blunted now. When the merman called her beautiful, butterflies, not tears, spiraled up inside her.

She didn't move when he leaned in even closer, and his hands settled on her hips, slippery hair shrouding them both. His sigh matched hers when his lips grazed her cheek, tickling her skin with the lightest touch as they mapped a path over the bridge of her nose to her other cheek before drifting up to caress her temple and eyebrows. She closed her eyes against their feathery pressure on her eyelids. Her lips parted as his mouth rested briefly on hers and stayed.

Did merfolk kiss?

The question drifted across her thoughts before fading. It didn't matter. If he didn't know, she would teach him and hold close in her dotage the wondrous memory of it.

He twitched against her when she took his bottom lip between her lips and lightly sucked, exhaled a moan when her tongue traced its outline, tasting a hint of brine. Strong hands dug into the folds of her skirt to hold her hips even harder, and he surged against her, the powerful flex of his tail almost carrying him out of the water.

Brida's eyes snapped open and she pulled away to stare at Ahtin who stared back with a gaze gone almost completely black. Heat poured off him like a furnace, and he loosened his grip on her body long enough to touch his mouth with one fingertip.

A series of clicks, much too rapid and unfamiliar for her to translate, spilled from him before he went silent, scrutiny never wavering as he searched for a word.

"Kiss," Brida told him. "That's a kiss."

"Kiss." He drew out the end of the word as if savoring its sound and texture.

She smiled a tentative smile. "You like it?" The gods knew she certainly did.

He wore the same look as when he licked the spoon she'd given him. A quick nod, and he reached for her, drawing her closer to him until the lower half of her skirts floated in the pool, drifting around him like a spill of blue ink in the luminescent water. "Land magic," he breathed across her mouth. "Teach me, beautiful Brida."

CHAPTER FIVE

"WHY DO HUMANS cover like this?" Ahtin picked at the folds of her skirt, rooting for the shape of her thigh hidden beneath the heavy wool.

Like the night before, they spent these hours together in the sanctuary of the cave lit by Ahtin's magic. And like the night before, they kissed and explored, learning each other's taste, the shape of leg and tail, shoulders and arms, cheekbones and necks, chest and breast.

Brida stroked a hand down his side, contouring her palm to the ridges of muscles that laddered down his torso to his narrow waist and the smooth flesh that denoted the beginnings of his tail. The heat of his body kept her warm in the chilly cave. "For protection and warmth. Our bodies don't get as hot as yours unless we're sick. Clothing keeps us warm and protects our skin from other things too." She nudged his chin with her nose. He obliged her by bending to eagerly press his mouth to hers, cool lips against hers, warm tongue sweeping the interior of her mouth.

She had taught him that the previous night, and he'd been an enthusiastic student of what he called her "land magic." Brida might have taught him even more were it not for the far-off hint of a whistle. Ahtin's fluke slapped the water, and his features had pinched with annoyance.

"I must go," he told her, leaning his forehead against hers with a sigh. "Come back, Brida?"

Caution dictated she should have said no, but she'd thrown that notion to the wind the moment she'd first seen him injured on the beach. "Tomorrow," she'd agreed.

He'd led her out of the cave, staying by her side as she waded back to the level, drier shoreline. No threatening dorsal fin raced toward her, nor had any appeared tonight, for which she was thankful.

None of this would last. She'd never been under the illusion that it could. Ahtin was a dweller of the sea and she a dweller of the land. They'd found literal common ground here, but her life was in Ancilar among her people and his somewhere in the Gray's liquid wilderness, with other merfolk and creatures savage and sublime. That he was even here now was a wondrous thing in itself.

She refused to think beyond this ephemeral moment, this hidden place where she and a fabled merman traded loving caresses. To him, she was simply beautiful Brida. Not Brida, alone and widowed, viewed by some as a woman to be pitied while they silently thanked the gods they weren't in her shoes. The memories she made with him would last her lifetime, gifts of value beyond measure, more precious even than the priceless pearl he'd given her.

He lifted her braid to wrap its length around his arm, letting it uncoil before catching it in his hand. He painted his cheek and the bridge of his nose with the end. "Swim in the water with me."

She shuddered at the idea. "The pool is freezing. At least for me." It was bad enough that her feet were submerged. If she didn't have them pressed to the sides of Ahtin's tail, they'd be numb from the cold. Wading all the way in was out of the question, especially since she'd have to strip to her shift so as to have dry things to wear during the trek home. "Just how cold can it get before you start to feel it?"

He shrugged. "We can swim in the waters when ice floats there, and we dive deep where it's dark and no sunlight can reach." A troubled expression settled on his features, and the hand on her thigh tightened for a moment. "But we don't stay in one place. Soon, all the mer will swim for warmer seas, where the women with child will birth their young."

The bottom dropped out of Brida's stomach. "How soon?"

"When the *aps* say so. They decide when the families make the journey."

They were migratory, just like the dolphins and the whales. She guessed it might be so. The idea lodged in the back of her mind like a splinter, making her wonder each time she traveled to meet him if he wouldn't be there.

Ahtin nuzzled her, rubbing his nose in the soft hairs that lay against her temple. "Swim with me," he whispered. "My magic will hold back the cold."

A tingling sensation spread across her feet, washing feeling back into her toes. Brida pulled away from him to stare at the pool. Ahtin's palm rested atop the surface. Runnels of fiery light coursed along the tendons and veins in the back of his hand, spreading up his arm. The water grew warmer by the second until it turned tepid.

Brida laughed, delighted, and kicked her legs so that water splashed behind Ahtin. "Amazing! So much good magic! Can all the mer do this?"

He grinned at her compliment, pale eyes glittering in the cave's half light. "When we must. It helps the laboring mer-women and the infants when they're born." He tugged on her skirts. "Now will you swim?"

With the pool now more temperate than a bath, she had no reason to refuse. She'd learned to swim as a child. Too many who lived by the sea lacked the skill and had paid the ultimate price.

Brida stood and stepped farther back from the pool's edge to shed her clothes. Ahtin watched her, silent, curious. Once she was down to her shift, she hesitated. The garment was thin and wouldn't drag her down in the water the way her heavier garb might, but it was still long and restricted the movement of her legs. She played with the neckline, considering. None of the merwomen she'd seen in the group who had come for him and his niece wore coverings across their breasts. The trappings of such modesty were a land dweller's concept, not that of the merfolk, who would find such covering not only unnecessary but also foolish. Raised within such a culture, Ahtin likely wouldn't make much note of her breasts if she bared them. Her legs though…that was another thing altogether.

Grabbing her courage with both hands and shrugging away her embarrassment, she stripped off the shift, letting it fall atop the mound of clothes at her feet. The cave's chilly air raised goosebumps on her skin from her ankles to her scalp, and she scampered toward the pool, hugging herself in a failed bid to retain her body heat.

Ahtin caught her, hands on her waist, and lowered her into the pool. He smiled at her happy sigh, letting her go when she pushed gently against his chest to paddle the pool's circumference. He joined her, sleek, and quick, and quiet.

As she predicted, his gaze flickered briefly over her torso before focusing on the wavering outline of her legs as she tread water. He reached down, grasping one of her knees to lift it for closer inspection. Brida grasped for the pool's stony shore behind her to keep the merman from her tipping her backwards. He flashed her an apologetic look before returning his attention to her leg, exposed to the air from lower thigh to foot.

"Two tails," he said, gesturing to her other leg still underwater.

Brida snorted. "Legs. They're called legs."

He repeated the word, then nodded to show either his approval or his understanding.

She pointed to her toes, wiggling them for emphasis. "Toes." Her foot jerked in his grasp while he counted the five digits with ticklish touches. At his inquiring taps on her skin, she revealed the name for each part of her leg. "Foot. Arch. Ankle. Shin. Calf. Knee. Thigh." Every touch sent sparks shooting through her body. Was it possible to catch fire while immersed in water?

The tell-tale series of low-pitched clicks started low in his throat, a vocalization of his growing arousal. Her lessons in kissing had taught her as much as they taught Ahtin. In those interim moments when they'd come up for air, she'd caught a good look at his erection.

Displayed with neither shame nor arrogance, his cock had

emerged from where it lay hidden behind the longer vertical slit in his tail. Pink in color and broader at its base than its tip, it had nudged the inside of her thigh covered by the fall of her skirt. They might be human woman and merman, of different origin with different bodies, but mating instinct possessed an accurate aim.

At the moment, his erection rubbed along her buttocks as he floated her on her back, and his breathing was as rapid as hers. He lifted her a little higher with one hand until the chilly air washed over her nicely warmed skin and pebbled her nipples. With the other, he stroked the line of her body from collar bones to the triangle of dark hair between her thighs.

Brida's breathy moan made the ridges marking his eyebrows arch and his lips curve into a pleased smile. He repeated the caress, pausing to trace the curve of her breasts and tease her nipples with the barest hint of a touch.

"You are made like the merwomen here. You feed your young the same way?" Brida nodded, hardly able to retain a thought for more than a moment. He continued his journey down her body, stopping once more at the juncture of her thighs. "Here you are different." She gasped as his fingers slipped lower, finding the entrance to her body. The heartbeat of her own arousal pulsed there, and her legs parted wider to give him better access. "Not so different, beautiful Brida," he said in a low voice before slowly sliding a finger inside her.

Brida's gasp echoed throughout the cave. She clutched his supporting arm with one hand and gripped his opposite wrist with the other, torn between wanting him to stop and urging him to keep going, use more than a finger on her. Use that lovely cock rubbing so teasingly against her backside, promising a pleasure she'd all but forgotten in the years since Talmai had died.

He played her body the same way she played her flute, with a combination of delicacy, prowess, and reverence, learning each curve and reaction as if she were the notes to a song. They floated in the water, Brida no longer on her back but pressed breast to chest with Ahtin, her legs wrapped tight around his middle, her hands clasped at his nape under the slippery cascade of his hair.

She explored his body in much the same way he had hers, hands marking a path over his shoulders, tracing the color divide that started just under his ears, transitioning from dove gray on his back to the pearlescent shade of ivory on his front, with its muted pastels shimmering just below his skin. "You're made like human man here," she said, running her hands down his arms and over his chest. "Different in other places."

She traced the helix of his ear, not smooth and rounded like hers, but rimmed with small bony points of various heights. His ear lobe was much smaller than hers, while the auricle was much bigger, almost completely covering the entrance to his ear canal. The low-profile dorsal fin along his back, and of course his tail, were the most obvious distinctions from a human, but Brida found that it was the shape of his ears that most sharply reminded her of their dissimilarities.

The thought plagued her for the time it took her to blink before she shoved it aside. Those physical disparities didn't matter. He made her remember happiness and spontaneity, reminded her that wonder existed in the apparent and the hidden. He made her spirit, so long asleep, awaken.

Ahtin thrust against her with a flex of his tail. "Different here as well?"

She dipped one hand below the water, reaching between their bodies to grip his cock and give him a quick stroke. His nostrils flared, and his fingers dug into her buttocks. "Only a little, and in a good way." She kissed him then, not just with her mouth, but her entire being, rejoicing when he enthusiastically returned her ardor, those humming clicks erupting from his throat to tickle her tongue and lips with their resonance.

Waves lapped around them as Ahtin spread her thighs, opening her wider so that his cock slid long and deep inside her in one smooth stroke. Brida groaned at the penetration, the fullness of him. She squeezed his waist with her thighs, swallowing his rushed exhalation mixed with a groan of her own.

The back of his tail tensed and contracted against her heels with each thrust, his breathing as stuttered as hers when they ended one hard kiss, only to begin another. Their bodies' positions and the rubbing of his tail against her pelvis in just the right way spiked sensations through her so hard that she climaxed before he did, nearly arching out of his arms with the intensity of her orgasm.

Ahtin soon followed her, his thrusts growing quicker, more forceful, punctuated by guttural sounds he purred into her ear even as he pumped his seed into her welcoming body. Afterwards, he stretched onto his back, with Brida atop him as they floated in the pool. He remained inside her, still semi-erect. Brida folded her hands across his chest to rest her chin on her knuckles and gaze at his handsome features, a little slack now with satiated pleasure. She suspected she looked much the same.

What a strange and marvelous thing she had just experienced. A small part of her feared she dreamed all of this: a merman, his magic, the discovery of the merfolk, Ahtin's strong body beneath her, inside her. Brida feared waking up to discover none of it was real—that life, as she had always known it before the storms had dumped seaweed and a wounded merman on the shore, continued on as it always had. Days of mundane existence and hard work ending in nights of solitary quiet in which she would wonder if she might go mad one day from sheer boredom.

"What are you thinking, beautiful Brida?" Ahtin's webbed hands skated down her back, one finger following the indentation of her spine.

She smiled. Dark thoughts had no place here or in this moment, and weren't meant to be shared. She brushed them away. "I like being here. With you. I wish we could stay this way for a long time." Forever, she thought but didn't say it aloud.

He frowned a little. "Why can't we?"

Struck by his question and his reaction, she shrugged. "Because dawn isn't far off. I need to be home before I'm missed, and no doubt your people wonder where you go to each night." In all honesty, Brida was surprised she hadn't seen even a hint of the merfolk so far besides Ahtin. Maybe they weren't as nosy and far less enamored with gossip than humans were.

His frown deepened, darkened. He abruptly rolled them, slipping out of Brida so suddenly, she gasped. She still floated in his arms, though now she faced him once more, treading water. "Do you have another mate?"

Her eyes rounded. Was that jealousy she heard? The idea stunned her. Was she wrong in her earlier translations when he described the habits of the mer? They found mates, but the unions were temporary, the only permanent, long-lasting relationship that of the merfolk to their familial groups led by their *aps*.

Brida stroked his arm in a soothing gesture. "I did, once. He died."

Compassion softened the pinched lines of his face. He grasped her hand and brought it to his mouth, kissing her fingers. His eyes darkened with a remembered sorrow. "I had a mate too, and a child. They died as well."

She pressed her palm to his cheek. It seemed Death was no more merciful to the merfolk than it was to humanity. "Losing one is terrible enough. Losing both, an unbearable grief."

He gathered her close, and they held each other until his magic faded, and the pool grew colder with every passing moment. When even Ahtin's body heat couldn't keep the shivers at bay, he swam with her to the rocky edge and helped her out of the water. She dressed quickly, shaking hands struggling with laces and clasps until she was finally wrapped in her shawl and her damp hair bundled in a kerchief she'd tied around her head to keep her ears warm. She wouldn't be totally dry until she got home, changed, and buried under her blankets, but it would do for now.

Once more standing on the other side of the bluff, with retreating tide stroking her feet, and the red edge of dawn just cresting the horizon, Brida blew a kiss to Ahtin. He returned the gesture.

"Come tomorrow, Brida." His farewell carried a tone she hadn't heard before, an unspoken promise, an assurance of deepening emotion. It made her soul dance and her heart clench.

"I will," she said. For as long as he and his kinsmen lingered in these waters, she'd return.

She watched him turn and dive into the waves, a flicker of pearl and smoke that quickly disappeared into the Gray.

The beach was littered with shells and empty of people as Brida made her way home. She'd gone a little past the tidal pools where Ahtin had stranded himself when a familiar, four-note tune drifted toward her from the sea. She spun around, lifting her skirts to jog in the direction of the sound, drawn by a powerful need to answer its call.

A merwoman swam toward her, and Brida recognized her as the obvious leader of the group who'd come to rescue Ahtin. If her guess was right, this was the *ap* of his family.

The two women, human and mer, met in the shallows. Brida regretted not bringing her flute with her. It made it much easier to communicate with the mer.

She needn't have worried. Her mouth fell open, and she gaped at the merwoman when the other told her in perfect, articulate words that any might hear in an Ancilar meeting hall "You are Brida. Ahtin told me about you."

If Brida didn't already possess proof of the fantastical, she'd swear she dreamed this scenario. "Are you his *ap*?" She did her best to repeat the front-forward sound Ahtin had made when he described the mer matriarchs.

The merwoman nodded. "And the grandmother of his

grandmother. I'm called Edonin in human tongue."

Brida marveled at Edonin's mastery of human speech, wondering who had taught her. Another human? Or another mer taught by a human? Or had she listened to the conversation of sailors and fishermen who sailed the Gray? "I wish I knew the language of the mer as well as you know ours."

Edonin's grave expression didn't change with Brida's compliment. Her features, lovely in the way of the mer, grew even more stern the longer she stared at Brida. "You put Ahtin in danger every time you meet him in the cave," she finally said, the statement more of an accusation.

Brida stiffened. She didn't need another to tell her what she already knew. That worry had fractured her sleep and plagued her thoughts during the days when she worked and wondered about him. However, neither she nor Ahtin were children, nor did they need a minder. Despite her irritation, she kept her voice neutral. "I don't mean to. And is it not dangerous in your world? Even more so? He told me what happened to his mate and child. The sea is no different from the land in that way."

The *ap* slapped her fluke against the water, revealing her own annoyance. "You saved him. I and mine are in your debt. You will always be safe with us in the sea, but Ahtin isn't yours to keep."

"He isn't my prisoner. His will is his own," Brida shot back.

"His will is to be with you. He can't." Another fluke slap. "He is merfolk. You are land dweller."

Brida had expected this from the moment the conversation started but was still disappointed by its appearance. "And no lesser for it."

Edonin's severe expression suddenly softened with a pity that made Brida's stomach twist a little. "You haven't asked what I told you those years ago when I saw you grieving on the shore."

Brida wasn't sure she wanted to know now. "I've always wondered," she said, careful not to reveal too much of her curiosity or her dread.

Judging by the enigmatic look in her double pupil eyes, the merwoman wasn't fooled. "I told you 'Edonin shares your grief, land woman.' She nodded when Brida's eyebrows arched in question. "I once loved a land dweller. When he was killed, a part of me died with him. He died because we refused to part, even when we knew no good would come of it."

The twisting in Brida's gut only worsened at the revelation. Edonin's warning didn't come from a place of familial intrusion or protection but from old heartbreak that, if the ap's tone was anything to judge by, still had not healed.

At Brida's silence, Edonin continued. "Our mistakes stay with us all our lives. Don't make the one I did. If not for Ahtin, then for yourself." She raised a hand. "Farewell, Brida."

The merwoman was nearly out of sight when Brida remembered something she had meant to tell Ahtin but forgot. Edonin's translation of her four-note tune to Brida alarmed her even more now that she knew what they meant. She called out to Edonin, relieved when the merwoman heard and swam back to her.

Edonin had warned that Ahtin courted danger by courting Brida, but Brida wondered if maybe the *ap* herself was at more risk and unaware of it. "I don't know if this will mean anything to you, but there's a land dweller in Ancilar who I think searches for the mer. Searches for you specifically. His name is Ospodine." At Edonin's puzzled look, Brida clarified. "Ospodine means 'horse of the sea.'"

A sound, desolate and stricken, erupted from Edonin's mouth. Her skin turned the shade of old hearth ash. Desolation, mixed with terror, darkened her eyes. She shuddered, the motion traveling from the top of her shoulders, through her tail, and into her fluke.

Shocked by the extraordinary reaction, Brida waded toward her. Edonin raised a hand to stop her. "Again, I'm in your debt." Her voice no longer carried the lyrical quality Brida had learned to associate with the merfolk. "I beg you, please, if you care anything for Ahtin—anything—stay away from him. If you care for your own life, stay away from the one you call Ospodine. I know him well, and wish with all my soul I never did."

At that, the ap sped away, the wake of her quick departure a cut in the waves that marked the direction of her path to the deep from which she'd come.

Brida, thoroughly frightened now, for Ahtin, for Edonin, and for herself, sprinted home, throwing the bolt to her front door as soon as she closed it behind her. Her body, still throbbing from Ahtin's lovemaking, now shivered as much from fear as from chills. Her instincts regarding Ospodine had been right. She had no idea what terrible thing existed between him and a merfolk matriarch, but Brida had no doubt that Edonin's reaction had not been overly dramatic or unjustified. Ospodine was dangerous. She only wished she knew exactly why.

She checked all her locks twice before changing into warm

night clothes and crawling into bed. Brida didn't know why she bothered. She'd have to be up in a couple of hours, and there was no chance her spinning thoughts would allow her to drift off. Moments after she nuzzled into her pillow she was asleep.

A sharp pounding awakened her to a bedroom bathed in punishing sunlight. Her throat was on fire, and every swallow was like downing a handful of ground glass. The incessant pounding came from inside her skull, but also from her front door.

She wove her way through the parlor on unsteady feet. "Who is it?" she croaked, surprising herself by the awful sound. Gone were the days when she opened her door without knowing her visitor first. Ospodine's trespassing had seen to that.

"Are you all right, Brida? Open the door." Norinn's exasperated command seeped through the wood. Brida yanked back the bolt and shoved the door open, squinting against the unseasonal brightness. The slant of the sun on the cobblestones told her it was well past morning and into early afternoon.

Her sister-in-law's irritation changed to concern, and she gently nudged Brida farther into the house, closing the door behind her. "My gods, you look ghastly. I think I've seen healthier looking wraiths. Are you sick?"

Brida shuffled back to her bedroom and collapsed on the mattress. "I must be. I feel like death." Inwardly, she wailed her frustration. Now was not the time to be ill!

"You look like it," Norinn blithely informed her. She tucked Brida's feet back under the covers, then adjusted them until Brida huddled under their weight, certain she'd never get warm.

Norinn pressed a hand to her forehead. "A fever as well." She clucked, reminding Brida of a disgruntled chicken. "Stay in bed. I'll make willow bark tea before I go." She clucked again at Brida's disgusted rumble. "Bad taste or not, it will help," she admonished. "I'll send Yenec over later with soup. She can mind the house for you while you rest."

Brida didn't argue. If she ever decided to take over the world, the first thing she'd do was enlist Norinn as the general to lead her armies. She drifted off to sleep, waking only long enough to down a cup of bitter willow bark tea at Norinn's urgings.

Night had fallen when she roused again, feeling fractionally better but still like Zigana Imre's brave mare had decided to stomp on someone else after the obluda and had chosen Brida as her next victim.

"*Come tomorrow, Brida.*" Ahtin's voice wove through her foggy mind.

"I'm sorry," she croaked. "So sorry."

Would he wonder why she didn't appear? Would he wait or search? She prayed not, especially after Edonin's warning.

Her niece Yenec entered the bedroom, balancing a tray with a bowl whose contents sent up ghostly tendrils of steam. The girl, oldest of Laylam's and Norinn's nine children, smiled as she set the tray down on the table close to the bed. "You're awake, aunt. That's good. How do you feel?"

"Terrible," Brida whispered, regretting it instantly as more of the glass splinters embedded themselves in her throat. "How long was I asleep?"

Yenec helped her sit up, fluffing the pillows behind her. "A few hours. You were restless. Dreaming and talking in your sleep. Who's Ahtin?"

Brida froze, then offered her niece a casual shrug. "I have no idea. For all I know I was dreaming about someone's sheepdog named Ahtin."

She spent the next half hour eating the soup Yenec prepared and drinking more of the vile tea before plummeting into sleep that left her more tired than rejuvenated each time she awoke. Four days passed before she felt well enough to leave her bed and sit at her table, and two more days beyond that before Norinn declared her well enough to take a much-needed bath. In that time, Brida fretted and worried over Ahtin. And said nothing to anyone.

By the time the next market day arrived in Ancilar, she was well enough to leave the house and vowed she'd return to the cave. She had no hope that Ahtin would be there. The weather was fast leaving autumn behind for winter with its bitter, gusting winds, snowfall, and sea ice. Edonin would have urged her extended family to migrate south to warmer seas, and Ahtin would have followed. At least she hoped that was the case. A part of her sorrowed that she hadn't had a chance to tell him goodbye, while another part feared he might think she'd abandoned him. But the greatest part prayed he had left with the others, finding sanctuary in safer waters, away from a man whose very name had made the *ap* blanch in horror.

Norinn had fetched her early in the morning, bundling Brida so thoroughly in layers of wool, she sweltered in the house and felt none of the cold, despite her breath steaming in front of her as the two women strolled to the market. Brida's larder was nearly bare, and she intended on using the money she'd earned from her spinning to restock. The pearl Ahtin had given her rested safely in a box buried in her garden at the base of a citrus tree. Reason dictated she sell it in the spring when she could travel to one of the bigger towns and find a jewel merchant who wouldn't cheat her too badly in the sale. Her emotions refused to consider the idea.

Norinn had wandered off to browbeat her favorite coster-monger into selling her produce for half the price that he was hawking it, leaving Brida to load her basket with those things she needed to fill her bare cupboards.

A voice she hoped she might never hear again addressed her. "Mistress Gazi."

Brida gripped her basket, took a bracing breath and turned slowly to face Ospodine. She stared at him without returning the greeting, uncaring that it was rude. This man had breached the sanctity of her privacy, nearly attacked her in Lord Frantisek's castle, and threatened her on the beach. She didn't owe him a thread of civility. "Leave me be, syr. I've nothing to say to you."

She turned her back to him and strolled to the next stall, hoping he'd go away. She hoped in vain.

He kept his distance but didn't leave. "I only wish to inquire about your health. I'd heard you'd taken ill."

Her skin crawled at the thought of him asking about her, or worse, lurking about to see when she might emerge. He believed she knew more about Edonin than she was saying, and now that suspicion bore out. She did know.

"I'm fine," she snapped. "You need not concern yourself." She moved to the next stall where the merchant sold brooms and washing bats. Brida eyed one of the stouter bats, wondering if she'd have to resort to clubbing Ospodine in order to for him to leave her alone.

"The sea air can be hard on the lungs in autumn and winter, especially at night." His oily voice oozed an unpleasant slyness. "Better to stay inside by the fire, don't you think? But you're a strong woman, befitting of your name. I've no doubt you'll be right as rain and playing your flute in no time. Good day."

Brida kept her back to him until she heard his footsteps walking away. Only then did she turn to watch him, made even more uneasy by his emphasis on her name. He hadn't gone far when he began to whistle, a discordant combination of notes that sound like nothing more than tuneless ramblings, but which swamped Brida with terror.

"Come tomorrow, Brida," he whistled as he sauntered off. "Beautiful, beautiful Brida. Come tomorrow."

CHAPTER SIX

S HE HAD COME full circle since playing her flute for Lord
Frantisek at Castle Banat a month earlier. From doing her
best to avoid Ospodine with his strange obsession, she now
sought him out, determined to learn what lit the fanatical gleam
in his eye each time they crossed paths and what lay behind the
sinister hint in his whistling of Ahtin's affectionate call to her.

"We'll wait for you in the bailey," Zigana Imre said, glancing
at Brida over her shoulder. The two women shared a ride
toward Castle Banat on Zigana's mare Gitta with Brida riding
pillion. She'd started her journey on foot in the late afternoon
once she managed to escape Norinn's hawkish scrutiny to return
to her house. Once again she sneaked out through her back
garden, only to go in the opposite direction of the cave where
she spent her nights in Ahtin's company.

Zigana had crossed paths with her not far from the base of
the castle bluff, riding Gitta back to the village. A widow, like
Brida, Zigana had lost her husband on the same ship as Brida
lost hers. Their casual acquaintance had become friendship,
strengthened by the bonds of common tragedy. Brida had
readily accepted the other woman's offer of a ride to the castle,
and Zigana didn't question why Brida walked there instead of
having her brother take her in his wagon.

The trip up the bluff road to the castle took a quarter of the time it would have taken her had she walked the entire way. She stared toward the Gray from her lofty seat atop Gitta, searching for a hint of pearlescent skin catching the last of the day's light or the flick of a tail rising above the waves. She prayed she'd see neither one, sick with a nameless dread that had plagued her since seeing Ospodine in the market earlier.

The sun set a little earlier each evening as autumn arced toward winter, and the red blaze of its descent turned the Gray bloody along its horizon. No different than any other fall afternoon, yet the sight now heightened her alarm along with her determination to confront Ospodine and demand he tell her exactly what he wanted from her. She carried the bone flute with her this time, willing to play any tune he demanded.

She no longer worried that Edonin would respond. The merwoman's expression had spoken more clearly than words what she thought of Brida's information, and Brida wondered what terrible connection Ospodine, an outlander in Ancilar, had with Edonin to inspire such horror, such anguish.

Some of the guards in the bailey were local men from Ancilar, and they hailed both women as Gitta trotted toward one of the hay racks set along one side of the stables. Brida shook the wrinkles from her skirt and recited in her mind what she'd say to the steward to convince him she was worthy of a few moments of Lord Frantisek's time. Luck, for once, played in her favor.

"The flute player from Ancilar," a familiar voice said from the other side of Gitta's big frame. Brida glanced across the horse's back to find his lordship gazing at her, a curious light in his solemn eyes. That gaze shifted, deepened, just as his voice did, when it landed on Zigana standing at Gitta's shoulder. "And Zigana. What brings you here? A visit with Jolen?"

Zigana avoided his gaze. "A favor for Brida. She's come to Banat to speak with you. I brought her so she wouldn't have to walk."

Undercurrents heavy enough to drown in flowed between his lordship and the woman who was his wife's bastard sister. Any other time Brida might have squirmed inwardly at the moment's awkwardness and made her excuses to find something else to do. However, she hadn't come to Castle Banat on a whim, and she needed Lord Frantisek's attention.

"My lord," she said, interrupting the silent exchange between the two. His eyes shifted from their heavy regard of Zigana to focus on her. Zigana snatched up Gitta's reins and led her to the farthest hay rack, out of earshot.

"Mistress Gazi, how may I be of service?"

Brida's eyebrows lifted. He did remember her name, and his courtly manner toward her eased her fretfulness a little. "My lord, I know Syr Ospodine is still your guest. I must speak with him on important matter as soon as possible."

She tried very hard not to reveal her distaste for the man in front of his host, but she needn't have worried. Judging by the lift of Lord Frantisek's upper lip, he shared the sentiment.

"He is indeed, Mistress Gazi. It has been long and long, and I count the hours until he tires of my hospitality. But he isn't here at the moment. You may find him walking along Madigan's Teeth. There's a path that winds down the bluff where the slope isn't so steep. You can reach it from the east side of the demesne. I can have one of my guards show you the way." He motioned one of the soldiers over, a man Brida recognized as the son of Ancilar's miller.

Brida glanced down at her shoes and inwardly sighed. She wasn't wearing the right footwear to go hiking along Madigan's Teeth, especially as it grew dark. The jagged landscape on that side of the bluff was a favored place for catching crabs and harvesting a type of mollusk that clung to the rock with holdfasts stronger than ship rigging. They also made the rock face slimy. Going barefoot was a fool's choice that guaranteed feet sliced to bloody ribbons by the sharp edges of the mollusk shells.

There was nothing for it. She'd pray they'd meet on the path as he returned, and if they didn't, then she'd have to be extra careful navigating the Teeth and dealing with Ospodine.

The miller's son, a lad named Endel, saluted his lordship then offered Brida a smile. "Welcome to the castle, Mistress Gazi."

"Escort the mistress to the Madigan path." Lord Frantisek eyed Brida. "He can go with you if you wish." A brief scowl flickered across his face. "It might be wise I think."

She almost refused, afraid too many might learn of the merfolk's existence in the waters or see Ahtin swimming in the waves. She discarded the idea. There were risks in everything, and after her last encounter alone on the beach with Ospodine, she welcomed the presence of a companion for this one. Besides, many a trick of the moonlight played on the Gray, and people imagined seeing things that weren't there.

She accepted the offer, then thanked Zigana for the ride, assuring her she need not wait for Brida's return.

"Brida." Zigana touched her arm. A shadow of memory passed across her face. "Gitta killed one obluda. Only one. Be careful."

Brida patted the other woman's hand to reassure her. If Zigana only knew how often of late Brida had visited the shore at night... Fortunately, the only sounds arising from the Gray had been those she heard all her life or Ahtin whistling her name in welcome.

With the darkness fast descending, Endel handed Brida a lamp and carried one himself to light their way down the path. The dirt road snaked down the slope between scrubby bushes that shivered in the wind. Madigan's Teeth lay ahead, rising sharply from the base of the bluff like fangs in a dragon's mouth, spaced with narrow gullies hollowed out by the eternal tide. Shallow stair treads of more stone jutted into the water, their surfaces adorned with clusters of mussels.

The Gray heaved toward the shore here, hurling breakers against the rocks with battering force as if protesting their intrusion into the water. Foamy remnants left by the dying flow of waves burst and bubbled in the spaces between the mussel shells or oozed back toward their source in a serpentine wash. The sea didn't just sing, it thundered.

A black silhouette stood just out of reach of the surf's swash, its long tunic flapping in the wind like a gull's wings. Brida recognized the narrow profile and slim frame. Ospodine.

"Stay here, keep watch" Brida instructed Endel. She didn't need him overhearing this conversation.

"But mistress." Endel tugged on her sleeve. "His lordship said—."

"For you to accompany me, and you have." She held her lamp higher so that he could see her smile. "You can see me quite clearly from here, and you're close enough to come to my aid should I need it."

He eyed her, then the place where Ospodine stood. "If you're sure," he conceded reluctantly.

She admired his commitment and his bravery. "I'm sure."

Ospodine turned his head a fraction and dipped his chin even less in acknowledgement of her presence. "I wondered if you might join me."

"Don't be coy, syr. You knew I would." She set the lamp down. "I'll not play this game of yours. You know I've some knowledge of the merfolk and their language, and I know you've been spying on me. Why?"

His smug demeanor took on a more contemptuous quality. Brida was reminded of their confrontation on the beach when he'd touched her elbow before yanking his hand back as if discovering she had fleas. "I think your knowledge of the sea people goes beyond understanding a few clicks and whistles, wouldn't you say?"

She refused to respond to his baiting. The idea that he might have observed her making love with Ahtin in the cave sent a surge of bile into her throat. She held it back by virtue of silent outrage. "Why?" she repeated.

Disappointed by her flat response, he gave up baiting her. "Because you're a means to an end." He pointed to her skirt pocket. "You brought the flute you used at the castle this time, didn't you?"

How had he known she carried it with her?

As he seemed in the mood to answer her questions, she pulled the flute from her pocket to show him. In the darkness, it seemed to glow softly in her palm, bleached ivory with a touch of magic humming through its striations. "How did you know?"

Ospodine didn't try to snatch the flute from her as he had at Castle Banat, content to stare at it with the same avid expression he'd worn then. "The flute's value to you is that your father made it, yes?" He continued when she simply stared at him. "It's far more than the clumsy desecration from a land dweller's carving knife."

Brida clenched her jaw to stop herself from sniping at him in return.

He turned back to survey of the Gray. "The bone he found came from the sleeping deep, off the remains of a being so ancient the oldest of the Elder races were infants, when humans themselves weren't even the lickspittle of a lesser god's after-thought. It's the remnant of an ancestor from where all sea people came. The mer, the yastri, the kyzyn." His sneering glance raked her from head to foot. "And somehow you, a filthy land dweller, ended up with it. The gods laugh."

Stunned by the revelation that there were other kinds of merfolk, Brida hid her surprise and returned his contempt with a once-over stare of her own. "Are you not a man with legs?" He spoke as if he were somehow separate from—and better than—those with whom he shared ground.

"Not always." He waved a hand down his front. "Before I became this abomination, I was like your lover. A merman of the Gray."

Brida lost the battle to remain impassive and gaped at Ospodine. She struggled to find words, shocked to her soul by his disclosure. Fluke or feet, this snide, arrogant creature was nothing like Ahtin.

Once her initial shock faded, she adopted a more stoic expression, one that no longer fooled the smirking Ospodine. "You still haven't truly answered my first question." She was a means to an end. What end?

"I need you to play the last two notes of that four-note tune. This flute will play them, and they will spread across the waters so that all the herds hear and know you call."

While Brida had no intention of offering up the flute to him, she was curious. "Why can't you play it?"

A bitter smile twisted his mouth. "Because I rejected the sea to walk the land. The flute recognizes this and rejects me in turn. No music, no notes will come from it if I tried to play."

His forthrightness carried a hidden edge to it. Brida sensed there was more to this than a merman abandoning his heritage to walk among men and later regretting it. Something much darker. Something terrible enough that the long dead remains of an origin ancestor refuted him.

"The merman won't come," she said, refusing to speak Ahtin's name. Ospodine had already helped himself to enough of her privacy. She pretended continued ignorance of the four-note tune's meaning. His request for her to play only the last two made her glad she'd warned Edonin of his interest. Those notes were her name.

He shrugged. "I don't care about your lover. It's his *ap* I want."

Never before had Brida wished her instincts had been

wrong. But they weren't. This wasn't some trophy hunter looking for a mythical creature to hunt and kill for profit or fame. Ospodine hunted with a more personal purpose. A more singular one, and it centered not on Ahtin but on Edonin. She shuddered inwardly, so very glad she had followed her gut and warned the matriarch about him.

Certain Edonin would ignore the summons, no matter how far or deep the flute's voice carried across the Gray or how many merfolk heard it, Brida didn't resist. "If she answers, will you then leave me be?"

"Yes."

Again his reply carried the knife's edge of a lie, an unspoken *"Unless..."* Brida glanced back to where Endel waited for her. She didn't think he'd be much help in a physical altercation with Ospodine. He was younger than the nobleman, bigger, but she knew without a doubt who was the more dangerous of the two. Still, she felt better having the guard there.

She took her time wiping the salt spray off the flute before playing a short lullaby to warm up the instrument. Ospodine shifted impatiently from one foot to the other, but stayed quiet. A glimmer of moonlight reflected in his eyes, revealing a hint of eye-shine at their edges. He might have forsworn all of his heritage. Not all of it had forsworn him.

The flute throbbed under fingers at her first exhalation of the two notes, as if welcoming a long-lost loved one. Unlike previous times when Brida had played the entire four notes of Edonin's message to her, the flute released the notes of the ap's name in an undulation of sound that swept across the rocks and out to the Gray.

Waves caved in on each other as if to capture the name and embrace it. Brida played Edonin's name several times until the very air around her hummed with the summons. Far in the liquid glass wilderness, something answered in a voice not of sound but of vibration that made the rock beneath her feet shiver.

Still, the *ap* didn't appear.

Ospodine's rapturous expression soured, then blackened. Brida stepped back. "Summon your lover," he practically snarled at her.

Brida glared at him. He was mad if he thought she'd use the flute to bring Ahtin here. Did Ospodine think her so stupid that she didn't readily see his objective? If he couldn't entice Edonin to answer him, he'd lure her. "No. I've done as you wanted, played the two notes. Whatever I'm calling chooses not to answer."

"Summon him!" His bellow might have pinned her ears back if the wind hadn't torn it to shreds.

"No!" Terrified now, she bolted for the path, calling her escort's name.

Agony exploded across her scalp as she suddenly went airborne before slamming into the ground on her back. Every scrap of air in her lungs rushed out of her mouth in a hard gust. She fought to draw in a breath, even as she was hauled to her feet and suspended just above a cluster of mussel shells by Ospodine's merciless grip on her plait.

Tears streamed down her face, and she could do nothing more than wheeze in pain when he shook her like a dog held by its ruff.

Ospodine pointed to Endel who hadn't moved. His empty gaze stared beyond them to the rolling Gray. "He can't hear you." Mockery oozed from every word, and he shook her again for good measure. "Ensorceled by your own playing. Now you know what true siren song can do."

He dragged her back across the rocks. Brida clawed at his hand on her braid, trying to keep him from scalping her even as mussel shells broke under her weight and shredded the back of her skirt. She'd lost the flute somewhere in the struggle and prayed it had fallen into the water.

Ospodine finally stopped, dropping her like a sack of refuse. Brida just missed smacking her skull on the hard surface. Wet heat tickled the back of her neck, and she touched the spot, following the line of its source into her scalp. Blood, dark under the moon's light, stained her fingers.

Her ordeal wasn't over. She'd hardly regained her breath and rolled to her hands and knees to stand, when Ospodine snatched her up by her blouse, his grip preternaturally strong and unyielding. He spun her to face him. She twisted in his grasp, desperate to free herself. He held her with little effort, the grin he wore one of pure malice.

"Lost the flute, didn't you?" His eyes shone almost yellow, reminding her of a wolf's gaze. He shrugged at her silence. "No matter. You can whistle his name. I've heard you." That shark's grin widened. "Ahtin, isn't it?" He laughed when Brida struggled even harder. "Sounds like Edonin finally got the fast swimmer she always wanted."

When Brida still refused to summon Ahtin, even by whistling, Ospodine gave an unconcerned shrug. "No matter," he said. "We can do it the hard way."

He overpowered her struggles, dodging the punches she tried to land on him, and bound her hands and feet. She screamed for help to no avail. Endel, still imprisoned by siren song, stared unseeing at the sea, unaware. Those in the castle were too far away to hear her, especially with the roar of the breakers as they hurled themselves against the rocks.

The bindings Ospodine used were neither rope, nor cord, nor silk, but threads of lightning bolts woven into sorcerous shackles. Vibrations traveled up her body, forcing her muscles to involuntarily contort and contract in places. More of the woven lightning coiled around her waist, spooling out to a silvery tether that ended in Ospodine's grip. The shark smile flitted across his face before he shoved her off the rock's flange.

Brida plunged into the surf and sank like a stone. The churning water shoved her one way and then the other amid a froth of bubbles and sand whipped into underwater whirlwinds. She held her breath, lungs on fire, and kicked her bound feet for the surface. Her chest felt close to bursting, her body's natural instincts screaming that she find air and breathe. Breathe. Breathe.

A tremendous force smashed her stomach into her backbone as she was yanked upward, clearing the surface in a cascade of seawater to fall on cold rock with a jarring thump. Brida opened her mouth to suck in a gulp of precious air. Her manacles sizzled against the skin of her wrists, and among the scents of sea and salt, she smelled scorched flesh.

Ospodine's sneering features filled her field of vision as he bent down to stare at her. "Do you think you're valuable enough to your lover to save from drowning?" He nudged her body with his foot. "What say you, land walker whore? Another dip in the Gray?"

Inwardly, Brida screamed. Outwardly, she inhaled until her ribs felt pressed to her shoulders. Once more, Ospodine tossed her into the water. Once more the churning spume flung her about in a blinding whirl.

She refused to give up, refused to give in to the drag of her skirts and the blackness closing around her as the air faded in her struggling lungs. She fought to reach the surface, each effort more feeble than the last.

A flash of something dark within the foaming water shot past her. The hint of a dorsal fin that pivoted and aimed straight for her. A betraying bubble escaped her mouth, and she gulped in seawater, surrendering her last gasp of air to the Gray.

The delirium of drowning mixed with her body's panicked struggle to survive weighted her down, and Brida felt herself sinking, sinking.

Hands gripped her hips, and a long, muscular body flexed against hers. The lightning bonds loosened, freeing her waist, hands, and feet, as her rescuer lunged to the surface, taking her as well. For a second time she hit unforgiving ground and promptly vomited sea water from her mouth and nose.

She lay on her side, but not alone this time, and the realization made her sob in defeat. Ahtin lay beside her, clutching her close as she gasped against him. Fingers caressed her head.

"Brida," he whispered softly. "I'm here."

"And the fish finally takes the bait." Ospodine's voice rang with gloating triumph. "I wondered how many times I'd have to dunk her before you decided to appear and play the hero."

It was a monumental effort, but Brida raised her head enough to see that the sorcerous tethers Ospodine had used to bind her had transformed and now bound both her and Ahtin together in a filigree net delicate as spider web, unbreakable as steel.

He used the most basic fishing wisdom. Bait the hook until you caught the fish you wanted.

Brida stroked Ahtin's cheek, still too starved for air to waste it on talking. Or whistling. She told him with her gaze what she couldn't yet say with words. *"Why did you come? You shouldn't have come."*

As if he read her thoughts, the merman spoke into her hair. "Because you are here. Where else would I be?" He chased the tear sliding down her cheek, kissing it away.

A new voice traveled across the waves, strident, commanding. "Release them!"

Brida tried to rise for a better look at Edonin, but the net entrapping her and Ahtin only allowed her enough movement to peek past Ahtin's shoulder and see the ap swimming toward them. Another movement in the corner of her eye caught her attention, and she jerked in Ahtin's embrace.

His hands pressed into her back. He said nothing, only gave a slight warning shake of his head. *Stay silent. Pretend you see nothing.*

Brida had expected a battalion of merfolk to join Edonin, but only she tread the waves. She, however, hadn't come alone. A pair of colossal black shapes cut a swath through the waves, huge dorsal fins, twice the height of a tall man, catching the moon's light on their tips before they dove beneath the waves.

The *ap* had brought sea wolves with her. For what purpose, Brida couldn't begin to guess, but their presence didn't bode well for Ospodine, who was, so far, unaware of their presence.

Ospodine, smug with his victory in luring the *ap* to him, executed a mocking bow. "Ap-Edonin. I thought I'd never see you again."

She stared at him, wearing that same look of anguish Brida had seen when she translated Ospodine's name for her. "I'd hoped never to see you again.

His face wiped clean of expression, except for a tightness around his mouth. "Is that any way to speak to your son?" he said in a hoarse voice.

Brida's mouth fell open and she stared at Ahtin, who showed no surprise at Ospodine's latest disclosure. This violent, entitled man was the *ap*'s son?

"I have no sons," Edonin replied, voice cold. "You murdered them both long ago when you sacrificed your brother to a riven mage for the chance to walk on land. How much of his soul and blood did that monster steal before his sorcery turned you? And now you have regrets?" Her fluke slapped the water twice, fury in the stiff set of her shoulders.

"You forced my hand!" Tiny bolts of lightning sparked off Ospodine's fingers. "You knew what I wanted yet you refused me Pneuma's Blessing." He panted, visibly working to control his rage. "Gulsuca was a half-blood anyway," he said with a sniff, as if that explanation justified his fratricide. He shoved Brida's legs with the toe of his shoe. "No better than this bitch. Worse even because he tainted our herd." He flung out his arm in a frustrated gesture. "How could you mate with a land walker?

"Because I loved him. And I loved the child I bore him. A spirit of earth and sea in the best way." The sorrow in her voice made Brida's eyes well with tears. Her sorrow sharpened to anger, turning cold as before. "You didn't just murder your brother, you desecrated him. Why would I ever welcome you back to these waters?"

Brida might have pitied Ospodine for his mother's rejection of him, if he hadn't tried to drown her. As it was, his forlorn look didn't move her, nor did it last. The haughty visage he showed to the world settled firmly on his features, utterly unrepentant for what he'd done. For what he was about to do.

"Because if you don't, history will repeat itself. You know this magic as well as I do, Mother. Used in the right spell, and the blood and soul of both elements can give one legs or fins. Gulsuca was convenient because he had both, but I don't need a halfbreed whelp to work this magic, just land and water, and I have both here. He pointed to Brida and Ahtin. "Their deaths will fulfill that requirement."

Edonin glided closer to the rock, dangerously close to where Ospodine stood. "If you do this and return to the Gray, all of ocean-kind will hunt you. I'll make sure of it."

Her threat, made in the gentlest voice, was no less terrifying for it. Brida believed her, and judging by Ospodine's pale features, so did he.

His jaw clenched, and his hands curled into fists. "Then I will swim the rivers and make of them my kingdoms." He bared his teeth at Ahtin and Brida when Ahtin suddenly issued a series of whistles and screeching pulsed calls that made Brida wince. She gasped when Ospodine reached into his long overtunic and brought out a knife, an athame with a black blade. He crouched next to Ahtin, bound tight in the sorcerous net, and pressed the blade's edge to the merman's throat. Ahtin hissed at him.

"Please don't do this," Brida begged him.

He ignored her, attention fully on Edonin who met his eyes with an unwavering stare. "Give me Pneuma's Blessing, Mother, so that I may become mer again."

Frozen in Ahtin's arms, Brida stared at the blade, the edge pressed hard against Ahtin's neck. A thin line of blood oozed over the steel where, to her horror, the metal soaked it up like a sponge, as if the athame drank from its victim. She almost added her voice to Ospodine's demands. Whatever Pneuma's Blessing was, she prayed Edonin would surrender it and save her grandson from the predation of her twisted son.

Edonin lowered her head, the sigh she emitted an echo carried on the wind across the face of the waters. A black shadow coursed below them, crossing paths with another of equal darkness. The merwoman touched the hollow of her throat with her fingertips.

Ghostly light pulsed beneath them, elongating into smoky skeins as she stretched her arm toward Ospodine. Gaze locked on the revenant magic, he stood to meet it as it snaked toward him. Brida sagged into Ahtin, hardly daring to believe they both managed to avoid having their throats slit, at least for now.

"The Blessing of Pneuma," Edonin said, and this time her voice enfolded them all. "All the magic of our herd spilled out before you, Seahorse. Passed from *ap* to *ap* and shared with all. Sea magic, long life, and we, the *aps*, the keepers of that birthright." As she spoke, age lines blossomed across her face, carving deeper with each word. Her cheeks sagged, and her eyes grew hollow. Her breasts flattened and her arms lost their firmness.

Ospodine changed as well as the misty tendril of ancient sea magic coiled around his hand to slide up his arm. His ears transformed, the once smooth helixes stretching to accommodate small spikes along their lengths. The hair of his eyebrows fell out, leaving behind bony ridges. He touched his changing face, trilling a victory tremolo in whistles he couldn't sound earlier, uncaring that his longed-for metamorphosis back to merman came at the price of his mother's life force.

She watched him from sad eyes in a sunken face. "The Blessing must be freely given, Seahorse, or it isn't a blessing."

Suddenly, the ghostly tether that connected him to Edonin solidified, becoming a thick rope tightening on Ospodine's arm. Edonin gave a quick jerk of her head. The rope snapped taut, yanking Ospodine so hard forward, he pinwheeled off the ledge and into the water.

Still trapped by the net, Ahtin managed to roll himself and Brida to a new position in time to see the spires of dorsal fins rise above the waves and speed toward Ospodine. He saw them as well and screeched his terror, an eerie combination that sounded both human and merman.

The Blessing of Pneuma was gone, spiraling back to its customary place, giving back the grace of the sea to one of its matriarchs. Edonin no longer looked the crone, but she still looked aged, not by the parasitic draw of stolen magic but by the actions of her son.

Ospodine flailed in the water, striking out for the ledge and the questionable safety of the rock flat. He made it, heaving himself onto its surface, murder in his gaze when it landed on Brida and Ahtin. He still clutched the athame and lurched toward them. He didn't get far.

Brida screamed when one of the monstrous fish, bigger than a fisherman's boat, surged out of the water onto the rock flat, its momentum and weight propelling it forward at the speed of a ship sailing under full mast. Its maw opened, revealing rows of cone-shaped pointed teeth, before it snapped closed on the back of Ospodine's tunic. Ospodine never had a chance to cry out. As fast as the creature appeared, it slid back in the water with its prey and dove. Its companion followed, dorsal spire shedding water as it rose, slicing clean as it sank, followed by the slap of a fluke the width of a barn door.

The ensorcelled net surrounding Brida and Ahtin turned to dust and was swept into the sea to join its creator.

Despite her shock at what she witnessed, and the events prior to it, she flung her arms around Ahtin's neck and kissed him. He returned her affection with gusto, pulling away only when an inquiring whistle sounded next to them.

Edonin swam to them, gripping the rock ledge with one hand, holding out Brida's flute with the other. "This fell in the water."

Brida reached for it, then drew back, remembering Ospodine's words. "I think it belongs more to the merfolk than to me."

Edonin's effort to smile failed. She placed the flute on the ground. "You are mer in your way, and you've earned the right to keep it. Play it should you ever need us. Play to remember us."

Brida wiped at her eyes. "I'm sorry you lost your sons." She was glad Ospodine was no longer a threat, but her heart ached for the ap's grief at losing her children.

Edonin emitted a trio of despondent clicks. "Ahtin would say Seahorse's death was just. I say it was merciful. He was born empty and sought to fill that space. Maybe now he's at peace, and I have avenged his brother's death."

She exchanged a series of rapid fire whistles with Ahtin before turning back to Brida. "My son saved you. The debt is paid." She raised a hand. "Farewell, Brida."

The ap swam away without looking back. Brida wondered if she'd ever return to the waters surrounding Madigan's Teeth.

A caress on her leg made her look down to find Ahtin next to her, balanced on his forearms. His tail arched his back, and the shallow cut from Ospodine's sacrificial dagger no longer bled, though it left a red mark on the merman's ivory skin. He nodded to where Endel now lay sprawled along the path. "Your friend?"

Brida gasped and raced to where the guard lay, no longer frozen in place by a siren's spell but sleeping the sleep of the innocent, completely unaware of what had just played out before him. Brida tucked his arms against his body and watched to make sure he breathed steadily. She'd have to invent a plausible story to explain why she was soaking wet, how her skirts ended up shredded, why Syr Ospodine was nowhere to be found, and why Endel was napping outside in the middle of the night. It shouldn't be too hard if she put some effort into it. She thanked the gods it was Endel who accompanied her here and not the far more astute Lord Frantisek.

She returned to find Ahtin floating in the water, waiting for her. Shrapnel from crushed mussel shells crunched beneath her feet, and she swept some aside to clear a spot for herself on the rock ledge level with the water. Seawater sluiced under and over her, cold enough to make her bones crack.

Ahtin curved an arm on either side of her legs and rested his chin on her knee. "I feared you had spurned me, Brida."

She wove his slippery hair through her fingers in a long caress and bent to steal another kiss from him. "No," she said when they parted. "I was sick. And then I was afraid. Ospodine knew about you. I prayed you and your family had already begun your journey south."

He nuzzled his cheek into her skirts, a frown drawing down the corners of his mouth. "We were leaving when Edonin heard your flute. She came back, and I followed. The rest continued south."

"And now she's gone to join them."

"Yes."

"And you will too." It was the way of the merfolk, and who was she to change it? Still, her soul ached at the idea of this inevitable parting.

Ahtin captured her hand to kiss each of her fingers, her thumb, then her knuckles and the inside of her wrist. "I can stay." He pressed her hand to his cheek. "I want to stay."

Brida sniffled and blinked back the tears threatening to spill down her face. "I want you to stay too, but sooner or later someone will discover you, and I don't want that to happen."

She traced the elegant line of his nose down to the fine curvature of his lips. "Your ap needs you. All of your family needs each other. The children your women will bear are going to need all the protection they can get." She stroked the high planes of his cheekbones. "I will miss this face." Her thumb pressed his lower lip. "This mouth." He covered her hand with his where it flattened against his chest. "This heart."

"I will return when the waters are warm again, beautiful Brida," he promised. "Come to the shore then. I will be waiting."

He pressed her hand even harder to his chest before folding her fingers over her palm. "My heart," he said softly. "Keep it safe."

No longer caring that tears streamed down her face and dripped off her chin, Brida repeated his gesture, pressing his hand to her chest just above the edge of her bodice before curling his webbed fingers closed. "My heart," she whispered. "Take it with you."

They kissed a final time before Ahtin launched himself into the surf and dove out of sight. Brida watched the fading wake of his departure, peering into the darkness for a final glimpse of him until her eyes ached. The Gray held its secrets close and showed her nothing more.

EPILOGUE

S UMMER RETURNED TO Ancilar on the back of an unexpected
gale that launched the Gray far onto the shoreline and
snapped trees under its might. In the aftermath, the villagers
crept out of their battered houses to survey the damage and
thank the gods the sky was once more blue, the sea calm, and
the temperatures warm.

Brida joined the rest of the villagers as they gathered at the
shoreline with their wagons, clearing away the debris strewn
from one end of the beach to the other. Most would be taken
back to the village for sorting and salvage. All the effort went
toward clearing the area for the safety of the horse shrimpers
who planned to start the trawling season in a few days.

Norinn helped Brida throw pieces of driftwood into the
dray. "Why is it all we ever do on this beach is work?" she said,
encompassing the length of sand and dunes with a sweep of her
hand. "Why not have a gathering? Build a fire. Bring food, play
music, dance. Lord Frantisek is always borrowing you and the
others to play at the castle. Why not play here for the neighbors?"

Those who overheard her comment embraced the idea, and
Brida was swiftly conscripted to play at the impromptu celebration that evening. She didn't mind. Winter had been a lonely

season, punctuated by bouts of melancholy that gave way to brief cheerfulness at the thought of summer's return. Brida missed Ahtin, missed him even more when she played her flute. She worried as well. His world was far more dangerous than hers, at least in her opinion, though hers didn't lack its share of evil men like Ospodine.

No one seemed to care that he hadn't returned from Madigan's Teeth, though his lordship had asked her twice if she'd seen him there. That somber gaze, deep as the Gray itself, had settled on her for a long moment until he finally said "Sometimes the sea takes what it wants with no apology for the theft."

At the memory of the great fish snatching Ospodine off the rock ledge as if he were a seal, Brida couldn't agree more.

Once the sun set, all of Ancilar gathered around bonfire stack they'd built. When two of the men set the kindling aflame with torches and fanned the flames to flare up the heap, everyone cheered. Children raced along the beach, chasing and being chased by pet dogs. The ale flowed, along with the gift of a cask of wine from his lordship on the bluff. No one worried about an obluda, especially after Zigana Imre dipped her hands in the shallow, then stood up with a smile and shake of her head. The Gray this night offered no threat to those who remained on the shore.

Brida played alongside a large group of musicians with various instruments and skill levels spanning from beginner to expert. She'd brought her bone flute, her most treasured possession now, and played all the songs the villagers knew by heart. Her lips tingled with the urge to play the two-note siren song: Edonin's name and so much more, but she resisted the temptation. That wasn't merely a tune. It was a spell, and a powerful one at that, and had no business at this gathering.

She did slyly incorporate the whistle that was Ahtin's name into three of the songs. No one noticed, but Brida stared beyond the crowd of villagers and the bonfire with its blaze of light, to the dark sea.

Was he out there? Had the merfolk returned? And if they had, had Ahtin forgotten her? Brida prayed he hadn't.

As the evening wore on, the women gathered sleepy children and rode back to the village. Some of the men went as well. Those who stayed sat around the slowly dying fire, swapping stories and boasts, all growing exponentially more outlandish in proportion to the ale imbibed.

Brida returned with Norinn to help her put her large brood to bed. She declined an offer of tea, claiming exhaustion and an aching back from a long day of cleaning up the beach. She returned home, and just like more than a half year earlier, she sneaked out her back gate, taking a path that avoided the bonfire and its admirers.

Ixada Cave no longer frightened her. She now welcomed its rumors of hauntings and doorways to dead places. It kept others away while Brida sat on the sand not far from the flooded entrance and serenaded the Gray with her flute playing. She did the same tonight, hoping against hope that she might hear an answering whistle.

The crescent moon, though bright in a clear sky, offered little illumination, and night settled heavy on the Gray and its bordering shoreline. Brida played a few more tunes, stopping mid exhalation during one as a sound drifted above the surf's rumble.

She didn't move, certain that if she did, the sound would disappear. The flash of a pale fluke striking the water made her heart leap. Streamers of seaweed hair glistened under anemic starlight, and a webbed hand rose in greeting.

Brida stood, laughing and sobbing at the same time. She brought the flute to her mouth with shaking hands and blew into the mouthpiece, playing a song of salutation and pure joy as she waded into the shallows.

The whistle came again, short and sharp, followed by a series of clicks that made her breath catch.

"Brida. Beautiful Brida. Did you keep my heart safe?"

About Grace Draven

Grace Draven is a Louisiana native living in Texas with her husband, kids and a big, doofus dog. She has loved storytelling since forever and is a fan of the fictional bad boy. She is the winner of the Romantic Times Reviewers Choice for Best Fantasy Romance of 2016 and a USA Today Bestselling author.

Find Grace on Facebook!
facebook.com/GraceDravenAuthor

More titles by Grace Draven can be found here:

gracedraven.com/books

A CURSE FOR SPRING

BY
AMANDA BOUCHET

A malevolent spell strangles the kingdom of Leathen in catastrophic drought. Prince Daric must break the curse before his people starve. A once-mighty goddess trapped in a human body might be the key— but saving his kingdom could mean losing all that he loves.

This is a stand-alone novella

Thank you for reading!

Dedication

For S & S
You bring me so much joy.

Acknowledgments

I'd like to express my thanks to Jeffe Kennedy, Grace Draven, and Jennifer Estep, three kind and talented authors who gave me the opportunity to work with them and learn from their experience. My thanks also to my editor for this novella, who prefers to remain anonymous, to Adriana Anders for her early feedback, and to Callie Burdette for always being there for me, whether it's for a morale boost or for an emergency proofread. Thank you also to my family, because I couldn't do any of this without you.

Prologue

PRINCE DARIC TOUCHED his fingers to the giant column of mist and then jerked them back. He stared at his fingertips, but nothing had changed. His skin hadn't reddened; the nails weren't blackened. Nothing, in fact, had happened.

With a nervous swallow scraping down his throat, he turned his head to check that no one had followed him from the royal encampment. The dying forest stared back with gnarled eyes, everything brittle, creaking, and ready to catch fire. Nothing disturbed the too-dry branches, but it was only a matter of time before someone noticed he'd snuck off and came looking for him.

They were still days from home after a long journey to neighboring Raana followed by a pilgrimage to their own sacred Wood of Layton. Negotiations with Raana's Royal House of Nighthall had not gone well, putting everyone in a foul mood, especially Daric's father. King Wilder worried for his people, and Queen Illanna Nighthall had shown more greed than humanity, as usual.

Every year had been the same since Daric's birth—ten years of drought. Fields grew drier, the people of Leathen thinner, and the royal coffers lighter as Daric's parents were forced to pay the surrounding kingdoms for water, grains, and provisions.

After another look around him to make sure all was quiet, Daric turned back to Braylian's Cauldron. A thick column of mist rose from the sacred circle, but he knew that at any second, the elements could shift, turning into violent flames, bolts of lightning fierce enough to blind a man, gales that whipped and wailed, or shards of ice that exploded upward before raining down like daggers.

Children were warned away from the Cauldron from the moment they could understand fear. At least once a year, Daric joined the rest of the royal family at the volatile stone-lined circle to pay homage to Braylian, the goddess of the elements and the divine creator of the four seasons.

Usually, he was not alone to come before Braylian and beg for the return of water to Leathen's lakes and rivers. And to his knowledge, no one had ever stood this close to the Cauldron. He was not too young to understand the consequences of this ongoing lack of true springtime. He saw the tension in his parents and the gauntness of his people. The fact that he and the drought were the same age made him even more determined to find a solution. Somehow, he felt responsible.

Gathering his courage, Daric stretched his hand into the mist again, this time losing sight of everything up to his wrist. It was cool, damp, and terrifying. He curled his hand into a fist and drew back. As he did, he could have sworn he felt a soft brush of fingers across his knuckles.

Daric shivered in a way he knew a brave young prince shouldn't, and had he been a hallerhound, he'd have felt the hair on the back of his neck rise and quiver.

He squared his shoulders. Raana coveted Leathen's orin

mines. No longer satisfied with simply purchasing the strong, versatile metal, Illanna Nighthall had just successfully bartered for a nearly untapped mine that hugged the border. She had one shaft now. Next year, Daric feared she would have another.

Why spring rains would still water and nurture the surrounding kingdoms but not Leathen was a mystery. All Daric knew was that Leathen had faithfully guarded Braylian's Cauldron for generations. It was time that Braylian returned the favor for Leathen.

"Braylian!" he called out, frightened, even though the stone circle seemed calm today. This was where spirits gathered, the seasons changed, and storms were born from nothing. "We need your help!"

No response came, and the mist remained quiet. He leaned forward, dipping his head into the column. To do so was bold and spine-chilling, but if the goddess saw him, maybe she would answer.

A thick gray cloud dampened Daric's skin with more wetness than he'd felt on his face outside of his own washroom since the last snows of winter, but he saw only fog in front of him.

Disappointed but also a little relieved, he straightened out of the column. Leathen's summer heat sucked the moisture from the land, its autumn storms sometimes ruined the crops the kingdom's struggling farmers managed to cultivate, and its harsh winter freezes left too many people huddled around kitchen fires, cold and hungry. The long, ground-watering rains of springtime had abandoned Leathen the moment Daric came into it.

He didn't know how, or why, but he needed to fix it before the drought forced his parents to sell their kingdom piece by piece to the power-hungry Queen of Raana.

An orin mine for water. More orinore for bread. When Leathen had no riches left, what would become of it?

Other kingdoms would turn covetous looks their way soon, just as Raana did. Land was land, even if it was dead.

Daric appealed to the goddess again, leaning once more into the mist. He knew his actions were dangerous. Reckless, even. But what good was a prince to a kingdom that might cease to exist?

He called to Braylian until he was hoarse. Finally forced to admit defeat, he withdrew his head and torso from the cloud and started back toward the royal camp, his heart heavy with failure.

A lilting female voice stopped him in his tracks. "Who calls?"

The sound was more water than words. Daric turned back in awe, seeing a hand emerge from the column. Small fingers mirrored the tentative movements he'd first made into the mist. As if she'd learned from him, she mimicked his gestures, eventually leaning forward. As she did, her upper body took form, solidifying. Every action matched his, except she was a girl. She was even his age, and the most ethereal, radiant being he'd ever seen.

She stretched out her hand more boldly. Beads of water dripped from her fingertips. *Rain.* It watered the dying ground between them, turning it vibrant and green.

Daric moved toward the Cauldron, his eyes wide and his pulse beating with wild hope. "I am Daric, of the House of Ash.

Are you Braylian?"

"I am her daughter," she answered. Her speech was slow, as if she were discovering language as they talked.

At the dawn of time, Braylian created the four seasons to help her govern the year. This daughter had new vines for clothing, silver waterfalls for hair, and eyes the color of the lakes he'd seen in Raana.

Spring! She had to be Spring! And she had not yet gone to her rest. This was her last day of the season. At dawn, Summer rose from her bed.

"Why have you abandoned my kingdom?" Daric asked. "Will you not water our fields again?"

"I have abandoned no kingdom," she replied. "I water all the lands that I see."

Daric frowned. "Then...do you not see Leathen?"

She looked as confused as he. She seemed to have no answer and withdrew into the Cauldron again.

"Please!" Daric dashed after her. He stepped partway into the misty column, forgetting about the stone circle he wasn't supposed to cross. "Can you see me? Can you see my kingdom?"

A vague form twirled in the cloud, rushing like a river, swirling like a tempest. He moved toward the shadow, and an icy sheet of water splashed across his face. He jerked back with a gasp.

"Do not step through, or you can never go back," she warned. "Braylian will claim you, and you will race across the land and sky as weather."

Daric retreated, his heart pounding in fright. The girl followed him halfway out. They began a gentle back and forth, almost a dance. She met his gaze, and her delighted smile put to shame the most beautiful of starlit nights.

"We're in a terrible drought," he said as they continued to sway together, sometimes Daric partway into the Cauldron, sometimes her partway out. "Can you help us?"

She threw a high-arching spray of water into the forest with a tinkling laugh.

"That's wonderful." Daric grinned. "But we need much more than that."

She shook her head. "I see only you and the magic of the Cauldron. Everything else is dark."

Hard hands suddenly ripped Daric away from her. He struggled but was no match for the large man dragging him back. He recognized Soren's gruff voice as his father's personal guard banded a heavy arm around his chest and told him to settle.

As though Soren's words broke a spell, people appeared around him. His mother stood only a step away, pale with terror. Beside her, his father swung a calculating gaze back and forth between Daric and the girl, the gears of his mind visibly turning.

"No!" cried Daric a split second before King Wilder surged forward and clamped his hand around the girl's wrist. With a decisive yank, he pulled her from the Cauldron.

She turned entirely to flesh as she crossed the stone circle. The vines covering her milky-white skin withered and died. Her silver hair stopped cascading water. Her eyes were the only part of her that still brimmed with moisture, and she stood there, shaking.

Daric shoved away from Soren and ran to her, throwing his

cloak around her shoulders. He tugged it closed to cover her, and she clutched at the garment, her legs trembling like a newborn foal's. She seemed barely able to hold up her weight, even though she was as slight as a sapling.

"Can you make it rain, child?" the king asked urgently, bending down close to her. "I will give you all that I have for rain."

She blinked at Daric's father, silent, and yet everything about her screamed out in horror. The tears in her eyes hit the ground, but they made no difference to the crisp brown moss still struggling to survive in Leathen's sacred forest.

Daric began to shake along with her. He'd failed, and he'd ruined spring forever.

She'd seen only him, and Daric only her. Some magic had blinded them, a curse for spring, and him, and everyone.

"Rain," he pleaded softly. Maybe she could still control the elements. Maybe she was still Braylian's daughter.

Sorrow filled the bluest eyes he'd ever seen. "Once, I might have been what you needed. Now, I am nothing."

CHAPTER ONE

"**R**AIN? ARE YOU awake?"

Rain cracked open her eyes at the sound of Daric's deep voice. Her lungs squeezed with joy and relief that he was home safely from his latest trip up and down the slippery Axton Peaks, although she simply mumbled something that sounded like *No* while her heart settled into a normal beat.

Daric slipped into her room anyway and stretched out beside her on the high bed. He was lying down but hardly still. Her prince was a constant explosion of motion, going everywhere as if his heels were on fire.

And he called *her* the storm.

"Happy birthday!" Daric turned onto his side, beaming at her.

"I'm sleeping." Rain refused to open her eyes enough to do more than watch him through her lashes. The day her adoptive parents had chosen as her birthday was a terrible day. It was the first morning of spring, and another long season of *nothing*. "But welcome home," she said with a budding smile.

"You're not sleeping. You're talking to me."

She huffed, unable to fault his logic. "We're not children anymore. You *do* know that it's highly inappropriate for you to charge into my bedroom like this? Especially at the crack of dawn."

"The crack of dawn?" Daric scoffed. "That was at least three minutes ago."

"You're impossible." Sighing, Rain resigned herself to facing the day—this day when everyone still hoped she'd do something amazing and wonderful, even though they'd stopped expecting it a long time ago.

At least Daric was back, which made it all more bearable.

She stretched the sleep from her limbs and opened her eyes, allowing herself to really look at him. Her chest knotted with the usual mix of elation, misery, and longing. His face was weathered from his latest journey, maybe even a little sun-scorched, and his blue eyes stood out with brilliance against his tanned skin. His dark hair had grown, now tumbling over his forehead in a way that made her want to smooth it between her fingers and brush it back. And his smile…

Rain's pulse sped up again. His smile was the same as always: warm and devastating.

"Did everything go well?" she asked.

Daric nodded. "The last two towns in the dry-belt now have their full supply of ice blocks. I inspected the containers, and they're all in good shape. It won't water their fields, but it'll give the townsfolk what they need to survive the upcoming season."

Several years ago, Daric had conceived of a plan to provide extra water for the towns around Leathen with the fewest natural depressions to collect rainwater and snowmelt from the winter. Under his direction, villagers had built huge watertight basins to hold blocks of ice that Daric and a team of soldiers regularly cut from the mountain lakes in winter. Each journey meant a difficult climb into the Axton Peaks, a long week of perilous work, and a treacherous descent with heavy sleds stacked with ice. While the weather was still cold enough to transport the frozen water, Daric brought it to the towns that needed it the most. There, it was stored and slowly melted as the weather warmed. With rationing, the ice provided enough water for areas hovering on the brink of disaster to survive the inevitably rainless spring while everyone waited for summer storms to help refill their water towers.

Daric had yet to lose a man on these dangerous but necessary outings, and Rain knew he'd jumped into holes in the ice more than once to pull someone out. People didn't die on Daric's watch, despite the winter elements sometimes doing their best to blow his team from the mountaintops. Rain felt as though she held her breath each time he left and only let it out again when he returned.

"Did you just arrive?" she asked.

"Last night," he answered. "But you'd already gone to bed."

That explained why he was clean-shaven and looked freshly washed. Polite and civilized were expected of Daric, but Rain enjoyed seeing him come home all bristly and wind-whipped and looking deliciously barbarous in his winter furs. Weapons strapped on. Somehow stronger and wider after each grueling, work-filled expedition. Eyes sparking blue fire from across the room.

She shivered just thinking about it, although with him beside her, she was anything but cold.

Rain sat up and wiggled back against the headboard. Daric did the same and then handed her a small box.

He grinned at her. "I would have offered you a silver necklace to match your hair, a sapphire ring to match your eyes, or a ruby brooch to match your lips, but Leathen has no riches left, so you'll have to make do with this." He tapped the lid of the box, his smile widening.

Rain smiled back, laughing a little. "You make me sound like a crown—silver and rubies and sapphires."

"Sadly, we don't have a single crown anymore, either. Besides, they were all gold, and you certainly don't have boring yellow hair."

The mood in the dawn-lit room abruptly soured as they both thought about who *did* have blonde hair—Astraea Nighthall.

"You don't have to marry her," Rain murmured, turning the unopened gift over in her hands. She watched the box, unable to look at Daric again yet. The near constant ache in her chest ratcheted up with a vengeance. She'd thought her heart hurt before? Lately, it was in constant pain.

"And do what?" Daric asked bitterly, some of the princely veneer slipping from his voice. "Run away?"

Steeling herself, Rain turned back to him. "Talk to your father. He can't possibly wish her on you." Astraea Nighthall was all that was spiteful, vicious, and petty.

Daric shook his head. "The contract has been negotiated. We marry. Our first child inherits both kingdoms. Raanaleath." He snorted. "It sounds like a disease."

Angry, unhappy Daric felt like a stranger by her side. These past few months, though, this surly prince had become more familiar to her. "At least Leathen won't be obliterated from the name entirely." Not like the name of Ash, which they were being forced to abandon.

He tried to smile and failed utterly. "Good point, Raindrop." Rain watched as he drew a deep breath and forced back his visible dread over the future that was slowly destroying them both. "Now open your present."

Rain swallowed the lump in her throat. If Daric could focus on today then she could, too. It was better than thinking about the vile Astraea in his bed.

She rubbed the velvet-covered box between her fingers. It was a daring red. She wasn't surprised Daric had chosen something he knew she'd like, even if the color was better suited to an experienced, married woman.

"I'm not certain today's a day to celebrate," Rain said.

He drew back, his countenance darkening again. "You're not to blame for any of this."

"Neither are you," she shot back. "And yet you'll be punished for a lifetime."

"If I hadn't dragged you from the Cauldron, you'd still be Spring. You'd still control the elements, make rain and wind and grow new buds into trees." He shook his head, his features contorting into something she saw more and more often these days—disgust.

Rain knew it wasn't directed at her, but it still hurt to see. She feared Daric would never stop blaming himself for what had happened. Not only to her, but the drought, the failing farms, the hungry people, the empty coffers, their dependence on Raana... Everything.

"*You* did not drag me from the Cauldron," she corrected.

"But my father..."

Rain put a finger over Daric's lips to hush him, warmth tingling down her arm at the contact. "King Wilder did what he thought was best, and I don't blame him, either. Your parents have been kind to me and have treated me as their own for the last fifteen years, despite my being a useless mouth to feed in their home."

"Useless mouth to feed?" Daric echoed indignantly.

His breath swirled around her finger, and the feel of his warm lips was one of the most intimate things Rain had ever experienced. Though they did almost everything together, they rarely touched except when dancing. But no one really danced anymore. There wasn't much to celebrate.

Rain dropped her hand. She remembered little of her life before she became flesh. She'd been ancient; she knew that. But she'd taken the form of a child to match the charming, earnest boy who'd called out to her that day. Awareness of her previous existence and abilities had been mostly stripped from her, and Braylian had refused to take her back into the Cauldron.

"What good am I?" she asked, knowing her tone matched Daric's recent bitterness. "Braylian brought forth a new Spring, and she doesn't see Leathen any more than I did. People are desperate and starving. I'm of no value to the kingdom. You're being forced to marry Astraea." Rain heard the near growl in her voice and didn't even try to disguise it. Raana's princess had been malicious as a child and age had only worsened her. On a royal visit many years ago, Astraea had snuck into Rain's bedroom one night and cut off her hair while she slept. She'd then used Rain's hair to make a noose to hang Daric's cat.

Astraea still gloated about it. *That* was who Daric was being forced to marry. *That* was who he'd have to endure so that Raana would create a canal to divert water directly into Leathen.

Raana's mightiest reservoir sat mockingly on the border, filled to the brim with precious water. All they needed was a year of digging to direct some of that water into the dry riverbed that wound like a desiccated serpent through Leathen's once-fertile farmland.

King Wilder had been trying to negotiate a canal with Raana for years, but Illanna Nighthall wouldn't agree to it, even when orin mines had still been a valuable bargaining chip. She finally had, but her price was Daric. With a marriage, the House of Nighthall gained the heart of the continent, and Daric could finally save his people, if not his kingdom. His entire life revolved around bringing them out of this seemingly endless drought. He would do it, even if it meant tying himself to that witch Astraea.

"You're of value to me," Daric said softly.

Rain bit her lip to keep from saying—or perhaps doing—something rash. In moments like this, she wished that Daric would lean in and kiss her. And if he didn't, that maybe she would find the courage to kiss him.

She let the thought seduce her and then pushed it away, as always. "And you're of value to everyone."

A shadow flitted through his eyes, the cloud of responsibility, and she wished she'd said nothing.

"Let's talk of happier things," Daric said briskly. "Open your present."

Rain brushed her fingers over the velvet again, wondering

what could be inside. When Daric said Leathen had nothing left, he meant it. Even the castle had been mostly stripped of tapestries, rugs, and furnishings and was in terrible condition, making cold mornings like this difficult to face. In return for the food Leathen so desperately needed, their neighbors, and especially Raana, now had everything the House of Ash could possibly sell or barter.

King Wilder had finally been forced to offer up the last thing he had of value: Daric.

If Rain had truly been a member of the Ash family, she supposed she would have gone first, likely to the House of Lockwood in the south to guarantee their continued friendship and assistance. They were the only ones with a marriageable male royal: a king much older than she who'd been widowed for years and whose heirs were daughters.

Any of the Lockwood princesses would have been better for Daric than Astraea. Regrettably, they were all married and also offered nothing in the way of easily accessible water.

"Your patience far exceeds mine," Daric said, reaching for the box.

Rain twisted away from him with a smile. "Don't you dare. I'll open it. Right now, I'm savoring it."

"Savoring the box?" His winter-blue eyes glimmered with roguish charm. "That's older than I am, you know. I found it in a wardrobe. I'm reusing it."

"It's lovely."

"And we'll both be old and gray before you actually open it," he grumbled.

Rain took pity on the impatient prince and lifted the lid.

Amid more red velvet lay a delicate starflower carved from white marble. Her breath caught. It was Braylian's mark.

"When I made it, I carved a small loop into the back so that you can slide a hairpin through it. See." Daric pulled a hairpin from his pocket, picked up the starflower, and slipped the pin through the loop. Clearly, he'd planned ahead.

Rain watched his deft fingers as much as the sparkling gift, too overwhelmed to speak. Early morning sunlight poured through the window—long deprived of curtains now—and glinted off the crystalline stone, making it glitter like snow on a winter morning.

Daric gathered a portion of her hair and attached the gift above her ear. "Like a snowflake on ice," he said, smiling as he adjusted a few sleep-tumbled locks and smoothed them down.

Rain shivered, not used to anyone else's hands in her hair, and least of all Daric's. She pressed her lips together, trapping her tears in her throat.

"Don't you like it?" Daric asked, a worried crease forming between his brows.

Like it? She loved it. She loved him. It was torture.

"It's the most beautiful gift I've ever had," Rain finally answered in a voice that thickened with every word. "Thank you."

Daric seemed pleased with her response, but then his expression turned troubled once more. "Wear it now, while you can, because you'll have to hide it after we all move to Nighthall."

"Why?" Rain asked, the thought of their family being uprooted two moons from now to live among vipers making her stomach cramp.

"Because Astraea will take it. She's always been madly jealous of you."

"That's ridiculous." Rain touched the starflower, wanting to look at it again but not wanting to undo Daric's careful handiwork. "She's a princess. Rich, powerful, and if one can ignore her inner ugliness, quite attractive."

Daric made a face as he hopped off the bed and moved toward the door. "I can't ignore it. I have names for Astraea but saying them out loud would tarnish your image of my princely manners forever."

Rain's lips twitched. "I'm certain my imagination can supply them without your help."

Daric's eyes sparked with genuine humor, despite the terrible union he faced for the benefit of his people. "I'm leaving so you can get dressed and come face the frigid breakfast room with me."

Rain got goose bumps just thinking about it. Even firewood was scarce these days, and they mainly kept it for the evenings, for a small moment of comfort and peace. This winter had been darker and colder than most, and while it was officially spring now, Rain doubted the new season would bring much improvement. Gradual warming, yes, but no rain, of course. Thankfully, snowmelt would at least help fill the natural water basins for the coming weeks.

Daric turned back to her from the doorway. "As for Astraea being jealous, you're of the House of Ash, and she knows she'll never have what you have."

"What's that?" Rain asked, her heart jerking uncomfortably.

"A family that loves you." Daric left and shut the door behind him.

Rain didn't try to stop the wetness flooding her eyes. She would cry rivers if only her tears would make the crops grow again in Leathen.

CHAPTER TWO

RAIN DECIDED TO grab the bag of books she intended to donate and take a brisk walk around the upper city of Ash before breakfast. Daric would wait for her, probably reading newssheets and cajoling the kitchen staff into making his favorite berrybread, and King Wilder and Queen Marla never emerged as early as Daric and Rain did. Rising early wasn't Rain's preference, either, but Daric couldn't seem to stop himself from waking her up in the morning.

Two guards fell into step behind her the moment she left the castle, which wasn't unusual but also wasn't truly necessary. Nothing would happen to an Ash in Upper Ash. The royal soldiers kept their distance even after she entered the busiest part of the city, and Rain spoke with passersby and shopkeepers who were opening up for business. Despite the brave front they put on, there was little in the way of foodstuff or wares in general. And hardly anyone buying. People were just scrambling to survive, especially after the harsh winter. Leathen was dying, choked by years of drought. Daric would be its saving breath.

Trying not to project too much melancholy since that wouldn't help the people of Ash or Leathen, Rain handed out the books she'd collected from the castle. Illanna Nighthall had been clear: the royal family of Ash would come to Raana with little more than the clothes on their backs, reinforcing their position as beggars.

She gave a set of novels to the Carpenter's Guild, although she feared the young apprentices would burn them in the place of firewood; poetry to the baker, knowing his wife would enjoy it more than he would; and a book of fairy stories to the cobbler's daughter. Now empty-handed and ready to go home to join Daric for breakfast, Rain turned and saw an elderly man racing toward her.

"My lady!" He frantically waved at her. "Stop!"

Rain waited and reached out a hand to steady him. "Are you all right?" She was concerned about how hard the old man was breathing.

"I finally understood... Prepared my student..." He doubled over, gulping down air. "Needed to find you... Or Prince Daric."

"Catch your breath," she said soothingly as she waved her guards away. She didn't need protection.

His hunched shoulders rose and fell on wheezing pants. Grizzled hair hung in stringy clumps down his narrow back, revealing a cloak that was torn in places. He spoke again without looking up. "Leathen doesn't have to become one with Raana. You must find the Barrow Witch. She has the strength."

Rain's heart leaped in her chest. "Not unite with Raana? The Barrow Witch?" She'd never heard of the woman, but sorcerers were best avoided—especially for her.

The man straightened, and unease jolted through her. His eyes swirled with the madness brought on by using too much magic.

Rain turned cold all over as a swift and powerful response

rose inside her. Instinctively, she beat it down. The only magic anyone needed from her was gone. What remained served no purpose other than to make her different from everyone else.

"Go to the castle and ask for Non. She'll feed you." Stiffly, Rain backed away from him.

"I'm not hungry, my lady. You need to listen." He closed the distance she'd put between them, and it was all Rain could do not to unleash something that could hurt them both.

He gripped her arms, his fingers like talons. *"Isme dolunde vaten crew."*

Magic snapped through her, itchy and hot. She didn't know the language of sorcery, at least not anymore, but the *feel* of his sentence still grew into an imprecise thought. Something about an offering. The idea chafed and hollowed and *hurt*.

"Release me!" Panic thumped inside her, trying to wrench open places she'd locked up. Rain struggled for control over magic that wanted to burst out and expose her to the world. She couldn't imagine what people would think if she let it out, especially Daric.

"Mockweed. Alderbank. The Blood of Braylian," the sorcerer said, adding new riddles to the foreign words still banging around inside her as if searching for an opening. She didn't understand them, but something told her she *could*.

Her two guards swooped in and lifted the old man away from her. Rain gasped in relief, and then Soren himself appeared from out of nowhere. King Wilder's personal guard growled like a hallerhound as he swept her behind him and shielded her.

"Soren?" Rain clutched the back of his cloak. "What are you doing here?"

"Buying boots," he answered, still half snarling as he turned to her. "We've a long journey ahead of us."

To Raana. Her insides dropped like a stone.

Rain swallowed and released her white-knuckled grip on Soren's garment. She had no desire to think about leaving. For the second time, she'd lose everything she knew and loved.

Soren still loomed protectively over her, a muscle ticking in his jaw as his narrowed gaze swung back and forth between her and the sorcerer. In a voice so gruff it scraped like an angry plow over parched fields, he asked, "Are you hurt? What did he say?"

Rain shook her head. "No. And I don't know. He made no sense." The guards still held the sorcerer between them. Soren would question him, but she needed to question him first.

She stepped forward, still shaken but now firmly in control of the part of her that wanted to answer magic with magic. Soren followed.

"What Barrow Witch? Where?" she asked. "What are you talking about?"

The sorcerer's gaze darted to Soren before coming back to her. "It's a curse."

Rain frowned. Everyone believed Leathen's absent springtime was a curse. They just didn't know how to break it.

"Remember what I told you. Bring everything to the Barrow Witch, and you might still save Leathen."

"How?" Rain asked.

"Take him to the castle," Soren rumbled at the same moment.

The sorcerer's madness-flecked eyes flared in distress. He uttered a solitary word in his mysterious language and disappeared. *Vanished*. The guards looked at their empty hands in terror.

Rain gaped. She'd lost him without answers. And she'd never seen such power—not in this lifetime. Just as frightening was the strong, cold echo of magic inside her. She wasn't a sorceress, though. She was something *other*.

SOREN DIDN'T LET her out of his sight until he'd deposited her in the breakfast room and told the king, queen, and Daric about the incident in Upper Ash. Three times. In detail. Now, it was Rain's turn.

"Repeat exactly what the sorcerer said to you," King Wilder insisted once again.

"Mockweed, Alderbank, the Blood of Braylian. He said to bring everything to the Barrow Witch—whoever that is—and that we might be able to save Leathen."

"Save Leathen from the drought?" the king asked. "Or from Raana?"

Rain shook her head. "I don't know." At this point, the two were the same anyway. "That's all he said."

Which wasn't true. She had no desire to lie, but she kept the odd words the sorcerer had spoken to herself. It was as though they were knocking on a door she knew she could open, but she didn't yet have the key. If she just held *Isme dolunde vaten crew* locked inside her a little longer, Rain thought she would understand.

"Mockweed grows in the Wood of Layton," Daric said.

"And if the Blood of Braylian is anywhere, it would be in Layton, too."

"What is Alderbank?" Queen Marla asked.

The king sighed. "It doesn't matter. These are the ramblings of an unwell person. Sorcery corrupts the mind, and if this man was as old as Soren and Rain say, then he was at least two decades beyond insane."

"That doesn't make what he said false," Daric argued.

"I know you hope for a way out of this marriage," Marla said. "But we have a solution for the kingdom. We must persist."

"A terrible solution," Daric muttered. His eyes flicked to Rain's. She saw anger in their blue depths.

She hated to think what this marriage was going to cost him. She knew what it was costing her.

"Nevertheless, it's the solution we've agreed to. We have no choice." Wilder sat at the table, having spoken in a way that clearly dismissed the topic.

Everyone sat down to breakfast in a solemn mood and with little appetite. There was no berrybread—perhaps they had no dried berries left?—and the tea was weak, at best.

They ate what they had, and what they could stomach, in silence. Rain fretted over her incomplete encounter with the sorcerer, and she knew Daric well enough to know he preferred to say nothing rather than let out the fury brewing in his chest. They both knew his parents had only ever tried their best. Wilder and Marla looked sad and defeated, which was as heartbreaking as the rest.

They eventually stood to go about their day, which at this

point mainly consisted of emptying the castle and distributing items around the city of Ash. At the doorway to the breakfast room, however, the king and queen stopped Rain and Daric before they left.

"We have a birthday present for you, Rain," Marla said.

Rain smiled. She knew it would be thoughtful, even if it wasn't much.

When the queen took off her ring—the one with the Ash-stone that had been in the Ash family since the dawn of Leathen—Rain's heart stuttered in her chest. "In two moons, we must take the name of Nighthall. We've negotiated something for you, though, so that you might keep the name of Ash."

A sick feeling welled up inside her. Rain knew it was an enormous gesture, but her soul wept for everything her family was sacrificing.

She shook her head, but Marla ignored her silent protest.

"Take it with you." The queen placed the jewel in Rain's hand and closed her fingers around it. "You'll be Queen Rain Ash, even in Parr."

Rain had no idea what Marla was talking about. "I don't understand."

Daric stared at his parents, his brows drawing down. Then his horrified gaze swiveled to Rain, and his voice dropped, turning raw and rough. "No. She's coming with us."

"Aldo Lockwood has expressed interest in the past. He's prosperous, powerful, and, to my knowledge, not unkind," Wilder said. "He wants Rain, and I've told him he can have her."

A haze seemed to cover Rain's vision. "Without even consulting me?" She wasn't sure if she was about to throw up, pass out, or simply catch fire from anger. A decision like that made entirely without her? Marriage to an elderly king she scarcely knew?

"He's three times her age!" Daric exploded.

For the second time that day, Rain started to shake. The House of Ash had always treated her like family, but there was no question of where she'd come from, either. There'd been too many witnesses to her "birth" for that. She was not their child. She was not Daric's sister. "I'm not of royal blood. He cannot want me."

"He does," Wilder answered. "And you have something better than royal blood. You're Braylian's daughter."

Did King Aldo truly believe that? Rain had no power, or nothing useful, anyway. Nothing she dared reveal or wield. She brought nothing of value to a marriage.

Daric raked his dark hair back, his face turning bone-white. "You can't force her to go south when we're all going north. It's not possible."

"Rain is young and beautiful." Marla laid a hand on Daric's arm and squeezed. "Aldo will dote on her, and maybe she'll give him the son he's always wanted."

Rain felt herself blanch. Her. The Queen of Parr. In Aldo Lockwood's bed.

Daric looked as sick as she felt. Despair and something much more powerful and volatile churned inside her. She bit down hard to keep both inside.

"It's time you two stopped living out of each other's pockets," Wilder announced with an abruptness that hardly masked his obvious discomfort with handing Rain over to a man who could be *his* father. "Daric will go north and gain Leathen a river. Rain will go south to Parr. It's final."

A disbelieving huff burst from her. Rain had never defied the king. She'd been a dutiful Ash since the day she'd become human. She'd never given the family the springtime they needed, but that wasn't from lack of effort. She'd tried— endlessly.

Her heart pounded out of control. What could she do? The king had already agreed to sacrifice his son, his position, his own *name* for the good of his people. She wasn't in the worst situation here. Some part of her recognized that Wilder was trying to protect her. He loved her and knew she'd be miserable in Raana.

Rain touched the starflower Daric had given her. *Braylian! Please find us another solution!*

As always, silence was her only answer.

CHAPTER THREE

WRATH ROSE UP in Daric with such blistering quickness that he could barely refrain from violence. He'd wanted to pummel his father only twice in his life. The first time was fifteen years ago in the Wood of Layton. The second was right now, in the bloody dining room. Rain stood beside him, as silent, horrified, and colorless as she'd been the day they'd destroyed her existence as a goddess.

"Rain will not go south to Parr. *That* is final." He hardly recognized his own voice.

"Daric, it's for the best," his mother said, trying a conciliatory tone that wouldn't work on him this time. It might never work again. She turned back to Rain and forced the Ashstone ring onto Rain's delicate finger, putting it in the place reserved for a betrothal ring.

Daric saw red, then black, and then Rain—with Aldo Lockwood thrusting over her in bed.

Jealousy like he'd never known grabbed his gut so hard he thought he might vomit.

"Soon, you'll both have children to bring you joy," his mother said, a brittle smile pasted on her face that looked like it made her just as ill as it made him.

"Children," Rain murmured. She could barely speak, which

was distressing in itself. She usually had plenty to say, although she was more reserved around his parents.

Daric snorted harshly. "Whatever children I have will likely be sadistic cat murderers, like their mother—if I can even manage to accomplish the necessary deed with that…woman," he ground out. What he really wanted to call Astraea wasn't appropriate in mixed company. "And Rain will be obliged to welcome an old man to her bed whenever he feels like it. He already has more children than teeth. He doesn't need more of them."

"Don't be vulgar," his father rebuked. "Rain will be much happier with Aldo than any of us will be in Raana with Illanna Nighthall doing her best to belittle us and dictate our every move while Astraea gleefully injects her venom into our daily lives."

"You mean Raanaleath." Daric couldn't contain his spite.

"The name hardly signifies," his father said.

"I'm glad you think so," Daric snapped, "since this aberration of a marriage is about to extinguish the name of Ash!"

"Not if Rain carries it to Parr for her children," his mother said, giving Rain a significant look, as if she should be proud to carry on the name of a royal line of failures.

"Go to Aldo, Rain. Take the Ashstone. Be an Ash. We've never asked anything of you," his father said, "except for this."

"Never asked anything of her?" Daric said in disbelief.

"Besides that." His father waved away the defining problem of both Daric's and Rain's lives. "And we stopped asking years ago," he said.

That didn't mean that Rain had stopped trying. Or that Daric didn't see it eating away at her to fail.

Rain stood like a petrified tree, but Daric knew she was no shrinking flower. She was trying to do her duty, and she would obey the people she cared about, even if it killed her.

He couldn't fault her, no matter how much he hated it. Wasn't he doing the same?

"Soren will go with you," his mother told Rain. "He'll look after you."

That awful feeling yanked hard at Daric's gut again. "Soren? He's half Aldo's age and you know he's—"

"Enough!" His father brought his fist down hard on the table. "The entire household goes with Rain. We've negotiated it with Aldo, and he'll take everyone from the castle. From cooks, to maids, to guards, to masons. Entire families that live and work here. That's one-hundred-and-thirty-two people that won't be starving anymore. And Rain will be surrounded by familiar faces."

A small gasp escaped Rain, and Daric knew the argument was over. She would never weigh her own wishes heavily against the welfare of so many people.

His heart twisted in agony. He'd known he'd lose Rain in a way when he married Astraea, but he'd never imagined losing her entirely. An abyss opened inside him and swallowed every hope he'd secretly held for the future.

But the sorcerer... If they could just... "We have two moons. Let us find this Barrow Witch."

"Out of the question," his father said. "There is no Barrow Witch."

"Because you know all the witches on the continent?" Daric

knew that sarcasm was unbecoming in a prince. He was beyond caring.

His mother looked as though she might argue for his plan, and he turned to her, but it was Rain who spoke before anyone else could.

"Let us go. If we haven't found another solution in the time we still have, we'll return to Ash and do what we must for Leathen." Rain looked at his parents in turn, and then at him, awaiting confirmation.

Daric's lungs seized. Rain had always been beautiful, otherworldly, and fierce in her own way, but right now, she was so stunning and determined that he could barely breathe.

His father eventually nodded. "Soren will put together a team for you. You can leave when you're ready."

Some of the knots in Daric's chest unwound until his father proved he was just humoring them. After all, the king hated the future they faced as much as Rain and he did.

"It takes twelve days to get to Nighthall," his father said. "Factor that into your travels."

In other words, Daric thought bitterly, into their failure.

CHAPTER FOUR

R AIN WAS MANY things, but reckless wasn't one of them. The only thing she'd ever done purely on impulse was dance with a boy, half in the Cauldron and half out, half element and half something more solid, so that he could see her and wouldn't be frightened by what she truly was.

What she *had* been: a deity with power over clouds and sunshine. She'd been the lightning that lashed the treetops as well as the kernels that sprouted into all things green and lush. She'd been whole storms, and she'd been each tiny speck of moisture. She'd run wild across the continent, but she'd kept the land in balance. Or so she'd thought—until Daric showed her otherwise.

Perhaps it was a blessing that she recalled only the larger picture of her existence as a season. It allowed her to be satisfied with her life in Leathen.

A life about to end as well.

Glumly, Rain flipped the pages of another musty old tome looking for mentions of the Barrow Witch, mockweed, Alderbank, or the Blood of Braylian.

Daric studied another book beside her, untouched mugs of ale and dinner plates in front of them. The candles had burned low and now flickered in a draft, throwing shadows across his face as he read. It was a face she knew better than any other sight, and yet there was something unfamiliar about it now, a hardness that told her Daric was a man who would face his responsibilities, no matter the cost.

He shoved the book aside and leaned back in his chair, scrubbing a hand over his eyes. "There's nothing of interest in here unless you want to know how to make a beeswax and ingeroot poultice."

"Useful for burns," Rain murmured.

"We don't have burns. We're facing disgusting marriages— which might be worse."

"Aldo Lockwood is kind. I could do worse."

Daric scoffed. "You could certainly do better."

"Well, no one else is offering." Rain glanced at him but turned away at the intense anger on his face. The blue of their eyes was nothing alike. Rain's was much darker. Right now, Daric watched her through chips of glacial ice.

This wasn't the man she was used to. He hadn't seemed half this furious when it was *his* marriage forced upon the House of Ash.

"He's a king. He's willing to take me and our entire house-hold."

"Who wouldn't take you?" Daric muttered.

A pinching sensation cinched around Rain's heart. If only Daric wanted her the way she wanted him. But then... That wouldn't help either of them at this point.

"Perhaps we'll find a solution. We have two moons. And if not... Aldo will be kind," she repeated.

"Aldo will likely die of heart failure the moment he sees you naked."

"Daric!" He'd never spoken to her like that.

"At least he'd die happy," he said under his breath.

Rain didn't know whether to laugh or cry, so she went back to the safety of the bland history book in her lap. She had a decent idea about what went on in the marriage bed because she wasn't stupid and she asked questions. But she'd never even felt another's lips against hers, because the only person she'd ever wanted was Daric.

There suddenly seemed to be a great deal wrong with that.

"I've never been kissed," she announced, closing the book with a snap. Maybe she needed a little impulsiveness in her life. What could it hurt? Everything she knew was about to be destroyed again anyway.

Daric scowled at her. "Good. No one deserves you."

"I'm a twenty-five-year-old virgin about to be married to a man who could be my grandfather."

"Of course you're a virgin. You're unmarried."

Rain rolled her eyes. "Do you honestly believe that every new bride is a virgin?"

"No. But I believe that you damn well better be."

"Are you?"

He looked shocked by her question. Then his color rose. "No."

He didn't elaborate. Rain felt a corner of her heart wither and die but soldiered on, because she knew what she wanted.

"Before I marry Aldo, I want to be kissed by a man who is young, vigorous, and attractive."

Daric's face turned to stone. "I'll be damned if I'm going to let you comb Upper Ash for a man to kiss you."

"And I'll be damned before I let you dictate my actions." Rain faced Daric's glower with a boldness born of knowing him better than anyone. He was polite and good, but he'd never let anyone run roughshod over him. Not even her, but that didn't mean she was intimidated by him. "That said, why would I need to comb Upper Ash for a candidate when I have you right here beside me?"

He stared at her. His throat bobbed. He looked almost…frightened. "Do you have any idea what you're asking?"

Heat coursed through her. "I'm asking for a kiss."

He shook his head. "You're asking to make the years ahead of us even worse."

Rain's eyes widened, and her pulse leaped to a harder beat. Was he saying what she thought he was? "You accepted your betrothal to Astraea, who is truly awful, but you've been vulgar and enraged since we found out about me being promised to Aldo. Why?"

Daric turned away from her. For a moment, she thought he might leave. "Because I can live with my own unhappiness, but I can't live with yours."

Tears stung Rain's eyes. "Your father is right," she said gently. "Do you think I'd be any happier at Nighthall, with you married to Astraea and me living in her shadow?"

Daric's head snapped around. He looked furious. "You outshine her by far."

Rain stood, her chair scraping back. "I don't know if you say that to be chivalrous and kind, or if you feel something…more. Speak plainly, Daric, or I might go comb Upper Ash after all for a man to do more than just kiss me before Aldo is my only option."

Daric stood, too, a head taller than Rain and a good deal wider. He stepped closer, backing her against the table. "You wouldn't."

Rain lifted her chin. No, she wouldn't. She would never dishonor herself, Aldo, or her family in that way, but Daric couldn't be sure of that. "Then kiss me yourself," she demanded.

"Don't ask me to do this," he choked out.

"Why? Would it be so terrible?"

"Terrible?" His brows arched in surprise. He lifted a hand. His thumb grazed her jaw, tilting her head back, and Rain's heart tumbled wildly. Daric's gaze shifted to the starflower still in her hair before his eyes returned to her face, haunted. "You're my one and only obsession."

Rain drew a sharp breath, the ember of hope inside her catching fire. She touched her hand to his chest. Daric was hard and strong. Aldo would be the opposite.

"Then kiss me." Boldly, she slid both hands toward his shoulders. She wanted to touch him, had yearned for this. "For I'm just as obsessed."

Heat and hunger blazed across Daric's expression. Then his face abruptly twisted. "I cannot." He stepped back.

Rain froze, hurt pounding through her like the downpours she occasionally dreamed she unleashed upon the kingdom—only to wake and find the land as dry as bone.

She swallowed, but her voice still shook. "You're making me feel very foolish, Daric."

"I'm the fool." His bitter tone coated the air between them

in frost, just as it had countless times over the course of this dreadful day. "I'm the fool for loving you from the moment I saw you—and wanting you more than my next breath."

Blood surged in her veins. Rain reached for him again. Those were the words she'd wanted—*needed*—for years.

Daric avoided her, shaking his head. His voice grew thick and hoarse as he said, "You're beautiful, desirable, strong, and kind. Any man would be lucky to have you even look at him. But I am the Prince of Leathen, and my life is not my own." He turned away. Daric left and didn't look back.

Rain trembled, heartsick. As his footsteps faded, she bit down hard on her lip to keep from sobbing. She'd rather draw blood than shed more tears, although neither would help her, Daric, or the kingdom.

CHAPTER FIVE

Daric paced his chamber like a caged beast, angry, miserable, and restless. If the palace hadn't been stripped bare of anything nonessential, he'd have picked up some useless object and thrown it against the wall for the sheer satisfaction of smashing something. He'd needed to fight more violent urges in the last day than he had in his entire lifetime. The desire to rip into something was overwhelming.

First, it had been his father. Then Rain. Then anything and everything, especially himself.

They'd been the best of friends forever, and Daric had been madly in love with her since they'd danced at the Cauldron, but he'd never imagined that Rain thought of him as anything other than a brother. It had been different when they were children and easy playmates with mostly innocent thoughts, but for years now, Daric had been careful to keep his distance—physically, at least. Whenever he touched her, even by accident, the longing just grew worse.

Tonight, he'd wanted to rattle some sense into her. Shake her. Hold her. *Consume* her.

He was tormented by thoughts of the kiss he didn't take, aroused to the point of pain. His heart ached, but so did another part of him, hard and heavy with want.

Rain's quick breaths fluttering across his jaw. Her lush mouth. Her eyes drifting closed...

Like a damnable curse, she'd offered up the lips he'd dreamed about kissing every day and night of his life.

Daric scrubbed a hand down his face and paced.

What had he imagined for the future? That Rain would remain his companion, his joy, while he did his duty and sired children with the vicious Astraea for the good of Raanaleath?

That Rain would comfort him? That she wouldn't marry and have children of her own?

That maybe they'd have a secret affair one day, sharing the intimate things he now knew they both wanted?

Heat swelled in his chest, but it warred for space with a large block of ice. Daric let out a vile curse. How could he be so selfish? Hadn't he already ruined Rain's life once?

He hadn't realized it before, or so clearly put it into thought, but he'd had it all planned out, to make the future bearable. *His* future.

Rain had a better option now.

Daric left his chamber in the pre-dawn dark without even a candle, sick at heart but determined to make things better. Rain was used to him waking her up. She wouldn't be frightened, and he had to tell her he was sorry for being so hard on Aldo, a man who was certainly better for her than a failed, soon-to-be-married prince without a name or a house.

Daric stood outside Rain's door for a moment, gathering the will to say what he must before lifting his hand and knocking. There was no answer. He nudged the door open, expecting to see her sleeping. Instead, he found a candle burning and an open book upon her neatly made bed.

A mix of fear and anguish hit him in a sickening rush. She'd left. He'd rejected her, and she'd struck out on her own. She'd gone on their last adventure without him.

Daric stalked into the room and shut the door behind him. He didn't believe for a firesnap that she'd gone to Upper Ash in search of kisses—and certainly not to Lower Ash, which sometimes bordered on dangerous. She'd gone looking for the Barrow Witch.

Had she taken Soren with her? Daric's chest clenched again hard, and jealousy cut through him, as biting as the winter wind. Soren had been in love with Rain for nearly as long as he had.

Still, with Soren was better than unaccompanied. His father's personal guard would protect her with his life. Envy aside, Daric hoped that Rain wasn't alone in the creaking wilderness that surrounded Ash in every direction. She knew how to ride and wield a blade or bow, but her caring nature made her an easy target for anyone trying to take advantage, and as always on cold nights with little moon, the hallerhounds would be out in hungry packs of hunters.

Desperate for any hint as to the direction she might have taken, Daric brought the candle closer to the book and read. The passage she'd left open was about the mighty waterfalls that had once poured down the Cliffs of Alder. The now-dry cascades were said to have protected a nearly inaccessible cavern far up the cliffside that contained a supply of rare bloodstones, a mineral used in breaking curses.

Daric held his breath and continued reading.

The deep-red gemstone takes its name from an arcane legend that whispers of Braylian cutting her finger on the jagged Heights of Alder while placing the gemstone on the continent.

He snapped the book shut. Rain had found the Blood of Braylian.

Daric tucked the old volume under his arm. It could contain other useful information. His mind spun a dozen different scenarios about what Rain had done in the hours since he'd left her. The Heights of Alder were four days northeast on horseback. It was a daunting journey on foot, and she'd never waste time walking when she could ride Arjun.

He checked Rain's wardrobe. Her heavy cloak and warm boots were gone.

He muttered a curse. Knowing Rain, she'd set a vigorous pace from the start.

Daric hurried to gather provisions. She could be leagues from Ash already, but he had the faster horse. He'd find her, and when he did, he'd give her the tongue-lashing she deserved for leaving without him. He only wished that once she was safe, he could make that tongue-lashing literal.

RAIN HAD NEVER considered herself a coward, but she had to admit, if only to herself, that she was terrified. Hallerhounds howled in the distance, yipping and growling around what was surely their ripped-apart dinner. It was closer to breakfast, but she didn't think hallerhounds cared when or what they ate—

only that the meat was fresh and bloody.

The night was darker than she'd imagined, and the sound of their brawling made her shiver. Eyes usually adjusted to the dimness and then shapes became clearer. Not tonight, with little moon and branches that were thick this deep into the forest, even if they were still leafless.

The wind howled louder than the hounds, and Rain drew her cloak more firmly around her. Spring had come to Leathen, in her way at least, but the air still smelled of her sister, Winter.

And Dawn was taking forever.

Rain had considered taking Soren with her, but she hadn't wanted to make him choose between abandoning her or abandoning his position. If he was to become her personal guard in less than two moons and for the remainder of their lives in Parr, though, perhaps he would have agreed to start sooner.

But Soren had an irritating way of making her see reason, and she hadn't wanted to be talked out of leaving without Daric. She'd been too angry and hurt to stop herself, and she hadn't wanted Soren to stop her, either.

Now, however, with the chill wind in her face, the haller-hounds at her back, and the night all around her, she wished she'd woken Soren. But he sometimes looked at her in a way that was disconcerting. He wasn't so old, and he was fit and handsome, but she wanted that same look on Daric's face, and she'd never had it.

Until tonight.

Rain worried her lower lip between her teeth. Daric had looked so torn and desperate. And she'd just left him. Without a word. Without a note. Without anything. That was terrible, in retrospect.

She sighed loudly enough to make Arjun's ears twitch. At least she'd left the book open to the passage she'd found about the Blood of Braylian. If Daric wanted to, he could join her.

A branch cracked, and Rain stiffened. The sound hadn't come from overhead but rather from just in front of her. She squinted, watching the narrow roadway, but the first light of day was still weak and gray and scarcely penetrated the darkness.

A figure she could barely see suddenly lunged at her. He waved his arms and shouted, startling Arjun into rearing. Rain kept her balance and lashed out at the man with her whip when he tried to unseat her. He frightened Arjun again, hitting her mount in the face, and the poor animal went nearly vertical.

She might have righted herself, but hands tore at her from behind and dragged her backward. Arjun landed on all fours and shied to the side, leaving Rain in a heap on the ground with two men looming over her. The horse raced down the path in the opposite direction, taking her provisions, extra clothing, sword, and bow and arrows with him.

Rain drew the dagger from her belt and swung her arm up, ramming the hilt into the face of the man behind her. He grunted harshly, and the hands gripping her shoulders loosened. She whipped around, bashing him in the head again with the heavy crosspiece. His eyes rolled up, and he went down, unconscious.

She turned to face the first man again. He leered at her with a rotten-tooth grin that sent a spike of panic through her. Something dangerous and powerful answered the distress inside her. It built beneath her skin, and Rain knew that now was not the time to stop it.

"I like a feisty woman, 'specially one with pretty silver hair and fine clothing. Who'd'a thunk? Fierce for such a small thing." His eyes glinted and it wasn't too dark to see his malice.

Rain had always kept a tight hold on whatever was left of her former self. That existence was gone, and there was no reason to frighten people with it, even horrible little princesses like Astraea. The magic left in her didn't water Leathen or make crops grow and prosper, so she'd seen no point in showing it. She didn't want people to fear her—not when she had to live among them. But this man could use some frightening.

"I am not small." Rain's words cracked out of her like lightning. "I am the storm you never saw coming."

He blinked in surprise. She advanced, and he stepped back.

Rain let magic swell in her veins, magic she barely knew how to wield or control since she never used it. Nevertheless, vines grew down her arms at her bidding, feeding on her own moisture and minerals until she felt prickly with thirst. One sturdy tendril of greenery circled her dagger, waiting. The other grew long, snaking toward the bandit.

He flinched in fear and turned to run, but Rain blew him to his knees with a gale that snarled around them. Trees creaked and leaned. Forest debris rose on violent whirlwinds and eddied into him. Whipped on all sides, he cowered, groveling on the forest path like a beggar before her altar. The good-natured woman she'd been for years stepped aside, making room for something terrifying.

She'd hidden this away, shunning it, but she instinctively knew this powerful being was only a pale version of what she'd been before. In the beginning, for years really, she hadn't even realized it was still a part of her. And when she did, she hadn't wanted to alarm Daric, or to be so very different from him. Long before that, she'd already wanted to keep him. Love him. She'd wanted him to love *her*.

Rain's head tipped to one side as she contemplated her attacker. She was not innately cruel and would rather nurture life than take it. Spring rain watered. But late frosts also killed new buds with a coating of ice, and sometimes, that was just the way of it.

The bandit shivered as she weighed her options, feeling her magic stretch and grow powerful. It was wild from disuse and aggressive from its sudden unleashing. It pulled her toward a wider perception than that of one person, where the world around her seemed increasingly distant but also more richly layered.

Rain sent a vine to coil around her attacker, loops upon loops to hold him in place while she decided. Life. Death. It was a cycle that never ended.

The man drooped and slumped to his side, motionless. Had her vines been too tight? Or was he simply cold and frightened?

She didn't know. In the end, she willed the vines out of existence, freeing him. She would leave his fate to Chance, who had once been her companion. The two unconscious brigands could live or die. The day might turn warm and save them. Or stay cold and take them. The hallerhounds might scent easy prey and eat them.

A familiar voice called through the forest, distracting her. Or maybe grounding her. Bringing her back to herself. Hooves pounded, but no threat poked at her suddenly heightened senses. In fact, she felt an overwhelming sense of protectiveness.

Daric.

Rain threw her hood back and let him see the woman he knew, corralling that other part of her. He galloped toward her, handsome and strong and visibly exploding with worry.

Dawn broke fully around them just as he reached her. He held Arjun's reins in his hand and brought both horses to a mad halt scant steps from her. Daric vaulted to the ground, grabbed her, and crushed her against him. A warm wave tumbled in Rain's belly. All parts of her leaned into him willingly.

"Are you all right? What happened?" He set her back from him, his frantic gaze darting to the men on the ground before coming back to her.

"I was attacked."

"Are you injured?" Daric's hands moved all over her, searching for wounds or wetness or perhaps for protruding daggers.

Rain stopped his anxious probing, holding his hands in front of her. "I'm fine. I fought them off."

He frowned deeply. "With only a dagger?"

She shrugged. "Daric, I'm fine. Thank you for bringing Arjun."

"I was terrified when he came galloping down the path without you." He freed his hands and gripped her face in a hold that was uncharacteristically intimate. He tipped her head from side to side. "I don't see any bruises. It appears you didn't need me."

She would *always* need him. "I'm glad you're here," she whispered thickly.

Daric scowled harder. "I'm furious at you for leaving without me."

From the look on his face, Rain believed him. "I can only hope your fury lasts as long as usual."

"I think my anger has already been overcome by terror." Closing his eyes, Daric leaned his forehead against hers, his breathing still rough and irregular. He never put them this close, and Rain realized that if she moved just a little, just a tilt of her head, she could kiss him. But he'd already refused her once, and she wouldn't take what he wasn't offering.

She stepped back, breaking the flustering contact.

Daric opened his eyes. A deep breath shuddered into him. "You figured out Alderbank and the Blood of Braylian."

Rain nodded. "I found the right book after you left the library, although Alderbank was an unfair clue. There hasn't been enough water there to make a riverbed in ages—not since long before this drought ever occurred."

"Why didn't you wait for me?"

Rain stayed silent. Didn't he already know?

Daric grimaced. His weight shifted. "What do we do with them?" He plowed a hand through his hair, his troubled gaze landing on the brigands.

Not that it should matter to their decision, but Rain didn't think the men were from Leathen. They hadn't known who she was, and her silver tresses were unusual. "Leave them where they are. I've no desire to decide their fate myself."

If the hard set of his jaw was any indication, Daric thought that sentence was far too lenient. Rain laid a soothing hand on his arm, thinking it was ridiculous that they almost never touched, especially when they'd only ever wanted or needed comfort from each other. Daric's fist uncurled in increments.

"Their blood should not stain our souls." And Rain was quite certain they would never again attack a woman. They now understood that powerful and fearsome things lurked beneath the skin of females.

Daric's nostrils flared, but he eventually nodded. "As you wish." He turned to gather Arjun's reins and handed them to her with a flourish. "Your horse, my lady."

"Thank you, kind sir." Rain mounted, their silly formality lightening her heavy heart, as she was sure Daric had intended. They'd played this game since they were children.

"Mockweed?" Daric asked hopefully as he slipped her booted foot into the stirrup for her. "Or the Barrow Witch?"

Unfortunately, Rain had no idea. The witch was a mystery, although logic pointed to her perhaps having taken up residence at the barrows in the Wood of Layton, and any mockweed they found at this time of year was sure to be dead and brittle. "My prince, we've only just begun this journey."

And she hoped with all her heart that it would be successful. Despite the increasingly disastrous last quarter century, Leathen was still the home of Braylian's Cauldron and the coveted heart of the continent, and the Ash family the most ancient and respected of the Houses. It made her sick to think about handing any of that over to Illanna Nighthall.

Daric mounted as well, and together, they rode toward the Heights of Alder to find the Blood of Braylian.

CHAPTER SIX

D ESPITE LIVING A privileged life compared to most, Daric knew hardship and crushing responsibility. Three days later, he decided that nothing had ever been as torturous as bedding down next to Rain each night and not reaching for her. He wanted to bring her into the warmth of his body, breathe in her scent as they slept, and hold her against him.

Oh, for the love of Braylian, he didn't want to just *hold* her. He wanted to roll her beneath him and kiss and touch and cover her.

But he would also hold her. He wanted to hold her forever—something he couldn't do if she was Aldo Lockwood's wife.

His stomach plummeted, killing his morning arousal.

Rain stirred in her sleep, huffing softly. She wasn't an easy sleeper—something he hadn't known. They never shared a room or tent or any quarters that could be considered intimate. They never traveled without guards and an entourage. They hadn't spent this much time together without anyone interrupting them in years, and never nights in each other's company. Even now, they'd intended to travel with guards—Soren and a team of warriors. No one, not even him, had meant for them to go on this quest alone.

He did, however, know what Rain looked like when she

woke: bleary-eyed, sleep-tousled, rosy-warm, and delightfully provoked. She didn't enjoy rising early, which seemed ironic for someone who had once embodied spring, but he was always desperate to see her in the mornings, to make sure she hadn't evaporated during the night, hadn't turned into mist and left him.

Having her with him day and night was reassuring in that regard.

Rain jerked in her sleep and mumbled something incoherent. Daric reached out a hand and touched her head. She settled instantly.

He wondered if she was dreaming about how she'd once roiled and rolled across the continent, a formidable daughter of Braylian. He saw relatively little of the powerful being from the Cauldron in her, but sometimes lightning flashed in her eyes, and it wasn't just an expression of temper. He wasn't sure what it meant, or if she was even aware of it.

That wasn't the only thing he'd noticed. She didn't seem to realize that the wind sometimes blew *from* her, not around her, or that the castle lawn wasn't still green simply because they were lucky, but because Rain trod upon it.

Unable to stop himself, Daric wound a long strand of Rain's silver hair around his fist. In the liquid pre-dawn light, it looked more like a waterfall than ever. He let her sleep. They'd been riding hard and had a tiring push ahead of them to get to the Heights of Alder before sundown. He only drew his hand back from her hair when the sun finally rose high enough to wake her.

Rain slowly opened her eyes, squinting and wrinkling her

nose. "Ermph." She rolled over, flopping an arm across her face.

"Good morning to you, too, Raindrop."

"What's good about it?" she grumbled. "I'm cold and stiff and—"

"As grumpy as ever?" Daric finished for her.

She sat up and scowled at him. "There's no reason to be so annoyingly chipper."

"I'm with you," Daric said simply. "Why wouldn't I be happy?"

She flushed bright pink, which delighted him more than it should have, considering they were both betrothed to other people.

Rain rummaged in her pack for a comb while he prepared their meal. She braided her hair and then wound it around her head like a crown, securing it with pins. As a finishing touch, she added the starflower.

Satisfaction welled inside him along with something frankly proprietary. Rain's daring request for a kiss—coming right on the heels of learning she was betrothed to Aldo—had unleashed something primitive in him that made him want to howl and curse and never let her out of his sight again.

It made him want to abandon his duty.

To resist hauling her into his arms, Daric handed Rain her breakfast. Her smile seemed shyer than usual and struck him in the chest. Was it truly possible to fix their problems without having to lose each other, Leathen, or anything else?

"When you look at me that way..." Rain's voice faded to a mere whisper. "I feel much warmer than this frigid morning should permit."

Pressure clamped around Daric's heart. The need to reach for her was a physical ache. In a cavern-deep rasp, he asked, "In what way is that?"

The flick of her eyes over him was like a warm brush of lips. "Like we shouldn't be dressing right now, but rather undressing instead."

Heat blazed through him, and his groin tightened fast.

Her suddenly roguish grin almost had him groaning out loud. "I believe I've shocked you, Daric. But if now's not the time for boldness, I'm not sure when is."

He swallowed hard. "I adore when you shock me. I'd have you shock me silly for the rest of my life."

"Really?" She sounded surprised.

"How could you doubt?"

"I know you'd keep your companion if you could." She shrugged. "I'm sure of that."

His brows collided in a frown. "You're more than my companion, Rain."

"Yet you refused to kiss me."

The thought of learning her mouth with his tortured him relentlessly. "If I kiss you," he said, his eyes riveted to her lips, "I'll never stop."

THEY PACKED UP and rode out with Rain in a restless mood. She'd always had some trouble understanding human emotion. Hers was human enough now as well, but she still felt as though she were learning, just as she'd had to learn to read and write, bow and dance, refrain from snapping others like twigs once she'd discovered she still could, and do all the things people did but that seasons did not.

Daric often defied her understanding, which made him even more appealing—and exasperating.

He wanted but wouldn't take. He longed but wouldn't act. He looked but wouldn't touch. It was frustrating, infuriating, body-heating...

Rain blew out a tense breath, wishing Arjun's rolling gait would soothe her as it often did. Nothing took the edge off her body or her thoughts. Things had certainly been easier before her betrothal had prompted her to show her true feelings to Daric—and revealed Daric's in return. Knowing the desire was shared only made the craving worse, but she also wouldn't trade the heady storm of sensations brewing inside her for anything. Liquid fire described it best.

Rain knew what would satisfy her—satisfy them both. Unfortunately, her prince was not cooperating.

She bit down on her lower lip, nibbling it between her teeth until it felt sore and swollen. She supposed she wouldn't love him half as much if he had no respect or honor.

"Finally." Daric heaved a sigh from beside her when they turned a bend in the road and saw the Heights of Alder.

The cliffs didn't roar with water as Rain knew they once had at the dawn of the continent, and the riverbed was mostly a dusty basin, but the ancient cascades still existed in the form of a glistening film that filtered down the imposing cliffside, leaving the craggy surface slick and mineral-stained.

On the positive side, the cave the book had mentioned was

clearly visible without any rush of water to cover it. Sadly, it was midway up and completely inaccessible.

"How in the name of Braylian are we supposed to reach that?" she asked.

"Climb?" Daric suggested.

Rain snorted. "And break our necks?"

He looked at her. "What do you suggest?"

She studied the cliffside. "Climb," she finally said, although she didn't like it one bit.

"I'll go," he said. "There's no reason for you to risk yourself."

"I'll go," Rain countered. "You're of more value. Astraea won't marry *me* and give water to Leathen if you're dead."

Daric's head canted to the side as he rather harshly said, "Aldo might provide it instead."

"Parr is half as rich as Raana in both wealth and resources. And don't snarl at me. I didn't ask to be married off."

A dark, foreboding look crossed Daric's face. Her kind prince was a lovely companion, but this intense man was someone who made her heat and shiver and ache. Although she tried to curb it, she always gravitated toward the heart-pounding and wild. In spirit, she remained untamed.

"We'll both go," Rain said. "I'd rather break my neck with you than live without you. In Parr. With Aldo," she added for good measure. The mention of her intended had the desired effect: Daric stopped thinking clearly and agreed to her plan with a muttered curse.

They left their horses and supplies at the base of the cliff, their mounts tied with loose ropes staked to the ground near some dry grass and the trickle of water that was the only evidence of the once mighty Falls of Alder. Not wanting to compromise their balance, they left everything behind except for a dagger each and a pouch to gather the bloodstone they needed.

The climb was difficult, terrifying, and slick. Rain was sore and trembling by the time they were only halfway to the cavern, and she wondered how she could possibly scale the rest.

"Go back!" Daric shouted from above. "I'll finish and bring you the stone."

She gritted her teeth and climbed to the next decent hand-hold. "Back is as daunting as forward."

"But it's half the total distance," Daric called.

Rain glanced down and then wished she hadn't. "Half is still more than enough to shatter our bones."

"Would you *please* stop talking about dying?"

"How can I? It's all I can think about!" Rain shouted back.

"I'll wait here then." Daric beckoned her upward with a tilt of his head. "You go before me."

He'd thought to show her the best path for climbing, but maybe it was better to know he was behind her. He could never catch her if she fell, but it might still be reassuring.

Rain nodded, saving her breath for climbing. Once she was past him, Daric began barking out directions, pointing out places for her to grip the cliff, which became more slippery the higher they ascended.

Rain finally threw a tired and heavy arm over the lip of the cavern. She struggled to pull herself up, her muscles quaking. She suddenly went nearly weightless as Daric gave her a hard shove on her bottom. She was too exhausted to care—or enjoy—that he had just firmly gripped her backside as he tumbled her shoulder-first into the cavern. She pivoted on her stomach, ready to reach out a hand to him.

Their eyes met as her head popped out of the cavern. Then something crumbled. Daric's eyes widened, and he started falling.

Rain's heart bucked violently. "Daric!"

His hands scraped over stone, all of him sliding until he flailed and lost his grip entirely. He soared backward, shouting her name.

Instinct grabbed her. Rain threw out vines from both hands to catch him. They wrapped around him, stopping his fall. He banged against the cliffside. Rain slid forward, nearly yanked from the cavern. She made the vines sink roots into the rock wall, working them hard and growing a hundred years' worth of grip in a second.

Her vision swam. Her whole body went dry, her mouth suddenly parched and dusty.

"Daric!" The vines had circled him unevenly from shoulders to thighs, and he bumped against the cliffside, one arm free and the other pinned to his side.

He groaned in response. She thought perhaps he was only half conscious, but then he shouted up, "Have you been keeping secrets from me, Raindrop?"

She made a strangled sound, neither a sob nor a laugh. If he could jest, he was fine, thank Braylian.

Rain detached herself from the vines that were now firmly anchored and summoned the reserves beneath her skin to grow a sturdy new shoot for Daric to grip. "Can you cut free from the ones around you and climb this?" she called down.

"I think I can reach my knife." He began to wriggle and twist.

Rain directed the new vine down to him, making it thick and branchy, and all the while anchoring it with thousands of small roots that cracked the stone. Her thirst turned desperate, her tongue sticking to her mouth. She'd never been able to produce water, and now the vines were taking all the moisture she had left.

Daric gave a triumphant shout when he managed to free his dagger. He wrapped the new vine around his arm for safety and began sawing his way out. Rain shook free of the greenery she'd made and stumbled to the side of the cavern to drink from the water sliding down the wall, lapping it up like an animal until her throat no longer burned.

As soon as she felt steady again, she watched Daric climb, nerves sinking little arrows into her abdomen. Her anxiety wasn't only for him as he worked to extricate himself from such a perilous situation. Sorcery frightened people, and anyone using magic regularly was known to go mad before they'd lived even half a normal lifespan. But she didn't utter chants or brew potions, and she didn't even know the language of sorcerers. Rain's magic was different, part of her very nature rather than fabricated by using outside forces. But would it still scare Daric?

She didn't know whether to reach for him as he climbed into the cavern, scraped and bloody in places, but whole. Alive. Her Daric. As he stood, relief overwhelmed her fears, and she strode forward.

Daric met her halfway and crushed her against him. "I thought I'd lost you," he said into her hair, his grip like a vice around her.

"Me?" She held him back with greedy arms. "I thought I'd lost *you!*"

His grip only tightened. "I would have haunted you."

Tears shuddered in Rain's throat. He haunted her already.

Daric loosened his embrace enough to look at her. "Why have you hidden this?"

She glanced at the vines around them. "Are you angry?"

"What's to be angry about?" He seemed genuinely perplexed she would think that.

"I-I never told you I regained some of my powers."

Daric looked at her oddly, as though his surprise were minimal. "Can you make it rain?"

She shook her head. "I've tried so hard. It never works. I'm sorry."

Rain had tried especially hard since negotiations had begun to marry her prince off to Astraea, but the results had been no better than in the past—or ever.

Daric lifted both hands and cupped her cheeks, his fingers raw and unsteady. "My life didn't flash before my eyes as I fell." His gaze roamed her face with an intensity that ravaged her heart and took her breath away. "I had only one thought. One regret."

"What?" Rain's pulse pounded like a tempest. Human bodies were so fragile. She remembered not having one, and now the one she did have felt as though it might shatter from heat and pressure.

"That I didn't kiss you when I still could."

CHAPTER SEVEN

R AIN SWAYED TOWARD Daric as he dipped his head. She'd been waiting for this moment forever.

Their lips hadn't quite touched when an accusing voice sent them rearing back from one another. "Not only do I find invaders at my back entrance, but now they start kissing?"

A crone dressed in ragged robes brandished a staff at them. "I'll teach you to come into my home uninvited!" She started chanting a spell that made the sphere at the top of her staff glow.

Just as Daric started to step in front of her, Rain blew the witch back with a stiff wind, pinning her to the wall of the cavern. The crone's weapon clattered to the ground, and the greenery that Rain had already created grew again, crisscrossing the woman and stopping all movement. The witch gaped at them, falling silent.

Daric turned his head and arched a brow in Rain's direction. "I'd like to come to your rescue occasionally. It would comfort me in my masculinity."

Rain's lips twitched. "Your masculinity is not in question, Daric."

"But I do so enjoy a damsel in distress." He was clearly teasing now.

"I'll swoon for you in a moment," Rain replied. "Let's just

see if this is the Barrow Witch."

"Barrow Witch?" the crone spat. "Does this look like a barrow to you?"

"Then I suppose that makes you the Cave Witch?" Daric asked.

In answer, the crone tried another incantation, hissing unfamiliar words that seemed somehow to Rain to relate to bowels melting. No wonder everyone hated sorcerers—and she should not have understood a word of that.

Isme dolunde vaten crew punched into her with new vigor. The sorcerer's words in Upper Ash had meant little to her at the time, leaving only the impression of hardship and the near certainty that she could decipher their meaning with time and effort. That impression deepened upon hearing the witch's chant. The language of sorcery became clearer, and Rain suddenly knew down to her very essence that there was a terrible choice to come.

Daric advanced and stuffed a wad of the woman's own tattered shawl into her mouth. The witch glared at them. Rain did her best to shake off the feeling of dread now weighing her down.

"Let's get a bloodstone and leave this place," Daric said.

The witch grunted muffled protests.

Rain hesitated. "She might know where the Barrow Witch is."

"The only barrows in Leathen are in the Wood of Layton," Daric said. "Near Braylian's Cauldron."

"She might not be home," Rain pointed out. "I think we should ask."

Ceding to her wishes, Daric turned back to the witch. "We may have started off on the wrong foot. Please forgive us for bursting into your home uninvited. We didn't realize it was occupied, and we all startled each other."

The crone narrowed her eyes, but she was listening.

Rain nodded for him to continue. Daric was nothing if not diplomatic.

"We need to find the Barrow Witch. Would you happen to know her?"

The old woman just watched him as he slowly reached out and removed the gag from her mouth.

"Do I look like I frequent barrows, you idiot? I'm a Cave Witch and therefore frequent caverns."

"I see," Daric said, all dignity, as usual.

Rain almost laughed at his unwaveringly cordial expression. She wasn't duped. To her, his face looked crisp, like a sour apple.

"We were led to believe this cavern contains a rare gem called bloodstone," Rain said. "We need some."

"Oh, do you now?" The witch cackled. "Well, I need a cook and a maid. Which one of you likes to stir the pot and who prefers to clean?"

"I think we'll just take a bloodstone," Rain said, losing some of her humor and patience.

The witch bubbled with unhinged laughter. "You'll never get one without me. Even with your magic that needs no words." She glared at Rain, as though trying to dissect her strange abilities.

The Cave Witch attempted her spell again, and Daric stuffed

the gag back into her mouth. "None of that," he said sharply. He turned to Rain. "Shall we?" He offered her his arm.

Rain took it. Side by side, they moved deeper into the cavern.

DARIC WAS STILL reeling, although he tried not to show it. The slight weight of Rain's hand on his arm was the only thing keeping him steady. He'd suspected that Rain still had some of her magic, but he'd never imagined she was this powerful. A true force of nature.

And he'd almost kissed her.

He desired her, admired her, *loved* her as intensely as always. Nothing had changed, except he was now more certain than ever that he didn't deserve her. No one did. He was a mere man, and he wasn't even sure Rain was mortal.

"Did you notice the witch said we'd come in through her *back* door?" Rain asked.

Daric cleared his throat. It seemed so tight all of a sudden. "I did. I'm hoping there's an easier way out."

Rain murmured her agreement as they were confronted with a fork in the tunnel, both options fading into complete darkness.

"There are two paths," she said, eyeing the set of torches on the wall. They were lit and ready for the taking, surely the Cave Witch's method of seeing her way around. "Should we separate?"

Daric hesitated and then shook his head. "I'd rather stay

together." His lips quirked, and he added, "I may need you to rescue me."

Rain huffed. She gripped his arm more tightly. "I'm nervous in the dark."

Daric knew that. It was unsurprising. The first time she'd ever truly been in the dark, not seeing the world around her, big hands had grabbed her and dragged her from the existence she'd known forever.

As always, the memory chilled him. At the same time, having Rain by his side was a source of endless heat and energy. It was in part this contradiction that had kept him from revealing his true feelings. Could she really love him as he loved her, with the kind of passion and devotion that burned a hole in one's chest and filled it with longing, when he'd been responsible for ending her life as she knew it?

She'd wanted a kiss, but that would never be enough for him. Rain needed to want more, *everything*, just as he did.

Daric took a torch from the wall. If he'd spoken up two years ago and Rain had agreed, he might have been able to convince his father to let them marry. Now, it was too late. They'd both been bartered away, him for a canal and Rain for her own safety along with that of the household.

"Your thoughts look darker than this cavern," Rain said, following him with the other torch.

Daric stayed watchful and alert as they moved deeper into a tunnel. "Do you have my mother's Ashstone ring with you?" he asked instead of addressing his thoughts. They were indeed dark and dismal.

She shook her head. "I left it at the castle."

"Promise me you'll wear it," he said, taking her free hand and squeezing. "If things don't go as we hope, it'll connect us. We'll remember how we once lived together in the House of Ash."

Rain stopped and swung an iron-hard gaze on him. "Don't give up before we even start."

"I'm not giving up," he hastened to assure her. He would never do that.

"You're giving me an odd look I don't like at all."

"You'll outlive me by far, Rain. Maybe by millennia. It'll be something to remember me by."

A storm flashed in her eyes. He saw it for what it was now. "I'm as mortal as you are."

"Are you though?"

"Yes," she said emphatically.

"Mortals don't grow vines from nothing and make gale winds blow."

Her budding anger abruptly disappeared, and her face fell. "Are you afraid of me?"

"Of course not." The need to wipe away her horrified expression made him pull the first thought from his mind. It was an inane one—inevitably. "Although I would think twice before turning you backside-up for a spanking."

Rain's jaw dropped. Heat billowed inside Daric like an inferno.

She laughed suddenly, the bright sound chiming through the cavern. "A little vulgarity suits you. Suits *us*," she corrected. "It's amusing."

"I strive to never bore you," Daric admitted, his voice

rougher than a rockslide.

The smile on Rain's lips widened, so beautiful it was heart-breaking. She started moving again. "I can safely promise, Daric, that you never bore me."

Every already raw and heightened emotion inside him swelled painfully. Rain was both his joy and his affliction. She was his everything.

CHAPTER EIGHT

RAIN WAS AMAZED. They found the bloodstones in a large chamber at the far end of the first tunnel they'd taken and didn't need to backtrack to try the other—or to explore any of the half dozen offshoots they'd seen. They'd briefly ventured down one transecting pathway because of the dim glow emanating from it and had come across the witch's living quarters. A high-up hole in the rock ceiling let in light and air and let out smoke from the kitchen fire. A long rope ladder hung from above and a clever drainage culvert ran underneath the hole and toward a descending passageway. The rope ladder was an encouraging discovery that relieved them both, although emerging on the clifftop would mean a lengthy walk back to the horses.

Their torches became unnecessary as they approached a wall nearly covered in bloodstones. The red crystals grew from heated fissures in the rock and glowed with a crimson thermo-luminescence.

"The gemstone is aptly named, it seems." Daric swept his gaze around the cavern.

Rain grimaced. "I feel as though the wall will spurt blood if we pull one out."

"There's a gruesome thought," Daric said.

The wall pulsed with heat and light, almost a heartbeat.

"And I agree," he murmured.

"The witch said we wouldn't get one without her, but this wasn't that difficult to find." Rain glanced from side to side, looking for clues. "That makes me nervous."

Daric studied the cavern as well, touching the bloodstone wall with tentative fingers. "Could the gems be cursed?"

Rain groaned at the possibility. She was thoroughly sick of curses.

She doubted that she—Spring—had been cursed, but rather thought a nefarious spell had been cast over Leathen. As far as she knew, she'd forgotten all about Leathen and skipped right over it with her weather from around the time of Daric's birth.

"According to the book you found, the Blood of Braylian is used for breaking curses," Daric said. "Can it also *be* cursed?"

"I don't know. What else could the witch have meant?" Rain asked.

Daric shrugged. "It could have been a bluff. Let's dig one from the rock and find out."

Rain wasn't sure that sorcerers bluffed. At the crone's age, could she even still think clearly enough for that?

Daric took out his dagger and started chipping at the base of a crystal.

Rain hovered near his shoulder. "Daric, be careful. I have a bad feeling about this."

He tossed her a reassuring grin. "Then be prepared to defend me, my lady. I know you're capable."

He could tease, but Rain couldn't smile. Her tongue stung with the acidic taste of worry.

Daric worked at the gem, chiseling and wiggling until it loosened. Slowly, he pulled the glowing crystal from the wall. Rain held her breath. The wall pulsed with inner light and the bloodstone throbbed in return, almost sentient. Daric held it out to her—and the crystal exploded into a monster.

Rain gasped and threw herself back from the towering creature. Daric leaped in front of her. It lunged, and a snap of razor-sharp teeth sent them scrambling in different directions.

"Rain!" Daric rolled under a swiping claw to get back to her.

The monster's furious roar slammed into Rain. Chilled to the bone, she drew her dagger. Demonic eyes rolled in a reptilian head. Its scales were blood-red. She'd never seen anything like it.

Daric swung his knife. It was all he had for a weapon. Rain sent out vines to tangle around the beast's legs. It somehow evaded capture, and her creepers fell to the ground, useless. *How could that happen?*

She blew her strongest gale, but it did nothing. The wind just bounced back at them, whirling around her and Daric.

True helplessness swamped her, dredging up more fear than she'd felt in years. She'd adapted. She'd thrived as a human. She'd even retained some of her magic. Now, she knew dread again—for herself and for Daric.

Rain drew her knife. Her hand trembled, and she gripped it harder. Terror had a distinct flavor. It tasted like waking up from the dark and realizing you were still in a nightmare.

"Run, Rain! I'll hold it off!" Daric's dagger whistled through the air in front of the monster.

And leave him? Never.

"The witch must know how to control it. Find her!" Daric shouted.

She shook her head. The beast would chase them down and rip them to shreds before they'd run ten steps down the tunnel.

"Go!" he cried, sweeping his knife in a wide arc when the monster sprang forward.

Rain stopped and watched, her eyes narrowing. Daric's blade should have swiped the creature's muzzle. His was a long dagger, almost a short sword, and the beast had lunged right at it.

"Did you see that?" She looked harder. "It wavered."

"What? Go!"

There it was again—an odd ripple when the creature moved quickly.

Rain jumped to the left, drawing the monster with her. Daric's shouts turned frantic, but Rain jumped back again almost as swiftly. The beast followed her movement, confirming her suspicion. It had flickered from one position to another and then back again. There was no in between, no solid movement.

"It's not real," she said, her panic subsiding. The ancient-looking monster hadn't touched them, despite the cold murder in its lizard-like eyes and its ferocious jaws snapping at them. It couldn't. "It's an illusion. It's a guardian, not an executioner."

Sure of herself, Rain lunged forward, rolled, and thrust her knife upward just as she landed between the front legs of the deception. Her blade sliced into nothing instead of hitting a scaly breast and muscle. The illusion disappeared from her vision, gone, as though it had never existed. The bloodstone lay on the ground beside her.

Triumphant, she turned to Daric and saw his face turn ashen with grief-stricken panic. Her smile died. *What happened?*

"Rain! Rain!" His eyes wild, his voice raw and terrible, he let out a bloodcurdling howl. He sprang forward, plunging his dagger toward her.

Daric's arm came down like a hammer. Rain threw her weight to the side, but his blade still sliced a burning cut across the back of her shoulder.

"Daric! Stop!" She twisted to look at him.

His hand went slack. His knife clattered to the floor of the cavern, and he stared at her in abject horror. "Rain? My darling, what have I done?" He dropped to his knees beside her. "Your shoulder." His cautious touch was shakier than a dead leaf in autumn.

"It's nothing." The wound throbbed, but that was all. "I'm fine."

"It's bleeding." He flinched, and she knew her pain was his. "You attacked the beast. You rolled right under it. I saw it rip you apart. I saw it kill you." Daric's voice veered toward guttural, and a sheen coated his eyes, turning them glassy in the dimness.

"It was a deception. Trickery." Rain picked up the bloodstone that Daric had dropped and showed him. "I saw through the illusion. And once I proved to myself that the monster wasn't there, it disappeared entirely."

"You mean you weren't *sure*?" he choked out.

Rain shrugged, although it hurt her shoulder. "This *is* a place of sorcery."

"I swung at the beast and felt nothing until I grazed you."

Daric glanced at the bloodstone. "That broke the illusion for me, too?"

Rain nodded.

He swallowed, and the vision of her gruesome death was still there for her to see in his eyes—as well as the fear that he'd hurt her.

She touched his cheek, pressing her hand against the beard that had grown while they traveled. "It's just a scratch, Daric, and now we have what we came for."

The crease between his eyebrows deepened. "I'm sorry."

I love you. "I know," she answered.

Rain's heart turned over heavily, churning with a mix of hope and despair about their future. She stroked his furrowed brow, smoothing a thick lock of hair back from his forehead. She let her fingers slide over one strong cheekbone and then traced the curve of his jaw, rough with whiskers. Her hand moved to his mouth. It was full and soft even though his lips were pressed together. Daric's eyes heated. His lips parted, and his breathing accelerated.

She'd never touched him like this before, the way she'd always wanted to, exploring the textures of his skin and the slopes of his features. The contrasts thrilled her and made her want to touch him everywhere. And to feel him touch her.

Heat spread through Rain. Tension gathered low inside her. Deep down, she ached for things she'd never experienced.

Daric's lids grew heavy. The low, vermillion light turned his blue irises wine-red, and Rain found herself wholly intoxicated. Her pulse beat hard enough to make her unusually aware of it. At her throat. In her thudding veins. Between her legs, where her body called to Daric.

She inched toward him. Daric lowered his head. He brought his arms around her.

A sharp ache flared in Rain's shoulder, and she sucked in a breath. Daric let go immediately.

"I'm sorry." He stepped back and scrubbed a hand over his face so hard it looked like punishment. "Let me tend to your injury."

"That can wait until we're safely away from this place." Rain wished she hadn't made a sound. Daric would have kissed her.

She waited, but he made no move toward her again. Sighing, she turned to the bed of gemstones.

"I think we should take another bloodstone." Letting their future partially hang on just one crystal they could break or lose wasn't an option.

Daric faced the pulsing wall. His mouth flattened. "I don't like it."

"You get the crystal out," Rain insisted. "I'll slay the illusion."

His brows drew together, but he nodded and pried at another stone. "Life would be easier—and possibly safer—if I were capable of denying you anything."

Rain didn't answer. Daric had done a fine job of denying her that kiss in the library.

As soon as Daric freed the gemstone and held it in his hand, it turned into a long, writhing, black-scaled serpent.

Rain jumped, leaping backward. She'd expected the same thing again, or at least something red. The snake struck at her, and she reacted quickly, her breath hammering out in fright as she backhanded the reptile, feeling her hand pass right through what should have been solid fangs and a triangular head. The illusion disappeared, and Daric still held the bloodstone.

"Great Braylian!" She blew out a shaky breath and then laughed a little wildly. "That was still terrifying."

Daric grinned at her, sliding the second crystal into his pouch to join the other. "Remind me never to anger you."

Rain snorted softly. "Remind the sun not to shine."

He arched both brows, looking playfully wounded. "Do I anger you daily, then?"

"No," she admitted. "You're my hero most of the time."

Daric reached out and touched her jaw, tilting her face up. Their eyes met, and Rain stopped breathing.

He stroked her cheek, his deep voice wrapping around her like comfort and a shelter. *Home.* "You're my hero today and every day, Rain. You saw through the first illusion. You got us the bloodstones we needed."

Tears stung Rain's eyes, and she fought them. If she lost Daric to Astraea Nighthall, her heart would break and she'd wither, just like Leathen.

Daric dropped his hand and turned to the exit. "Let's leave this place."

Rain nodded and led the way toward daylight.

CHAPTER NINE

DARIC WAS RELIEVED to finally reach the horses. It was long after sunset, and he gathered what water he could from the abysmal stream at the base of the Heights of Alder while Rain freed the Cave Witch from her green bindings with only a thought. Now, the irate hag spit curses at them from the cavern entrance—though luckily not in a language that could hex them.

They mounted and departed by tacit agreement, despite the darkness and Rain's injured shoulder, riding until they were more than a league away and well out of the witch's purview. The abandoned and near-empty farmhouse they found made a decent shelter. It had three walls and half a roof, in any case.

"It'll be warmer tomorrow," Rain said, sniffing the air.

"Tonight is still frigid." Daric wrapped his extra cloak around her shoulders. They were hours from any town or inn, or he'd have tried to find them better accommodations. That was the thing about sorcerers: they were mysterious, generally unpleasant, and lived in the remotest areas.

He trusted Rain's instincts, though, especially about the weather. They might wake tomorrow to the first real spring day of the season, if one could call it spring with no moisture.

"I need to tend to your shoulder." Daric wished he'd been able to do so long before now. He fetched a rickety milking stool from a gloomy corner and set it near the campfire. "Sit."

Rain looked less than enthusiastic. "It's fine."

Daric wasn't arguing about this. It was happening. "Your blood-encrusted tunic is stuck to the scab, and I'm going to have to cut the material off you. Now sit."

Rain's delicate eyebrows swept up in astonishment. "When did you become so overbearing?"

"Amiability is overrated if it means the people you love die of infection," Daric informed her flatly.

Her mouth puckered as though she might argue, but then she tossed both their cloaks aside and sat, her back to him. "Happy?"

Now, isn't that a complicated question? "Not entirely."

After a moment, Rain sighed. "Me either."

The future returned like a shroud, dark and weighty upon them. It even blocked out the moonlight, forcing Daric to rely solely on the fire he'd built to see what he was doing.

He used his dagger to slice Rain's tunic down the back and then gently peeled the material away from her shoulder. He tried not to let the sight of her naked back distract him, but her pearlescent skin and the subtle curve of her spine were heady reminders that they were alone and she was partially bared to him.

"Daric?" He heard the hesitation in her voice.

"Yes?" It was torture not to touch her.

"Does it look bad? It doesn't need to be sewn, does it?"

He cleared his throat before answering. "No. I just need to clean it."

"Are you unwell?" She frowned at him over her uninjured

shoulder. "You sound hoarse. I hope you haven't caught a chill."

"Believe me," he murmured as he carefully tugged the last bit of tunic loose from the scab. "I'm excessively hot."

Rain slipped her arms free from the sagging tunic but held the ruined garment in front of her. "I'm cold." She shivered when he brushed her hair aside.

"This will warm you." With a stick, Daric reached for the cloth he'd put into boiling water. He let it cool for a moment before wringing out the excess and then gently pressing the steaming material against Rain's injury.

She moaned a little. "That does feel good."

Daric was incapable of responding. He renewed the cloth and finished cleaning her shoulder.

"You're good at this," Rain said. "Do you have experience as a healer that I don't know about?"

"Unfortunately, no. I'm using what I hope is good sense."

"This is one of those moments when you should have reassured me with a small falsehood," she teased.

"I'm reserving my wicked untruth for this."

"For what?" she asked.

Daric uncorked the small flask of spirits he'd brought out of precaution. He never drank the stuff, but he knew how the shrewdest of healers used it to prevent infection. He soaked a clean cloth with the strong-smelling liquid and then took a deep breath, steeling himself.

"This won't hurt at all," he lied, pressing the cloth to the slice across Rain's shoulder.

Rain screeched. Daric winced but held on to her other shoulder to keep her steady. An owl hooted in the distance.

She finally let out a slow breath, relaxing her tense back. Daric removed the cloth. The injury bled only minimally, not flowing but rather forming a new scab.

"It'll be difficult to bind," he said, inspecting the long but shallow cut.

"Just let it dry. I can hardly feel it." Rain gathered the cloaks and arranged them in front of her.

"Turn your back to the fire, then. To warm it," Daric suggested.

Rain nodded and turned. Daric stood beside her in silence.

"You're awfully quiet," she eventually said.

That was because every instinct that railed at him was physical. Hold her. Touch her. Kiss her. Raw desire speared him. He didn't want to talk.

To focus on something other than Rain's bare skin by firelight, Daric began making camp for the night. The horses were already corralled in the farmyard. He laid out bedrolls and blankets. Food was next. He handed Rain bread, cheese, a small pouch of dried fruit, and a little weak tea, brewed right in their cups.

The distraction hardly worked. The need he felt for Rain consumed him. His desire had always been on a tight leash and buried under the truest of friendships. These past days had snapped the leash and unearthed the truth. He wanted her in every way possible. Forever.

But if he made her truly his only to lose her…

He didn't know how he could go on.

He already didn't know how to face a future without her. Everything had changed the moment his father had announced her engagement to Aldo Lockwood. Daric's engagement to Astraea was repugnant, but he'd stupidly believed it would hardly come between Rain and him. Astraea didn't signify in his heart. Rain would have stayed with him. They would have continued as usual.

What an ass he'd been.

"Stop staring at me, Daric."

He blinked and turned away. "Of course." He left to collect more firewood.

THE HEAT IN Daric's eyes could have started a forest fire. Rain took a deep breath. Then another. It took three to settle her racing heart. As soon as he disappeared around the corner, she gently probed her injury to make sure it was dry, pulled on a clean tunic, and then settled her cloak back around her. She returned to her seat by the fire, waiting for Daric, her thoughts in turmoil.

If she'd beckoned to him just then instead of sending him outside, would he have come to her? She wanted him more than anything, and in all ways, but he was right: they weren't free, and duty was a heavy burden.

Before, the obligations had been all Daric's. Now, responsibility was hers as well. She would soon be the last Ash, honor bound by fifteen years of love and obedience to carry on a name that was only hers because the king and queen had declared it.

King Wilder could be heavy-handed, but he was a good man governed by fair principles. He was correct to say that Daric was selfish to want to keep Rain with him when she could have a better life in Parr with Aldo Lockwood. A husband. A kingdom. Safety. Her own children. Kindness and possibly even affection.

But she was also selfish, because she wanted to stay with Daric.

Only the thought of saving their entire household and a contingent of soldiers from losing their livelihoods and positions made her hesitate.

Rain squeezed her eyes shut, trying to block out the feelings that battered her. Life had been much less complicated before emotion played a role in it.

She hardly remembered that time in her existence. It was vague and shapeless, too vast for what she was now, leaving her with only fragments of memories—impressions more than anything—and piddling power she innately knew was laughable compared to the might and ferocity of a season.

Daric eventually returned with enough wood to keep them warm all night. He stacked it near the fire and then sat across from her.

"Why did you name me Rain?" she asked, watching him over the flames that danced between them.

"Why?" He frowned at her. "Do you hate it?"

"Not at all. I think it fits, all things considered."

Some of the new sticks must have been highly resinous or else damp from the patches of snow outside. The campfire popped and hissed before he answered. "At first, everyone kept asking you to make it rain. *Rain. Rain.* They said it over and over, like a chant. Or a supplication." He lowered his gaze and stirred the fire. "It began to sound like a name to me, and you didn't really have one."

"I was Spring," she said.

"That's not truly a name, either."

Rain thought about it. No, it was a *thing*. She'd been an entity, not a person. "I prefer Rain, anyway. It's far prettier."

Daric smiled, but his eyes remained on the fire. Stir. Poke. Why wouldn't he look at her?

"How's your shoulder?" he asked after a while.

"It's not bothering me. You must be a good healer."

"It's all in the inventive use of strong spirits," he said, although his joke sounded halfhearted.

"Better than drinking it," Rain answered. "We might lose our inhibitions."

He finally looked up, his eyes a scorching mix of smoke and fire. Hotter than the blaze between them. "Are you shy around me, Rain?"

A honey-like warmth spread through her. "I find I am more so now than I was only a handful of days ago."

Daric's lips parted. His eyes glittered, and he looked ready to leap across the fire and devour her.

Rain's insides swooped and fluttered. "What's our next move?" she asked, abruptly changing the subject. The direction the conversation was taking wouldn't help either of them. "Mockweed? The Barrow Witch?"

Daric studied her a moment longer, utterly still and concentrated, then he tossed the stick he'd been holding into the fire. "Mockweed grows in the Wood of Layton—in summertime, anyway. Any barrows we have in Leathen are also there, not far from Braylian's Cauldron."

"Then we should go west to Layton," Rain said.

Daric nodded. "And hope we find the Barrow Witch—and that she doesn't curse us." The hot, possessive spark still in his eyes made her belly twist with something raw and carnal and overshadowed his attempt at dry humor.

"What will you do?" Her voice grew husky, some inner beast roaring at her to move the ground and sky to keep Daric. "If we succeed in breaking the curse on Leathen?"

"What will I do?" He smiled a little, just the edges of his mouth curling up as his blue gaze brushed over her, soft but heavy like velvet. Then need sharpened his features, and Rain shivered before he even answered. "If you're willing, I'll kiss you until you can't breathe, learn you inside and out, and make you mine forever."

CHAPTER TEN

R AIN WAS A tightly wound-up ball of nerves and desire by the time they reached the Wood of Layton. Prolonged time alone with Daric was wreaking havoc on her body. How was it possible to physically ache for something she'd never known? Intense sensations leaped inside her like cloud-to-cloud lightning, shooting bolts of heat and longing through her with nothing to ground them.

The sacred forest creaked and groaned as usual, matching her stiffness after too many days on Arjun as well as her brittle mood. Daric showed signs of irritability also, and they snapped at each other occasionally only to converse easily again moments later.

Their new dynamic felt more natural than the courteous and always careful way they'd always interacted. That had been real, too, but with a varnish that had kept them shiny and bright in each other's eyes. She preferred the Daric she saw every day, all day—the Daric difficult circumstances and this journey had revealed. He was still everything she wanted, but Rain had discovered sharp edges that made him even more appealing. And when Daric looked at her now, his jaw often set at a hard angle and his penetrating gaze not hiding the force of his desire, Rain could barely catch her breath and wanted only one thing:

for him to touch her.

"We're deep enough into the woods to find some mock-weed now. You know what it looks like, right?" Daric asked.

He glanced at her, but his eyes didn't linger. They were sweeping the forest for threats. Many of Leathen's wild animals had retreated to the Wood of Layton over the years of drought, and even the well-trod paths had turned dangerous.

Rain nodded, shaking off her daydreams—although anxious and alert felt like poor replacements. "It grows low to the ground and has puffy yellow flowers that make me sneeze in summer. But we'll only find last year's dead plants. It hasn't bloomed again yet."

Despite the curse, things *did* grow in Leathen. Three seasons provided their habitual weather, and plants and forests and farms hung on, surviving in the way of the gradually starving.

"The flowers are seasonal, but the leaves don't wither. The rest of the plant winters over."

Rain was surprised. Who knew Daric was such a botanist? "Do you suppose it will matter if there's no flower?" she asked.

"Your disappearing sorcerer said mockweed not mockweed *flower*," Daric said with a shrug.

Rain frowned, trying to recall exactly. "He didn't have time to elaborate. Two guards had him, and Soren was snarling."

Daric's gaze swung around sharply. "Did Soren follow you?"

She shook her head. "He said he was on an errand."

Brittleness crept into Daric's expression. "He's in love with you."

"Soren?" Rain tried to muster up some shock, but deep down, she knew that already. The only real surprise was that

Daric had mentioned it. "Does that bother you?"

"It does if he goes with you to Parr," Daric bit out.

"If I go to Parr, I'll be married to Aldo, and I would never be unfaithful."

A dark laugh escaped Daric. "Aldo will be dead soon, and Soren still has years of vigor in him."

Rain tried to let what he was implying slide right off her, but she couldn't entirely. It stuck. Soren wasn't the man she wanted, but he wouldn't be a terrible alternative if Daric were truly lost to her. "If you're forced to marry Astraea, would you be unfaithful to her?"

Daric's eyes flared with barely suppressed anger and enough need to make her blood run hot. "In a heartbeat—if I have you to comfort me."

His words shot like an arrow to the space between her legs. Rain's muscles clenched. Before she lost her courage, she notched up her chin and asked, "What's to stop us from starting now?" She knew she *should* go to Aldo a virgin, but she didn't always do as she ought.

Daric's face turned blank with shock, then his color heightened significantly. He stared at her, and Rain waited for his answer, her heart banging against her ribs.

DARIC THOUGHT HE might die of heat and want and frustration and fury. *What's to stop us from starting now?* She acted as though that were a simple question.

Rain wasn't asking for a kiss anymore, although a kiss

wouldn't have been anything close to simple between them, either. She was asking to start something much bigger, much more consuming, and with consequences that stretched from one edge of the continent to the other.

In a voice gone thick and hoarse, Daric finally managed to answer. "I can find a way to go forward, Rain. But I could never go back."

Rain visibly swallowed. She nodded and turned back to the path, her fingers tensing on Arjun's reins until they whitened.

Before Daric could think of a more neutral topic to distract them both back to better spirits, a stiff breeze began to blow, making his mount, Wylar, dance and quiver. The wind didn't abate, turning colder and more violent and forcing them to tug their cloaks firmly closed and pull up their hoods for protection.

"The weather is fickle," Daric said. "This morning was pleasant."

"We're subjected to whatever's strongest around us," Rain answered. "If the north wind blows hard, we get the colder, more volatile air from Raana. If the weather to the south is powerful and enduring, we get whatever comes up from Parr."

As usual, Spring didn't even know Leathen was there, leaving an empty hole to fill with whatever pushed the hardest.

Daric glanced at the cloudless sky. The wind whistled a dismal song through the leafless branches. "Do you remember that darkness? That void where Leathen should have been?"

"Vaguely," Rain said, hunching inward. "I don't know why Braylian let it happen. She's there, all-knowing. The seasons... We couldn't confer with one another or compare knowledge of the continent. I didn't have a voice, or even know words, until I decided to speak to you, and while one daughter is active, the other three are dormant."

Daric fell silent, an unpleasant twinge stabbing at him. It was guilt, but not regret, exactly. The combination chafed. He couldn't be happy he'd altered Rain's existence so drastically, but he also wouldn't change what had happened.

Now, he might lose her anyway. The thought hollowed him out and left him empty.

Daric leaned over and gripped Arjun's reins when a gust of wind upset the horse. "Should we stop and find shelter?" he asked, having to raise his voice above the gale that was only worsening.

Rain nodded, and Daric dismounted. He led both horses toward a rocky outcropping that would at least block the wind that was howling down the path straight at them.

That howling? Daric frowned. *Was it only the wind?*

Rain's head snapped up. "Hallerhounds!" Her eyes widened.

Daric started to jog, leading them faster toward the minimal shelter he'd spotted. At least they'd have one less side to protect from wild animals.

The howling grew louder, as did the sound of heavy paws crashing through the forest.

"Hurry, Daric!" Still astride Arjun, Rain drew her bow and nocked an arrow.

Daric raced through the undergrowth with Rain and the two horses. He swung their mounts around at the rock formation, crowding the frightened animals against it. "How many? Can you see?" he asked as Rain dismounted.

"Nine. Maybe ten." Her bow in hand, she placed herself in

front of Arjun and Wylar. Daric did the same, drawing his sword and dagger.

The outcropping blocked the worst of the wind, but it still whipped and tore at them. They stood together, Rain already narrowing her eyes down the length of an arrow. Daric didn't do anything asinine such as demand that Rain get behind him. They were days beyond that. He was glad Rain was done pretending to be less than she could be.

The pack of huge, dog-like creatures approached and surrounded them on three sides, their razor-sharp claws clicking on the roots and rocks of the forest. The animals inched nearer, their ruffs rising. Rain released an arrow, bringing down the one closest to her, and chaos erupted.

A hallerhound leaped at them. Daric swung hard enough to nearly cleave the beast in half, his every instinct sharpening into one fierce thought: protect the woman next to him. With a twang of her bow, Rain felled another. Daric swung again, severing a jugular. Blood sprayed, its coppery tang a bitter perfume in the air around them. Whimpers, snarls, and growls mixed with his own grunts, pounding breath, and hammering heartbeat. Utterly calm and silent beside him, Rain loosed another arrow. In this storm, she was the eye and he was the maelstrom. With a snarl to rival the hallerhounds' growls, Daric focused on the next threat, his sword arm a blur and his knife at the ready.

The animal onslaught was brutal and continuous, but they fought back with equal ferocity. Rain lashed out with a vine, knocking a massive creature off balance. Daric lunged forward and skewered it with his dagger. Rain let fly another arrow.

Shoulder to shoulder, they guarded their horses—and each other.

At last, only two hounds remained, crouched low and baring their teeth, but now hesitant. Rain incapacitated one with a rope of greenery that tied its legs together. It collapsed, jerking and twisting in a violent effort to break free. It was no use and the animal surrendered, its flanks heaving.

That left a single adversary. Daric sliced his bloody sword through the air with whistling menace. The final beast's ears flattened. It hugged the ground, cowering.

With a beckoning yip toward its immobilized companion, the last hound ran away. Rain slowly unraveled the vine from the hallerhound on the ground, her expression so hard and deadly that the animal knew exactly who ruled the forest.

The creature scrambled upright and bounded after its fleeing packmate, disappearing into the woods in near silence.

CHAPTER ELEVEN

THE FEROCIOUS WIND finally calmed enough for them to leave the shelter of the rocky outcropping and head toward more substantial shelter. Shadows stretched longer, creeping in with the chill of evening. The forest grew dimmer, its habitual creaking keeping Rain on edge as she and Daric made their way to the nearest treehouse.

Hallerhounds had terrorized people for centuries. Long ago, generations before Daric, the House of Ash had built elevated shelters throughout the Wood of Layton. The regularly placed treehouses protected the royals and their entourages from animal attacks at night during their pilgrimages to Braylian's Cauldron. The mostly unfurnished rooms saw no regular upkeep and were often home to small creatures, but they were always stocked with blankets and oil lamps, and there would be a nearby enclosure for the horses.

It wasn't the thought of more hallerhounds that scared Rain right now, however. Each time she used her power, with every new vine she created, *Isme dolunde vaten crew* dug into her mind a little deeper. She'd already feared its roots were poisonous, but as she and Daric rode toward the treehouse that would be their last stopover before Leathen's barrows and Braylian's Cauldron, she finally understood what the combination of sounds truly meant—and how just four small words would destroy them.

The sorcerer in Upper Ash had given her the final ingredient to break the curse on Leathen, but it wasn't a simple offering they had to make, as she'd originally suspected. It was a sacrifice. And whoever spoke the words to Braylian both gained exactly what they wanted, and lost what mattered most.

"What's turned you so silent?" Daric asked as they approached the treehouse.

These past few nights in the sacred wood, they'd had somewhere more comfortable than the ground to sleep and more than a campfire to drive back the darkness. But they'd stayed in separate rooms, across a massive tree trunk from each other. Tonight, their last night before this quest likely ended, Rain would make sure they slept together.

"I've just realized something." She turned to Daric, his beloved features harder to look at suddenly. They burned through her, searing a scar across her heart. Winter-blue eyes, strong jaw, thick dark hair, that heavy lock always tumbling over one eyebrow. The way he looked at her... Rain dropped her gaze, trying to hide her sorrow.

"Mockweed." She grew a plant in the palm of her hand. "No need to go searching."

Daric grinned. "You never cease to amaze me."

She handed him the flower, not letting her return smile waver. "Keep it with the bloodstones. Tomorrow, we'll find the Barrow Witch and break the curse together."

"It seems rather simple in the end, after all these years of doing nothing."

"Not nothing, Daric. Everything we could. And we only just

received the clues pointing us in the right direction." Rain forced now dreaded words around the rising lump in her throat. "There's one more thing. A chant. I heard it from the sorcerer."

Daric's brow furrowed. "In Upper Ash?"

She nodded. "I kept it to myself because I didn't understand it."

"And now you do? How? What is it?"

Rain saw the confusion in his expression—and the hurt that she'd once again held back from him. *"Isme dolunde vaten crew."* Her heart ached, pounding. "The more I use my power, the more I understand the language of sorcery."

Daric's frown deepened. "What does it mean?"

"It's simply to formally present the bloodstones and the mockweed to Braylian." The lie rose up in Rain and fell from her tongue like acid. "Harmless, but we need it along with the other things when we ask her to break the enchantment."

Daric tucked the plant she'd given him into his pouch, seeming less worried after her explanation. "Not sure why a goddess wants a weed, but magic is a strange business."

"It is," Rain agreed. One that was tearing her apart, even as it made her stronger. "We'll find the Barrow Witch. She'll help us. You'll say those four words tomorrow, Daric, and break the curse on Leathen. You've been working toward this your whole life."

He nodded, repeating those raw and awful magical words back to her. He knew them now and could utter them without trouble.

A shadow crossed his features again as he watched her. "You look too somber for this happy news. We're almost there, Rain.

We've almost done it."

Somber didn't even begin to describe how she felt. Understanding the sorcerer's words had opened a chasm inside her and set her adrift. But Leathen would survive without her. The kingdom couldn't survive without its prince.

That conviction calmed her, left her resolute and sure of herself. "I want you to know that I would never, ever, have shown myself to you that day at the Cauldron if I hadn't wanted to," Rain said.

Daric shrugged a little stiffly. "But you didn't want this." He waved a hand in the air, seeming to encompass him, her, Leathen... Everything.

She thought back to that Time Before. *Want* hadn't been a concept for a season, as far as she could recall. What a boring existence it must have been, with no one to talk to, nothing to discover, no desires or needs, no fears or pleasures.

"The first time I remember wanting *anything*," she told him in a voice thick with emotion, "was the day I saw you."

Daric looked at her gravely. He reached out, feathered his fingers across her cheek, and tucked her hair back. "You're my every dream and desire."

Rain's heart swelled to near bursting. She was done waiting. Done hoping. Done playing by Daric's rules, because his weren't the only ones that mattered. "Tomorrow, we save Leathen, but tonight is ours."

His eyes turned wary—and burning. "Raindrop?"

"You secure the horses." Rain slid from her saddle in front of the treehouse. "I'll light the lamps in the room we're sharing."

WHEN DARIC ENTERED the room she'd chosen for the night, Rain had an almost worrying glint in her eyes and wore an expression that barely sidestepped aggressive.

She held out her hand to him. Daric took it, and she tugged him closer.

Her silver hair was down, cascading around her shoulders like a river. She'd even removed the starflower, which she'd worn every day and night of their journey. Her eyes flicked up, meeting his, and they were like dusk, both dark blue and on fire. A knot tightened in his chest. He loved her more than anything.

She unclasped his cloak and began loosening the laces of his tunic.

"Rain?" Daric's mouth went dry, and his voice croaked like a lad's. He ached from the need to touch her.

"I'm counting on you to guide us, Daric. I mean... I understand the basics."

His pulse pounded, heavy with desire. There were four walls. A bed. Privacy, even from the stars above them. And Rain was making herself perfectly clear.

He couldn't resist smoothing his hands into her hair and weaving the silken strands between his fingers. "We have to break the curse first. We'll be each other's reward for saving Leathen."

"Right now, Daric, I need you more than Leathen does."

A wild burst of heat tore through him. He struggled against raw craving but felt his control slipping when Rain plucked at the laces of her tunic. The front gaped, revealing pale skin and the upper swells of her breasts, round and perfect.

Daric stared, mesmerized. He was two ragged breaths from undressing her entirely. His hands slipped to her shoulders, half pushing the material off, half trying to keep it on her.

"There could be consequences." Daric's hands flexed on her shoulders. "And if we fail, I'll have to marry Astraea." He already loathed the idea. Now, he could hardly contemplate it.

Rain stepped back and took off her clothing piece by piece until she stood naked before him. She was exquisite, so unbearably tempting. She was everything he'd dreamed about and more. If anything, her skin was smoother and her body more made for worshipping than he'd even imagined. The sight of her before him like this would haunt him forever if they were forced to live out their lives separately.

But then, as she backed right up against the bed she'd prepared for them, she made him a promise. "You won't marry her. I won't let that happen. Tomorrow, this ends forever."

She was the most glorious being he'd ever laid eyes on, powerful in ways he knew he'd never truly understand, and when she vowed with such absolute certainty that he wouldn't have to marry Astraea, Daric believed her. And it freed him.

His control evaporated. Rain was his. She always had been. Just as he was hers and would be forever.

Daric stripped off his clothing, and the way Rain looked at him made him believe he might almost be worthy of the goddess before him. "I love you more than all the magic and might in Braylian's Cauldron."

A shiver rippled over Rain, making her skin pebble with goose bumps and her nipples harden. "There's nothing I wouldn't do for you." Her eyes glistened with unshed tears, and Daric believed that promise also.

He would do everything in his power to deserve her and the love she offered. He hadn't kissed Rain before for fear of losing his mind to wanting her, but he couldn't deny her—or himself— any longer. His devotion had always been there, laid out at her feet. Now, he couldn't wait to spend the rest of his life proving how wholly his heart belonged to her.

Daric reached for her, that first touch of naked skin scalding and wonderful. His heartbeat accelerated. Rain wasn't ignorant, even in sexual matters, but she had no experience. He knew he needed to be gentle and go slowly. Daric had little experience himself. He'd had exactly one encounter and had spent the entire time fantasizing about Rain, which had left him with a hollow feeling that lingered. Trying again had seemed pointless. Rain was the only woman he wanted.

Daric dipped his head and kissed her neck and shoulder. He trailed his mouth toward her jaw, soft as a feather. Her pulse fluttered, and she gripped his arms, drawing him closer. Her short, quick breaths warmed his skin, and then their lips met for the first time ever.

His blood ignited. With a deep rumble, Daric hauled her against him. Rain moaned into his mouth, her body scorching. She wrapped her arms around his neck and claimed him back, that first crush of lips hard, frantic, and intense enough to set alight the treehouse. Heat surged through him, stealing his breath, stiffening his cock, and setting his heart to pounding.

She broke away with a gasp. Both their chests heaved. Their eyes met, and Rain's gaze was hot enough to sear him to the bone and leave him in ashes. Daric swept her into his arms and laid her on the bed. She reached for him, and he stretched out beside her, pouring a lifetime of passion into every kiss and an eternity of want into the reverent way he touched her. Rain rolled toward him, nestling inward, and kissed him back with a fever that made him delirious. Daric rocked against her. A harsh breath groaned out of him. She was soft and smooth and hot as a bonfire.

"I've dreamed of this so often," he murmured between deep, soul-altering kisses.

"I feel you pulsing against my belly," she whispered.

"I want you so much, I hurt."

Rain lifted her hips, pressing into him. "I want to help."

"You are." He kissed her. He wanted to kiss her a thousand times for every beat of his heart. "You're the ache and the cure."

Daric bent his head and nuzzled her breasts. His hands skimmed her ribs. Rain shuddered, breathing faster. Already drunk on the taste of her, Daric took her nipple into his mouth and gently sucked. She groaned, arching against him and tilting her head back, her hair like a cloud around them.

Sensation rushed down his spine and flooded his groin. Everything tightened. His heart hammered and Daric pulled back, his jaw clenching. He let out a slow, shuddering breath and moved his hand down Rain's body. He needed to bring her pleasure now, because he had no illusions about how long he would last once she was beneath him.

CHAPTER TWELVE

RAIN STOPPED MOVING and held her breath when Daric's hand drifted between her legs and he touched her where they would soon connect. She knew the basics about coupling. She'd seen animals mate—dogs and horses didn't care about privacy—and she'd seen servants kissing when they thought no one was looking. She hadn't known, though, that a man stroked a woman like he was playing an instrument, and that it was fantastic.

Rain gasped and quivered at his light, exploring touches and then moaned and sought firmer contact when his fingers turned bolder and more adept. Heat coursed through her body, increasing with every kiss and caress. She ground against his hand, tension gathering like a whirlwind inside her.

A deep groan resonated in Daric's chest. His tongue tangled with hers, and Rain thought she might fly apart under the mounting pressure. Every movement they made was instinctual. She knew the steps without thinking. It was the hottest, wildest dance of her existence, and she wanted it to last forever.

Daric stroked her inside and out and then slipped and slid his fingers over a spot that made bright bolts of pleasure arc through her like lightning.

"Am I doing this right?" he asked, sipping kisses from her lips and drinking her breath in.

Rain arched off the bed, clutching his shoulders. "Yes! Don't stop!"

He kept going, and Rain shattered apart. Her cry was silent, or perhaps deafening. She tensed as a breathtaking climax pulsed through her in waves and then sank into the bedding, boneless and floating.

Daric moved over her, and she felt his hard tip gently prod her opening. She tilted toward him. Daric closed his eyes, and when he opened them again, they were as dark as the night sky and stark with intensity.

He brushed a warm, coaxing hand down her body before guiding her knees higher around him. In a strained whisper, he rasped, "Steady, darling. This may not be comfortable."

Rain nodded. "I know it's only the first time, and only for a moment." She was well aware of rumors concerning lovemaking, especially for virgins, but so far, everything she'd heard had underrated the act tremendously.

Daric's expression held a wealth of tenderness and the promise of scorching encounters for years to come. Rain wanted nothing more. Her prince. A lifetime together. Children. Love. If only that were possible.

She blocked those thoughts, refusing to give them power. Their future heartbreak had no place here—not when Daric was slowly pushing inside her. Sensations rioted through her, some pleasant, some not. She inhaled deeply, trying to relax. She wasn't afraid, but her muscles stayed taut.

Daric took her head in his hands, holding her steady. As he looked down at her, the discomfort gradually faded.

Rain gave him an encouraging smile. "I'm fine, Daric. It's all right."

"This won't last long." He kissed her before he started moving. "Next time, I'll do better."

Rain nodded. She understood, and she was ready.

Daric's measured movements quickly became unsteady. He thrust faster, harder, and then he shuddered. He groaned her name as he stiffened all over, the sound seeming to tear straight from the center of his body.

Rain clung to him, so close she could feel the heavy thud of his heartbeat. They stayed joined, Daric surrounding her. Their lips brushed and pressed, and she wrapped herself around him, as elated as she was devastated. She wanted to remember the feel of him. His weight. The love in his eyes. The way he kissed and touched her. Memories to take on a journey into eternity.

"Again," she murmured, her voice nearly breaking.

Daric gazed down at her, already hardening once more inside her. Locking eyes with her, he began moving, and what started as gentle worshipping slowly turned into fierce possession—and both were exactly what she needed.

CHAPTER THIRTEEN

ARIC AWOKE EUPHORIC after his night with Rain. Everything was finally coming together. Everything he wanted and needed was within reach. Even the Barrow Witch was as easy to find as they'd hoped. She was their age, not at all insane yet, and willing to help. In fact, the slender woman with rosy cheeks and dark hair had been waiting for them. She'd studied magic under the sorcerer who'd found Rain in Upper Ash. Together, the two of them had discovered the way to break the curse.

The witch invited them inside her home—one of the large earthen mounds dotting the forest not far from Braylian's Cauldron—and as he and Rain took a seat at the Barrow Witch's table, Daric wondered if Rain would eventually suffer the dire consequences of using magic. She'd never mentioned it and didn't seem worried, but she'd also hidden her power from him until now. He'd guessed at it without ever guessing the *extent* of it. Now that he knew, thoughts of the illness of the mind that ultimately plagued all sorcerers haunted him.

Daric glanced at Rain as she described their journey to the witch, who listened with avid interest. Rain's magic didn't require chants and ingredients. It was simply a part of her. He hoped that would make a difference.

While Rain spoke, Daric laid out the pieces they'd gathered. The mockweed was withering but still hearty enough, and the bloodstones glinted dully in the weak light filtering in through the open doorway of the barrow. The witch's home was tidy, if austere. And, he imagined, very cold in winter. He saw no remnants of the ancient culture that had built these mounds as burial grounds, either time or the witch having swept the barrow clean of the bones and ghosts that had once occupied it.

"I'm glad you listened to my mentor and came to me," the Barrow Witch said. "Most people would have shunned him. You did not, and for that, we can all be grateful."

"We have everything your teacher mentioned," Daric said. "You're the final piece of this puzzle."

She reached out and reverently touched the gems they'd brought. "Bloodstones. The curse is strong, but the Blood of Braylian is stronger. And you have two crystals, which is impressive." She gave them an assessing look, as though she might know what the Cave Witch had put them through with her enchantment.

"And the mockweed?" Rain asked. "We don't know its purpose."

"Mockweed, when combined with other curse-breaking elements, reveals the face of the person who cast the spell to begin with." She turned to Daric. "You'll finally know who cursed you."

"Me?" He frowned. "Leathen was cursed, so that spring wouldn't come here."

"In this case, you and Leathen are synonymous. But no—you were cursed as an infant. I can see it in your aura."

Daric's initial confusion swiftly turned to rage. He knew who'd visited Leathen shortly after his birth, a cold queen who'd looked upon his cradle with her snake-like smile in place as she'd struck.

"Illanna Nighthall did this." His fists clenched in fury. "And then she slowly drained Leathen of riches and resources until its coffers were as dried up as the soil, and we had no choice. The marriage..." He looked at Rain, seeing his own horror reflected in her eyes.

"Astraea is only six months older than you are." Rain's face leached of color. Even her lips looked bloodless. "Her mother planned this from the start!"

"Who else? She choked us in exchange for water and bread. Bought our orin mines. Took our wealth. And when we had no other options left, she arranged for a marriage that would give her grandchildren two kingdoms with only the Nighthall name attached." Daric let out a bitter laugh. "I will punish Raana for this."

Rain laid a cool hand over his and squeezed. "First, Daric, let's break the curse."

The touch of her hand returned his focus. Break the curse. Marry Rain. Give Illanna Nighthall what she deserved.

"Tell us what to do," he said to the witch, steel in his voice. Soon, Raana would feel his blade.

"We take the bloodstones and the mockweed to Braylian's Cauldron and lay them on the stone circle like this." The witch arranged the pieces on the table to demonstrate, facing the sharp tips of the bloodstones out and placing the mockweed across them. "But sixteen stones make up the great, curving border of the Cauldron. They each serve a different purpose, and the purpose rotates among them. The stone needed for breaking curses two moons ago might not be the same one needed today. I'll have to perform a difficult ritual to reveal the stone currently tied to maledictions."

Daric nodded. "I'll reward you for your efforts."

The Barrow Witch smiled vaguely. "I'm tied to the ground under which I live. I do this for Leathen."

Daric acknowledged her words but still planned on making her underground home more comfortable if he could.

"And when everything is set up correctly, we explain the enchantment to Braylian and ask her to break it?" Rain asked.

"It's almost that simple." The witch's gaze moved back and forth between them. Her eyes were the color of grass and soil—and seemed suddenly haunted. "If Braylian hears you, fire will erupt from the Cauldron. Then you must speak the words, the ones to—"

"We know them," Rain interrupted. "We know the phrase to accompany our offering."

Daric looked at her oddly. She was usually too polite to interrupt anyone, but he'd seen how the language of sorcery chafed her. Rain shivered, and Daric tucked her against his side, wanting to comfort her.

The Barrow Witch watched them, her expression inscrutable, or perhaps a little sad, and Daric began to suspect he was on the outside of something he needed to be a part of. He couldn't be sure. His thoughts still boiled angrily at Illanna Nighthall, and wrath possibly clouded his judgment.

The witch shifted her gaze to the open doorway and the

forest beyond. "Who'll say it, then? Who will present the offering?"

Rain clamped her mouth shut and looked at him.

"*Isme dolunde vaten crew.*" Daric murmured the words she'd taught him yesterday so that Rain wouldn't have to say them. His mouth puckered. "Is it supposed to taste this sour?"

"All magic tastes rotten," the witch answered. "That's why it eventually rots *you*."

Daric had no intention of becoming a sorcerer or succumbing to their curse—and he wanted to know Rain's opinion on the strange words.

"Rain?" he prompted.

"Yes." She glanced away from him. "They taste foul to me as well."

RAIN HAD LIVED her last day as human, and she had no idea what Braylian might do with her next. Her one regret, the dread making her heart twist and jerk, was losing Daric. But she'd loved him in every way possible—and been loved in return. Could a woman ask for more, or better than that?

She'd known joy, fear, excitement, sadness, affection, desire. Rain was complete, just not anywhere near ready for this life to be over.

And Daric... How would he fare? He had so much passion in him that it could easily turn to rage and despair.

Braylian's Cauldron was no strange place to her. She'd lived in it once. She'd also paid homage to the great goddess from outside it, watching elements erupt from the circle as she'd prayed alongside her adoptive family. The people of Leathen came here to worship, in awe and fear and hope and hardship. She'd been no different from them these past fifteen years, no different from anyone else asking for Braylian's blessing.

It was a calm day, both for the weather and for the Cauldron. Rain and Daric hung back while the Barrow Witch performed her mysterious task of discovering which of the stones making up the wide circle held the key to breaking curses. Daric had the objects they needed, and Rain stood beside him, wishing they could have had another night together, just the two of them, tangled and touching and loving each other more than anything.

The witch finally backed away from the Cauldron, pointing an unsteady finger at a stone that suddenly pulsed with darkness. "There." Her voice was reed-thin and exhausted. She stumbled over to a large tree and sat, slumping almost lifelessly against it. As they watched, her skin turned ashen, and she seemed to age a decade. Gray streaks now patterned her hair, and Rain knew without a doubt that the witch had sacrificed more than they'd ever intended.

Perhaps she'd known what this day would cost her, just as Rain did, and had accepted her role anyway.

Visibly worried about the witch's condition, Daric took off his cloak and tucked it around her. She didn't stir, clearly depleted by her long and strenuous ritual.

Rain and Daric approached the Cauldron together. When they reached the stone they needed, she turned to him and lovingly touched his face. "A kiss," she whispered, her heart splintering. "For luck."

Daric gently drew her closer. His lips brushed hers and Rain clung to him, sealing their mouths together. The kiss turned deeper, a little frantic, and she feared her desperation had begun to show. She was deceiving him, and he might never forgive her. But springtime would come to Leathen again. Daric wouldn't marry Astraea. He would punish Raana and make Leathen the most powerful kingdom on the continent again.

Daric pulled back too soon, his eyes glittering with a mix of desire and determination. "Will you marry me, Rain? The moment we return to Ash?" He kissed her again, quick and hard this time. "Please say you'll be with me—always."

Instead of euphoria, nausea churned inside her. She chose her words carefully. "Nothing would make me happier than being with you forever. I love you, Daric."

Smiling, he tucked her hair back. "I love you, too, my silver raindrop."

Tears burned in Rain's throat. In a flash of memory, Daric was young again, calling desperately into the Cauldron. It had been impossible not to go to him then, just as it was impossible not to help him now.

Daric bent and laid out the bloodstones and the mockweed as the Barrow Witch had instructed. He straightened and gripped Rain's hand, bringing her fingertips to his mouth and kissing them. "And now it ends," he said.

She pressed her lips together to prevent her breath from shuddering out. Then she nodded. "Talk to Braylian. Explain the curse."

Facing the Cauldron, Daric called out to Braylian. Years ago,

Braylian hadn't heard him—or else had ignored his pleas. She, Spring, had left her seasonal wanderings and come instead, seeing nothing but a handsome young prince amidst a strange and impenetrable darkness. He'd shone so brightly that she couldn't resist.

Now, Daric once again explained the curse, told of the crippling drought, and begged for springtime to return to Leathen.

When he finished talking, fire erupted from the previously quiet Cauldron. It shot high, a ferocious and roaring inferno reaching for the sky with angry fingers. In all their years coming to the Cauldron with supplications and apparently useless offerings, Rain had never seen anything like it. This time, Braylian had heard them.

Daric's eyes met hers, his bright with triumph and the reflection of the blaze before them. Rain lifted her chin and smiled in encouragement. She would leave him with bravery as well as sorrow. "Say the words. End the curse, Daric."

"*Isme dolunde vaten crew*," Daric called out solidly, his voice carrying above the firestorm in the Cauldron.

I sacrifice that which I love most. The bloodstones were to get the goddess's attention, the mockweed to reveal the source of the curse, and the words in the language of sorcery... They offered an exchange of sorts. Daric was asking for something, which meant he had to give something up. And not just anything—the thing he loved above all else. Rain had no doubt it was her, which was both a comfort to her breaking heart and a dagger straight through it.

A great force pulled at her, ripping her from Daric. Rain screamed. It was too soon! Now that it was upon her, she wasn't ready—not for this end, not for Daric's desperate yell, and certainly not for the terror in his cry when the fire seized and engulfed her.

Energy exploded through Rain, transformative and fracturing. All sound from her lips stopped. She lost form and features. Everything she'd been since the moment she'd decided to look like a human girl, so she could dance with a human boy, disappeared in fragments. She rose toward the sky in a great ripple of power, but even as she soared once again as she had before, something of the person she'd become remained, clinging to an essence that now stretched far and wide across the continent. That part of her belonged to Daric. It still beat like a human heart, steady and strong. The rest of her was Spring.

Above Leathen, Rain gathered herself into a low, churning cloud pregnant with water. *How many times can a heart break? For how long?* She unleashed her tears, and they were the first spring showers the kingdom had seen in Daric's lifetime.

Braylian had taken her back. She was enduring again. Timeless. A season like three others. But she'd forgotten nothing. Rain wept, watering Leathen with a heavy, miserable, persistent downpour that splattered the ground below her.

In the sacred clearing, Daric turned his face up to the raindrops and howled like a dying animal.

She rained harder. Thunder was her only way to scream, so she split the sky with bolts of lightning and their tremendous cracks cried back at him.

Their hearts broke together. Hers would break over and over, and until the end of days was a terrifyingly long stretch of forever.

CHAPTER FOURTEEN

D ARIC STOOD BEFORE the Cauldron. The final day of spring was almost over. Four years had passed since he and Rain broke the curse, and he was once again back at the stone circle. He'd built another shelter. As usual, Braylian would blow it down the moment he left the clearing for longer than a few hours. He did get called away. He wasn't fully free to live as a savage and ignore his name and kingdom, but when he could, he made his home next to the Cauldron. It brought him closer to Rain.

Everything had changed that day, especially him. Glittering parties and cozy family evenings now graced the House of Ash again—and sickened him more than anything. He'd done his duty and would do his duty in the future. For now, his parents were healthy and ruled wisely. When that was no longer the case, he would take their place. The only thing he wouldn't do was produce an heir for Leathen.

The mockweed had indeed revealed Illanna Nighthall's treacherous face, although he'd barely seen it through his tears and misery. When Daric had finally brought himself to leave the clearing and the Cauldron—*to leave Rain*—he'd focused and honed his anger and desperation until it was as sharp as a blade, and then he'd stabbed Raana.

The remainder of that first spring, with his heart wrecked and his spirit in agony, he'd plotted and struck, driving his army halfway to Nighthall with a gale and a tempest leading each attack. That summer, he'd secured Raana's lake district for Leathen and taken back every single orin mine his father had relinquished. By autumn, Illanna's struggling army had retreated to the capital city, and by winter, he'd defeated her last battalion. He took Nighthall on a frozen afternoon and plunged a cold dagger into the chest of the wicked Queen of Raana. A knife through her heart for the knife through his.

He hadn't turned his blade on Astraea, despite the temptation and his brokenhearted fury. She knew he could, though, and she'd sheathed her claws in the interest of not dying. He had a contingent of guards watching her in her gloomy, inhospitable castle, making sure she didn't touch sorcery, although he didn't think she had her mother's predilection for it. Astraea was cruel but not clever—and now lived as a prisoner in a land he'd conquered.

By the following spring, the second without Rain, Daric was no longer considered pleasant, fun, and easy-mannered. His people started calling him the Hallerhound Prince, and not only because of the way he bayed his misery into the Cauldron. He sought solitude and snapped and snarled at anyone who came near him. His kingdom was secure, largely expanded, and headed toward unparalleled prosperity, so he prowled the Wood of Layton, alone with his memories.

Each year since he'd given the bloodstones, the mockweed, and his precious Rain to Braylian, Spring had watered Leathen until the rivers nearly overflowed and farmers had to scramble between storms to do their planting. Rain wept her unhappiness for three moons, nearly drowning the kingdom. Then she slept while Summer brought them plentiful crops. She slumbered through Autumn's crisp days and bountiful harvests. She slept while Winter allowed his people to rest once again in happy plenitude before crackling hearth fires—satisfaction and comforts that Daric refused for himself. He chose to winter among the beasts and blizzards of Layton.

He'd considered punishing the Barrow Witch for allowing Rain's deception, but helping them end the drought had hastened her fall into insanity. She'd used so much sorcery that day to locate the curse stone that her decline had started early and struck her like a thunderbolt. Now, Daric hunted for her when he was in the forest, and she cackled and cawed and lived like a wild bird, hopping in and out of her barrow.

He was sorry for her. They'd all lost more than they'd imagined that day. The gain had never once outweighed his heartbreak.

Rain's next sleep was almost upon them. Daric reached a hand into the thick cloud rising from the Cauldron, desperately hoping that cool feminine fingers would brush his skin in a loving caress and that a beautiful silver-haired woman would appear before him. She'd smile, join him, and he'd be complete again, not this hollow shell, not this man whose nightmares echoed with words he never should have spoken.

Isme dolunde vaten crew.

He hadn't been offering Rain. He would *never* have sacrificed Rain, and she'd known it.

Daylight waned, the healthy, leafy branches of the trees

around the Cauldron blotting out what little sunlight remained on this last day of spring. Daric turned Rain's starflower over in his hand. She'd left it in her saddlebag, and he'd rubbed the carving so often between his fingers that the shallower details on the flower had faded. Her hairpin still dangled from the loop, sometimes pricking him. He'd taken a few strands of silver hair from it, but those he kept in a safer place.

Rain would be dormant for the rest of the year soon. He'd still call to her. He'd call and call, but she would never answer. And next spring, she would wake again and pour her unhappiness down on Leathen. The farmers still cried tears of joy when spring rains started, but Daric watched the drops fall in torment. His love was gone, and he'd never accept it.

RAIN'S NEW SISTER was jealous and possessive. She didn't understand why she had to share her season. Rain tried to communicate with her, to explain that they could work together, but this new Spring didn't understand the idea of producing those kinds of thoughts herself—or have any interest in listening. Rain shaped clouds into people she loved and missed, and her sister blew them away with disapproving gusts. Rain moped on clouds of gloom, and her sister threw down rainbows from her darkness simply to contradict her. Rain cried in gentle, steady streams while her sister did her best to cut through her clouds with violent weather.

After three seasons of bickering, Rain, who remembered her name, her life, her love—*everything* from her time in Leathen—

claimed her land with the explosive force and fierce determination of a goddess much older and stronger than any spring infant. The sister born when Rain left the Cauldron, this child who hadn't even lived the span of a human lifetime, ran to Braylian when Rain banished her from Leathen.

Braylian chose not to intercede, for Rain's sister still had the rest of the continent, and Rain cared nothing about what happened in Parr or what used to be Raana, or anywhere that wasn't *her* Leathen.

Her heart broke every time and somehow harder each time she saw Daric at the Cauldron. He barely resembled the prince she'd known. He was leaner, tougher, shaggier—more jagged all over. His eyes glinted like chips of blue ice, but they'd once held warmth despite their cool color. Now, they held only rage and bitterness.

Rain longed to go to him, to help him somehow. She was desperate to show herself and speak, even if she couldn't touch him. Braylian wouldn't let her. The great goddess stopped her with harsh elements every time Rain tried to take shape at the Cauldron. After being burned, battered, and overcome too many times to count—and seeing Daric also violently blown back by the tremendous force of Braylian's power—Rain finally stopped trying and simply watched Daric from afar, giving her tears to him instead.

He'd turn his face up, and sometimes, she knew they wept together.

And when he told her it was too wet, that the land was flooding, she did her best to dry the eyes she didn't truly have anymore and let the sun peek through, thinking not of loss but of happy memories.

Just hours from now, she would sleep. She'd spend three seasons without Daric, without being able to see him or watch over him. Four years ago, she'd sent thunder and lightning along with his army into Raana. She'd lashed storms down on his enemies. She'd done her best to protect him and Leathen. But a lot could happen while she slept, and it terrified her each time the Great Rest claimed her.

From the ground, Daric called her name until he was hoarse. He always did, his anguished rasp scraping across bark and branches. She'd been transformed into something without form, but heartbreak wasn't physical. It was her soul that cracked and suffered.

Daric suddenly howled and threw her starflower into Braylian's Cauldron with a curse that rattled the forest. Rain gasped, her shocked inhalation sucking at leaves that abruptly shook and churned upward.

His gaze rose sharply. Daric's eyes narrowed. "Rain?"

Focusing on the starflower, Rain gathered all her power and barreled toward the Cauldron. Painfully hot flames shot up to deter her. She fought and dodged them. She had to save the carving. It belonged to her and Daric.

Pressing downward like a tornado, she blew out and crushed Braylian's fire with her own formidable weather. Rain was just one season compared to the mighty goddess of all the elements, but she was *determined*.

The two ancient and savage forces clashed in the Cauldron. Rain doubled her efforts, drawing strength and courage not from knowing she was a deity but from the stubborn resolve she'd learned from humans, that boldness of spirit that embodied fight and sacrifice and hard, unwavering purpose.

Smoke and ash suddenly took the place of violent struggles—a war turned silent. She'd done it. She'd overcome Braylian. Extinguished her fire!

Rain took form in the center of the Cauldron. She stood on trembling legs and stared at Daric. He was so close, so close she could almost touch him.

He stared back. Then he roared and leaped for her. Rain bent and snatched up the starflower just as Braylian fought back, hard and fast, her flames surging high to reclaim her daughter.

Rain dove out of the Cauldron, fire licking her feet. Daric caught her and raced away, his broad back shielding her naked skin from the inferno Braylian hurled at them.

He set her on her feet at the edge of the clearing. Rain wobbled, unused to legs and the need for balance. Daric steadied her. He gripped her arms, his blue eyes wild and haunted. "You're real."

"I...think so," Rain answered.

"I love you. So much." His voice cracked, and Rain let out a sob. He held her face in his hands and kissed her. The kiss was hard but tender, heartbroken and unsteady. "Don't leave me again. I won't survive it."

"I love you. I've been miserable without you." The words trembled out of her, as shaky as her new limbs.

"These years without you..." Daric shook his head, his breath shuddering violently.

Rain wrapped her arms around his neck and kissed him. Their lips collided, and warmth bloomed inside her, the heat of home and life and love, and she realized more than ever how cold and lonely she'd been without Daric.

She drew back to look at him, still shaking, her hands in his hair. She couldn't stop touching him. "You threw away my starflower."

"It was yours. I didn't know how else to give it back to you." He took off his cloak and wrapped it around her bare shoulders.

Fire popped, and they both looked at the Cauldron. As they did, the flames settled. The blaze turned into something resembling softness, and Rain instinctively knew that Braylian had forgiven her for rebelling. The goddess wasn't angry. She understood that her daughter wasn't hers anymore, and that Rain's heart and spirit had belonged with Daric's since the day they'd danced as children.

A triumphant, last sunbeam of the day hit the clearing at the same time as a wisp of fog. A rainbow shot through the moisture, and Rain threw her head back and laughed, happiness bursting out of her.

"Are you doing that?" Daric grinned along with her. It was the first time she'd seen him smile since the day she'd left him.

Rain shook her head, her heart healing as she gazed at him. "That's my little sister, claiming Leathen before she sleeps for the next three seasons."

"Spring will still see us? This hasn't changed anything?"

"Spring will come to Leathen when she should," Rain answered, trailing her fingers through the dark beard she would enjoy feeling all over her body as soon as she could. "And I have no doubt the little imp will split clouds over my head whenever she can. I probably won't be able to leave the castle between the winter and summer months."

Daric gazed at her in confusion.

"We fought violently over Leathen," Rain explained. "I took it, of course."

"Of course," he murmured, his expression saying he believed she could do anything.

"My prince." Rain held out the starflower to Daric, now cool marble again.

He took it, and she angled her head for him. Daric slid the starflower into her hair, pinning it back the way he had the morning of her birthday. It was the symbol of their love, and the sight of it disappearing into the Cauldron had given Rain the strength she needed to fight her way back to him.

"You're several years late for your wedding." Daric's rusty attempt at humor tangled in his throat.

Rain slipped her arm through his and tugged Daric toward the shelter he'd built, already eyeing the furs she could see piled up inside as bedding with great interest. "The wedding can wait until after I've had my way with you."

A spark found its way into Daric's eyes again—the first in a long time. "I'm at your service, my lady."

EPILOGUE

One year later

"WERE YOU AWARE that an infant can squall louder than one of your sister's storms?" Daric asked, placing the little silver-haired bundle into his wife's outstretched arms.

Princess Cassia Starflower Ash immediately began rooting around for her mother's breast.

"My goodness, I've only just fed her." Rain looked in concern at her perfectly red-faced, grunting daughter.

"She's voracious," Daric said, feeling slightly less harried now that Rain was done with her bath and could nurse their daughter. He'd tried everything. Singing. Bouncing. Swinging. Cuddling. Cassia had wanted nothing but her mother.

He understood. He'd felt that way for years.

"Voracious." Rain glanced up with a sly smile after Cassia had found what she was looking for. "Like her father."

The teasing heat behind her words sent an instant bolt of desire through him. "I'll show you voracious," he teased back with a low growl. "As soon as Cassia is asleep, and my hearing goes back to normal."

Rain chuckled. The sound would never cease to amaze him, not only because it was beautiful, like dewdrops on spring flowers, but because he'd once thought he'd never hear it again.

His heart still exploded with joy and relief each morning he woke up next to his stunning, powerful wife. The only woman he'd ever wanted.

"My parents have promised to take her out for a stroll after her nap and let us collapse from exhaustion."

Cocking her head to one side, Rain gazed down at their infant daughter. Cassia was two moons old, incredibly demanding, and growing like a weed in summer. "It's odd, wanting a respite and yet not wanting to let her out of my sight."

"They'll take good care of her," Daric assured her, smoothing Rain's damp hair back when it slid forward. "I've never seen more proud and doting grandparents."

She looked up again. "They're wonderful with her." Rain bit her lip, and her lake-blue eyes roamed over him with blatant interest. "And I'm not all that exhausted," she added.

If Cassia hadn't been between them, Daric would have pounced. He was still the Hallerhound Prince, after all, not quite tamed and definitely not placid, even though he'd started looking and acting more civilized again. Their time apart had given them both an edge that would never disappear entirely. Desperation had left its mark on him, and he still woke some nights in a sweat, his heart pounding a hole through his ribs and his voice raw from shouting for Rain.

But she was there now when he woke from his nightmares, right next to him, soothing his fear and anguish with soft words and hot touches. They'd twine together like vines, and he'd make love to her with an intensity that bordered on broken. But every day that went by, he felt less like he might shatter, and more like everything in his life was whole again, including him.

"She's asleep," Rain whispered. "That didn't take long."

Daric took Cassia and gently laid her in her cradle. He went back to his wife and pulled her into his arms. "She just needed you to comfort her."

Just as he did. As he always would.

Rain smiled, and when she did, no matter where they were, inside or out, day or night, it was as though the sun came out to shine upon him.

About the Author

Amanda Bouchet grew up in New England where she spent much of her time tromping around in the woods and making up grand adventures in her head. It was inevitable that one day she would start writing them down. She writes what she loves to read: epic exploits, steamy romance, and characters that make you laugh and cry.

A French master's graduate and former English teacher, Amanda lives in Paris, France. She met her husband while studying abroad, and the family now includes two bilingual children who will soon be correcting her French.

Amanda is the *USA Today* bestselling author of The Kingmaker Chronicles: *A Promise of Fire*, *Breath of Fire*, and *Heart on Fire*. Her fourth full-length novel, *Nightchaser*, comes out in January 2019.

For more information about Amanda and her books, please visit amandabouchet.com. You can also follow her on Facebook, Twitter, Instagram, Goodreads, and BookBub.

THE DRAGONS OF SUMMER

An Uncharted Realms Novella

BY

JEFFE KENNEDY

As unofficial consort to the High Queen, former mercenary Harlan Konyngrr faces a challenge worse than looming war and fearsome dragons. His long-held secrets threaten what he loves most—and he must make a choice between vows to two women.

Takes place after The Arrows of the Heart

Thank you for reading!

Credits
Line and Copy Editor: Rebecca Cremonese

Dedication

To everyone who loves Ursula and Harlan,
and asked for more.

Acknowledgements

Many thanks to my Fabulous Assistant Carien, who suggested several ideas that made this novella come to life—and who caught some egregious typos.

Thanks to Marcella Burnard and Jim Sorenson who provided very helpful feedback on the story and made it ever so much better.

So much love and appreciation to Rebecca Cremonese, for crying at all the right parts, and for being a sap in exactly the perfect way.

CHAPTER ONE

"INSPECTING THE DEFENSES yet again?"

Ursula's question startled me, as I'd been so deep in thought I'd missed her approach. From my vantage on the walls of Castle Ordnung, I'd been contemplating the lush, green, and apparently peaceful countryside. The early onset of summer seemed to please the locals. For farmers and merchants, the fair weather brought welcome warmth for crops and dry roads for trade.

For a warrior like me, dry roads meant enemy forces could reach the seat of the Thirteen Kingdoms all that much more easily—and fair weather only made it easier to pillage freely and set fire to the rest.

I didn't let Ursula see she'd surprised me—or the dark direction of my thoughts. As High Queen of the Thirteen Kingdoms, she had enough to think about. "It pays to be thorough," I told her, making sure I looked relaxed.

"And here you're always nattering at me to delegate. Don't you have lieutenants to handle this?" she asked in an arch tone, her gaze as piercing as a hawk's. Sometimes her eyes are steely, like the sword she'd slept with when I met her, and other times they soften to gray with hints of blue, like the fog that rises out of the valleys of the Wild Lands in the mountains beyond

Ordnung.

I've never told her that, as she'd be embarrassed—and would likely try to hide that softness from me. My Essla—as her sisters called her, an intimate nickname I loved—learned long ago to compensate for her early wounds with tensile strength and hardening her heart.

Her tough resilience only added to Ursula's unique beauty. The rising sun set her deep auburn hair on fire, gilding her high cheekbones and that strong nose I'd set with my own hands after her father broke it. Dressed for court—though she had yet to don her crown—she wore a streamlined and high-necked gown of black velvet. A bodice of worked silver hugged her waist and flared over her elegant breasts, finishing with stylized caps at the shoulders. One of her mother's rubies glittered at the low dip in the center, where a pendant might rest on another woman.

Overall, the bodice gave the impression of armor, and Ursula's sheathed sword hung from the belt incorporated into the metalwork, the ruby in its hilt a perfect match to the one at her breast. The split skirt of the gown parted to reveal narrow silver leggings and high black leather boots beneath, allowing Ursula the freedom of movement she craved, even though she'd be waging battles of wits in the day ahead, not of arms.

We'd only returned a few weeks back, to fortify Ordnung and for Ursula to direct war strategy from the seat of the High Throne. To Ursula's vocal and caustic dismay, she had also returned to a veritably endless supply of gowns appropriate for court. The dressmaker, Denise, and her army of seamstresses had been hard at work during our journeys, creating formal garb so well designed for Ursula that she couldn't find fault with them, beyond that they weren't her preferred fighting leathers. With no excuses to do otherwise, Ursula had conceded that particular battle and looked more often the High Queen these days than road-worn warrior princess.

She always looked beautiful to me, so unlike the meek, submissive, and gentle-voiced women of my homeland. In fact, in all my travels, I'd never met another woman like my Essla, another lover of the sword, and as determined as I to wield it for justice.

Just as the first time I'd laid eyes on Ursula, my heart swelled in my chest, filled with the undying love I'd sworn to her service. I'd never regret that I'd given up loyalty and all connection to the blighted homeland of my birth when I'd sworn the *Elskastholrr* to Ursula. That vow—which must be freely given and never requested—had become my compass and foundation.

But I did sometimes wonder how much of the love I felt for her grew from the tattered shreds of guilt and remorse where the love for my sister Jenna had once lived in my heart—and had been ripped away when she disappeared.

In countless small ways, Ursula reminded me of Jenna, whom I'd never forgotten, though I had finally stopped searching for her. I'd kept her existence and fate my personal secret all these years, locked in a box in my heart, where no one could ever open it.

Where the wounds inflicted by the cruel world had nearly killed Jenna before our insane escape attempt, they'd honed Ursula into a weapon. Jenna had possessed no fighting skills, no knowledge of the world outside the Imperial seraglio. Both princesses and heirs to powerful parents, Jenna and Ursula could not be more different.

Perhaps Jenna had survived to go on and find something of Ursula's ferocity. Probably that was a foolish and idealistic hope. Jenna was no doubt dead. Yet I couldn't help wishing otherwise.

"Harlan?" Ursula asked, when I failed to reply to her question. She tipped her head, studying me with a too-knowing gaze, a wealth of other questions crowding her simple asking of my name.

I shook my head, willing the old memories, the miasma of nostalgia—and dread of the future—to go back to the shadows where they belonged. She'd asked me about delegating, a rich question coming from her, who thought she had to handle every cursed thing herself.

"You put me in charge of Ordnung's defenses," I reminded her. "And I'm very good at my job. Let me decide what can be delegated and what requires direct supervision."

She smiled slightly, more of a thin-lipped grimace than anything, as she stepped up to stare out over the walls and the road to the township along with me. "It wasn't a criticism," she replied mildly. "I've received a message from Andi," she said, seeming to change the subject, though I knew this must be why she'd sought the solace of the walls.

"Ah. And how is my heart-sister?" The message held bad news, no doubt, as we seemed to have only that variety of messages lately. And, as Queen of the Tala, Andi lived at the heart of the brewing storm.

Sure enough, Ursula huffed out a sharp, impatient breath,

stepping away from me. "Carelessly overextending herself, as usual."

"Sounds like someone else I know," I replied, smiling easily when she glared at me. "I have to point out that you're supposed to be resting before court, not checking up on Ordnung's defenses."

She narrowed her gaze at me, eyes sharpening. "How do you know I didn't come up here looking for you?"

I lifted one shoulder and let it fall. "Did you?"

Giving me that thin-lipped smile, she turned to sweep her gaze over the pastoral scene below us, if one could consider a fully-armed castle with guards at high alert 'pastoral.' "I thought you'd be drilling with the guard," she admitted. She was scrupulous about being honest with me, determined to never again cross lines she thought had nearly destroyed our relationship before. Though I'd explained countless times that nothing could damage my love for her, the rejected and abandoned child who still lived in Ursula's heart would never believe it. All I could do was give her that love without reserve or qualification.

"And before you get annoyed with me," she said, bristling at my expression, "I wasn't checking up on the defenses so much as..." she trailed off, searching for the right words.

"Reassuring yourself that all is as it seems?" I suggested, and held out an arm for her, so she'd lean against me for a bit. She gave me a relieved smile, real affection in it, coming to me with at least that much trust.

"You always understand me—often before I understand myself." She snuggled against me, letting out a long breath. "I hate that the practitioners of Deyrr can mess with our minds.

I'm more comfortable with an enemy I can predict. And one I can skewer with my sword."

I hugged her close, her slim form and long bones nearly delicate, though I knew better than most how fast she could strike when provoked, and how lethally. "I do understand—and agree," I told her.

She tipped her head against my cheek, so I kissed her temple, giving her the comfort she'd never ask for, her fiery hair always surprising me with its silky texture. It had grown longer since I'd met her. Tamed for court by her ladies, it lay in sleek waves and ended in wisps down her neck.

"Andi reports that the Tala are gathered and the navy assembled," she returned to her point. "Now that Karyn and Zyr have recovered somewhat from their ordeal, Kiraka has been interrogating them about what they found."

I grunted in sympathy. Kiraka was an old dragon—literally— and as cantankerous as they came.

"It's bad." Ursula said it so softly I almost didn't hear. "Andi expects an attack on Annfwn at any time."

"But the magic barrier is still holding, yes? The Dasnarian navy is still on the other side."

"At last report that seems to be the case, but the ships are massing there as if they expect that to change and soon."

I held her, glad she'd come to me. "We have a lot of might on our side, too. We've done everything we can to prepare."

"I know."

She did. We'd both known most of this. The waiting was what wore on us. She shook herself and stood straight. "Andi warned me to expect attack here. The Deyrr sleepers might have infiltrated deep into all the Thirteen Kingdoms. They're waiting to spring some sort of trap on us all, or they would've attacked already."

"If they do we'll fight back. We're ready for them—and not so easy to surprise."

With a brief smile, she turned back to gaze over her realm. "I wish I could be so sure. Of everything."

Something about the way she said that—some intuition perhaps—sent a brush of alarm that made my short hairs prickle. Something else was on her mind, and it wasn't good.

Chapter Two

"IT ALL LOOKS so peaceful," she said, gazing out, still skirting the heart of the topic. "So… normal. Like I recall it being back in the day, in Uorsin's early years." She waved a hand to disperse the shades of all that had happened later in the tyrant's rule.

We didn't talk much about her father, the late High King Uorsin, and for good reasons. In fact, it said something that she'd mentioned him voluntarily at all. Just speaking his name put unhappy lines around her mouth, signs that the emotional wounds he'd given her had cracked open to seep pus and old blood. She liked to see herself as whole and healed. I knew her better than that.

I set a hand on the small of her back. Through the flexible silver bodice, Ursula's lean and strong muscles were as tight as I'd anticipated. My Essla is built like a racehorse, all slender speed and alert readiness—and she's equally as high strung. She tried to hide the strain of rule from me, the anxiety she felt for her sisters and her realm, pretending she didn't need me or anyone. Still, she leaned in to my touch. Gratifying, given how long and patiently I'd worked to earn her trust.

"Things were good then, in the early days?" I asked leadingly, willing to accept this conversation instead of the one that clearly weighed on her.

She frowned slightly, watching something on the road. I followed the line of her attention and found nothing salient, so she must have been seeing images play out in her memories, frowning as she always did when she remembered her father.

"Maybe I just have the idea things were good because he said so all the time," Ursula said slowly. "Uorsin was a great one for singing his own praises. But that's how I remember things, back when Salena was alive, when Andi was still little, and before Ami was born. Abundant and peaceful."

"Those were the years right after the Great War ended," I noted.

She huffed a sigh of acknowledgment. "Exactly, which would play in. If nothing else, Uorsin put a stop to the blood-shed and conflict. He built the roads and mandated that everyone use Common Tongue. In those early years, he accomplished a great deal, and most of the kingdoms prospered. People were relatively happy."

"People think that war stimulates trade," I reflected, "when the underlying truth is that the *end* of war allows trade to rebound."

She nodded, her gaze unfocused, attention still on the past. "I'd come up here to the walls sometimes, just to watch the road and all the people living their lives."

Their normal lives, she meant and didn't have to articulate. "You wouldn't have been ten years old yet," I observed as neutrally as possible. She so rarely spoke of her childhood that I treaded carefully when she did, even when I wasn't certain—as I was now—that she was building up to something else entirely.

"True," she replied, then fell silent, brooding, so I moved fully behind her, working my fingers into the gaps of her bodice to loosen the knots I could reach. She rolled her shoulders with a murmur of relief, and continued. "Truly, back then I came up here mostly to figure out what Andi saw in it. Even at barely four, she had a knack for slipping away from her nurses. We'd always find her up here or on one of the towers, staring out like she'd lost something."

"Was that before she had her bedroom in the tower?"

Ursula flicked me a wry glance over her shoulder. "Yes. The tower bedroom was a solution to the problem of her forever running off. With the views from the windows, she was at least content to stay in her room and look out from there. That changed, of course, once she discovered horses—and proved remarkably good at evading notice to ride off for hours in unpredictable directions. If we'd known then that we were dealing with a budding sorceress, we might've done things differently, but Salena would've been the one to know that and…" she shrugged.

"I might point out that you were but a girl yourself and bore no responsibility for what your mother and father should've handled, as parents and as king and queen."

"There you would be wrong. Taking care of Andi and Ami was always my responsibility, whether they liked it or not. And the Thirteen are my responsibility." Her face hardened, and she turned to face me. "You're worried about something. That's why you keep coming up here. But not about war. What aren't you telling me?"

I shouldn't have been surprised at what she noticed. Even

apparently and thoroughly preoccupied with matters of court and defense, Ursula missed very little. "This is simply a good place to think," I hedged, hoping that might be enough to deflect her.

She leaned back against the parapet, facing me with crossed arms. "You think and think, yet you never tell me what plagues your thoughts. Don't you think it's about time you changed that?"

"You don't need to worry about me," I told her, a weak defense, but I didn't have a better one.

She laughed, short and without humor. "First, that's not true. Second, I do worry because I love you, and I'm reliably informed that it's not only natural to worry about the people we love, it's usually expected. Third, that reply was an evasion."

I raised an eyebrow at her. I might've left the Imperial Palace of Dasnaria far behind in my misbegotten past, but I'd been around plenty of rulers in a variety of lands and I knew how to handle an irritated monarch. More, I knew Ursula. Better than I knew my own heart. "You have plenty on your mind and I can handle myself."

"Another evasion," she shot back. Debating with Ursula often felt the same as sparring with her, though it was rarely as enjoyable since the odds of getting my hands on her were much lower in a debate.

My own irritation rising to meet hers, I gave her a long, very calm look. "I appreciate that you love me enough to worry about me, but it's simply old memories plaguing me, like a bad joint that aches when the weather changes."

"Tell me anyway." She raised her brows in challenge, but

her voice held an almost pleading note.

Uncertain of my footing, I wondered where this was going. She didn't usually press like this. "Essla, there are things my vows prohibit me from speaking of. I can't tell you."

Her winged eyebrows lowered, forking into a dark frown. "Those vows again." She spat the words as if they were distasteful.

"Those vows again," I agreed. I found I'd folded my own arms in a mirror of hers, unconsciously harmonizing with her even when she pissed me off. Too late to undo it without tipping her off. "They are nothing important, especially compared to your other concerns. My secrets have nothing to do with the security of your realm. You needn't be concerned that I would keep something from you that you need to know."

Her frown cleared, leaving her expression carefully blank, though her lips parted slightly to draw in a quick breath before she firmed her mouth and her gaze went steely. "I see," she replied in a neutral tone. "I suppose I'd foolishly believed I could listen to your worries as you've so often listened to mine. I apologize for my presumption." She stood to go.

I cursed myself. I'd hurt her, thoughtlessly and clumsily. Putting a hand on her arm, I stopped her. "Essla, I'm sorry."

She stared past me, her throat working as she swallowed whatever words sprang to her lips. When her gaze met mine, her eyes had gone silvery with the sheen of tears she'd never permit herself to shed. "We're all growing further apart—have you noticed? Dafne is preoccupied with her pregnancy and translating for Kiraka. Ami is ensconced at Windroven with her lover and the children—I'll never pry her out of there."

"And Andi?" I prompted. Of everyone, I knew Ursula missed Andi the most.

"More like our mother every day," she replied, weary affection in her voice. "Of us all, she's carrying the heaviest burden, so I do my best not to add to it. Everyone is devoting themselves to preparing for this war. We all know that Annfwn will be where Deyrr attacks. And here I sit in Ordnung, doing nothing, far away from it all."

"You're hardly doing nothing." I could only wish she'd do a bit less. "You wake before dawn and rarely go to sleep before midnight."

She shook her head, studying her boots. "All meetings and talk, talk, talk. I've lost most of my Hawks to other duties—Jepp and Marskal off fighting the battles I used to."

I understood what she meant. She and I, both creatures of action, accustomed to leading from the front. But being High Queen meant she'd had to return to Castle Ordnung and direct strategy from safe inside walls. As for me, my Vervaldr had all been released from their contracts, some almost certainly returned to Dasnaria, while others were absorbed into Ordnung's guard, or dispersed into other parts of the troops we had amassed in defense of the Thirteen Kingdoms.

Though I'd taken over for the unfortunate Lord Percy, one of the first victims of Deyrr's occupation of Ordnung and former Captain of the Guard, I had no real title or role. I wasn't fool enough to believe that I could ever be more than Ursula's unofficial consort, nor did that bother me. That was the nature of the vows I'd given her, to support her in any way I could.

That also meant keeping her safe.

"You're needed here," I told her, emphasizing what she already knew. "You're too important to risk on the front lines of this fight."

"I know that in my head. My heart is another matter." She took a deep breath, uncharacteristic vulnerability in her eyes when she met my gaze. "Speaking of which, I didn't expect you to disappear on me."

The vague dread coalesced, sharpening into wary surprise that she'd say such a thing. "I'm right here," I said, and turned her so she faced me, squeezing both shoulders so she'd feel it.

"Are you sure?" She studied me, emotion banished, all keen observation. "You haven't been the same since my injury."

Shocked, I let go of her, sudden cold numbing my fingers nerveless. The events of that terrible day flooded back in excruciating and vivid detail. The heat of the tropical sun and the pitch of the Tala ship beneath my boots, rocking in the gentle waves. The eerie silence and the sharp scent of blood, raw meat, and entrails spilling from Ursula when the High Priestess gutted her. How I stood there frozen, helpless, unable to move in the slightest. All those years I'd built my strength, honed my skills, to make myself into warrior enough to protect the woman I loved and it had all been for nothing.

I hadn't been able to protect Ursula any more than I'd been able to save Jenna. Fury and fear warred in me.

"Your *injury?*" I sneered the word, unreasonable rage firing in me that she could speak of it so casually. "Let's rephrase for accuracy. You mean when you very nearly *died.*" So pale and weak in my arms when she collapsed, her blood pooling on the deck around us. If not for magical healing, she *would* have died there. For long moments, I'd been sure she was gone. And I'd been helpless to do anything about it.

A flare of unhappy triumph crossed Ursula's face. She was too much the warrior not to be pleased with her accurate piercing of my emotional armor, and too much the woman who loved me not to be sorry about it. "I didn't die."

"It was a near thing... *and* you're still not totally healed."

She opened her mouth to protest and I cut her off with a chop of my hand through the air. "Don't lie to me," I bit out. "You don't have your former strength and speed. Your color still isn't right, and you won't *get* better when you work yourself to the bone and refuse to rest."

"My kingdom faces attack from a two-pronged enemy, either of which could devastate us entirely on its own, and they've joined forces. I've been betrayed from within, I'm still new to my throne and utterly out of my depth. I can't afford to rest."

"I understand that," I ground out. "But you can't afford not to rest. If you don't care about yourself, at least think about the people who love you."

"I love you, too," she replied seriously. "Because of that, I'm suggesting that whatever is going on inside your head is getting to you. Normally you're very good at leaving the past where it belongs, but lately you're letting it eat away at you. You were the one to teach me that ignoring emotional wounds weakens us. If you won't talk to me about it, then find someone else to listen."

I scrubbed my hands over my scalp, willing my brain to kick in with a reply to soothe her. "I just worry about you is all," I said. "There's nothing else that needs discussing."

"Like I worry about you?" She parried.

"No." I called on the meditative calm of the *Skablykrr* that had always served me so well, but couldn't grasp it, my hand groping in the mental dark and coming up empty. "That's different," I threw out, a poor defense and we both knew it.

"Is it?" she asked coolly, neatly knocking that aside and leaving me open.

I had no answer, nothing else to offer. She dipped her chin in wry acknowledgement, then shrugged it off. "You're a stubborn man, Harlan, and I've got other things to do this morning than bash my head against this particular wall."

She put her hand to her sword and took a few steps, then changed her mind and turned back to me, a certain resolve in the line of her jaw.

I knew that look well, though it usually meant she'd decided to draw a metaphorical dagger she'd hidden up her sleeve in dealing with a recalcitrant ambassador or courtier—and the strike of that hidden weapon would inevitably be devastating. Though I'd seen her use it on others, she'd never turned it on me. She'd softened me up, deflecting and tiring me, all in preparation for this particular blow.

She scanned the immediate area, checking that the guards still gave us privacy, making sure her battlefield remained clear.

I braced myself. This would hurt.

"I know about Jenna," she said.

CHAPTER THREE

NO AMOUNT OF bracing could've prepared me for that.

Hearing the name I hadn't spoken—or heard anyone else speak—in over twenty years fall from Ursula's lips shocked me as little else could. She'd timed her attack perfectly, distracting me by evoking the fear for her that plagued me, outmaneuvering me, then slipping under my guard to deliver that strike directly to my heart.

She watched me with keen attention, no doubt cataloguing every whisper of reaction. I'd had to fall in love with a woman with an intellect as razor sharp as her sword. I should've known she'd ferret out my secrets eventually.

Even those I'd vowed to keep, because they weren't only mine.

"How?" I finally managed to ask, once I had the breath to sound reasonably in control of myself. "Kral told you," I realized, my thoughts finally catching up.

My brother Kral had unexpectedly defected to our side of the war, becoming the only member of my family I didn't have to dread facing on a battlefield. He also formed the third point of our lethal family triangle: Kral, Jenna, and me. The bad blood had festered between us for years until we agreed to put it away. Not that we'd actually dealt with it. I'd thought he didn't care to discuss it any more than I did.

"Not Kral." Ursula replied, confirming that. "He's as tight-lipped on the topic as you are. Jepp told me."

"Jepp," I echoed, feeling thick and stupid. Former scout in Ursula's elite troop of Hawks, Jepp had inexplicably fallen in love with my domineering and arrogant brother, and was the reason he'd left the Empire. She didn't give up her footloose ways and settle down—she hadn't changed that dramatically—instead she sailed the seas with Kral on his ship the *Hákyrling*. And Ursula had restored Kral's title and status as General, but of our forces in the field. The *Hákyrling* was patrolling the magic barrier, watching for incursions from Deyrr and monitoring the build-up of the Dasnarian navy.

Surely Jepp hadn't learned about Jenna from Kral. Ah... but, Jepp had gone to Dasnaria as a spy. She'd been to the Imperial Palace.

Acutely aware of Ursula's scrutiny as I put it together, I sat, the weight of the past and the secrets I'd carried so long suddenly feeling too heavy to bear. "Jepp learned the story in Dasnaria." I nodded to myself when Ursula's expression confirmed it. "Who told her?"

"Your *other* sisters, Inga and Helva—more sisters I had no idea existed—told her the whole story. She reported it to me."

I winced, rubbing my eyes with one hand, bracing myself on the wall with the other, as I felt oddly dizzy. Of course Jepp had reported everything to her captain and queen. "How long have you known?"

Ursula's mouth thinned, not pleased with that response. Truly I was lucky she hadn't cut my throat in my sleep. The last time she'd discovered I'd kept a secret from her about my family—that I was a former prince of the imperial household in Dasnaria—she'd drawn blood, then coolly cut me out of her life. Not that she'd had much luck with that. As she'd noted, I could be a stubborn man.

"I debriefed Jepp on the Tala ship while I was recovering from my *injury*." She raised a brow, daring me to quibble with the term again. I wouldn't. I needed to pick my battles with her very carefully now.

I nodded, assimilating all of it. That had happened months ago. All this time, Ursula had known and said nothing. I could take comfort that she'd continued to share my bed and welcomed me with her body, but I could see now that we hadn't been quite the same—and that I'd been too preoccupied to notice.

"It seems then that the distance between us isn't entirely of my own making," I said, more of a feint than a strike, just to test her defenses.

Her jaw tightened, her thumb caressing the faceted ruby in the hilt of her sword. "I'm right here," she said, tossing my words back at me. "And I've given you plenty of opportunities to tell me all of this. Including just a moment ago."

She had, I realized, asking me all those leading questions about my family, about the bad blood between me and Kral. Asking me to confide my worries in her. And I'd deflected them all, out of habit, in part. Also out of the comfortable assumption that she didn't know that history. Over time it had been easier not to talk about *any* of the sisters I'd left behind, when I talked about Dasnaria at all. That's the great problem with lies of

1

omission—over time, they begin to feel less like lies than an alternate truth, one that becomes a façade that weakens with age.

Because I hadn't replied, she continued. "Jepp explained that these vows of yours are related to this family history, so I should give you latitude for that—in fact, she thought long and hard whether to tell *me* everything she knew—but I've had a lot of time, and enforced inactivity, to contemplate this and I think there's a lot you could have confided in me, had you chosen to."

I couldn't argue with that. The fact that Jepp had considered not reporting everything she knew... that would've lodged in Ursula's heart, and craw, as well. I'd well and truly fucked this up.

I spread my hands, making myself meet her penetrating gaze. "I apologize. I'm at fault and I don't expect forgiveness."

She stared at me, unrelenting. "You do that so easily, but I don't think this is that simple for me."

"I'm surprised you haven't tried to kill me," I ventured, trying for the joke.

"I thought about it," she answered crisply, but without her usual fire. Then she looked away. "I don't understand why you wouldn't at least tell me about Inga and Helva. *Brothers.* You only ever mentioned brothers. You know *everything* about me— things no other living person does, because you wouldn't settle for anything less—and you didn't trust me with the smallest thing. All I can think about is what else I don't know about you. I'm not at all sure where to go from here."

"Court should be starting soon," I offered, still hoping for levity. The other possibility, that I'd destroyed her trust in me, didn't bear thinking about. Ursula didn't trust easily. What another woman might be able to forgive and forget would feel like the ultimate betrayal to her.

She leveled an icy glare on me. "As you so love to say, they can hardly start without me."

I braced my hands on my thighs, studying them. "Why to-day?" I asked.

"Excuse me?" She'd drawn her High Queen imperious attitude around herself like a protective cloak, the offense clear in her voice. When I looked at her, she'd indeed straightened her spine, looking every inch the warrior queen.

I barreled on, eager to at least extract myself from this corner she'd boxed me into. Standing, I gestured to the heights of Ordnung's walls, arguably one of the very few places we could speak without being interrupted or overheard by the ubiquitous staff and anxious courtiers who plagued every moment of Ursula's day. She'd picked this spot and plotted her attack, meticulously planned and devastatingly thorough.

"Why did you choose today to confront me with this, when you've known for months?" I clarified. "You could've told me you knew long before this, instead of asking leading questions, testing me. You let me hang as you reeled in the rope."

"Don't you dare try to turn this back on me," she warned, quiet fury in her tone, her fingers sliding down to curl around the hilt of her sword. She stood just outside my reach, were I to draw my own broadsword on her—a distance she knew precisely from all the times we'd sparred.

"Will you draw on me?" I asked softly. I didn't think she would. We'd come a long way with each other, and she'd promised never pull a weapon on me again. Not a physical one, anyway, or rather, not with lethal intent. But my Essla was a woman of strong passions and not always predictable. I could best her with my strength where she outmatched me in speed.

I, however, could never harm her. Not physically. In her righteous anger, she might have no such scruples with me.

"I'm tempted," she replied.

"Then do it," I dared her. Better to fight it out and get it done.

"You'd like that, wouldn't you?" Then she sagged, releasing her blade and lifting her hands to her face. "It would be *easier*. I'm aware that's one of the ways you manage me."

Reflexively, I stepped toward her, to comfort her, to—

"Don't." Her hard voice cut me short. She dropped her hands and gazed at me. "To answer your question, two reasons why today. The first..." Her voice shook as it never did, and she firmed her jaw. "I think I couldn't stand it anymore. I promised you a long time ago that I wouldn't walk away again without letting you explain, but I waited every day for you to tell me about this—even pieces of it—and day after day you pretended it wasn't there, carving a hole between us. Yes, it would be easier to call you out, to match blades and see who takes first blood, but that would be redundant. First blood is yours. This cut me, Harlan. Cut me to the quick and I'm still bleeding."

"Essla, I'm sorry," I said, fully realizing the weakness of those words, how ineffective to express anything at all.

"I'm sure you are." She smiled slightly, but it didn't touch the sorrow in her eyes. "And I wish that could be enough for me. Maybe it's a flaw in my character, but it isn't enough. There aren't that many people in my life I can believe will always tell me the truth—now more than ever. You were one of those people."

The past tense hit me like a knife to the kidneys, and I groped for breath to reply.

"You have a choice, I think," she continued. "The second reason is that starting two weeks ago I received a series of messages from Dasnaria, relaying information supposedly leaked from the Imperial Palace."

I grappled with that equally astonishing news—as well as the fact that she'd kept it from me. "How do you know that's where it's from?" I asked.

"I don't have a way of verifying, do I?" She snapped. "The information is coded to make me think it comes from someone in your family. 'From inside the fist,' it said."

The stunning blows kept coming. That would indeed imply from a Konyngrr—the silver fist being our family emblem—as Ursula knew, but few others would.

"If it's legitimate, I think the messages come from one or both of your sisters."

"My sisters?" I echoed, pondering the absolute implausibility of that.

"Aspects of the messages are decidedly feminine. What are the odds it's them—or perhaps another female *associate* of yours?" she pressed. "What can you tell me without violating your *vows*?"

"I..." I didn't know what to say. Mostly I wanted to fight back, to growl at her not to interrogate me like one of her subjects—especially that jab about some unknown female associate—even as I knew I deserved every bit of it. "It's not easy to untangle those threads, what I can and can't reveal. That's why I never mentioned any of my sisters, because it was easier to put everything about them behind the same door."

She nodded slightly, unsurprised. "I think you have to consider that your loyalties are divided. We face a war with your family and—"

"There is no question that my loyalty lies with you," I interrupted her furiously.

She held up a hand, icily calm. Quite the reversal for us. "I've given this a lot of thought," she reminded me. "You need to do the same. You've withheld information from me that's arguably critical to this impending war. I know you want to believe that the *Elskastholrr* you swore to me makes everything clear cut, but you have other vows, too, ones you made before that to keep your sisters secret. Which vows take precedence, Harlan?"

Flummoxed, I had no reply. I didn't need one, evidently, because she nodded again, smiling sadly. "There is no easy way out of this," she repeated. "If you have to leave in order to reconcile your conflicting interests, I'll understand."

Leave? The thought of leaving her shredded my heart. "How can you even think I would?" I asked, my voice coming out ragged. "Or could?"

"We always knew our love affair might be short-lived," she replied, softly, with deep sorrow. "That our differences might end at exactly this sort of conflict. I told you from the beginning that I belonged to the High Throne first, and because of that I'm a warrior for my kingdom, and only incidentally a woman."

"And I told you that's only because you don't put the woman first," I said with more bitterness than I'd intended.

"You're absolutely right." She inclined her chin, acknowledging the problem, but not apologizing. "I don't put the woman first. I can't, and I never will. I don't want you to leave. You'll tear my heart out and take it with you if you go. But I belonged to the High Throne from the day of my birth, and I can't let you stay if you're a threat to it."

CHAPTER FOUR

S HATTERED, I WATCHED her stride away. The guards came to attention, saluting as she passed, the warm breeze catching the long coattail skirts of the black velvet gown, making them snap like the tower pennants, the silver of the leggings flashing in the cuts, black boots making crisp sounds now that she wasn't being stealthy. She looked long, lean, and as dangerous as her sword.

How cleanly she'd cut out my heart, taking it with her and leaving me hollow.

Every muscle and nerve in my body urged me to run after her. To say what, though? In her usual fashion, Ursula had sliced to the bones of the problem. I'd never thought of my loyalties as divided, but they were. With another woman, that wouldn't matter. The way we felt about each other would outweigh everything else. Another woman wouldn't allow a matter of principle to override her heart.

But then, I hadn't fallen in love with another woman.

It had only ever been Ursula for me, and always would be—despite those past vows.

Pledging the *Elskastholrr* to her had been an easy decision. I'd been a simpler person then. A mercenary captain, disinherited from my past. The secrets I'd carried hadn't been so heavy, and it had been easy—that word again—to let them lie buried. Easy at that time to forget I'd ever been anyone else.

In its purest form, the *Elskastholrr* exists only in the heart and mind of the one who vows it. Ursula, heir to the throne of a tyrant, beloved of her people and obvious choice as their savior, had been a fine recipient for my vow. After witnessing the abuse of power in far too many forms and places, I had no desire to be king, but I would happily serve as kingmaker. In that crystal moment of decision, I saw a scenario where I'd serve out my vows and Ursula would never know about the *Elskastholrr*.

Deceptively simple.

I had told her, eventually, because she'd asked—and because I'd been unable to resist the temptation to have her. Nothing had remained simple for me after that. And, now, like the undead creatures animated by Deyrr's cursed magic, the events of the past trudged relentlessly forward to convene with the present.

There is no easy way out of this. Ursula had the right of it. Even if I could mark the boundaries of the vows in my mind, tell her everything but the essentials I'd sworn in blood and flesh never to reveal, the secrets I kept would still lie festering between us.

When I pledged the *Elskastholrr* to Ursula, I hadn't given those other, older vows I'd taken to protect Jenna a second thought. I'd had no expectation that Ursula would become my lover, that she'd return my love. A mercenary in love with a princess—nothing should have come of it.

Kral had himself a good laugh about it when he found out. Though with his practical, ambitious nature, he'd always thought the *Elskastholrr* a hopelessly romantic and self-destructive tradition anyway. He'd never see his way to being so selfless that he'd pledge himself to a woman for the rest of his life, whether she returned his regard or not. Though Jepp may have changed that. She wouldn't want eternal devotion so much, but she *would* demand commitment—at knife point, if necessary.

Being honest with myself, I'd have to admit that I'd embraced the hopeless, even punitive aspects of pledging myself to an impossible love. Though I'd pursued Ursula, I hadn't hoped for more than a night or two in her bed to sustain me. *We always knew our love affair might be short-lived.* I huffed out a laugh, a despairing edge to it that made a nearby guard look at me sharply.

I hadn't known that she hadn't had any real lovers before— or that in enticing her to unfurl her tightly closed heart, I'd become the sole caretaker of her intimate self.

Ursula would say this is why I shouldn't have vowed myself to her without even having a conversation first. She'd have a fair point, too, except that I suspected we could've conversed for years and I wouldn't have learned what I needed to know.

I knew I could spend the rest of my life with her and not be able to predict where her canny mind would go next.

Knowing her as I did now, however, how things had fallen out between us was all too predictable. I'd breached her walls and found my way to the heart of her as no one else had. Ursula didn't trust or love easily, but when she did, she committed herself entirely, with unflagging loyalty and determination.

Her own version of the *Elskastholrr*, in a way.

I had no doubt that if I did leave, she'd never give her heart again. She might eventually agree to a marriage, perhaps even take another man to her bed to produce an heir of her own body for the High Throne and the realm she loved above all else. But she was the kind to give her heart only once. Another way that she and I were the same.

From the beginning I'd been cognizant that if we succeeded in putting her on the High Throne, she'd one day make a marriage of state and not to me, a foreign mercenary. I would handle that eventuality when it happened—though the thought of another man making love to my Essla filled me with protective fury.

How could another man understand her particular fragility? Especially since she hid it so well under that tough skin and slicing wit. She'd be so easy to injure. If she succeeded in sending me away, and she married another, I wouldn't even be there to help her through that painful transition.

No matter what, I needed to make sure I stayed. I'd have to do what I could to bridge this chasm I'd created.

The great irony was that the vows I'd taken no longer served any real purpose. I couldn't reveal where Jenna had gone, because I didn't know. I'd once had guesses. We'd planned to flee together to Halabahna, to see the elephants, but I'd looked for her there and never found a trace of her.

Elephants. Had Jenna ever found them? For a long time I'd thought if I looked where elephants are, I'd eventually find her, but no.

I had to face that she'd probably died long ago. Or been captured, enslaved. An extraordinarily beautiful young woman with no ability to defend herself... It was a mark of my foolish idealism that I could even entertain anything but the worst fears for her fate. I'd likely never know what happened to her—and that I'd kept these heavy, destructive secrets all this time for no reason at all.

An alarmed shout went up from the lookout.

I spun, drawing my broadsword as I did, gratified that my sweeping glance verified all the guards in sight did likewise, brandishing whatever weapons they used best. The shout came from the highest tower, from a young woman I knew to be one of Jepp's protégées, a scout for the Hawks. She waved a flag in a complicated series of dips and twirls—one of their cryptic codes I had yet to learn—and I scanned for the nearest Hawk commander. Brant. With a gesture I summoned him and he came at a run.

"Report," I ordered.

He turned to watch the flag. "Unidentified movement. Request to be alert. Shadows in motion."

Shadows in motion. "Nothing more?"

Brant shook his head, eyes still on the lookout. "Message is repeating. I'll go see if I can find out more from Dary."

I grunted acknowledgement, scanning the shadows in question. The bright summer morning left few enough of them, but corners of the courtyard remained filled with deep shade cast by the high walls. I saw nothing unusual—certainly nothing to swing my sword at—but Ursula's Hawks weren't given to flights of fancy or false alarms.

With the enemy we faced, formless and born of darkest magics, anything odd could be an attack. Far better to err on the side of caution. Ursula was right that Annfwn was the apparent focus of Deyrr's enmity, but Ordnung remained the capital of the Thirteen Kingdoms. Deyrr wanted the heart of magic, but Emperor Hestar would want the High Throne. Because the two had joined forces, anything could happen.

Still, I felt more and more like a fool, seeing nothing strange or alarming, pointing my sword at shadows. We all did, bristling with weapons and anxiety, while the merry sounds of trade and a fine summer morning rang out from the road and township.

A metaphor for my current situation if ever there was one.

"Captain." Brant returned from conferring with Dary. "Recommend we stand down from high alert but increase eyes on the situation. Dary saw something she can't explain—like smoke or fog in the shadows—but it hasn't recurred. She asked me to relay her apologies for a false alarm, which I will, though I don't think they're necessary. She's as sharp-eyed as they come and solid with it."

"No," I replied, sheathing my broadsword and rubbing a hand over the back of my neck where the hair prickled with chill foreboding, even as the sun made my skin slick with sweat. "No apologies for a report made in earnest. Call on whoever you need to help watch. Dogs, too."

"Dary suggested some of the hunting falcons, as they're good with picking out small movements in bright daylight."

"Do it." He saluted and I returned it, then went to report the incident to the woman currently considering kicking me out of her bed—and her life.

When I reached the throne room, Ursula had already convened court and sat on the High Throne. The setup had changed since the early days when I first arrived with my Vervaldr, hired by Ursula's father to shore up what I quickly understood to be his mad and crumbling grip on power. In those days he'd sat on an iron throne flanked by four others, all empty.

One had been vacant for twelve years, once belonging to Salena, the dead sorceress queen, and the other three to her daughters, all away from Ordnung for various reasons. I'd thought I'd grown open-minded since leaving Dasnaria, but I'd been astonished to learn Uorsin's heir was his eldest daughter, an unmarried woman.

When she returned home, striding down the center aisle of court, covered in road dust, eyes steely with resolve, and proceeded to engage in a battle of wits with her father... well, I'd understood. And fallen hard.

Unlike Ursula that day, I didn't approach the High Throne down the center aisle, but took the long way around the assembled courtiers, keeping to the shadows in my own way, I supposed. It bothered Ursula far more than it did me that I had no official place in her court. As the youngest of seven legitimate sons born to my father, I'd been a prince in the Imperial Palace, sure, but one largely ignored in favor of those with a far greater chance of becoming emperor. When I'd been a boy that had rankled.

Discovering the kind of lives my sisters led had given me sorely needed perspective on just how fortunate I'd been.

When I reached my usual post at the side and foot of Ursula's throne, she gave me a narrow glance from the side of her flinty eyes. "I didn't expect you here," she murmured.

"It's where I belong," I replied simply, repeating a truth I'd had to drum into her thick skull. Folding my arms, I settled into the relaxed stance I could maintain for hours—and often did when court dragged on for a ridiculously long time. So determined not to repeat her father's mistakes, Ursula rarely cut off the petitions when any rational person would. Another consequence of her being away from Ordnung for so long—the business of the kingdoms, major and ridiculously minor, had piled up. The King of Carienne, Groningen, had handled a great deal of it as regent in her absence, but many people held onto their petitions, awaiting the return of the High Queen, certain they merited her personal attention.

In my opinion, very few of their urgent requests truly rose to that level. But that was another difference between my homeland and this realm. In Dasnaria, His Imperial Majesty the Emperor would never trouble himself with such trivia. He relied on his nobility to govern, which inevitably led to corruption and abuse of power.

Surely there had to be a middle ground between the two extremes.

Ursula delivered her decision on the current question. While Shua—the cleric who'd taken on Dafne's role—shuffled documents and prepared to call the next petitioner, Ursula flicked another glance at me. "What's wrong?" she wanted to know.

When I gave her a placid, questioning look, she made an impatient sound and gestured me to approach. "I know the difference between you being pissed at me and there being something of concern. Tell me what happened."

Chapter Five

THUS OFFICIALLY SUMMONED, I stepped up the dais to her throne. When she'd removed the vacant thrones, she'd replaced the imposing and unyielding one of her father's with a wooden one that gave a nod to the other half of her heritage. A gift from the Tala, it had been created from wood and magic. Not carved, but grown into its shape, the mahogany hardwood flowed without seam or nail, a bloodred nearly black, into the form of spread hawk's wings. The arms and feet of the great chair echoed talons and the winged back provided a striking frame for the High Queen's imposing presence.

By staying one level below her, I observed protocol and avoided appearing to loom over her. "Nothing urgent," I replied. "Dary spotted something strange in the shadows, but it seemed to disappear again."

Ursula considered that with interest. Even now she knew all of her Hawks by name. "Dary has sharp eyes. Almost as good as Jepp. Still it would be helpful to augment the watch with some of the shapeshifters Andi promised to send."

"We're bringing in dogs and falcons," I reported, "but supplementing with shapeshifter eyes would be ideal."

She considered me. "Perhaps you could travel to Annfwn with the message. Andi might take that more seriously."

I caught and held her gaze, delicately setting my mental feet on the narrow line between subject and lover. "Don't send me away."

"Would you go if I ordered it?" She sounded idly curious. And didn't fool me for a moment.

I simply saluted her with the *Elskastholrr*, not with a blade—even I didn't draw on the High Throne—but with two fingers against my forehead in lieu of a blade. The essence of the vow is in the physical demonstration and, indeed, no words go with it. The intent lies entirely in the heart and mind.

She read it in me with a flicker of resignation, and broke her gaze away to the patiently waiting courtiers. "As you were," she told me, the quiet words speaking volumes.

I'd returned to my place and she to the business of the realm, when the warning bells sounded from the walls. First-level alert. The courtiers erupted into shouts of panic.

Drawing my broadsword, I positioned myself in front of the throne, scanning the room for signs of attack before glancing back at Ursula, who'd leapt to her feet, her own sword in hand. "You know the drill, Your Majesty," I declared loudly enough for all nearby to hear.

Members of Ordnung's guard and Ursula's Hawks, a protective cadre I'd personally chosen, formed a circle around the throne, more running into the room.

She glared at me in impotent fury, but in this situation our hierarchy reversed itself. As much as she might resent it, the focus of Ordnung's response to attack had to be protecting the High Queen. We'd fought about it at length—usually with most stimulating results—and she'd at last conceded responsibility to me in a state of emergency.

Satisfied with her protection, I nodded at the ranking commander. "If you don't hear the all-clear, take Her Majesty to the safe room."

She saluted in the Hawk's style, fist over heart.

"Harlan!" Ursula's voice cut through the chaos.

I looked to her, braced for argument, but she set her jaw. "Be careful."

"Always." I grinned at her, her exasperated glare giving me heart, then took off running down the center aisle, courtiers scurrying still to both clear the way and move closer to safety. One part of my mind—the part that had made the Vervaldr the best mercenary troop a fortune could buy—noted what worked in our emergency plan and what didn't.

Courtiers, curse the lot of them, acted more like terrified chickens than anything. A few, the savvy and those experienced in the conflicts that had shaken their kingdoms over the last years, handled the crisis with efficient, even cynical calm. Most, however, had gone straight into panic and hindered the rest.

Next time—if we had a next time—I'd have troops assigned to crowd control. The former dungeons, now a growing library, made for excellent safe rooms. The deepest and most difficult to access was reserved for Ursula and the best of her elite guards, but no reason the courtiers couldn't be sent directly to the rooms that ringed it. More buffer against the enemy reaching the High Queen.

A grim smile stretched my lips as I shouldered a panicked young diplomat aside, his pile of scrolls scattering across the floor, and I imagined him giving his life to protect his liege.

The savage fantasy helped vent my frustration. Truly Ursula should be in the safe room already, but—as with all things to do with her—I'd also eventually compromised. She'd successfully convinced me that it would make her look weak if she ran and hid at the first alarm, but she'd promised to go at the second-level bells, or in the absence of an all clear. Theoretically.

I'd believe it when I saw her do it. She refused to drill in worst case scenarios.

My own handpicked team fell in behind me as I barreled out of the throne room and into the formal courtyard of the castle. Composed of Vervaldr, Hawks, and a few others, these fighters all either augmented my own strengths or compensated for my weaknesses. At least, those weaknesses I could do anything about. The biggest one should be in a safe room and wasn't.

Deliberately, I cleared my mind, reciting the mantras of the *Skablykyrr*, the ancient words tolling in my mind and driving out everything else. I needed to fight and kill, to do and be nothing else but the intelligence behind my blade.

Taking the fastest route, I climbed the ladder to the walls, peripherally aware of the precision teams who raised the ladders for my comrades to climb, then lowered them again. We'd been able to drill *that* much.

Brant awaited me as I topped the wall. "Dragon, Captain. Approaching from the west." He pointed and I followed the line of his finger.

A densely dark flying creature flew steadily toward us. With the long-winged silhouette of a vulture, it seemed to be no bigger than that—until I mentally measured it against the mountains. Enormous. Still distant, but rapidly gaining.

"Sand at the ready?" I jogged beside Brant.

"Yes. And water."

"Water won't work on dragon fire. Neither will arrows. Save those. Use the ballistae."

"Already armed and waiting for range."

I didn't know if we could do much damage to an attacking dragon on the wing, but we'd certainly find out. We reached the guard station below the lookout tower. Dary was still up there, using her flag in crisp, unhurried communication. "Get Dary down," I told him.

"Sir, if there's another—"

"If there's an attack from another direction, it will be nothing compared to dragon fire. Get her down. Everyone not on the ballistae takes cover."

He saluted and obeyed, signaling to Dary and passing along my orders. I squinted at the dragon, growing ever larger, like a slowly falling star whose explosive landing could likely make Ordnung into a crater. The words itched to jump out, to order the second-level warning bell rung, but I couldn't be sure yet—and Ursula wouldn't easily forgive a false alarm.

On the one hand, all the living dragons we knew of were friendly. On the other, I'd seen firsthand what Kiraka, one of those "friendly" dragons, had done to Ursula's Tala cousin Zynda. She'd been immolated and survived only by magic and possibly—literally—divine intervention.

I stared at it, willing my eyes to see more than they did. I beckoned to Dary. "Is the dragon a bronze color?" I demanded.

"No, Captain. Black, or very deep blue. Hard to tell at this distance with the light the way it is."

I nodded, biting down on the frustration. Dary had good eyes indeed if she could see that much—and she must've picked out that it was a dragon, not a bird, when it had been merely a speck in the distance, given its rate of approach.

Kiraka was bronze, so that ruled her out. And the friendly dragon liberated from under the dormant volcano at Windroven was silver. At least they did us the favor of being different colors, much good may it do us.

Compared to the bedlam indoors, the walls were eerily silent. The township, alert to the bells of Ordnung, had gone quiet as everyone took shelter. Even the traffic on the trade road had halted, horses and oxen unharnessed and taken to cover, people crouching under wagons where necessary. The courtiers could learn from them.

Otherwise the quiet was broken only by the snap of Ordnung's pennants in the wind, and the occasional scrape of a foot or weapon as we waited in tense readiness to fight an unstoppable enemy. One pass of dragon fire could wipe out half the soldiers on the wall.

"Track that aim," I called out as the dragon veered from its direct approach. The crews on the ballistae were ahead of me, using the swivel mounts to good purpose. The dragon swung east, banking with spread wings on a glide, its massive shadow passing over us as its bulk blocked the sun.

"Nearly in range," the near-end ballista crew leader called.

"There's a rider," Dary called out from her perch standing atop the parapet. Not at all under cover but at least not so easy a target as on the lookout tower.

I squinted at the dragon, barely making out a figure on its

back. If it was one of the Deyrr sorcerers, they could wipe our minds and make us happy to die by dragon fire.

"Correction." Dary had a hand up, ticking fingers to show three. "Multiple riders."

"Count of five to range," the crew leader announced.

"Stand by to launch," I ordered, starting the countdown in my head.

"Rider appears to be signaling," Dary called.

Four.

"Can you make it out?" Brant asked.

"Not easy at this distance, sir."

Three.

"Could be spellcasting," I warned.

"Best guess," Brant ordered. "Now."

Two.

Dary's face was pinched in concentration. I didn't know how she could see anything. "On my signal," I told the ballista crew.

One.

"We have the target, Captain."

"Wait!" Dary nearly leapt off the parapet. "It's Lieutenant Marskal."

"Are you sure?" Brant snapped.

"His personal signal, sir." She did leap off the parapet, running up to me, dark eyes large in her tight face. "Don't shoot, Captain. I'd stake my life on it."

"Stand down," I ordered the ballistae crews, who leapt to disarm the weapons. "But keep the alert. You're staking the lives of everyone in Ordnung, Dary—not just yours."

"Yes, sir." She spun to watch the dragon as they closed the

distance, no doubt having observed our disarming. Then she pumped a fist in the sky. "It *is* him. And Scout Jepp and General Kral."

This day got better and better. At least we wouldn't die by dragon fire.

"Stand down to normal alert," I called. "And send for Her Majesty. I'll meet her at the castle gates. She'll no doubt want to see this."

CHAPTER SIX

HER SWORD SHEATHED at her hip, tri-point crown glinting, and a phalanx of her personal guard trailing, Ursula strode through the outer gates, sharp gaze fixing on me for a long, inscrutable moment before she scanned the scene. Without a flicker of surprise, she took in the unprecedented sight of the enormous blue-black dragon gently wafting to settle on the expanse where tradesfolk and visitors to Castle Ordnung typically pastured their horses. Defying all common sense, the immense creature hovered like a hummingbird, setting itself down precisely and gently, though the great leathery wings stirred dust into whirlwinds.

"Who is it?" Ursula inquired, as if receiving an ambassador in court.

"Marskal, Jepp, and Kral, on an unidentified dragon," I replied, with some bemusement, shaking my head for the absurdity.

"What kind of world are we living in that we even use phrases like 'unidentified dragon,'" she muttered, sliding me a look.

I laughed under my breath, glad to connect with the woman behind the regal mask. "You got here fast," I noted.

"I followed our agreement," she countered.

"The letter of it, anyway." I said it mildly enough. Had she remained in the throne room until I sent word, it would have taken her twice as long to arrive, even at a dead run. I'd timed it.

She elected not to reply, apparently absorbed by the spectacle of Marskal sliding down the dragon's extended leg, followed by Jepp and Kral. My brother wore fighting leathers in the Hawks' style, rather than the Dasnarian armor he'd affected for longer than he'd kept his loyalty to the Empire, though he carried a broadsword as I did. He caught my eye, gestured at the dragon, and shook his head.

I dipped my chin. We lived in interesting times.

Marskal turned to look at the dragon and held out a hand, as if to a lady love, and the immense creature vanished, replaced by Zynda. Clad in a simple, pale-blue silk gown, her long, black hair streaming down her back, the Tala shapeshifter smiled radiantly, and placed her hand on Marskal's arm.

Ursula let out a short breath, too quiet for anyone but me to hear, and too subtle for anyone who didn't know her as well as I did to understand it as sheer vexation. Even knowing shapeshifters could perform such tricks didn't make our minds assimilate such impossible-seeming transitions. Never mind the additional headaches that receiving friendly but gigantic monsters at Ordnung would cause.

With Marskal and Zynda in the lead, Jepp and Kral following behind, the foursome strolled up to us. Arm in arm, they might be honored guests arriving for a ball.

"Your Majesty." Marskal bowed, then saluted in the Hawks' fashion, fist over heart, Jepp echoing the salute. Kral inclined his chin, an expansive gesture of respect for him, while Zynda smiled easily. Extracting her hand from Marskal's arm, she embraced Ursula, kissing her on the cheek.

"It's good to see you, Cousin," she said.

"Likewise," Ursula replied, smiling with warmth, unbending for the first time in hours. "Though I rather didn't expect to see you on two legs again. Or possibly at all."

Marskal made an odd choking sound and cleared his throat. Zynda shot him an amused look over her shoulder. "Things went better than we hoped," she said, "though it takes a bit of explaining." She arched her finely etched brows in significance, and Ursula took the hint.

"Let's retire to my council chambers," she declared, loudly enough for all to hear. "Court is postponed until afternoon." She caught my pointed glance, but ignored my unspoken opinion that this would be a good opportunity to cancel court entirely for the day. Determined to work herself into the ground.

We passed through the deep outer walls of Ordnung, the gated entrance tunnel casting a deep, cold shadow, a reminder that the warm summer was still tentative and new. There hadn't been enough time for it to fully banish the winter chill. Zynda strolled beside her cousin. Jepp and Marskal, likely out of long habit, marched side by side, conversing quietly, which left my brother and me to bring up the rear.

Hlyti seemed determined today to demonstrate that I couldn't leave the past behind. Though hlyti isn't a deity so much as the force of destiny in Dasnarian thinking, it is capricious, so I sent up a prayer that it would treat us as kindly as possible.

Kral had aged since that last night that all three of us were together. Of course, we'd both aged in the ensuing years. Jenna, however, remained locked in my mind looking as she had that night, forever a girl of eighteen, the last time I laid eyes on her. Unbelievably lovely, even with her ivory hair cropped short—an attempt at disguise—her deep blue eyes enormous in her delicate face, she swam in my clothes. Though four years her junior and nowhere near my adult bulk, I'd already outweighed her by half again as much.

The long sleeves of my shirt at least covered the raw wounds on her wrists and the other injuries she bore on her willowy body. Nothing could hide the haunted look in her eyes.

She'd been happy, though, as much as she could be. We both were, giddy with the prospect of imminent escape, and we'd been ravenous when we'd ordered the meal—food we never ended up eating, because Kral had found us.

I'd learned many lessons that night, all of them deeply painful, and just as deeply embedded.

"You're quiet, rabbit," Kral observed in Dasnarian, and I looked over at him. The age difference between us had vanished over the years. Four years meant little for men our age. Back then, it had meant everything. Though he was a bit younger than Jenna, barely more than a boy himself that night, he'd been far harder than either of us, already chiseled with the cutting edges our parents had carved into him with relentless purpose.

"You're the garrulous one, shark," I replied in the same language. The language of home, bittersweet to me, with its twin threads of cruelty and nostalgia interwoven.

He snorted, eyes lingering on Jepp in front of us. She'd softened him considerably. Immeasurably, really, as I'd never have predicted Kral would turn his back on the ambitions he'd given up his humanity to pursue. He wasn't the same viciously triumphant young man who'd held me at sword point and gloated over his victory.

Nor was I the weaponless fourteen-year-old boy who'd faced the devastating failure to save his sister from her terrible fate. Though Kral and I had made amends when we encountered one another again, it had been more of a tourniquet to stop the mortal blood flow that threatened to taint the present as well as the past. We'd agreed to move forward, as the men we'd become.

But that night hung between us still, hampering easy conversation. I'd think he didn't feel the pain of that unhealed wound as I did, except for the way he searched for things to say to me.

"I've had word from our sister," Kral said, jolting me out of my thoughts. He'd spoken quietly, as if we could be overheard though he still spoke in Dasnarian. All of our companions had picked up varying degrees of our language, so his discretion was well deployed.

Kral's mouth twisted as he gauged the look on my face. "Not *that* sister. Inga."

Ah. "And?" I prompted.

He gestured ahead at Ursula's straight spine. "You'll hear in the debriefing."

"Then why mention it now?"

"Maybe I wanted to see if you'd think I meant Jenna."

Twice in one morning. Hlyti had taken a broadsword to me, done with playing. I said nothing. Could say nothing.

"Silent as a boulder, peaceful as a tree," Kral observed with some cheer, probably pleased at having drawn blood. "The *Skablykrr* does all those dour monks claim, making you silent as the grave that Jenna likely found—"

He didn't complete that foul sentence, breath knocked out of him by the stone wall slamming into his back, his head clapping against it hard enough to daze him. Face pale, icy eyes for once lacking arrogance, he gaped at me over my broadsword laid against his throat.

I could kill him. Silence his mocking superiority for all time.

"Harlan."

Ursula's implacable voice cut through the snarl of my thoughts and jagged emotions. I became aware that Jepp held a dagger to my throat. Marskal on my other side, calming hand on my shoulder. Ursula stepped beside Kral, catching my eye, flicking a warning glance at Jepp, whose dagger point pricked my skin uncomfortably.

"You've gotten faster, brother," Kral wheezed from a tight throat, straining back from my blade, palms raised in surrender.

"Don't speak of her." I said it in Dasnarian, using words of command and warning.

Kral opened his mouth and I sank the blade against his throat, still the flat, but enough of an edge to draw a trickle of blood.

"Harlan," Jepp said evenly. "Don't make me choose between my lover and my queen."

I ignored her. And Ursula, calm and steely as she stared me down.

"Understood?" I asked Kral.

He closed his mouth. Nodded as much as my blade would allow.

I dropped the sword, releasing him, stepped back and sheathed it. Jepp moved immediately to his side, a dagger in each hand, big dark eyes hard on me. She also assessed me with some surprise, a new caution. Finishing the dance, Ursula moved to my side, Marskal still on the other, hand on my shoulder.

"Not speaking of her changes nothing," Kral said to me, still in Dasnarian, rubbing a hand over his throat and inspecting the blood on his fingers. "Some day you're going to have to face the reality that she is—"

I lunged at him, barehanded, but Ursula and Marskal were ready this time. He caught me in a hold—a Dasnarian one I'd taught him, Danu take the man—and though I could've broken it, given a moment more to muster my superior strength, Ursula interposed herself between me and Kral, knowing I'd die before I hurt her.

"What in Danu's freezing tits has gotten into you?" she hissed at me. Beyond her, Jepp kept a wary eye on me, but conferred in furious whispers with Kral.

I took a breath, reaching for the *Skablykrr* calm Kral had mocked. "It's been a thrice-cursed trying day," I muttered at her.

Her expression softened and she laid a hand on my cheek, a rare gesture of public affection. Especially considering that her retinue of guards, along with a good portion of the gate guards, now surrounded us, weapons drawn.

"I apologize," I said to her, and stopped there, hoping she'd understand all the words I couldn't say. Marskal, feeling the killing rage leave my body, relaxed his choke hold and, with another firm and reassuring clasp of my shoulder, stepped back.

"We'll talk later," Ursula promised. She moved back enough to take in both Kral and me at once. "General Kral, please accept the High Throne's apology for violating a truce of hospitality."

Surprised, he looked to her. "Your Majesty." He inclined his head. "No apology needed. I should apologize for baiting my brother. An old argument that elicits… unpredictable reactions."

"Get more predictable, both of you," she replied crisply.

"Yes, your Majesty," I bowed to her, then straightened. Habitually, my hand moved to give her the *Elskastholrr* salute, a promise and reminder, a grounding return to center—and for the first time since I'd made her that promise, I hesitated.

I didn't know if she realized I'd stopped myself, that the conflicts and doubts had seeded themselves in me so deeply that I wasn't sure of myself anymore. She might not have observed it since she'd turned away, dismissing the guards and thanking them for their alert attention. A duty that should've fallen to me, had I not been the cause of it all.

"As we were then," she declared, gesturing Jepp and Kral to precede us. "Perhaps you should attend to other duties," she said quietly to me. "Burn off some steam."

Marskal lingered close, ready to enforce her commands, no doubt.

"Your Majesty," I said, accepting the implicit judgment. As much as I wanted to affirm—perhaps have her confirm—that my place was at her side, I was in no shape to be in the same room with Kral. "I'll be working out in the training yard if you need me."

I left before she could tell me that she didn't.

CHAPTER SEVEN

"**Y**OU SHOULD TRY playing *I Eat You*," Zynda said, walking beside me. I didn't realize she was there until she'd spoken—a daunting indicator of my level of distraction.

"Shouldn't you be going to the council chambers?" I asked her mildly, to cover the surprise that she'd snuck up on me. Twice in one day, between her and Ursula.

To be fair, the Tala shapeshifters move uncannily fast and silently. Kral was right—I had gotten faster, entirely from sparring with Ursula. Even as a partblood who couldn't actually shapeshift, she could move like lightning striking. Zynda was not only a fullblood, she was likely the most talented shapeshifter alive. It didn't pay to forget that, as much as she seemed to be a graceful and lovely woman in human form, she was also the dragon. Not to mention any number of other lethal and predatory forms I'd seen her take.

She smiled at me, all blue-eyed beauty and friendliness, no frown of concern for my previous behavior. "I will go there. Eventually. But they don't need me for the talk-talk-talking. I loathe that stuff anyway. I'm just the transportation."

I snorted, the half-laugh another surprise. "And I'm just a mercenary soldier."

Her smile took on a rueful twist. "None of our lives are as

simple as they once were. But, in fact, Jepp and Kral are the messengers, and Marskal knows everything I do." She shrugged in her languid Tala way, pushing her hair off her shoulders and stretching her arms up to the sun. "Sparring with you gives me an excuse not to have to be inside those horrid stone walls any longer than necessary."

"Are we going to spar?" I asked.

"Yes, thank you!" She smiled radiantly, as if I'd invited her. "When you mentioned the training yard I figured I could be useful, so my cousin won't worry that you're going to kill your brother. Do you want to talk about it?"

"No," I replied definitively.

"Good. I'm a terrible listener." She laughed when I slanted her a glance. "We all have our strengths. If it were me, I'd rather try to kill something than talk about my feelings, too. I'll teach you to play *I Eat You*."

We'd reached the training yard, now empty with everyone either retired for midday meals or at their guard stations. I'd been planning a good workout, it was true—alone, so I could fume to myself—but sparring with a shapeshifter of Zynda's caliber could be interesting. "All right. What are the rules?"

"Quite simple. I shift to a form, try to best you in it. You counter with something that can top that."

"I can't shapeshift," I pointed out, somewhat unnecessarily.

"But you have many weapons and fighting techniques. Basically, it's a test—which of my forms can best you, which of your weapons can best me. And remember, I heal when I shift, so don't worry about pulling your strikes." She grinned. "Do your worst, mercenary."

"I don't heal magically, so watch your claws, shapeshifter."
This began to sound fun. With my blood still hot, I drew my
sword, swinging it to loosen my muscles.

Her smile took on a feral edge. "Just try not to actually kill
me. Marskal would be most put out and we don't need any
more manly displays today." With that taunt, she shifted into a
tiger. I barely registered the sight of the big cat—astonishingly
orange, ribbed in black warning stripes, mouth opened in a
mighty snarl that had frozen plenty of warriors in their shoes—
before she leapt at me.

I barely dodged those lethal claws, coming up under her
belly with an upward, two-handed heave of the broadsword that
connected with a satisfying bite. Or started to, because she
vaporized at the edge of my blade, becoming a raptor that dove
with a shriek. Talons slashed down my upraised arm before I
countered with a hastily drawn short blade, my broadsword
heavy in one hand on a backstroke too distant to bring it to bear
in time.

Next time, I'd make a pile of weapons to access. A bow or
spear would be handy. The raptor—was it an eagle? I couldn't
get a clear look at her and it didn't matter—buffeted me with
stunning blows of its wings, hooked beak going for my eyes. I
dropped the sword, as it was too big for close infighting like this,
and seized the bird by the slender neck, squeezing.

And found myself embracing a fucking grizzly bear. My
fisted hand slid uselessly off the thick throat as the bear roared in
my face, stopping my heart, and then wrapped its great arms
around me in a deadly vise so that my spine cracked, the fanged
jaws closing over my head. I was done for. I'd be so done for if

this was to the death.

But I still had my dagger and I drove it up, into the soft cavity under the rib cage, into its heart, putting all of my muscle into it. Hot blood gushed over my hand, along with entrails and the scrape of bone resisting, then cracking. I roared, too, into the bear's steaming maw, my defiance and rage in the face of death.

And it was gone.

Zynda—remarkably composed in her pretty blue dress, hair sleek and flowing—stood barefoot before me with a slender hand pressed over her heart. Her eyes huge and dark blue as the deepest ocean regarded me with shock. "Moranu, Harlan—I told you not to kill me!"

I looked down at my dagger hand, covered in blood and gore. Why did the fleshly aspects of the bear remain when the animal itself had vanished? In this, too, I shared Ursula's uneasiness with shapeshifting. A profoundly strange magic. "You had my entire head in your jaws," I pointed out, very reasonably. "All you had to do was bite down a fraction more to end me."

"Yes, but I didn't," she snapped. Then burst out laughing. "Well played, Dasnarian. I'm only glad Zyr didn't see this. He'd never let me hear the end of it. Beaten by a mossback."

I found myself grinning back at her and rolled my head on my neck, feeling the bear's bruising grip in my spine. "My ancestors thank you. I'm sure more than one faced an actual grizzly in the forests of Dasnaria."

"Two out of three?" she suggested with raised brows.

It had felt good not to have to hold back. "You're on. But I'm stockpiling some weapons for this round."

"Sure." She pretended to examine her nails like a lady of court. "But I won't go so easy on you this time."

"Same," I told her.

"When I suggested you burn off some steam, I didn't mean get yourself killed," Ursula said with considerable asperity as she walked into her chambers.

She would've been informed that I'd requested a Tala healer to attend my worst wounds, so it didn't surprise me that she already knew. Just as well that I'd gone to her rooms and not elsewhere. I'd considered it, whether I'd be welcome in the chambers that had been hers long before her father hired my Vervaldr to defend Ordnung. Ursula referred to them as our rooms, but I was careful not to. Finally I'd decided that she'd tell me in no uncertain terms when she wanted me out.

She'd left the decision in my lap, so I'd keep that tactical advantage.

"I didn't get myself killed," I replied mildly. "As you, with your acute observational skills, can no doubt confirm for yourself."

"How is he?" she asked the Tala healer, Kelleah, ignoring me entirely.

"A few broken ribs, a lot of lacerations, some internal bleeding. Nothing I can't fix, given a few more moments of quiet," Kelleah replied, voice vague and green eyes sharp. A wide-shouldered and big-bosomed woman with an unusual amount of red in her Tala dark hair, Kelleah possessed both the gentle, nurturing qualities of a healer and the no-nonsense conviction of those who put their calling above all else. Andi had sent her to be Ordnung's healer, remarking that Kelleah would be up to the challenge of defying Ursula when necessary.

Duly rebuked, clearly not happy about it, Ursula divested herself of the trappings of her public persona. First she tossed the crown aside, then removed her jewelry, treating her mother's rubies with a reverence she hadn't shown the crown. She unbuckled her sword belt from the metalwork bodice and set the whole thing—sword still sheathed—on the table. One of her ladies approached at her glance and undid the fastenings of the bodice, taking it away.

Apparently Ursula planned to stay in for a bit. I couldn't decide if that boded well or ill for me. At least she was unarmed. With external weapons, anyway.

She stretched—nothing like Zynda's languid movements, but like a warrior relieved of armor—and prowled to the window behind me. Her soft bootsteps on the thick rugs continued, and I pictured her pacing restlessly. Kelleah's healing magic swarmed through me, an odd prickling heat that made me profoundly sleepy and restless at once. I resisted the sleepiness, focusing on the surging energy. I'd need it for whatever confrontation Ursula planned—almost certainly not of the enticing variety. Alas.

Tala healing—we all knew from experience—tended to arouse sexual desire along with the renewed wellbeing. The more intense the healing, the more extreme the ensuing arousal. Except when the patient nearly died, as Ursula had. Then it was all they could do to muster the will to live. Aha—and that memory worked to dampen any ill-considered desire on my part.

I sincerely doubted Ursula would appreciate any seductive moves from the man she thought had betrayed her and had lost his temper, shaming her royal hospitality.

"There," Kelleah declared, rubbing her palms together briskly, the green of her eyes dimming as she allowed the healing magic to settle inside her again. "You'll be just fine, Captain Harlan." Her gaze darted to Ursula, still standing rigidly by the window. "At least physically." She winked encouragingly and stood. "Your Majesty," she said, by way of signaling her withdrawal, and strode out.

Servants passed her, bringing in platters of food and wine, then also left, closing the doors and leaving us alone.

"Didn't you eat yet?" I asked Ursula, surveying the spread, and the midafternoon sun.

"Yes. And no." She sounded distracted, deep in thought, but came over to sit opposite me. With her crown removed, she'd been running her hands through her bloodred hair so it stood in unruly tufts and spikes. Endearingly so. Her composed expression and shuttered gaze didn't show it, but the mussed hair gave evidence of her agitation.

I reached over the table and took her hand, so wiry and strong, callused from wielding her sword. "I'm sorry if I worried you. My wounds weren't that severe. Under other circumstances, I'd have dealt with them on my own. I only asked for Kelleah in case there's an attack. I need to be in top form."

She squeezed my hand, meeting my eyes—hers indeed filled with worry. "It's not that," she said, then amended, withdrawing her hand. "Well, hearing that Zynda had torn you up enough that you called for Kelleah didn't help my appetite. But, no, I had no stomach to eat with the others, and I knew you hadn't eaten. Due to the aforementioned and ill-advised battle to the death with the best shapeshifter living."

"It wasn't a battle to the death," I corrected, filling my plate. Magical healing left you hungry, too. "We only sparred."

"Sparred," she echoed, the neutrality of her tone an accusation in and of itself.

I quickly checked her expression, but it revealed nothing. "Yes. A game, nothing more."

"Oh, it was more than that. It was foolish and irresponsible," she bit out "Either of you could've killed the other and we need you both in the war ahead. One slip, Harlan, that's all it takes. One wound mortal enough that she can't shift in time or the Tala healer can't reach you. For a *game*. She wasn't supposed to be out there with you anyway. *Sparring*."

I watched her closely as she finished by spitting the word through tight lips. We *had* been foolish and irresponsible, Zynda and I. She'd beaten me two rounds out of three—the third time only because she pulled out the dragon form—and I'd been the one to insist on a fourth, with the dragon off the table as the worst kind of cheating. That last match had indeed nearly killed us, both of us carried away in our determination to best the other. We'd finally conceded to the tie and she'd had to lend a shoulder to help me stagger back into the castle.

Ursula, however, was more than worried, more than aggravated with me. Something had her in a quiet fury, something newer than this morning's trials.

Ursula and I usually sparred together, and it often led to sex. It hadn't occurred to me that she might see my sparring with Zynda as another betrayal. "Are you jealous?"

"No, I'm not *jealous*," she sneered, lathering a slice of rye bread with fresh butter. Then she sighed, closing her eyes briefly. "All right, maybe a little jealous."

"Essla…" I wished I still had ahold of her. "I'm in no way attracted to Zynda. You are the only woman I want. Ever. You're everything to me."

She met my gaze wryly. "So you're forever telling me. And it's not that. I'm more…bothered that you sparred with her instead of talking to me about what's going on." She held up the honey-stick, the thick liquid forming golden teardrops, pointing it at me to forestall any explanation. "I'm also envious that you two got to be outside, playing games, while I was stuck in the council chambers talking obnoxious politics."

I chewed thoughtfully. The butter tasted of sweet clover, redolent of summer, and the warm afternoon sunshine brought in the sounds of furious birdsong and the faint echoes of music and laughter. Ursula didn't have Andi's same drive to be outdoors, to live outside of walls, which seemed to be character-istic of the Tala, but she had enough Tala in her to feel the pull. When she'd been her father's heir, Ursula had traveled exten-sively through the realm, leading campaigns or exercising Uorsin's diplomatic overtures. On our travels, we'd been outside more than in.

Since returning to Ordnung and taking up the weight of her crown again, it had been the reverse. She'd barely been able to enjoy the summer weather at all. No wonder she acted so caged lately. Maybe I could do something about that.

Though not today.

"I take it the politics were obnoxious enough for you to cancel court for the afternoon?" I asked carefully.

"As obnoxious as they get," she agreed, then poured us both wine, filling the goblets to the rim. An ominous sign for so early in the day. "You and I need to talk."

Chapter Eight

H AD THERE EVER been another phrase to strike such terror in a man's heart? I could've wished to be more clear headed, free of the dregs of the healing magic, but I'd brought this on myself and I'd withstand the storm.

"All right," I said, helping myself to more food, acting as calm as possible. "You know I always enjoy conversing with you."

She slammed her palms on the table, jolting the dishes and destabilizing the wine pitcher. I caught it before it toppled, setting it back carefully and eyeing her. "Stop managing me," she ground out. The measured words might as well have been shouted.

I put down my food and rubbed my palms on thighs. "I'm not managing you. I'm doing my best to keep this conversation calm and reasonable."

"Oh, is that so?" Her eyebrows climbed along with her tone. "You mean, calm and reasonable like when you attacked Kral?"

Setting my teeth, but keeping my jaw relaxed so she wouldn't read that tic of mine, one she knew well, I picked up a fresh slice of bread and began to meticulously coat it with an even film of butter. Witness my manful control. "I apologize for that lapse. He goaded me in exactly the way he knew how to get to me."

"Then it had to do with Jenna."

Three times. Jenna's name spoken aloud for the third time in one day.

Though I'd thought I'd left Dasnarian superstitions behind, I reflexively scanned the room, half expecting her ghost to appear, summoned by the incautious incantation. Would she rail at me? Weep, perhaps, and rightfully accuse me of having been too weak and stupid to save her?

The butter tasted sour now, the fresh-baked bread like ash. I set it aside and scrubbed my hands over my face. "Yes," I replied. "It had to do with her."

Ursula sat back in her chair, angling it so she could extend her long legs, crossing them at her booted ankles. "You once told me that old pains fester like unhealed wounds, that we think they've healed, but they've only scabbed over, with the pus growing in the dark. Until something happens to break them open."

I eyed her. "There are few blows that sting more than having one's own words flung back in one's face."

She smiled slightly, more a grimace of sympathy. "I know that well, as you do it to me all the time."

I laughed a little, dry and without humor.

"That was a lot of pus I saw today," she said.

I gazed back at her, and she refilled my wine cup, which I'd already emptied. Another bad sign. "Is this what you wanted to talk about—or is it whatever news Jepp and Kral brought?"

"Both, actually." She had unhappy lines around her mouth. "They are … intertwined."

I nodded, not understanding, but wondering. Kral needling me about Jenna after all this time hadn't been a coincidence. In my experience, very little in life is a coincidence. I blame hlyti.

"I did cancel court this afternoon," Ursula continued, "so you and I can sort all of this out. I can't... I need to lock this part of my life down before I can deal with anything else."

A profound failure on my part, a failure to the *Elskastholrr* that I caused her difficulty instead of being a solid foundation. "Which first, then—yours or mine?"

She regarded me calmly. "I'm sorry to force you into this, so your choice."

Time to clean up my own mess, then we'd see if we had anything left in us to address whatever news Kral had brought that was dire enough for Ursula to cancel court.

"I was fourteen years old," I told her, "and the youngest of my siblings."

As I spoke, it seemed the formal chill of the Imperial Palace settled around us. The opulent carpets that muffled the bootsteps of the men and silenced the barefoot tread of the elegant women. The scent of jasmine and the delicate chime of jewelry as they drifted past, wreathed in colorful silk, gazes demurely averted. Mysterious and enticing.

"Six brothers," Ursula prompted, bringing me out of the reverie.

"Yes, and three sisters. All of us born in four years to three wives."

"Your father was a busy man—and his wives hard-worked."

"Yes." I splayed my hands on the table, so like my father's. Big and blunt. The hands of a warrior, not a statesman. The hands of a brutally cruel and domineering man. "He became emperor later than he wished—having spent many years in various wars, adding to the empire for his father—and set to making heirs with due diligence."

I lifted my gaze to hers, and raised a brow. "In Dasnaria, the emperor is not only divine, but expected to demonstrate his manly virility by producing as many children by as many women as possible."

"Of course," she replied softly, eyes a softer gray now with sympathy at whatever she saw in mine.

"Of course," I echoed, wryly. "So, that number doesn't include the multitudes of illegitimate half-siblings I have. I have no idea how many. Of the ten legitimate children born to his three wives, we are in order of birth: my eldest sister—whose name I've vowed never to speak aloud, but that you know—then Hestar, Kral, Inga, Ban, Helva, Mykal, Leo, Loke, and myself."

"So many," she murmured and picked up her wine, though she didn't drink. "And which are your full siblings?"

"Hestar—now emperor—Helva, Leo and Loke. Those last two are identical twins." I smiled despite my grim mood, remembering the trouble the golden twins of mischief had gotten into.

"You're full brother to the Emperor of Dasnaria," she mused, looking into her wine. "Does that mean anything significant?"

"It doesn't change anything materially, no. For the most part, birth order decides the hierarchy, though the status of the mother does, too. My mother was second wife."

"Was?"

"Died long ago." I met Ursula's intent gaze evenly. "My mother was named Jilliya. She was never in good health, not as long as I can remember."

"She bore five children in four years. Even with two of them twins, that would be enough to ruin the health of any woman," Ursula pointed out.

"True. And Hulda, first wife, had a deft hand with poison."

Ursula's mouth parted slightly, but she took that in, drinking a good draught of her wine. She drank less now than when I met her, which I liked to think I'd influenced, if only by helping her find other ways to unwind enough to sleep. I didn't begrudge her the choice this afternoon. Didn't begrudge either of us.

"So much you've never told me," she commented.

I laced my fingers together into one fist, steadying it on the table. "I'm sorry for that. I'm telling you now. Everything I can speak aloud. Whatever you want to know."

"All right." She inclined her head. "So Jenna was your half-sister and—does it hurt you for me to speak her name? You flinched just then."

I blew out a breath, aware it came out shaky. "No. It's... just shocking. To hear it. So is the past tense."

"I apologize. That was thoughtless of me. She *is* your half-sister."

"Yes. My half-sister. Kral's full sister, both of them born to Hulda. And past tense is likely accurate. She almost certainly died two decades ago. It's a... reality I've never quite grappled with." A headache throbbed behind my eyes and I squeezed the bridge of my nose between thumb and knuckled forefinger, aware of the moisture there. Soon I'd be sobbing like a toddler.

"Harlan." Ursula sounded broken, as she so rarely did. She stood beside me and her hand covered mine. I opened my arms to her and she slipped onto my lap, all delicate bones and yielding softness. She leaned into me and I buried my face against her silky hair that looked like blood and fire, but tasted of grace. "You're the one who's good at this," she finally said. "Do you want to stop or keep going?"

"The wound is open," I replied with grim determination, "so let's continue purging the pus."

"All right then. So, as eldest child born to the first wife, Jenna would've been heir, had she been a boy."

I smiled, brushing my lips against her forehead. The sharpest of minds—and practiced at keeping track of royal politics, much as she groused about it. "Correct. So Hestar was heir, with Kral in second place—though a close one, with his mother being the Empress. I didn't understand much of this back then. I was a boy, the baby, and I was entirely caught up in training to fight well enough that my brothers couldn't beat me into letting them run my life—and with the enticing prospect of bedding my first woman on my upcoming birthday."

She laughed, sweet against me. "I can only imagine your devotion to that particular threshold."

"Yes." I tipped her chin up and kissed her, needing it. To my great relief, she returned the kiss, opening her mouth to me and winding her long arms around my neck. I sank into her, savoring her intensity and passion. So rarely did I have her undivided attention. She smiled at me, caressing my cheek with her rough fingers, all womanly softness for the moment, all mine. For the moment.

"I was a callow youth," I continued, thinking back to my past self. "Self-absorbed as adolescents are, terribly spoiled as the baby of the family. When it came time for my eldest sister to be married, I was filled with excitement. There would be parties and I would get to see her, Inga, and Helva again for the first time in seven years."

"Why so long?" Ursula interrupted with a frown. "Didn't you all live in the Imperial Palace?"

"Yes, but the Imperial Princesses all remained in the seraglio. I spent my early years in there with them, the other wives and ladies, and my mother. Around age seven, though, the boys leave the seraglio to begin to learn to be men, and the girls stay behind." I smoothed the line between her brows with my thumb. "It's a strange practice, I know—and one I can't abide now—but back then I was actually jealous of my sisters that they got to stay. The seraglio of the Imperial Palace is still one of the most beautiful places I've ever seen. An enclosed world, lush and tropical, with lagoons and palm trees. We played all day and were indulged in every way. Leaving it... well, that was a cold awakening to what felt like a much harsher world. I would cry myself to sleep at night—silently, so my brothers wouldn't hear and use it against me—missing my mother and my sisters. I felt sorry for myself." I laughed, a bitter edge to it, for my selfishness.

"Of course you grieved," Ursula replied, still frowning. "Ripping a child that age from everything he's known would be terribly traumatic."

"And yet, I was a privileged idiot because I didn't understand that I was the lucky one. I still had no idea when seven years later my eldest sister turned eighteen and her marriage was arranged to one of our father's favored subject kings, Rodolf of Arynherk. I was more excited for that wedding—for all my siblings to be together—than I'd been for anything in my life." The jubilation of my younger self shamed me now. "Until I began to listen to the talk in the training yard, the way the other men snickered about Rodolf, speculating about what he'd done to his other wives, four of them, all dead young. They called him Bloody Rodolf, and the things they said about him, dark things, sexual things..." I had to stop, unable to say them aloud, especially not to Ursula, who'd suffered at the hands of a monster, too.

But she lay soft against me still, calm and understanding. "For a boy who had yet to lie with a woman that had to be shocking to hear."

"Yes." I wrapped my arms around her, as if I could protect her from her past, protect Jenna from the terrible things I had been powerless to prevent. "I'd had a boy's ideals about women and sex, that it would be all about soft skin and perfume and gentle delights."

"Like the seraglio had been in your childhood," she murmured.

"Ah." That hadn't occurred to me. "I suppose so." I tucked that idea away to examine later. "So when Inga and my eldest sister emerged from the seraglio for the first time in their lives... I learned so much that night."

About beauty and power.

And betrayal.

CHAPTER NINE

"THEY WERE BOTH astonishingly beautiful," I remembered. "As elegant and polished as the wealth of an empire could create. My eldest sister had inherited her mother's beauty—and Empress Hulda was famous for her ivory hair and extraordinary deep blue eyes. On top of that, my eldest sister had lived all her life indoors, with only magical light, away from the sun, so her skin was fair and unblemished, her hair only shades darker. And they'd dressed her in white silk, diamonds and pearls. She took my breath away." I frowned. "I don't mean that to sound…"

"It doesn't," Ursula murmured. "She was dazzling. Your beloved sister and the epitome of feminine beauty. You probably worshipped her."

"I did, yes." I rubbed my hand along her back, grateful she understood. "I was in awe of her and I wanted to save her. I warned her about Rodolf, told her she should break off the engagement. But she wouldn't listen. I figured it was because I was only a boy and not worth paying attention to.

"She married him, and they stayed in the Imperial Palace for a week. She was always either with *him*"—my voice shook, and I had to steady it—"or in the seraglio where I couldn't go. Everyone was so happy, celebrating the royal wedding. When I asked about her, everyone told me not to worry, that she was fine.

"But we had a reception for her that last night before she left on her wedding journey to travel with him to his kingdom—a party for her that she actually got to attend—a *party*. And, oh, Essla..." I had to pause to catch my breath. "She was so changed. He'd broken her. They'd covered her pretty skin with makeup, but I could see the bruises beneath. And her klút—her gown—covered more of her, and they'd given her gloves to wear under her wedding bracelets, but I could tell by the way she flinched, how she hunched into herself that the cur had hurt her in terrible ways."

Ursula made a sound, and I stopped, fully aware of the parallels, how Ursula had submitted to whatever her own father expected of her. "Is this too difficult for you to hear, given what Uorsin did to you?"

"It's not easy," she admitted, still not looking at me. "I want to say I'm over that and it's in the past, but we both know that would be a lie. And what happened to me was nothing like this. I want you to keep going. I begin to understand, though, how you could see so much in me, so easily."

Not easily. Nothing about Ursula had been easy. I squeezed her reassuringly, then relaxed my hold. "I asked her if he'd hit her and she *laughed*. Laughed in my face, and I realized that what she'd been through was so much worse than that. I wanted her to appeal to our father, her mother, to Hestar, heir apparent. I begged her to tell them, to show them her injuries."

"She told you they knew and it wouldn't matter anyway," Ursula guessed.

"How did you know?"

She shrugged a little, her cheek against my chest. "You were a sexually innocent boy of fourteen. If you could see it, imagine how much better the adults could recognize the signs. If you'd heard the gossip, then everyone knew about Bloody Rodolf. Jenna probably understood far better than you did how little recourse she had."

"What you and my sister saw so clearly came as an astonishing blow to me. I spoke to our father, to Hestar, to Kral, and my other brothers about the situation and... they didn't care. She was an Imperial Princess and must do her duty to the family and the empire. We all served the Konyngrr fist; a woman's lot fell to her. She accepted it—why couldn't I?"

"Because you've never had it in you to accept injustice of any kind," Ursula replied. "One of the many things I love about you."

I breathed in her scent and the reassurance that she could still speak so easily of loving me. So surreal to be telling this story after all the years of silence, but I couldn't imagine anyone else I'd rather tell. Could have told, for that matter. "My sister— she told me to forget her. And she said..." The anguish knotted my throat. "She told me goodbye, and said that if I want to do something for her, to treat the women in my life well in her memory."

"And you have," Ursula said softly. She must have been weeping because my shirt had gone damp under her cheek. "You are the best of men, Harlan. She'd be so proud."

I kissed her forehead, beyond grateful for those words. "But the story doesn't end there."

"Of course not," she said, her voice dry now. "Because you're you."

I chuckled, relieved to feel my chest relax. "Well, and I was an impetuous young man with more ideals than sense. But I also was an Imperial Prince, and I used that status to bully the Arynherk guards into allowing me to join their entourage. I stayed out of Rodolf's sight, not that he'd pay much attention to a minor princeling like me, and kept to the middle-ranking officers—intimidating them with liberal use of my father's name and probable wrath, avoiding anyone with enough rank to know I shouldn't be there."

"Nicely played." Ursula's admiration did excellent things for my ego, even for something I'd done long ago.

"I'm surprised in retrospect that I pulled it off."

"Youthful bravado goes a long way."

"Very true. My sister, when she saw I'd come along, very nearly gave it all away in her panic. She wanted to protect *me*, begged me to go back before I was found out."

"I can understand that," Ursula commented.

Of course she would, being the eldest sister, always taking care of the others. "But my mind was made up and I refused."

"Stubborn, even then."

I let that go as true enough. "The farther we traveled from the Imperial Palace, the laxer the seraglio rules were in the noble households where Rodolf planned to overnight. In the smaller manors and keeps, it's simply not practical or healthy for the women to live in a closed set of rooms all day, every day. That openness would work in our favor. I also knew once we reached Arynherk, I'd be dealing with people loyal to Rodolf, so if I was going to help my sister escape, then it had to be before then."

Ursula sat up and looked at me. "You helped her to escape?"

"Of course." I frowned, puzzled. "That was my plan all along."

"Oh, thank Danu," she breathed and framed my face with her warrior's hands, kissing me deeply. "I can't stand suspense. Tell me she escaped with you."

"She escaped with me."

Ursula let out a long breath. "Unreal. You are a remarkable man."

I smoothed a wayward lock of her hair back from her temple. "Thank you, but I was mostly insanely lucky. When I look back at all the ways my plan could've failed..." I shook off the specter of those nightmare scenarios, some that still visited me in harrowing dreams.

"I broke her out in the middle of the night and we traveled through... a cold climate." I hedged my way judiciously through the details I'd sworn not to reveal. "And made for a... place where we could travel out of the empire."

Ursula settled back against me. "This is like a riddle. I'm guessing you went through remote countryside, probably crossing mountains if it was so much colder, to a coastal city where you could sail elsewhere. Smart plan."

"Not so much. As with all plans, but especially those contrived by inexperienced fools, it went awry." I sighed heavily. "I need to move."

She obligingly stood, uncoiling herself with grace and a hint of the speed from her shapeshifter heritage. Taking the opportunity, she refilled our wine goblets and met me by the window with them. Handing me mine, she touched hers to it in grave salute. "To an idealistic boy who did what no one else had the courage to attempt."

I smiled slightly, mostly to please her, and sipped, steeling myself for the next part. "We couldn't travel as swiftly as I'd assumed. My experience had been with other men, ones properly dressed for bitter weather and skilled at riding. My sister... she had never even sat a horse before. Though I'd found outdoor gear for her, it had all been designed for men." I swallowed some wine, grateful for the way it blurred the sharp edges of those desperate memories.

"And she'd been hurt," Ursula supplied, gaze full of sorrow.

"Yes. The women... they used teas and a soothing smoke to ease pain. Another aspect of life in the Imperial Palace I'd been aware of but never thought through." I lifted my wine in grim acceptance. "My sister had been drugged into a stupor and I made her give up the smoke and tea so she'd be alert for the escape."

"You had to." Ursula nodded crisply. "No choice there. And she did it, which speaks to her strength of character."

If only I'd known someone like Ursula then. I could've used her clear thinking. "She was so brave, Essla. She never once complained, but she was in terrible pain, injured far worse than I knew, where no one could see."

Ursula nodded, understanding, the ghost of old pain tightening her face. I nearly asked again if I should stop, remembering what she'd told me about herself, how she'd been so young, and she'd bled, telling no one. She wouldn't thank me, though, for treating her as too fragile to hear this.

"I didn't know until we reached the hunter's cabin I'd been making for. We'd made it away clean and rode through the night, but morning would bring discovery of her absence and inevitable pursuit. I'd hoped to rest a few hours, then continue. But her saddle blankets…" I rubbed a hand over my face, wiping away the cold sweat. "Soaked in blood."

"Not surprising, really," Ursula said the words very softly, laying a hand on my arm and stroking me. "A young and virgin bride and a man of Bloody Rodolf's reputation…"

"Yes, well." I wrapped my hands around the goblet, holding onto it. "I didn't know that. I wasn't even entirely clear on how women differed from men, other than ribald jokes and improbable tales. But I had to do *something*. She was so pale and weak— even I could see she'd die if we kept going that way."

"What did you do?" Ursula asked, the knowing in her eyes.

"She was ashamed, embarrassed, didn't want me to know and certainly didn't want her baby brother seeing her that way." It had been so surreal, her embarrassment and mine, along with the keen awareness that her life, at the least, rode on both of us setting those niceties aside. My lovely sister, and the savagery of what he'd done to her tenderest, most intimate self.

"He'd torn her badly, in her sex, so I sewed her up. I knew enough of field dressing wounds, how to clean them, of stitches and so forth. What I didn't know was…" I gave Ursula a look I hoped was wry, though it felt like it fell short. She only watched me with solemn attention. "I didn't know what a healthy woman's sex should look like," I explained. "I didn't know what was a natural opening and what—" My voice broke.

Ursula took my goblet, set it aside, and drew me into her

arms; so much slighter than I, but strong enough to hold me as I dropped my forehead to her shoulder. "Oh, Harlan," she murmured. "You are an incredible man, then and now. And she lived. That's what matters."

"She lived. And I made myself some promises that night."

"You swore to learn your way around women so well that you would know what to do both to give them pleasure and to heal?" Ursula suggested, a wry knowing in her voice.

I lifted my head and kissed her forehead. "Yes."

"I can vouch for your success." She kissed me, a tender brush of her lips against mine, gentle in a way she rarely was. "What then?"

"We were extraordinarily lucky—or so I believed—and though we stayed in that cabin for days, long enough for her to heal sufficiently to at least ride, we weren't discovered. We made it to my planned destination, and I paid for passage on transportation to leave in the morning. My sister had shorn her distinctive hair and we'd found a sympathetic blacksmith to cut off her wedding bracelets, and unchain her ring. We'd—"

Ursula held up her index finger, stopping me. She'd broken that finger a few times in sword practice or battles, and it had a crooked bent, as if it asked a question. "Cut off her bracelets, and... unchain a ring?" she inquired, a hint of danger beneath the smooth surface tone.

I sighed. She was going to hate this. "Dasnarian wedding bracelets are an old tradition. They're jeweled and very pretty— all different designs—but traditionally they're locked onto the bride during the wedding ceremony, never to be removed." More like manacles than jewelry, it had occurred to me much later in life.

Ursula assimilated that with a cool and remote expression, saying nothing.

"The ring... Well, Bloody Rodolf had this extraordinary diamond ring, an Arynherk tradition, that he gave my sister to go with the bracelets—and attached to them by a chain. They all had to be cut off and the jewels were going to pay for our new lives."

"'Our'?" She still sounded distant, mastering her revulsion, I knew.

"I planned to go with her. My sister... she knew nothing of the world. She'd been raised very deliberately that way. I'd never thought about it—as I'd never thought about so many things back then, in my selfishness—but she'd been educated only in pleasing her husband. You know already that Dasnarian women can't handle money or make trade transactions of any kind, by law of the empire, but my sister couldn't even count."

"Of course you had to go with her." Ursula picked up her wine again and sipped, considering me, her thoughts obscure.

"And I had no wish to return to my life," I admitted. "I couldn't be a part of a family who did that to their own. I wanted nothing more of being an Imperial Prince and all that entailed."

"Which is why you were so angry with me the day Kral arrived at Ordnung, and I called you Prince Harlan Konyngrr," she noted.

"Yes." I grimaced, acknowledging. "You understand more now why I am not... entirely rational on the topic."

"I do." She gazed out the window at the lovely summer

THE DRAGONS OF SUMMER

afternoon, her profile sharp, her bearing so regal. "I won't beat you up about this, but you could have explained. It would've helped to know before now."

I brushed a hand over her hair, less an apology than an effort to demonstrate what I had no words to express. She gave me a sidelong look, and shook her head. "Finish it. What happened?"

"Kral found us."

"Kral." She pressed her lips together. "I see."

"He tracked us. Caught me naked in the bath, my weapons on the other side of the room."

She winced in sympathy and I knew she, of all people, would understand that level of nakedness, of powerlessness.

"He intended to escort us back to face our father, said all would be forgiven if we gave him no trouble. My sister, of course, would be returned to her husband, who owned her under Dasnarian law."

Ursula set down her goblet and leaned against the window sill, breathing the fresh air, her knuckles white. "I'm sorry I stopped you from killing him," she said conversationally.

"No, it's good you stopped me."

"Oh, right." She gave me a lethal smile. "Because now we can go kill him together."

CHAPTER TEN

S HE MEANT IT, too, gray eyes sharp as a silver blade. No matter that Ursula claimed the priorities of the High Throne overrode all else, where she loved, she loved fiercely and without reservation. And as Danu's avatar, she couldn't abide injustice, especially wrongs against other women. I laughed, running a hand down her back, more in love with this warrior of a woman than ever.

"Jepp would never forgive us," I pointed out.

"Jepp," she said reflectively. "How she can love a man like that?"

"Because he's changed." I held up my hands when her gaze narrowed and sparked. "He has. You have to realize he was only a youth, too. At seventeen, he had years of bulk and fighting skill on me, but he was, if anything, more selfish, more narrow-minded, able to see only one path, one ambition."

She snorted, but didn't interrupt.

"He believed that he'd be made heir in Hestar's place, as a reward for bringing us back."

"Would your father have done that?"

I lifted a shoulder and let it fall. "Who knows? Kral believed he would, and his mother Hulda molded him to want nothing but that, except perhaps her approval—which, along with her love, hinged entirely on Kral ascending to the throne instead of Hestar. Kral...didn't have it in him to have compassion for our sister. None of us were raised to have compassion for the weak, or for the women we believed existed to slake our needs and nothing else."

She contemplated that—and me. "However did you emerge from that as the man you are now?"

I refilled my goblet and hers. "I broke into pieces and put myself back together in another pattern."

"I see. So, Kral had you trapped and captive...?"

"Kral underestimated her. It never occurred to him that she'd act without my help, so he left her for the night in her own room at the inn and made me sleep in his." I raised my brows. "Anything else wouldn't have been proper."

"She escaped in the night?" Ursula breathed, a hint of delight in it.

"She did." I couldn't help smiling also. "She must've climbed out the windows and made her way over the rooftops. No one saw or heard a thing. She was a dancer, did I mention that? I saw her dance the ducerse the night before her wedding, and she was stunning. You would appreciate the athletic skill of it. She wore bells, but danced so that they remained silent until she allowed them to chime." I shook my head, remembering Jenna, her ivory hair like a banner of silk, gleaming with pearls and sparkling with diamonds, dancing as I'd never seen anyone dance, before or since.

"In the morning she was gone, leaving only that diamond ring behind. She arranged it just so, in the carcass of the fowl Kral had eaten for dinner. You should've seen Kral's face." I laughed, and Ursula laughed with me, the light of vengeance bright in her eyes.

"Good girl," she murmured. "Good for you." Her expression sharpened. "Surely Kral searched for her."

"Of course—and dragged me with him, also of course. She wasn't on the transportation I'd booked. No one had seen her."

Ursula looked interested, loving the puzzle. "She left the diamond but had the other jewels, and you have to be talking sailing ships. So, she set sail for somewhere else."

I lifted one shoulder and let it fall. "Or she was enslaved."

Ursula frowned, shocked out of her reverie. "Excuse me?"

"You, yourself, accused me of being from a race of slavers when we first met," I pointed out. "While not entirely accurate, it's also not entirely untrue. My sister was a lovely, nubile young woman, clearly of gentle birth, with no protection, no way to defend herself beyond a few last-resort moves I showed her with a dagger."

Ursula smiled briefly. "Of course you did. But she might've found friends. There are good people in the world, too."

I touched her cheek. "You are the idealist, though you try to act so tough."

She narrowed her eyes in menace. "I *am* tough."

"You are," I conceded. "My sister… was not." I could only wish she'd been trained as Ursula had, to be a warrior, to survive.

"I don't know, Harlan." Ursula thoughtfully turned the goblet in her hands. "The woman you describe is no fragile flower. She gutted it out on that ride, gave up the drugs when she had to be in horrendous pain—climbed out a window and disappeared. She sounds like a survivor to me."

"Then why didn't I find her? Why didn't she find me?" I tossed back the rest of my wine, the grit in the dregs of it scraping my throat.

"I take it you looked."

"Later, yes. After I left the third time."

"The third?"

"Yes. So, once Kral—to his intense fury and frustration, which I greatly enjoyed—couldn't find any trace of our sister, we journeyed back to the Imperial Palace. No surprise, though I went peaceably enough, all was not forgiven." I smiled without humor as Ursula's gaze darkened. "My father, the emperor; Empress Hulda; my brother Hestar; Kral—they all brought considerable pressure on me to reveal where my sister had gone."

"You didn't tell them you didn't know?"

"Sure I did. They didn't believe me. If I hadn't helped her final escape, then they'd have to accept that a young woman, barely more than a girl, whom they'd devoted enormous effort into molding to be obedient and helpless, had somehow succeeded at defying them all. Which is more likely?"

She nodded, slowly, then looked at me with concern. "What pressure did they put on you?"

I lifted a shoulder and let it fall. "It was long ago, and the young man I was no longer needs defending."

"I'll decide what needs defending. What pressure?"

"The usual, Essla," I told her wearily. "What you'd imagine—beatings, flogging, starvation, back-breaking work, humiliating me by stripping me of rank, of what little power I possessed."

"I'm so sorry, Harlan," she murmured, looking bereft.

"As I said, it was long ago, and it did a great deal to strengthen me. I learned a lot about myself and what I could withstand. I discovered they couldn't do anything to me that I wouldn't willingly suffer, as I always had in my mind's eye how much worse my sister had suffered, simply for existing. Eventually, however, they discovered something I couldn't bear."

"Your mother, and your other sisters," Ursula guessed, then smiled ruefully at what she saw in my face. "Standard technique for breaking someone, yes? If you can't break them, hurt someone else in their stead. I bet it worked, too."

"It did. You know, through all that, I still hadn't seen Helva. She was only fifteen and not old enough to leave the seraglio and attend the wedding *festivities*. But they brought her out to be flogged. Her and Inga both. I couldn't stop it."

I thought I'd done well, making it through the story thus far—past what I'd thought were the worst parts—without giving into the wracking grief. But the stricken look on Ursula's face did me in. I'd shed tears for her before, and now she wept for me, mirroring my terrible sorrow.

"I couldn't stop it," I told her again. Suddenly weak with the memory, I slid down the wall to sit on the carpeted floor. Ursula sat with me, her silver-clad legs crossed under the split gown, looking almost girlish, nothing of the regal queen or vicious warrior in her now.

She took one of my hands in hers. "No, Harlan, you couldn't have stopped it. They did it, not you. You bear no guilt for this."

I nodded so she'd feel better, though I knew the guilt was in fact all mine, and knuckled away the tears. "Fortunately, they didn't whip Inga and Helva much." I barked out a laugh, bitter. "*Much.* How's that for temporizing?"

"It's meaningful," Ursula insisted. "Your sisters were young, naïve, tender—it would've been easy to make them cry without hurting them severely, especially if the goal was to goad you."

"I'm not sure that helps."

"Set it aside for now, but you might find it does help, over time."

"When did you get so smart?" I touched her cheek and she smiled at me, watery.

"From being around you, obviously." She cocked her head. "Why didn't you lie, give them some story for where she'd gone?"

"Two reasons: first, because I didn't know. I was afraid of inadvertently putting them on her trail. Second, I knew it wouldn't end anything. When they didn't find her, they'd just come back to me, and do it all again, only escalating faster. The Konyngrrs don't give up easily." I gave her a humorless smile. "I come by my stubbornness honestly."

"So you had to stop it. The *Skablykrr* training."

I sobered. "Exactly. I stole out of the Imperial Palace for the second time in my life—which, as you may recall from Jepp's reports, was by no means an easy task—and I spent six months with the monks of *Skablykrr*."

"And no one found you?"

"Oh, they knew where I was, all right, but even the emperor didn't dare violate the sanctity of the *Skablykrr*. And when I returned to the Imperial Palace, they left me alone."

"But you left a third time. The final time."

"Yes. I couldn't live there. Couldn't be part of any of that any longer. I stayed a few months, recruited some friends, and we stole away. Had some adventures." I grinned, crookedly, and she smiled back. "I traveled the world, looking for my sister. Eventually I formed the Vervaldr, taking any job in a place I hadn't yet searched. Later I ended up here, thinking I might find her somewhere in these lands. Instead, hlyti has guided my footsteps to you."

"And your family just let you go?"

"Oh, they'd stripped me of my rank and disinherited me already. And they knew they'd get nothing out of me since the vows I'd taken couldn't be broken."

"*Couldn't?*" she repeated with emphasis.

I cupped her hands in mine, looking into her gray eyes, so keen and troubled. "*Can't.* It's nearly a magical binding—could be magical, for all I know—but the information I consigned to secrecy is beyond my ability to speak. I literally cannot say my eldest sister's name, or certain details I omitted. Even telling you all of this has been … painful in a way I can't quite describe."

"Thank you," she said gravely, gripping my hands. "I apologize that I ever doubted you."

"You had good reason," I said gravely. "I'm sorry for it."

She shook her head. "No, I don't think I did have good reason. But I can promise I'll never doubt you again."

I frowned a little. "Don't be hasty in—"

"I swear," she interrupted me viciously, "that I will never doubt you again, as long as I live. In the name of the boy you were and the girl she was, and the man you've made yourself into, and the woman she is, out there somewhere, I so swear."

My heart, so raw and bleeding, felt as if it swelled in my chest. "I love you, Ursula, with everything in me. The *Elskastholrr* is a vow like the others, something that cannot be broken, but even if it could be, I'll always love you. You are the best part of me. You can send me away from you, but know that it would end me. Nothing they could do to me could break me, but losing you from my life surely would."

She let go of our joined hands to crawl back onto my lap, straddling my outstretched legs and framing my face in her hands. The summer sun set her hair on fire and her eyes shone as clear and bright as Danu's sword. "I will never send you away, Harlan. You might wish to go, but it would break me to lose you, too."

"I'll never leave you willingly," I breathed, her lips coming tantalizingly close.

"Don't make that promise just yet," she urged, "but would you make me forget, for a while? I want to be only us, if only for another hour."

I didn't ask what she meant, for I knew we had yet to get to the second issue she'd closeted us to discuss. Instead I did as my queen commanded, taking her fierce mouth with mine, savoring her heat and flavor, relishing how she surrendered to my touch. My Essla, who melted only for me. Her lips parted, bringing me in, her hands working to unlace my shirt, caressing my chest. She'd long ago discovered how her calluses aroused me and she used them to good effect, with urgency and skill.

I groaned, loosing the chains I'd kept on the desire evoked by the healing, the need flooding me. For her and only her. My warrior queen. With a growl, I tumbled her onto her back, catching her wrists and pinning them. She glared at me in defiance. "Do your worst," she hissed, using her lithe strength to attempt to squirm out of my grip. Not quite shapeshifting, but slithery and as difficult to contain.

I bared my teeth at her. "You awakened the dragon, little hawk, and I plan to eat you alive."

CHAPTER ELEVEN

S HE FOUGHT ME. Never an easy conquest, my warrior queen, but I had ahold of her and wouldn't let her go. The struggle roused us both to panting, the fire burning hot between us. I'd first seduced her by enticing her into a fight, earning first her respect, then her heated surrender.

It had been the end of a long and subtle siege. A brilliant stroke of strategy on my part, one I had no qualms in congratulating myself on, figuring out I'd have to batter down those walls she'd built so long ago to keep anyone from hurting her again. Sometimes she came to me easily, with the soft kisses and sweet yielding of long familiarity.

Other times she insisted I fight my way through, proving to us both the intensity of our need—mine to have her, and hers to admit me to the inner circle of her trust.

With teeth and hands, I tore away her clothing and her reserve, driving her wild as I did, until I had her naked, all long-limbed, lean woman. My Essla doesn't think she's beautiful, but only because she can't see herself as I do. Her long, elegant legs, her slim, rangy body, very nearly delicate, if not for the wiry muscles and the scars of many battles, like a tiger's stripes, evidence of her ferocity. Pinning her, I took the prominent nipple of one of her small breasts into my mouth, locking it against my palate with my tongue and allowing my upper teeth to scrape her tender flesh.

She threw back her head, swanlike throat exposed, and arched her spine, crying out in her pleasure. The sound might carry through the open windows, but we'd both passed the point of caring. I slid down her body, tracing the lines of her rib cage, the narrow waist I could span with my hands, and lingering over the quivering muscles of her abdomen, still too hollow.

The scars there had faded extensively with the magical healing, but remained pinker than the older ones. Obviously not the work of a blade, the scars knotted like an exotic blossom, petals curling from where the High Priestess of Deyrr's clawed fingers had plunged through Ursula's flesh like melted butter.

"Harlan," Ursula said, her fingers stroking through my short hair, all soothing and sweetness, battle fire forgotten. "I'm alive. I'm fine. They're scars only."

I looked up her long body, to where she'd raised herself up on one elbow to look at me when I'd paused so long. She regarded me with concern.

"I know," I told her. "I tell myself that. All the time."

She sat up, drawing me with her, stroking her hands over my chest and shoulders. Not to arouse this time, but in comfort. "I understand better now what it meant to you to be held helpless by the High Priestess's magic, not to be able to act to protect me."

My breath caught hard and agonizing in my chest, my heart straining with it.

"But it wasn't your fault," she insisted, remorseless and intent, ducking her head to catch my gaze and hold it.

I shook my head slowly. "It feels like it was."

"I get that, but it's not real."

"I swore to protect you when I swore the *Elskastholrr*. I swore to myself that I'd never stand by and fail to act when someone was being wrongfully hurt." The cries and broken weeping of my sisters echoed in my mind. They hadn't begged—nor had they ever looked at me—but they had eventually wept. The whipping master knew his job too well.

Ursula's mouth, hot and avid on mine, broke through the agonizing reverie. "None of us is invincible," she murmured against my lips. "All we can do is our best. And your best, my mighty one, is astonishing. We've made it through fights no one should have lived through." She pushed me onto my back, divesting me of my clothes and following with mouth and hands, conquering me. Making me forget. "We did it by fighting together. You at my back and me at yours."

Her hands found my rigid cock, gripping firmly, teasing in their feminine roughness. I caught my breath again, but in shock at the sheer rush of pleasure, my heart hammering now with lust. She straddled me, glorious in the pour of afternoon sunlight, Danu's chosen, and lowered herself slowly onto my cock, eyes erotically silver. So fierce and beautiful. Mine. I gave myself over to it, the sense of coming home, of her slick heat enclosing me, internal muscles clasping me.

"I don't care about your vows," she said, fully seated on me, unmoving. "Any of them. It's not your job to protect me. We protect each other. Take care of each other. Don't leave me."

"I never have. Never will," I promised, my brain fogging, my control fraying. "What else do I have to promise for you to move already?"

She laughed, delighted, throwing her head back in utter ease. So far she'd come from the rigid and scarred woman she'd been, so afraid to touch and be touched. People did heal. They did survive to live. To live good lives, despite everything.

Ursula rocked herself on me, a mischievous smile quirking her lips. Playful and pleased with herself. "You feel so good inside me, maybe I'll just stay here." She leaned to run her hands over my chest and shoulders. "Keep you here like this forever, for me to feast on."

I'd let her, too. There was nothing I wouldn't give her. "I love you, my hawk."

"And I love you. I'm grateful every day that you found me, that your hlyti guided you to me." Undulating her hips, her smile turned sensual, her internal muscles rippling along my shaft to shattering effect.

"*Luta!*" I growled, all control lost. Grasping her hips, I held her as I thrust up into her. Startled, she dug her fingers into my forearms as she convulsed, clinging to me for balance, as an anchor. I thrust again and she cried out, a soft mewl of helpless pleasure she never made at any other time. A sign that she'd dropped the last of her walls and admitted me to the most private, vulnerable part of herself.

Shifting to cup her head and brace my weight, I rolled her onto her back, savoring the way she wound her long legs around me, capturing me in place even as she gave over the rhythm to me. Languid with her surrender, she draped her arms around my neck, eyes half closed as she savored the slide of our bodies.

She'd often told me she loved the press of my weight on her, the solidity of full skin-on-skin, so I gave her that—finding that sweet balance of being heavy without crushing her.

Watching her face, I adjusted the depth and drive, finding the ones that would unwind her, taking her apart bit by bit. Her nails bit into me as she climbed higher, legs grappling me, her body vibrating with tension. Silvery eyes glinting through lowered lashes, her face softened in need and love. If I ever doubted, I'd only have to watch her in these unguarded moments to see her heart and what it held for me.

My own climax gathering, I counted dynasties, an old habit to stall orgasm, accelerating my pace. She arched, convulsed, clinging to me as if she'd fall, crying out my name. Giving over, I followed her, driving myself into her sweet sheath, emptying everything I'd ever been, ever loved and suffered.

Giving it all to her.

Elskastholrr.

"AND HERE I'D intended to distract *you*," she said throatily, some time later.

I'd rolled onto my back again, as post-coital crushing is far less erotic, draping her over me. She lay in boneless abandon, her head nestled in the hollow of my shoulder, her favored spot. I traced the lines of her body, savoring this rare moment when she was utterly relaxed and without care.

If I could have her that way all the time, I would. But then she wouldn't be the woman I'd fallen in love with—a kindred spirit. Both of us shouldered the burdens of caring for those we loved, of fighting for the just cause, preventing the power-mad from consuming everything in their unfeeling greed.

"You're right," I said quietly. "We protect each other. You are no soft and sheltered maiden. I've known that all along. I fell in love with you the first time I laid eyes on you because of that."

She propped her chin on my chest, looking up at me. "Not because I reminded you of her, of what your eldest sister suffered—not even a little?"

I combed my fingers through the silky fringe of her fiery hair, admiring the sharp mind beneath. "I didn't know that about you when I first met you," I pointed out.

"You knew." She regarded me solemnly. "You've always been able to see through me."

Not always. It would be an excellent skill to have, however. "I think you would've liked each other, you and my sister."

"I look forward to meeting her someday."

"I think I have to face that she's gone forever. That it won't happen." When Ursula opened her mouth, I headed off the argument. "But you would've liked each other. Though you're very different, you share the same sweetness, the same purity of a truly good heart."

"I'm not sweet, Harlan," she said, and her voice held a hint of hardness, the first of her defenses going into place again.

She started to move and I held her there. Not fighting my grip, she subsided easily, her expression holding a question. "Don't go yet," I said, not sure what else I could say. *Don't say the words that will end this forever.*

"I'm not." She glanced out the window. "But we have formal dinner this evening, with our guests—including your brother, unless you've changed your mind about killing him?" She raised her brows at the question, humor in her eyes.

I laughed, loving her all the more, impossible as that seemed. "No." With a sigh, I released her and sat up. The idyll couldn't last. "I lost my head this morning. It won't happen again."

"I think you get a pass on that one," she replied, strolling naked to the washbasin, her tightly muscled buttocks flexing with her warrior's stride, the subtle flare of her hips swaying slightly. She tossed me a wet cloth, and I caught it as I stood, using it to clean myself and watching her dress again in the outfit she'd had on before.

Not a good sign, that. She'd have to change to a more elaborate gown for formal dinner, but she'd chosen her court garb instead of a lounging robe for the interim, which meant she wanted to feel armored for this battle with me. Salena's rubies glinted with a fiery gleam at her ears and on a bracelet she donned again, taking comfort in her mother's jewels.

With a mental sigh for it, I donned my own clothes, including my boots, since she had. "All right, then," I said, sitting again at the table and serving us both with more food. We'd barely eaten before. Knowing Ursula, she'd be too busy watching the political currents and guiding discussion to eat much at dinner. "Out with it. What is this terrible news?"

Chapter Twelve

"I MENTIONED THIS morning that I've been receiving messages from Dasnaria," she began in a neutral tone, gaze on her food, not me.

"That you believe might be from Inga. You didn't say why, other than that they sound feminine in tone."

She flicked me a glance, both of us recalling that conversation and how it had ended. "Jepp said that Inga indicated she would remain in communication if she could."

I sat back, surprised. Jepp hadn't told me that, though she'd relayed greetings and good wishes from Inga and Helva both. "Is there a reason you didn't tell me that?" I inquired, as evenly as possible.

"Yes," she replied in the same tone, "because I paid less attention to it than I should have. It didn't occur to either Jepp or me that Inga meant she'd send coded information on the politics inside the Imperial Palace. I underestimated her."

I nodded, accepting that. Inga had changed a great deal then, from the girl I'd known, if she'd indeed decided to betray the empire and had worked out a way to do it. "How is she getting messages out?"

"An excellent question and one I don't have the answer to. The messages arrive with other ones from within the Thirteen, marked as personal correspondence, written in Common Tongue, and apparently full of gossip from a cousin by marriage."

"You don't have any cousins who aren't Tala," I mused.

"Exactly. So she knows enough about me to include that information to tip me off. She also regularly speaks of my consort's continuing good health, she and her sister sending him love and the best of wishes."

I closed my eyes briefly, the surge of old affection taking me unawares. Until that moment I hadn't realized how much I missed them. Perhaps coming to terms with losing Jenna, letting her go after all this time, allowed me to remember the good parts of our lives, and how I'd loved my other sisters, too.

"She also warns me that my consort might face some sort of competition," Ursula continued, her tone exceedingly neutral. "With the code she's using, it hasn't been clear to me what she meant—a threat against you or something else. That's another reason I haven't mentioned it to you." Her eyes were clear and without guile when I looked at her.

I continued to play this her way. "What sorts of competition does she describe?"

Ursula gave an irritated shrug. "It's couched in silly phrases; you likely to lose a tournament—when we know you don't participate in such things—or being disqualified from some sort of gaming championship. Nonsense."

I grunted noncommittally, beginning to form an idea of what might be coming.

"Now Kral has received a formal communication, delivered to the *Hákyrling*, from your brother, Emperor Hestar."

Glad I'd had the wit not to be caught with food to choke on or wine to spit, I shoved my plate away and leaned my elbows on the table, cupping a fist in my hand and propping my chin on them. That way I'd be less likely to strangle her. "It's taken you *this* long to mention that?"

Her eyes snapped sword-sharp with irritation. "If you'd controlled your temper—words I *never* thought I'd have to say to you—you would've been there to hear the news at the same time I did. Then you had to dash yourself brainless against a shapeshifter and we had a lot of old secrets to clear off the table, which was also your doing. Don't second-guess me in this, Harlan."

I took a breath and let it go. "Fine. What does this communication from my esteemed brother offer?" I knew what it would be, from Inga's hints, in my bones—from knowing my family so well, perhaps—and only needed to hear the words.

"It contains an offer of alliance. A marriage of state, between me and your brother Ban."

And there it was. It almost didn't hurt, I'd been braced for that particular blow for so long. "Don't accept Ban," I told her. "He's never been right in the head. Hold out for Mykal, or one of the twins."

She gaped at me. I didn't often catch Ursula flat-footed. Sadly I couldn't enjoy it this time. Determinedly I bit into a leg of meat, chewing, counting the beats of silence until the explosion.

"That's your response." She was entirely astonished—and quiet with it. I would've preferred the explosion.

"Yes—the best advice I can give. Ban was born wrong. He's

fine in body, but not all there in his mind. Though that might be useful for your purposes." As soon as the words escaped my mouth, I regretted them. So much for keeping my cool.

"I don't deserve that," she said quietly.

"No." I blew out a breath. "I apologize. Though offering you Ban *is* an insult. Mykal or one of the twins would be more fitting for you to marry."

"Harlan. I'm not marrying any of them."

"What did Hestar offer?"

"What?"

I wiped the grease from my hands, giving her a knowing look. "A marriage of alliance with Dasnaria gets what for the High Throne of the Thirteen Kingdoms?" I phrased it deliberately, if unfairly prodding her, emphasizing where we both knew her responsibilities lay.

"Independent ally of the empire," she replied, eyeing me. "One hundred years of that status, with options to renegotiate. Protection from the Temple of Deyrr."

"A good offer," I acknowledged. "Better than I expected."

"If Hestar doesn't renege."

"He won't. Not on the letter of the agreement. Konyngrrs revere a good contract." I smiled at her in reminder of the Vervaldr's initial contract, how Ursula had pored over it, looking for loopholes, and how she hadn't believed at first that I'd written it. But she didn't smile at the old joke.

"And Deyrr?" she asked pointedly.

I lifted a shoulder and let it fall, contemplating. If I focused on the politics, I could set emotion aside. Giving Ursula advice was part of supporting her as I'd sworn to do. "I imagine Hestar will be very careful of exactly what he promises regarding Deyrr. From what we know of the movements of the High Priestess and the previous actions of the temple, I doubt Hestar has as much control there as he'd like. It's entirely possible this offer is a sign that he recognizes he needs this alliance—and your assistance—to tear Deyrr from his own throat."

"What possible assistance can I offer the Empire of Dasnaria?"

"You rule Annfwn," I pointed out. "The Tala are the descendants of n'Andana, ancient enemy of Deyrr. Arguably a successful enemy, as they made the deciding move in their long war by taking magic out of circulation and starving Deyrr of magic. In Hestar's place, who else would you bet on to contain Deyrr other than the people who did it before?"

She had an arrested look on her face, thinking through the ramifications, then wrinkled her nose. "Logical, except I don't actually rule Annfwn. Even Andi and Rayfe are hard-pressed to govern that lot of anarchists and iconoclasts."

Though I appreciated her attempt at levity, I didn't take the distraction. "Hestar doesn't know that. Something has pushed him to this point and it's an opportunity you can't afford to pass up."

Fury crossed her face like a summer squall, quickly passing. "How can you suggest that so calmly?"

I only wished I felt calm inside, but I could present the façade to ease this for her. Sliding a fruit tart onto her plate, I bit into one of my own. Fresh strawberries, first of the season, and a fair amount of sour with the sweet. "We always knew this day would come," I said after swallowing, since she'd left the question out there for me to answer, staring me down. "You've known all your life that part of being heir to the High Throne meant making a marriage of state."

"That changed for me when I committed to being with you," she replied, an edge to her voice. "I've told you that countless times."

"Essla." I set down the tart and took her hand. It lay limp and cold in mine, nothing there for me to grasp. "The *Elskastholrr* is about me and my own internal compass. Nothing changed for you. Your loyalty has always been to the High Throne first, as it has to be. You said as much this morning."

"I was angry."

"Yes, but you also know it's true."

"I don't know that."

"Oh, will you abdicate then? Step down and hand over responsibility for your Thirteen Kingdoms to... well, let's see." I pretended to think, letting go of her hand to cross my arms and rub my chin thoughtfully. "Andi is next in line, but she's preoccupied with defending Annfwn and we need her there as she's our best sorceress. Never mind the political unrest it would cause, putting a shapeshifting sorceress on the High Throne. Then there's Ami, who's come a long way but would be the first to tell everyone she's not equipped to be High Queen—and who you noted won't be pried out of her cozy nest in Windroven. Astar is your official heir, of course, but I'm not sure a toddler on the throne during a time of war is a good—"

"Just stop it," she cut me off, scowling. "Do you always have to be so thriced logical about every Danu-cursed thing?"

"Yes." I took up my strawberry tart again, savoring the

sweet that came with the sour. "I do, because you're the passionate one in this relationship. You are the fiery blade while I'm the cool water of reason."

She narrowed her eyes at me. "Says he who declared I'd unleashed the dragon and promised to eat me alive."

I waved that away. "That was sex."

"And who came close to killing his brother this morning."

"A temporary lapse."

"Who was passionate enough to save his sister and gave up everything to start a new and better life."

"She gave up *her* life," I answered. "She gave up *everything*. How could I do less?"

Ursula sat back, weary, grief in her eyes. "Harlan—how can you want me to marry another man, your own brother?"

"All I want is to do my best by you, and you need to do your best by your realm. That means accepting this alliance. You'd be marrying into the imperial family of the Dasnarian Empire, gaining a century of reprieve and very likely averting a war. That is a service to the High Throne that will save countless lives and bloodshed. There really isn't a question here of what you should do."

"I could marry you," she pointed out. "You're full brother to the emperor."

"No, I'm not. I was disinherited, stripped of rank. In the eyes of my family, I no longer exist."

"If I'm married to you, and they want this alliance, they might reconsider that."

Unfamiliar bitterness rose along with my gorge and I regretted drinking so much wine earlier. "I wouldn't have them," I bit out.

"Not even for me?" she asked, cagey now, neatly boxing me in. "You say you'll do whatever I need, but you won't take back a title that matters nothing to you? Won't take the opportunity for them to restore what's rightfully yours, something they should never have taken from you, particularly since you acted only in the best interests of another member of the family?" Ursula tipped her head in thought. "I wonder what Jenna would say you should do?"

I stared at her, astounded. Flummoxed. She'd outmaneuvered me again and I'd never seen it coming. If only I could go back to bed and magically start this entire day anew. "This is why you wanted the story about my eldest sister before you told me about the marriage offer."

She smiled thinly. "You're not the only one who's learned a few things about managing an obstinate spouse."

"I am not your spouse, hawk," I ground out.

"Oh, rabbit, you most surely are. All that's lacking is the actual contract and I happen to know you've a deft hand with those." She raised her brows as she scored the point, letting me know she hadn't missed my earlier reference to that.

"A missing contract creates a rather large hole."

"Easily fixed. You're going to marry me, Harlan, tonight. Your brother will stand witness for you and Zynda for me. Then Kral can deliver the news to Hestar that I'm fortuitously already married to a Prince of Dasnaria, and we can hammer out an agreement of alliance."

I had no words. "Ursula. I—"

I don't know what I would've said, because the lookout's alarm shout and the pealing of the warning bells—straight to second-level alarm—dashed everything else from my mind.

CHAPTER THIRTEEN

B OTH ON OUR feet in the same movement, we grabbed the weapons we always kept at hand as we dashed through her rooms and into the hall. Side by side, we ran through the arcade and her private courtyard, taking the shortcut to the walls, her innate speed making up for my longer stride.

A roaring shadow passed over us, an inferno of flame heating the summer air to crackling. Zynda in dragon form, blazing a swath through the summer sky at an enemy I couldn't see without stopping to scrutinize. Glad she was on top of our defense, and that I could recognize her now, I made a mental note to establish a system for us to warn of friendly dragon approach. It didn't bear thinking what a dragon bent on destroying us could do.

Shouts over the cacophony of the alarm bells greeted us in the outer yard as Ursula's protective guard formed around her. Other fighters streamed in from various quarters, some still buckling on weapons. "To the walls," she commanded crisply.

I turned to her. "You know you should go to—"

She rounded on me with a vicious glare. "Don't do this now. I'm done with being protected. This is *my* castle, *my* realm, and I'm done cowering indoors while you all fight for me."

I reassessed, taken aback by her vehemence, then nodded

and tapped the flat of my broadsword to my forehead. "*Elskastholrr*," I told her, and she grinned, a feral baring of teeth.

"Damn straight."

"Your Majesty!" The current gate commander dashed over. "Permission to close the gates?"

We exchanged a glance. The alarm bells had been ringing only a minute or so. "Do we have people outside still making for the castle?" she asked.

"Yes, but—"

"Gates stay up until they're all in," she ordered, turning her back and running for the walls.

We climbed the ladders swiftly, taking in the scene. I couldn't make much sense of what I saw at first. Smoke rose from the fields and orchards, thick and unnaturally coiling, dimming the air and swarming over people on the road—running either for the safety of town or the castle walls—or over people lying immobile. Zynda the dragon turned on wingtip—which seemed to bring her dangerously close to the ground—her silhouette against the afternoon sun very nearly vertical in the sky, Marskal clearly outlined on her back.

Brant ran up to us, out of breath. "Captain!" For a moment I didn't know if he meant me or if he'd reverted to the Hawks' habit of calling Ursula "captain." In the heat of the fight, it didn't matter. "Attack by unknown entities."

"Be more specific," Ursula snapped, eyes on the scene, also scanning.

Was the smoke...feeding on the people who were down? Clouds of it coalesced around their fallen forms, while other masses seemed more condensed, taking shape. They seemed almost humanoid, except terribly distorted, with missing limbs in places, appendages in others that looked more animal. Or like nothing natural at all.

"Can't." Brant replied. "Looks like smoke, but with particles like ash. Drops people where they stand. We can't pinpoint the source and—"

I swore, viciously, and they both turned to me in expectation. "Ash," I spat out. "Curse us for worse than fools. Those places are where we scattered the ashes of the unidentified dead."

When they stared blankly, I clarified. "After Illyria's defeat, all of the people she converted with her Deyrr magic—we burned them when the pieces kept coming."

"I remember that," Ursula said. Brant nodded, though he hadn't been one of the Hawks then. It had been terrible, soul-crushing duty and my Vervaldr, with the great gift of not recognizing most of the victims as friends and family, had handled the bulk of it.

"Some victims were identified and their ashes taken home to family graveyards." I waved my broadsword at the unusually fertile fields and orchards this summer. "The rest we spread on the tilled earth, as is traditional in Dasnaria. Stupid and short-sighted."

Ursula spun to survey the area. Zynda dove and flew so low she could only glide, as a downstroke of her wings would hit ground. "You're saying that smoke is the undead ash, rising again?"

"The remains are still coming," I replied grimly. "Even as ash. Unforgivably stupid of me to keep it so near the castle."

"My people would have done the same," she replied absent-ly, attention keen on the people fleeing the attacking smoke. Assisted by squads of Ordnung troops, some of the people on the road had unharnessed their horses from the laden wagons, riding full speed for the castle gates. A group of young women in pretty gowns ran, ribbons streaming. One lost her hat and it flew to the road behind her. She started to turn, but a soldier passing her on horseback shouted and pointed at the gates, then charged a cloud of smoke that had descended on the hat. "Ashes to earth, the cycle of life," Ursula added.

"Only this ash has nothing of life in it," I observed.

"What of the people down—what does the smoke do?"

"Near as we can tell it suffocates them," Brant answered. "Before they drop, it seems like they can't breathe."

"Does anything stop it?" she asked, her gaze on her fallen people. The soldier who'd charged the cloud of smoke was in trouble, he and the horse spinning as the smoke raked them with claws that should've been insubstantial but had them convulsing.

"Nothing so far," Brant answered. "Weapons pass through it."

Ursula dug her fingers into the parapet as she leaned over, clearly wishing to leap over it and into the fight. "All advancing on Ordnung. The walls won't keep it out."

"No, Your Majesty."

"Dragon fire might do it," I said, pointing as Zynda came around. She spouted a blast of flame through a cloud of ash where there weren't any people. We all leaned forward to watch. The ash disappeared in the flame, but in the wake of her passage, the air eddied with oily black shadows, the ash condensing again into coils, then into humanoid shape—and continued to move toward the castle.

"No good," Ursula murmured. "Why this, why today?"

"Does it matter?" Brant muttered darkly.

"It might. This is magic. You fight magic with magic. The ash has been there since last autumn. Why did it wake today?"

"It's midsummer," Kelleah said. She returned our surprised gazes with imperturbable calm. Of course she would've come to the walls, in case anyone needed her healing skills, not knowing we had nothing to fight. Would she be able to help the fallen? We'd have to retrieve them first, risking more of us.

"Midsummer," Ursula echoed, realization in her voice.

"You call it the Feast of Danu, and Danu is your goddess, not mine," Kelleah supplied, a pointed reminder.

Ursula had discussed—and quickly dismissed—celebrating the Feast of Danu, but the holiday had fallen out of fashion with the population under Uorsin's rule. He'd promoted worship of Glorianna and Her church as the primary religion for the Twelve Kingdoms. With so much else to do and really no one to champion the event, any thoughts of celebrating Danu's Day at midsummer had faded before they'd fully formed.

"But even in Annfwn we observe the longest day of the year," Kelleah noted. "As it's a day full of the potent magic of life."

"Enough to raise the undead," Ursula murmured, eyes still on the running women. Mounted soldiers had picked up two, but three others still jogged slowly, hampered by their pretty summer gowns. "The question is how do we put them to rest again?"

I measured the distance with her, and the relentless pace of the smoke creatures, many of them congealing into shape now. They'd soon reach the castle. How do you wall out something like that? Unless we could find a way to nullify it, the stuff would slowly suffocate everyone in Ordnung.

"We can't put them to rest," I realized. Ursula glanced over at my abrupt tone. "The ash has to be utterly destroyed," I told her. "Here and everywhere."

She blanched, swiftly following my meaning, then turned to one of her guard who also ran messages. "Have Shua draft a proclamation, short, as many copies as possible to be distributed throughout Mohraya as quickly as possible, and then beyond. Any ashes of victims of Illyria that have been buried, scattered, sealed in crypts or urns—whatever it might be—should be avoided or kept locked away. Anyone in possession of these remains should notify Ordnung so we can deal with it."

The guard took off at a dead run and everyone looked at Ursula expectantly for the solution. She looked to me. I had nothing.

"Zynda can magic it away. I've seen it," Jepp said, arriving out of breath with Kral behind her. He met my gaze steadily, tossing me an ironic salute, gaze going to the scene below and eyes widening in incredulity.

"Call them in," Ursula ordered Brant.

He relayed the message to Dary, once again atop the watchtower, who employed her flags to signal Marskal using the Hawks' code.

"You can call them in," Kral drawled, "but your precious

sorceress refuses to use the power, remember?"

"She doesn't like to *abuse* the power." Jepp rolled her eyes at him. "Something you could stand to learn, Your Imperial Highness."

He narrowed his eyes at her, then lifted a shoulder and let it fall, laughing. "Not so much of a danger anymore, as I no longer possess that title. All your fault, hystrix."

"You too?" I asked, somewhat surprised—mostly at how little my brother, who'd once held ambition above all else, seemed to care.

"As our esteemed elder brother recently took pains to remind me," Kral replied, gaze icing as he met mine. For a moment we shared a strange camaraderie, both exiled princes, stripped of our titles. And both strangely in this place.

Wind from Zynda's wings buffeted us, and we all reflexively crouched. Marskal slid down the dragon's extended leg, landing neatly beside us on the wall. He used a network of ropes that made a sort of harness on her great body.

"Nicely done," I told him.

He nodded in appreciation. "We've been working out the system. Hoping to use similar harnesses with other winged shapeshifter and human-form fighting pairs in battle."

The dragon became a hummingbird in midair—an astonishing collapse of size—who then zoomed in to hover beside Marskal before transforming into Zynda.

"I notice you didn't try *that* form against me," I noted.

She grinned. "Too easily eaten, even by a mossback."

"Enough banter," Ursula ordered crisply. "Zynda—Jepp thinks you can use Tala magic to destroy the ash, which we believe to be the risen remains of Illyria's undead."

Zynda's easy smile vanished as her gaze went to Jepp, contemplating the scout. "Hmm," was the only sound she made.

"Did your dragon fire work on it?" Jepp asked pointedly.

With an annoyed turn to her mouth, Zynda shook her head. "You saw it didn't, which is irritating, because dragon fire works on *everything*. The ash does avoid my magic-nullifying presence though—we noted that much."

"But goes right back when you've passed," Ursula said.

Zynda acknowledged that glumly.

"Zynda." Marskal took her by the shoulders, facing her with a serious expression. "You've said that you don't like to use sorcery because it takes creatures out of the cycle of life—but Illyria's undead are already unnatural. Wouldn't eliminating that ash be restoring balance?"

She frowned at him, searching his face. "A neat argument," she finally replied, "and I'm not sure your logic is entirely correct, but you all seem agreed there's no other way to stop this stuff?"

"No," I answered, taking charge as Captain of Ordnung's defense. "And it's coming this way. It doesn't matter if we close the gates, the walls won't keep it out. If you won't do this, Zynda, then we need to come up with other options fast or everyone here will die."

"I'd be happier with an enemy I could cleave with my sword," Kral growled.

"Or take apart with daggers," Jepp added.

Ursula threw them both an appreciative look. Something settled inside me, a realignment of sorts, that we were all the same side. Hlyti had guided my footsteps to this time and place—and these people—but so too had it brought Kral. Two points of the triangle, bound together.

With a third still out there. For the first time in years and years, I entertained hope that Jenna might also find her way here. If we survived this.

"I'll do it," Zynda decided. "Though I'm unprepared, so it will take a bit to build the necessary power to clear an area this big."

She became a hummingbird again. Jewel bright, she zoomed to the watchtower, where hopefully Dary wouldn't be too startled.

Ursula shaded her eyes, staring up at the tower that now held two women. "She didn't wait for instructions," she complained.

"She knows what to do," Marskal murmured beside her, mirroring her stance. "Your Majesty," he added belatedly, then grinned at whatever Ursula muttered under her breath at him.

"She's used a lot of magic today already," Ursula noted, a hint of worry in it, "lots of shapeshifting and healing." She deliberately didn't look at me. "I hope she's up to this."

"She is," Marskal replied definitely. "Dragon form has launched her into a new level of ability—beyond what any of us might have predicted."

"Is that so?" Ursula looked over to me at last, raising her brows. "Finally, some good news."

I smiled back at her.

She and Marskal fell into conversation, discussing counter-measures should Zynda's effort fail. He summoned several

Hawks and they sent them running with messages to secure people in parts of the castle without outside egress.

I scanned the strange battlefield, the fallen on the ground, the prowling smoke creatures. Groups of guards herded people toward town, giving rides to stragglers. A cadre of messengers on fast horses burst from the castle, moving too fast for the smoke monsters to catch them, the dust of their wake quickly settling, unlike the unnatural ash. We could take Ursula out of the castle the same way. I glanced at her, taking in her wide stance on the walls of Ordnung, in her element as she made fast decisions and crisply issued orders.

I'd never pry her out of her castle either.

The only people left on the road were the three young women, who were clearly winded but still struggling up the incline to the castle gates. A cloud of clawed creatures emerged from a copse of trees, advancing on them from the side. All the other troops were engaged elsewhere, leaving them unprotected.

Measuring their relative speeds—the exhausted young ladies in their fancy slippers not meant for such rigor, and the billowing humanoid ash figures—I knew the women would never make it.

I couldn't stand by and do nothing. With Ursula focused on protecting Ordnung, I stepped back, then shimmied down the nearest ladder and ran.

With any luck, I'd be back before she noticed I'd left.

CHAPTER FOURTEEN

I BOLTED THROUGH the gates, with a snapping gesture recruiting two more gate guards to accompany me. They obeyed with practiced alacrity. With the incline in our favor, we raced for the young women. Their faces red with exertion, they cried out when they saw us, holding out their arms in stark fear.

Younger than I'd thought. No more than girls, perhaps in their first pretty grown-up dresses, thinking they'd have nothing more than a sweet summer afternoon outing. That's what they should've had. Nothing more than seeing the market and flirting in their summer frocks. Not this vile attack.

The two guards with me each seized a gratefully squealing girl, swinging her into their arms and running for the castle. The third girl, in a white dress with pink rosebuds, lagged behind. As I ran toward her, I saw she'd lost her slippers—or they'd fallen off in pieces, because she'd run her feet raw, blood and dust caking her feet.

The smoke creatures reached her as I did, the oily ash cloud snaking around her, the distorted faces snarling silently. She screamed, a piercing sound of agony and despair. Reaching into the cloud, I tried to yank her free of it by seizing her wrist, the resistance as strong as if actual men held her. She cried piteously as I wrenched her shoulder.

Thrice curse it. Because I had to try, I swung my broad-sword over her head through the murky figures. It passed through them as if I sliced at nothing, the unimpeded swing nearly taking me off balance. Recovering, with no time to sheathe my sword as the girl now hung limp in the cluster of shadow shapes, I tossed it aside and reached in for her.

The smoked slimed over my skin, the ash like grit in my eyes and nose. Memories and emotions not my own filled my mind—violence, despair, and a grinding need to reach Ordnung, to devour the living. My lungs strained for air, my heart booming in my chest, struggling to pump blood growing thick and oily, as I wrestled the creatures for the girl.

Digging in, using all the strength I'd built over the years, fiercely glad for Kelleah's healing that had me in top form, I took one step back, then another, dragging the girl back. Some of the writhing creatures came with us, but the others dug in also. Good for me as that allowed my head at least to pop free, and I took a deep breath of clean air, like a drowning man barely able to push his face above water.

The girl had gone entirely limp, dead weight in my arms, and I struggled back with all my might.

A warrior's howl cut through the thick silence, the oily smoke parting around me as a sword cleaved it. The Deyrr creatures released their grip so abruptly that I fell back, the girl cradled in my arms.

"Give her to me," a woman in silver armor demanded.

I blinked at her in confused disbelief. Kaedrin, warrior priestess of Danu. Her brown eyes snapped with impatience in her lean face. "Give her to me," she repeated.

I relaxed my hold, and Kaedrin snatched up the girl, taking off at a run. Kelleah waited a safe distance away, wheeling to match Kaedrin's stride, already laying hands on the girl, a green light emanating out.

Skull throbbing, heart still pounding and lungs tightly laboring for breath, I tried to stand but barely managed to sit. Until I saw Ursula.

A whirlwind of black and silver, rubies shining like beacons of fire, she spun faster than a hummingbird's wings, slicing again and again at the increasingly indistinct figures. With each pass of her sword, the vaporous shapes lost human form, reduced to swirling clouds. The ruby on her sword hilt glowed with light brighter than dragon fire—but that seemed to burn the ash away as she defended me.

I struggled to my feet, trying to call for her, no breath to do it with. Reaching for her.

Ursula.

Essla.

Danu save her.

Even as I thought it, a deep blue glow washed over me, the feel of it somehow the same as the depths of Zynda's eyes. My lungs abruptly cleared, strength returning to my limbs.

The blue wave of magic expanded, pushing out until it blended with the deep blue midsummer sky. With a palpable pop, it vanished again, leaving the fields clear. The taint of ash gone again, so only golden light of the long, light-filled evening ahead remained to fall over the growing fields and ripe orchards.

Abruptly bereft of an opponent, Ursula lurched much as I had, gracefully regaining her footing in a spin that brought her to face me, a wild expression on her face. One that crumpled into relief when I opened my arms to her.

I grunted as she launched herself at me, a lithe arrow of a woman, bracing myself to absorb the impact as she rained kisses on my face, wrapping her long legs around my waist and clinging to me with all the considerable ferocity in her.

"I could fucking kill you," she said between kisses. "What in Danu's freezing tits were you thinking?"

"That I had to do something," I said. I stopped her with a long kiss, waiting until some of the tension dissolved in her body and she relaxed in the surety of my embrace. Then looking her in the eye, I offered a rueful smile. "I couldn't just stand there and do nothing."

"I know." The knowledge showed in her steely gaze, and she sighed heavily. "You wouldn't be you if you could."

"But what in Danu were *you* thinking?" I growled, letting my fear for her turn into righteous anger. "You had no business coming after me. The High Throne comes first!"

She met my gaze evenly. "It should. I know that in my head. But in my heart, it's not true. I'll never be able to just stand there and do nothing if you're in danger."

I laughed a little at how neatly she threw my words back in my face, my own heart squeezing at the staggering impact of her declaration.

"I wouldn't be me if I could," she added, with a quirk of a smile.

Unable to frame a reply, I kissed her long and deep. When we came up for air, I set her on her feet and surveyed the area. We both retrieved our swords.

"Why did your sword work and mine didn't?" I wondered aloud.

"Salena's rubies, I think," she replied. "The thought came into my mind, bright and clear, that the rubies would disperse the magic. I needed magic and that was the only thing I could think of."

"You think Salena infused them with some sort of defensive magic?"

"Why not? The Star certainly is magic. And our mother was very specific about those rubies being distributed among her daughters. We know Salena saw far into the future."

I took her hand and we turned toward Ordnung's white towers, climbing the hill together. People streamed past us, going to collect the fallen.

"You're going to marry me tonight, yes?" Ursula asked, though it sounded more like a demand than a question.

"It's not the best decision for the throne, for the alliance with Dasnaria," I cautioned her.

She threw me a blazing look of scorn. "Do you have any other objections, besides that?"

"No." I raised her hand and turned it over, brushing a kiss over her callused palm, delighting in the shiver that ran through her. "In this, as in all things, I am yours to command."

EPILOGUE

"**Y**OU EVER WERE the luckiest of us," Kral commented, signing his name with a flourish. "Landing in honey, after all your protests to the contrary."

I grunted in non-reply, hoping he'd drop the subject. No such luck because Kral's grin sharpened knowingly, fully his namesake the shark, scenting blood in the water. My blood.

He leaned in, dropping his voice to a conspiratorial whisper and switching to Dasnarian. "Tell me, rabbit—you had this planned all along. All that *Elskastholrr* nonsense. It was all part of an elaborate scheme to get you to this point, wasn't it?"

"Of course." I spread my hands at the spare chapel of Danu, lavishly heaped with summer blossoms and dripping with garlands, the air sweet as honey. "I intuited decades ago that Dasnaria would go to war with an obscure coalition of kingdoms where an eight-year-old princess would end up as High Queen. I figured back then that if I studied the art of *Skablykyrr*, I could work my way into her confidence and one day manipulate her into marrying me as part of an alliance to fend off conquest."

"Exceedingly clever," Kral agreed, clapping me hard enough on the back that I had to brace myself. Then he sobered. "It might not work."

"No." I scanned the small assembly, everyone in their finery, awaiting only Ursula's arrival. Kaedrin prayed quietly at Danu's altar, ready to perform the ceremony. She hadn't explained her abrupt reappearance, except to say that Danu had guided her to us because she'd been needed. The empire required only a contract, and Kral and I had drafted one—to his infinite amusement, as it bore only superficial resemblance to a traditional Dasnarian marriage contract—but Ursula and I would be wed by a priestess of the goddess of warriors as befit us both. "It likely won't satisfy Hestar, but Ursula is determined and I cannot refuse her."

Kral lifted a shoulder and let it fall. "You wouldn't be a Konyngrr if you'd stand back and allow another to take your woman, no matter the stakes. It is, after all, a grand Dasnarian tradition to make exceptionally foolhardy political choices for the sake of love. It seems your Ursula will fit right into the family. And this will surprise Hestar, so that makes it even better."

"Will you be willing to lie and say the wedding—and this contract—predate his offer?"

Kral showed a smile full of white teeth. "Oh, baby brother, I will savor every moment of defying and lying to Hestar. That fucker."

I laughed, the amusement full-hearted, and I clapped him on the back, satisfied to see him lurch forward before he caught himself. "I'm glad you're here," I told him, surprising myself that I meant it.

"I am, too." He sounded subdued, uncharacteristically so, and met my gaze. "I want to offer apology, for what I did to you and Jenna."

My heart caught, as it always did at the sound of her name, even though it had been said aloud so many times today that it should have lost its potency. It seemed Kral and I stood together again at that inn, Jenna a white ghost between us, all of us so painfully young.

"I forgive you." As I spoke the formal words, something seemed to let go inside me. "None of us are who we were then. All joking aside, none of us could have foreseen where we'd end up. Certainly not here, like this."

"True," he mused thoughtfully. "We cannot retrace those footsteps...and yet, I wish I could make amends with Jenna. I can't give her back what was stolen, but I wish her happy and would do whatever she asked of me. I owe her that."

"Jenna?"

We both turned to see Kaedrin standing there, a quizzical look on her face. The silver-haired warrior woman looked between the two of us. "I apologize for interrupting and eavesdropping. I don't understand Dasnarian, but I heard a name I know and wondered. I knew a young woman, long ago, named Jenna. Not a common name in the Thirteen Kingdoms, but she was also Dasnarian."

This pivotal day hadn't finished with me, apparently, holding yet one more shock to turn my blood to water. I stared at the priestess, unable to summon thought. Fortunately, Kral had no such issues. "Where did you know her?"

"She trained for a while at the Temple of Danu in Ehas," Kaedrin said. "My sister priestess brought her there—Kaja, who was Jepp's mother." She gestured toward Jepp, who stood conversing with Marskal, both of them smart-looking in the formal uniform of the Hawks.

"Ehas?" I repeated, able to grasp at least that nugget of information. Surely Jenna hadn't been in Ehas all this time. And at the Temple of Danu. It didn't bear considering.

"Yes." Kaedrin returned her gaze to me, her face clear and unlined, despite her age. "It had to be, oh, more than twenty years ago, but I remember Jenna. So lovely, so determined to learn to be a warrior of Danu."

Now Kral gaped along with me. "She became a warrior of Danu?" I asked, trying to imagine it.

Kaedrin smiled, enjoying our bemusement. "Indeed. She was a dancer—I don't know if you knew that—and many dances have their roots in martial forms. Kaja taught her to use knives instead of jewels within the forms she knew and I helped fill in the holes."

At last I could move. "Kaedrin," I said, and her eyes widened at the urgency in my tone, "is she still in Ehas?"

She looked rueful, shaking her head. "No. She only stayed a short time. She was running from something, which I suspect you know, so she changed her appearance and her name."

Disappointment, a sodden and familiar weight, returned to fill the spaces lightened by hope. "No wonder I could never find her," I commented.

Kral's hand fell heavy on my shoulder, and he looked at me with shared feeling. "It was too much to hope," he said, "that we might recover her after so long."

Kaedrin watched us, a canniness in her gaze. "I know where she went," she offered.

Slowly, afraid of shattering the fragile possibility, we both turned to look at the priestess, cautious, Kral's hand still on my shoulder. Neither of us seemed able to ask the most important question.

"At least, I sent her news of Kaja's passing, and I have reason to believe she received it," Kaedrin added that last enigmatically. "Do you swear before Danu that you mean her no harm?"

I went down on one knee without a thought. To my surprise, Kral joined me in the same movement. In one voice, we swore it together.

Kaedrin smiled with a soft radiance unusual for a follower of the sharp-eyed goddess. "I think Kaja would be pleased. She always promised to continue her service as Danu's handmaiden, to help us along as she saw fit. I shall give you the information, Harlan, as a wedding gift. And her new name: Ivariel."

Ivariel. I took it in, a name I could use like a balm to heal those old wounds, so recently purged.

Kaedrin's eyes lifted to the chapel entrance. "Time to begin," she said.

I rose to my feet and turned, absorbing the final stunning blow of the day—this one a punch of glory. Ursula stood framed in the chapel doorway, a vision of bright light and surpassing loveliness.

She wore a gown I'd never seen—a spectacular work of art, made entirely of finely worked metal feathers, all in shades of bronze, copper, and gold. The high collar rose to frame her long throat, a ruff of the metallic feathers radiating out from a deep bloodred at their base that matched her hair and picked up the gleam of Salena's rubies in her necklace and at her ears. From there the gown flowed in gleaming layers, sweeping down into a long, trailing skirt. Zynda, also dressed in a coppery gown, finished arranging Ursula's train and, giving her a kiss and whispering something that made her cousin smile, slipped aside for me.

I moved forward to this stunning woman who'd somehow become mine. She wore her crown and a regal smile, though a hint of uncertainty ghosted in her gray eyes.

"No sword?" I asked.

She smiled a little. "I thought I owed you that. I can come to you without weapons and trust that I'll always be safe. Tonight I'm a woman first. With you, always the woman first."

Always she knew how to outmaneuver me, taking my breath away with a few words. "I haven't seen this gown before," I commented.

"No, you haven't, because I hid it away," she replied, almost shyly. "Just in case."

"You've always been an excellent strategist," I conceded.

"Do you like it?" She asked, hesitant with the question.

"You are more beautiful in this moment than I have ever seen you," I told her gravely. "Ursula, my Essla, will you marry me and be my wife?"

The uncertainty fled, and she smiled in truth, all woman and not the queen. "Yes. Yes, I will, if you're sure?"

"I'm sure," I told her and offered her my arm.

She didn't take it right away. "I know I pushed you into this."

I laughed, took her hand and placed it firmly on my forearm. "Oh, my little hawk, you should know by now that you can't push me into doing anything I don't want to do."

With a wry smile, she huffed out a laugh. "I do know that." She narrowed her eyes. "No wedding bracelets, though, Dasnarian."

"No one could chain you, my Hawk."

Her answering smile faded as she studied me. "Why do you look so strange? Something has upset you."

She saw through me so well. "Kaedrin knows where my sister is. Her name is Ivariel now."

Ursula's eyes widened in shock. "I sense Danu's hand in this," she murmured.

"I believe that may be so."

"We'll look for her," Ursula said. "Whatever you need."

"Thank you, love." I turned her to face Danu's altar and we walked toward it, side by side, partners in this, as in all things.

Kneeling before Danu, we bowed our heads to Her clear-eyed justice and wisdom, listening as Her priestess bound us together in law and spirit as we'd long been in our hearts.

Though we had the shortest of nights to celebrate together, I fully intended to savor every sweet moment of it.

About Jeffe Kennedy

Jeffe Kennedy is an award-winning, best-selling author who writes fantasy, fantasy romance, and contemporary romance. She serves on the Board of Directors for SFWA as a Director at Large. She lives in Santa Fe, New Mexico, with two Maine coon cats, plentiful free-range lizards and a very handsome Doctor of Oriental Medicine.

Jeffe can be found online at her website: JeffeKennedy.com, every Sunday at the SFF Seven blog, on Facebook, on Goodreads and on Twitter @jeffekennedy. She is represented by Sarah Younger of Nancy Yost Literary Agency.

More titles by Jeffe Kennedy can be found here:

jeffekennedy.com/category/books

Made in the USA
San Bernardino, CA
28 December 2018